Regency Reputations:

Men About Town

JANICE PRESTON

MILLS & BOON

First Published in Great Britain 2022
By Mills & Boon, an imprint of HarperCollins*Publishers*
1 London Bridge Street, London, SE1 9GF

www.harpercollins.co.uk

HarperCollins*Publishers*
1st Floor, Watermarque Building,
Ringsend Road, Dublin 4, Ireland

REGENCY REPUTATIONS: MEN ABOUT TOWN © 2022
Harlequin Books S.A.
Return of Scandal's Son © 2015 Janice Preston
Saved by Scandal's Heir © 2016 Janice Preston

ISBN: 978-0-263-30444-2

MIX
Paper from
responsible sources
FSC® C007454

This book is produced from independently certified FSC™ paper to ensure responsible forest management.

For more information visit: www.harpercollins.co.uk/green

Printed and Bound in Spain using 100% Renewable electricity at CPI Black Print, Barcelona

RETURN OF
SCANDAL'S SON

For Elizabeth Bailey,
whose encouragement and advice during my early
writing attempts was invaluable.

Chapter One

April 1811

Eyes streaming, coughing and choking, she tugged at the window, but it refused to budge. The floorboards scorched her feet and she could hear the ominous roar of the fire below. Dragging the pungent air deep into her lungs, she screamed.

'Ellie. *Ellie.* Wake up!'

'What?'

Eleanor, Baroness Ashby, roused to the gently rocking rhythm of her carriage. She stared groggily into the anxious eyes of Lucy, Dowager Marchioness of Rothley. Eleanor levered herself upright on the squabs, her nightmare still vividly real.

'You screamed. Was it the nightmare again?'

Eleanor drew in a deep breath—fresh, clean, untainted. 'Yes. I'm sorry if I frightened you, Aunt.' Her heart slowed from a gallop to a fast trot. 'Everything seems so real in the dream. And I can never get out.'

'Well, we must be thankful you escaped the real fire, my pet. It doesn't bear thinking about, what might have happened.'

'Milady?' Lucy's maid, sitting on the backward-facing seat, opposite Eleanor, leant forward.

'Yes, Matilda?'

'Is it true someone set fire to the library deliberately?'

'Yes.'

Eleanor did not elaborate. Someone had broken into Ashby Manor—her beloved home—at the dead of night, piled books into the middle of the library floor and set fire to them. The whole east wing had been destroyed. All those beautiful books!

'I *told* you.' Lizzie, Eleanor's maid, also travelling in the carriage to London, nudged Matilda. 'If milady had not woken up when she did, she'd be—'

'Lizzie!'

Lizzie cast an apologetic glance at Eleanor as she subsided into silence. Eleanor needed no reminding of what would have happened had she not woken when she did, two weeks before. She shuddered, recalling that terrifying moment when, climbing from her bedchamber window, her searching toes met empty space where the top rung of the ladder had, only moments before, been placed against the wall by her head groom, Fretwell. If Lizzie had not come looking for her when she did… Fear coiled in Eleanor's belly. Lizzie had arrived just in time to see a shadowy figure knock Fretwell out cold before flinging the ladder to the ground.

Who was he? Was he really trying to kill me?

They had been unable to find any trace of the culprit. Fretwell had not seen him, and Lizzie's description was so vague it was no help at all, but there had been no further incidents and no one could recall seeing any strangers in the vicinity.

'I hope Aunt Phyllis will be comfortable staying with Reverend Harris,' Eleanor said to Aunt Lucy, keen to distract them all from the events of that night. Aunt Phyllis—Eleanor's paternal aunt—had lived at Ashby

Manor all her life and had helped raise Eleanor after her mother left when Eleanor was just eleven. She had also been Eleanor's chaperon since her father's death three years before.

'Oh, I make no doubt she will thoroughly enjoy her captive audience,' Aunt Lucy said. There was no love lost between Lucy—the older sister of Eleanor's mother—and Aunt Phyllis. 'It's the Reverend and his wife I feel pity for. Still, it is to my benefit that she refused to accompany you to London, my pet. I shall enjoy the opportunity to get you settled at long last.'

Eleanor shook her head, laughing. 'You know very well the only reason I am going to London is to escape the building work at home. I have no wish to find a husband.'

Unless I fall in love with someone and he with me. And that is unlikely in the extreme.

'You will feel differently if you meet someone who sets your heart a-flutter,' Aunt Lucy replied, her dark eyes twinkling.

'You take a different view of matrimony to Aunt Phyllis,' Eleanor replied. '*Her* only concern is that any suitor should have the correct breeding and be wealthy enough to add to the estates.'

'Ah, but she does not have to live with your choice. You do. Believe me, you do not want to be trapped in a marriage with a man you cannot respect. Or one who is unkind.'

Aunt Lucy fell silent and Eleanor guessed she was thinking back to her own unhappy marriage. The late Lord Rothley had been a violent and unpredictable man.

'No, indeed,' Eleanor said, heartened by the realisation that her aunt would not spend the Season trying to pressure her into a match she did not want.

'Where did James say our house is?' Aunt Lucy asked.

Eleanor fished Cousin James's letter from her reticule

and smoothed it, scanning the lines until she came to the relevant section.

'Upper Brook Street,' she said. 'I hope it will prove suitable.'

James, upon being told of the fire, and Eleanor's desire to visit London for the Season, had taken it upon himself to lease a house on her behalf. *Thereby making certain I do not land on his doorstep*, Eleanor had sniffed to herself upon receipt of his letter. Ruth, his wife, had clearly not mellowed towards her yet.

Relations between Eleanor and Ruth had been strained ever since Ruth had discovered that Eleanor, and not James, would inherit Ashby Manor and the title, becoming Baroness Ashby in her own right after her father's death. The barony was an ancient title—one of the oldest in England, created by King William I—and, as was often the case with such ancient baronies, the title devolved upon the 'heirs general' rather than the nearest male relative.

Marry in haste... Eleanor allowed herself a quiet smile. In her opinion, Ruth only had herself to blame for trapping James into marriage before she had ascertained the truth of his prospects. Eleanor was just relieved she had seen through Ruth's brother, Donald, on the eve of their betrothal, although the scandal when she rejected him had revived the old stories about her mother's disgrace.

Blood will out, Aunt Phyllis's voice echoed—the same refrain having been drummed into Eleanor ever since her mother created a scandal by running off with a rich merchant fourteen years ago. Eleanor was determined never to give the *ton* any cause for such salacious gossip about *her*. She forced her attention back to Aunt Lucy's contented chatter.

'Upper Brook Street is more than acceptable,' she was saying. 'I've always loved the Season—nothing can quite compare. Let us hope you have a happier time of it than during your come-out. I told your papa and that sourpuss Phyllis you weren't ready for society. You were too young, too shy. And that was hardly surprising, given your poor mama… Well! I shall say no more on the subject. Oh, I can't tell you, my pet, how delighted I am. Between you and me, this is just the remedy I need. I was bored to death at Rothley. I've come to the conclusion I'm far too young to retire to the dower house, despite what that reprehensible son of mine says.'

It was early afternoon on their first day of travel when a deafening crack jolted Eleanor from her daydreams. The carriage lurched violently sideways, slammed to a stop and then, very slowly, tilted until it fell on to its side with a crash. Eleanor flung her arms around Lucy to cushion her as they tumbled over to land on the side of the carriage. Lizzie and Matilda landed beside them in a tangle of arms and legs, shrieking hysterically.

Hip throbbing from the impact, Eleanor pushed herself up, still clutching Lucy.

'Oh, my life! Oh, my head… We're trapped! Milady, milady…oh, how shall we ever get out?'

'Gunshot! Highwaymen! Highwaymen! We'll be robbed and murdered, and no one to save us. Oh, dear Lord…'

'Lizzie! Matilda!' Eleanor raised her voice to be heard over the wailing of the two servants, who were still huddled together, eyes tight shut. 'Do please stop that infernal noise. Is either of you hurt?'

'My head…oh, milady—blood! I shall bleed to death.'

Eleanor twisted to look at Lizzie, who was clutching her head, a look of horror on her face. There was a minor cut on her scalp, which, like all scalp wounds, bled freely.

'Nonsense, Lizzie. Do please calm down. Here, take

my handkerchief and press it to your scalp—it's only a tiny cut.'

Aunt Lucy had wriggled free from Eleanor's grasp and was talking to Matilda.

'Aunt? Are you all right?'

'Shaken up, my pet, as are we all. But not hurt, thanks to you. You provided a soft landing, for which I am vastly grateful. And Matilda seems uninjured, just shocked.' She grimaced at Eleanor as, at the sound of her name, Matilda burst into fresh sobs. 'And you, Ellie? Are you hurt?'

'I banged my side, but nothing broken, thankfully.'

'What on earth do you imagine has happened? Oh, do hush, Matilda. Really, there is no lasting harm done. We are all still alive.'

'I cannot imagine, although Lizzie is right—it did sound like a gunshot.' Eleanor strove to speak calmly, to conceal her fear and the panic lurking below the surface. Were they being held up?

She looked up at the window above their heads. The carriage, despite being on its side, was still jerking and she could hear the men outside trying to calm the horses. She manoeuvred herself upright, her legs still shaky from the shock of the accident, and braced one foot on each side of the door frame that now formed the floor. There were some advantages in being tall, she thought wryly, as she shoved at the door above their heads. It crashed open, provoking another series of jerks from the horses, accompanied by a frenzied whinnying. She stuck her head through the opening, but was unable to see much. She shouted and the grizzled head of Joey, Eleanor's coachman, appeared over the side of the upturned carriage.

'Joey, thank goodness. What happened? Help me out, will you?'

Eleanor reached up and grasped Joey's hands and, with

much heaving and kicking, she was hauled out of the carriage and helped down to the ground. She took in the scene, gasping at the mayhem.

The lead pair plunged and scrabbled to regain their footing against the weight of the wheelers, both of which were off their feet. The offside of the wheelers was lying prone, blood pumping from its side, and the nearside of the pair, lying half beneath its teammate, eyes rolling wildly, was making intermittent half-hearted attempts to struggle free. Fretwell was trying desperately to free the lead horses, sawing at the leather harness with his knife, whilst the footman, Timothy, who had also accompanied them on their journey, was at the leaders' heads, trying, not very successfully, to keep them calm, whilst dodging their flailing hooves.

Eleanor was about to go to his aid when Joey clutched her arm.

'We just come round a sharp bend, milady. Get back there, lass, make sure nowt's coming. Last thing we need—another pile up.' Stress made the old coachman revert to speaking to her as the child he once knew.

Eleanor looked back, past the carriage, and only then did she appreciate the peril they were in. They had come around a sharp bend just before the carriage had overturned and the vehicle now blocked most of the road, which was enclosed by dense woodland. She shuddered at the thought of what that woodland might conceal, but there was no time to worry about that now. Surely any vehicle coming around that blind bend at even a modest speed would be upon them before they knew it. Picking up her skirts, Eleanor sprinted back along the road, suddenly aware of the approaching thunder of horses' hooves.

Her heart leapt with fear. The horses sounded almost upon her, but were not yet in sight. Pain stabbed in her side. She could run no faster. The driver was unlikely to see her in time to react, he was travelling so fast. She did the only thing she could to avert disaster. She ran into the middle of the road, arms waving, just as a curricle drawn by two black horses raced into view.

Curses filled the air as the driver hauled desperately at the reins, slewing the curricle across the road as they came to a plunging stop, missing Eleanor by mere inches. Lungs burning, legs trembling, she could only watch, mute, as a groom jumped from his perch and raced to the horses' heads. The driver speared her with one fulminating glare, then tied off the reins and leapt to the ground. Eleanor hauled in a shaky breath, flinching at his livid expression as he strode towards her.

Chapter Two

Eleanor stumbled back as the irate driver, frowning brows beetled over penetrating ice-blue eyes, loomed over her.

'What in God's name were you trying to do?' he bit out. 'Get yourself kill—' He stopped abruptly as his gaze slid past Eleanor to the scene beyond. He grasped her upper arms, steadying her as he searched her face.

'Are you hurt?'

Eleanor shook her head.

'Good. Now, I need you to stay calm and be strong. Go over to Henry—' he indicated his groom '—and tell him to come and help me, whilst you hold my team. Can you do that?' She nodded. 'Good girl.'

He stepped around her and strode over to the stricken carriage. Eleanor, still in shock, stared after him for a few seconds, then, shaking out of her stupor, she did as instructed and went to hold his horses as the stranger took charge with an ease that spoke of a natural leader.

Good girl? Who does he think he is? He cannot be much older than I am.

The minute those uncharitable thoughts slipped into her mind, she batted them away. Never mind that he had relegated her to the role of helpless female, she must remember he was only trying to help. Like a knight in shining armour. She bit back a smile at such an absurd thought.

In her experience, men rarely felt chivalrous towards tall, independent and managing females such as herself.

The stranger's presence focused the servants and the leaders' traces were soon cut, allowing the horses to stand and be calmed. Whilst they were occupied, Eleanor gathered her courage and forced herself to study the surrounding woodlands for anyone who might be lurking. She saw no one…no movement.

Timothy was dispatched to a nearby farm, just visible through the trees, to summon assistance, and the injured horse was examined. A heated discussion appeared to take place between the men before the stranger placed his hand on Joey's shoulder, bending down to speak in his ear. He pushed him gently in Eleanor's direction whilst nodding to Fretwell, who extracted a pistol from behind the box of the carriage.

Joey stumbled over to Eleanor, tears in his eyes. 'They're going to shoot her, lass. My Bonny. She's been shot and her leg's broke. There's nowt we can do to save her.'

'Oh, Joey, I'm so sorry. I know how you feel about the horses.' Eleanor's vision blurred. 'Don't look.' She clasped his arm and turned him away from the grisly scene. A few seconds later a shot rang out and they both stiffened. Then Joey sighed.

'That's that, then, lass…beg pardon, I mean, milady.' He straightened. 'There's still three horses there needing me. I must get back.' He began to walk away, then stopped, looking back at Eleanor with troubled eyes. 'Oh, milady, who d'ye think could do such a wicked, wicked thing? Shooting at an innocent animal is bad enough, but that shot could've killed any one of us.'

His words echoed as Eleanor watched him return to the other men, who were now heaving Bonny's carcass from on top of her teammate, Joker. A chill ran down her spine as she saw Fretwell reload the pistol and pace slowly back along the road, gazing intently into the dense woodland along its edge. Eleanor pulled her travelling cloak closer around her, as if it could render her invisible.

Joker scrambled to his feet as soon as he could and stood, shaking, allowing Joey to clasp his drooping head to his chest whilst he murmured into his ear. Henry returned to take charge of the curricle and pair and Eleanor made her way slowly towards the men and the carriage.

She was self-consciously aware of the stranger's scrutiny, which she returned unobtrusively. His curricle and pair were top quality, but his clothing—a greatcoat hanging open over a loose-fitting dark blue coat, buckskin breeches and an indifferently tied neckcloth—was not of the first stare. No gentleman of her acquaintance would settle for comfort over elegance. His build was athletic, his face—sporting a slightly crooked nose that had surely been broken and badly set in the past—was unfashionably tanned and the square set of his jaw somehow proclaimed a man who would be ill at ease in society's drawing rooms.

He would make a formidable opponent. The words crept unbidden into her head. Opponent? Mentally, she shook herself, irritated that she imagined menace all around her since the fire.

She braced her shoulders, lifted her chin and met the stranger's stare. Cool blue eyes appraised her, sending another shiver whispering down her spine, this time of awareness. His features spoke of strength and decisiveness and, yes, even a hint of that menace she had imagined earlier. His eyes narrowed momentarily before he smiled. It transformed his face—still rugged, but softened as his eyes warmed.

'I thank you for your assistance, sir.'

He bowed. 'It was my pleasure, ma'am.' His smile widened. 'I have long dreamed of rescuing a damsel in distress and now—' his arm swept the scene '—my dream becomes reality.'

Eleanor glanced at his face, suspecting him of mockery, but the candour of his expression and teasing light in his eyes appeared to hide no malice.

'Nevertheless,' she said, 'I do thank you and I am sorry to have so nearly caused another upset.'

'You did the right thing. There could have been serious consequences had you not been so decisive. Or brave.' He studied her anew and she recognised the devilish glint in his eye as he added, *sotto voce*, 'Or foolhardy.'

Eleanor stiffened and opened her mouth to retaliate, but he was already spinning round, his attention caught by a faint shout from within the overturned carriage.

'Good heavens!' Eleanor put her irritation aside as she remembered Aunt Lucy and the two maids, still trapped inside. 'Sir, might I impose on you once more?'

'Who is in there?'

'My aunt and our two maids.'

The stranger leapt on to the carriage, knelt and reached down through the open doorway to help out Aunt Lucy, Lizzie and Matilda before lowering them safely to the ground.

He was certainly accustomed to taking charge, Eleanor thought, watching him work, wondering who he was and where he came from as Aunt Lucy joined her, pale and shaken.

'How are—?' Eleanor got no further.

'Who is our rescuer, I wonder?' were the first words Aunt Lucy uttered, in a sibilant whisper. 'I wonder where he is from. He is very attractive, in a *manly* sort of way, is he not, Ellie?'

'Hush, Aunt Lucy. He'll hear you,' Eleanor hissed as

he strode towards them, his greatcoat swinging open to reveal muscular, buckskin-clad legs. He was hatless, and his dark blond, sun-streaked hair fell over his forehead at times, only to be shoved back with an impatient hand.

'It seems I am in your debt again, sir,' she said.

'I repeat, no thanks are necessary. It was…is…my pleasure. If I might introduce myself? Matthew Thomas, at your service, ladies.'

Aunt Lucy, her small dark eyes alight with curiosity, replied, 'Lady Rothley.'

Mr Thomas bowed. 'I am honoured to make your acquaintance, Lady Rothley. And…?'

'Allow me to present my niece, Eleanor, the Baroness Ashby.'

Mr Thomas bowed once more. 'Enchanted, Lady Ashby.'

As he straightened, his bright eyes locked with Eleanor's, appreciation swirling in their depths. Eleanor's insides performed a somersault. Oh, yes, she agreed silently with her aunt, he was certainly attractive. She switched her gaze from Mr Thomas to Fretwell, who had returned and now joined them, a frown creasing his brow.

'Fretwell, I do hope this hasn't aggravated your head wound. It has only just healed.'

'I'm all right, milady, barring a few bruises. Lucky nothing was broken; leastwise, nothing human,' he added gloomily.

'Indeed, it could have been much worse. What—'

'Milady—' Fretwell shot a suspicious glance at Mr Thomas before lowering his voice '—if I might have a word?' With a jerk of his head he indicated the far side of the road.

Mystified, Eleanor excused herself and followed him. 'What is it?'

'We must get away from here as soon as we can, mi-

lady,' he said. 'It's not safe. You're too exposed and we
don't know who *he* might be, either. He appeared very
timely after that shot, don't you—?'

'Fretwell! Surely you're not suggesting the horse was
shot deliberately?' Eleanor denied Fretwell's suspicions
despite her own doubts. 'Why would anyone—?'

'After the fire, milady, it seems a mite coincidental.'

The fire... The by-now-familiar coil of unease snaked
through Eleanor. Irritated, she suppressed it. It was her
duty to maintain her composure in front of her servants.
If they began to view her as a feeble woman, their respect
for her, and her authority, would soon diminish.

'Nonsense!' she said. 'There is nobody there—it was
surely a stray shot and, as for your suggestion that Mr
Thomas might have had any part in it, I'm surprised at
you. You are not normally given to such flights of fancy.'

Fretwell reddened, but stubbornly held her gaze. 'Be
that as it may, milady, I know what happened to me the
night of the fire. That was no accident. It was deliberate.'

'Very well, I shall take care, but please keep your conjectures to yourself. I don't want Lady Rothley upset and
there is no reason for Mr Thomas to become further embroiled in our problems.'

Movement further along the road caught her attention.
Her footman was on his way back, accompanied by another man leading a pair of draught horses.

'Come, Timothy is here now with help. Let us go and
sort the carriage out, then we can all get away from here
and put your mind at rest.'

Although how she was to contrive that, with a damaged carriage, she could not imagine. Aunt Lucy, Lizzie
and Matilda, the latter still sobbing into her handkerchief,
were sitting on a grass bank a short way along the road. Eleanor, more shaken by the accident than she would admit,

wished for nothing more than to join them, leaving the men to cope.

But this was her carriage, her horses and her servants. Ergo, her responsibility.

She joined the men, ignoring the curious looks of both Mr Thomas and the farmer, a wiry, weatherbeaten individual of few words, but surprising strength. Her own men knew better than to question her desire to be involved.

It soon became clear that Mr Thomas still considered himself in charge and Eleanor, at first bemused at being relegated to a mere onlooker, grew increasingly indignant at being totally ignored.

She stepped forward, preparing to assert her authority.

Chapter Three

Matthew Thomas studied the overturned carriage.

'Tie the chain there,' he said to Timothy, pointing to a position on the spring iron at the rear of the carriage and trying to ignore the baroness, who was clearly itching to get involved.

'Timothy,' she said in an imperious tone, after the footman had attached the chain, 'you ought to attach that chain further forward—it is too near the back there.'

Matthew straightened from checking that the chain was secure and turned to face Eleanor, lifting a brow.

She raised her chin, holding his gaze in typical aristocratic haughtiness.

'If you pull from there it will surely pull the carriage around, rather than upright,' she said.

He felt his temper stir and clamped down on it hard. He was not the wild youth he had once been and the intervening years had taught him to control his emotions, particularly in fraught situations like the present.

'When the other chain is attached—as it will be shortly—towards the *front* of the carriage, it will counteract the pull on *this* chain. And pull the carriage upright.'

He deliberately blanked his expression, hiding his amusement at her indignation as she drew herself up to her full height—which was considerable, for a woman. She was barely four inches shorter than his own six feet. Her bright blue cloak had swung open to reveal a curvaceous figure, which Matthew perused appreciatively before returning his gaze to clash with her stormy, tawny-brown eyes. Her dark brows snapped together in a frown.

His interest had been aroused the minute he had leapt from his curricle and stared down into her face, pale with shock. She was strikingly attractive, although not a conventional beauty—courageous, too, leaping in front of his horses that way. His heart had almost seized with terror as he had fought to avoid her. Admittedly, he *had* been springing the horses—keen to test their paces—but that fact had not mitigated his fury, which was fuelled as much by the fear of what might have happened as by anger.

Now his interest was still there, but tempered with reality. He could admire her beauty, as one might admire, and even covet, a beautiful painting or a statue. But he would admire from a distance. He was no longer part of her deceitful world. He turned his attention once more to the stricken carriage.

'We will need some poles to lever the carriage as the horses pull,' Eleanor declared some minutes later.

Matthew once more stopped what he was doing. He took a pace towards Eleanor, catching a glimpse of—was that fear?—in her expression as she retreated. Then her lips tightened, and she stepped forward, bringing them almost nose to nose. Pluck? Or was that merely her innate feeling of superiority?

'If—' he kept his voice low, in order that the others shouldn't overhear '—you are so keen to help, might I suggest you go and hold the horses so Henry can come and assist? Unless, that is, you really *are* capable of putting your shoulder to the carriage as the horses pull? I would suggest, with the utmost respect, that you are neither built, nor dressed, for such an activity.'

'Hmmph!' Her gaze lowered.

'Good point about the poles, though, my lady.' He waved an arm to the rear of the carriage, where two stout poles lay on the ground. 'The farmer, as you can see, has thought of everything.'

She followed the direction of his gesture. A flush coloured her cheeks.

'Oh.' There was a pause. Then, 'I hadn't noticed them.'

Shame pricked Matthew's conscience. He had not meant to make her feel foolish. He should not have risen to her arrogance—it was not her fault she was a part of that world he so despised. He reminded himself she must still be in shock after the accident.

They were still standing very close, her perfume tantalising his senses—floral notes interwoven with the undeniable scent of woman. A wave of desire caught him off guard and he spun away, forcing his attention back to the problem at hand.

The carriage was pulled upright with much heaving and straining, and they examined the extent of the damage. One wheel would need replacing, but the rest of the damage could be repaired. Try as he might to ignore her, Matthew was constantly aware of Eleanor's presence. He could *feel* the frustration radiating from her as she peered over his shoulder at the carriage.

'There's a wheelwright in the village over yonder,' the farmer, who had introduced himself as Alfred Clegg, said. 'I'll send word. The horses can go in the home paddock for the time. Where're you folk heading?'

'We have rooms bespoke at the White Lion in Stockport,' Eleanor replied.

The farmer scratched his head, peering at the sky. 'That's a tidy way, mum. And it looks like rain.'

'Do you have a carriage or some such that you could loan or hire to us?'

''Fraid not, mum. The missus is to market today in the gig. Hay wagon is all I got.' He looked at her dubiously. 'It might do for your luggage, and mebbe the maids there wouldn't object, but…' He paused, shaking his head. 'Anyways, my horses couldn't get all the way to Stockport and back—they'm built for power, not speed.'

'It so happens that I have a room reserved at the Green Man in Ashton tonight,' Matthew said. 'It is much nearer than Stockport and it is clean and comfortable—I'm sure there will be enough accommodation for us all. The hay wagon is an excellent suggestion for the luggage and the servants and I can take the ladies in my curricle, if they have no objection to squeezing in.'

He looked around the group as he spoke. Approval shone on the faces of the majority, the exceptions being the baroness, who looked mutinous, and Fretwell, who was eyeing him with deep suspicion. Lady Rothley had joined them in time to hear Matthew's proposal.

'That sounds an excellent suggestion, Mr Thomas. Do you not agree, Ellie?'

Matthew returned Lady Rothley's smile, praying she would not recognise him. He had known her sons, of course—wild rakes, the pair of them—but he was certain he had never met the marchioness. It was many years since he had been cast out from the world these ladies inhabited and, although in his youth he had borne a striking resemblance to his mother, he had lived a full and eventful life since then. He suspected the similarities were no longer so apparent. At the thought of his mother, his heart contracted painfully before he dismissed his weakness with a silent oath. His family had not believed his innocence; they had banished him from their lives and forgotten his very existence. Bitterly, he forced his black memories into the box where he confined them and slammed the lid.

'I should prefer to continue as planned to Stockport, Aunt,' Eleanor was saying. 'Fretwell, you may as well stay here—if Clegg does not object—and then take the remaining horses home tomorrow, as planned, as long as they are all fit.'

The farmer nodded his consent.

Fretwell scowled, shooting a suspicious glance at Matthew. 'I think I should stay with you, milady. For protection,' he muttered.

Matthew felt his brows shoot up. What was he missing here?

'No, Fretwell, I will not alter my plans. I shall hire another carriage to convey us to London. Joey, you can also stay on here and oversee the repairs. I shall arrange for a team to be sent out so you can follow us down to London with the carriage.'

She was certainly a lady used to having her own way, Matthew thought, listening as she set out her expectations. Fretwell was clearly unhappy with her decision, but he raised no further objections.

'I shall hire a chaise at Ashton to take us on to Stockport,' Eleanor continued, 'as Mr Thomas has offered to transport us as far as there.'

Her clear reluctance to spend the evening in his company irritated Matthew. Who the hell was Lady Ashby to dismiss him as a nobody? She appeared to believe that he was not worthy of her time or attention. Tempted to just forget her and be on his way, he paused. Lady Ashby needed dislodging from that high perch of hers. Besides, some female company that evening would be a welcome change to his planned solitary dinner. And she was without doubt prettier than the locals in the taproom of the Green Man, where he would most likely end up after his meal.

His devil got the better of him. He lifted one brow in deliberate provocation before directing his words at Lady Rothley.

'With everyone so shaken, you will be far better advised to remain at Ashton tonight, my lady. I'm sure you will find the Green Man to your liking, and, forgive me, but you look as though you would welcome a fireside to sit beside and a warm drink.'

'That is an enticing prospect, Mr Thomas,' Lady Rothley said, with a warm smile.

Eleanor's lips tightened.

'Excellent,' Matthew said. 'That's settled, then. I shall convey you and your niece in my curricle, and the servants and luggage can follow on in Clegg's wagon.

'Of course—' he switched his attention to Eleanor, grinning at her poorly concealed pique '—once we arrive at the Green Man, should you *still* insist on continuing your journey then you must do so.

'Shall we go?'

Chapter Four

The journey to the Green Man was both uncomfortable and, for Eleanor, disconcerting. The vehicle, designed to seat two comfortably, was a squeeze for three and, to her vexation, Matthew handed her into the curricle before Aunt Lucy, leaving her squashed in the middle when he leapt aboard the other side. Her objection that her aunt would feel safer sitting between them was summarily dismissed, both by Matthew and by Aunt Lucy herself, who appeared to thoroughly approve of their rescuer.

The heat of his touch through the fine kid of her gloves as he handed her into the curricle sent an unsettling quiver through her, despite her irritation. Quite simply, Matthew Thomas rattled her, with his knowing smile and the tease in his voice and his undeniable masculinity.

During the drive, Aunt Lucy was uncharacteristically quiet.

'Are you sure you were not injured, Aunt?' Eleanor asked, concerned.

'Yes, I am sure. Do not mind me, my pet. I am a little tired, that is all.'

Her lids drooped even as she spoke. Eleanor squeezed her hand. They had all had such a shock. She, too, felt drained, but Matthew's rock-hard thigh pressing against hers and the heat radiating from him ensured she remained on edge. Try as she might to focus on the road ahead, her attention kept wandering to his hands, gloved in scuffed leather, as he handled the ribbons with dexterity, controlling his highly strung pair with total confidence.

'How long have you had them?' she asked, indicating the jet-black horses trotting in front, their powerful haunches gleaming in the late afternoon sunshine. 'They look...' She hesitated, appalled by what she had almost said. 'That is, they are a splendid match.'

'They look...?'

What a careless slip of the tongue. Eleanor firmed her lips, conscious of his head turning and those blue eyes boring into her.

'They look too good for the likes of me? Is that what you were about to say?'

She had struck a nerve there. She risked a sidelong glance. 'I meant no offence.'

'It is as well I took none, then, isn't it?'

She did not quite believe that. For several minutes there was no sound save the horses' hoofbeats. Eleanor bit her lip.

'You are quite right, nevertheless,' Matthew said, eventually. 'They are far superior animals to anything I usually aspire to and, in answer to your question, I have owned them since last night.'

Eleanor bit back her exclamation of surprise. For an unfamiliar team they were going very sweetly indeed. Matthew Thomas was clearly a skilled whip...but he had no need of her praise to boost his already puffed-up opinion of himself. She kept her gaze fixed firmly on the road ahead.

'Take care, my lady,' Matthew said, after a couple of beats of silence, amusement threading through his voice. '*You* are determined not to admit your surprise, but I must inform you that *I* interpret your very silence as a compliment and a welcome salve to my bruised pride.'

'They have obviously been extremely well schooled,' Eleanor replied tartly, exasperated by his ability to read her thoughts.

Matthew shouted with laughter. '*Touché*. An impressive put-down.'

Eleanor arched one brow, but could not prevent a corner of her mouth from twitching. 'When you warrant a compliment, Mr Thomas—whether for your driving skills or for any other purpose—please be advised that I shall not stint in offering one. Until then…'

Silence reigned for a moment, then Matthew laughed again.

'You are a hard lady to please,' he said. 'Let me see…' from the corner of her eye Eleanor saw him lean forward and glance across at Aunt Lucy, who appeared to be dozing '…you almost cause an accident by running in front of my curricle—an accident that was only prevented by my superior driving skills. I cut your injured horses free, rescue your aunt and maidservants, help pull your carriage upright, and now I am transporting you to an inn to recuperate, and *still* I do not warrant any praise for my actions. Tell me, Lady Ashby…' his voice lowered to a husky whisper as he put his lips close to her ear '…what, precisely, can I do for you that *will* earn your approval?'

Eleanor suppressed a quiver as his breath tickled across her sensitive lobe and caressed her neck. Risking a quick glance, she could see he was fully aware of the effect he was having on her. She stiffened, her earlier amusement vanquished. She ignored his question.

'Do you travel far, sir? I do not believe you said where you are heading?'

'No, I do not believe I did.'

He did not elaborate, and Eleanor gritted her teeth against the extended silence, raising her chin and keeping her eyes riveted to the road ahead.

Eventually, he sighed in an exaggerated fashion and continued, 'I stay at Ashton for two nights. After that, I plan to visit Worcestershire before I return to London.'

She itched to question him further, but held her silence.

'Do you travel to London for the Season, my lady?'

'We do.'

'And do you go every Season?'

'We do not.' Two could play at being evasive.

'Have you travelled far today?' His voice quivered.

'From Lancashire.'

'North of the county or south?'

She slanted a suspicious look at him.

'Is that where you call home?'

His voice was now definitely unsteady. Eleanor stifled her *hmmph* of irritation.

'You, sir, are being deliberately provoking.'

His laugh burst free. 'Pax. I could continue this game of question and answer all day, but I suspect you do not share my enjoyment of the ridiculous. I shall not bore you with further impertinent questions.'

Unreasonably, Eleanor was stung by his assumption that she lacked a sense of humour. She was unused to this kind of byplay between a man and a woman and she was aware her embarrassment caused her to appear stiff and unfriendly. Although why she should care about his opinion of her, she did not know. However well he spoke, he was not of her class. She wondered what he was—a prosperous farmer, perhaps, or a merchant or a military man?

She felt his eyes on her and risked another sideways glance. He captured her gaze—his eyes warm, his expression open. His easy smile transformed his face, giving him a charm that Eleanor found instantly appealing. To her confusion, she read admiration in his regard and her blood heated instantly at the notion. She felt a telltale blush creeping up her neck and cheeks and, uncertain, she tore her gaze from his.

She was her own woman—rare in this day and age—in control of her own life and finances, answerable to no one, not even her trustees since she had reached her twenty-fifth birthday. She was strong and decisive when running her estates, responsible for not only her own comfort and lifestyle, but also the livelihoods and well-being of everyone who worked for her, plus their families—a responsibility she discharged with assurance. However, for all her outward confidence, she found herself regressing to the awkward, tongue-tied girl of her past in the presence of Matthew Thomas, simply because he was passing time with a light flirtation. Her experience with Donald had caused her to doubt her judgement of men and their true intentions. And had Aunt Phyllis not warned her time after time of the danger of showing too much encouragement to any gentleman?

'If you truly wish to earn my approval, sir, might I suggest that you keep your eyes upon the road? We have already suffered one upset today.'

She fixed her eyes once more on the road ahead and it was with relief that she saw the Green Man come into view.

As they pulled up in the courtyard of the inn, Aunt Lucy came to with a start.

'Of course,' she said, 'it could have been another attempt on your life, Ellie.'

Chapter Five

Matthew, on the verge of springing from the curricle, paused, his interest roused.

'Aunt Lucy! That is preposterous. Bonny's death was an accident.'

'You cannot be certain of that, Ellie. What about the fire at the Manor? Someone set that fire and lurked around to see what happened. He brained Fretwell to stop him rescuing you, in case you had forgotten.'

'Brained…! Aunt! What a thing to say.' Eleanor's voice lowered, holding a clear warning. 'Mr Thomas does not want to hear those wild conjectures. I'll warrant it was as I said—a burglar, and Fretwell was simply in the wrong place at the wrong time.'

'A burglar? In the library? Why would a burglar deliberately set fire to a pile of books? You must not dismiss this as coincidence.'

Eleanor glared daggers at her aunt, who took no notice, continuing, 'Your bedchamber is directly over the library and now a shot is fired at our carriage. Who knows what their intention was, but you are a common factor to both, you cannot deny it.'

'I think you have been indulging in too many Gothic novels,' Eleanor said. She laughed in a dismissive fashion, but Matthew caught the haunted look that flashed across her face. 'That sort of thing simply doesn't happen in this day and age. Do you not agree, Mr Thomas?'

Matthew completed his descent from the curricle. Eleanor was regarding him with her brows raised, clearly awaiting his agreement, but he was by now intrigued. He would not be pressed to give his opinion before he knew the facts. He did not doubt that, beneath her dismissal of her aunt's words, Eleanor was more troubled than she would admit.

'I should prefer to hear the full circumstances before passing comment, my lady.'

He assisted Eleanor from the curricle, biting back a grin when she snatched her hand from his as soon as she was on solid ground, her cheeks now glowing pink. She was certainly a woman of contrasts: one moment acting the *grande dame*, the next blushing like a schoolgirl. Not the response he expected from a married woman. Most likely her husband was one of those aristocrats—plentiful enough in the *ton*—who did not inconvenience himself with romancing his wife. A sad waste, in Matthew's opinion.

'In the meantime, ladies,' he continued, with a pointed look at the innkeeper, who had emerged to welcome his guests, 'I think we should continue this discussion inside, in private.'

Eleanor turned to the innkeeper, but Matthew stepped forward to forestall her. He might not dress the gentleman, but his upbringing—slowly stretching and awakening after what seemed like a long sleep—dictated that he, as the man of the party, should deal with innkeepers and their ilk.

'Good afternoon, Fairfax. We shall require two additional bedchambers for the ladies, plus accommodation for their servants, who will be arriving shortly. I trust there is room to accommodate the whole party?'

Fairfax's face fell. 'I'm sorry, sir; would that I could accommodate you, but the place is full to the rafters.' His voice dropped discreetly as he shot a sideways glance at the two ladies. 'What with the prize fight tomorrow, sir, I doubt you'll find a spare room anywhere in Ashton tonight.'

Matthew swore beneath his breath; the fight had slipped his mind after dealing with the aftermath of the accident. The illicit match was the reason he had returned to Ashton after the successful conclusion of his business in Rochdale.

Eleanor stepped forward, interrupting his reflections.

'It appears we have no choice but to continue our journey after all, Mr Thomas,' she said, with barely concealed satisfaction, a distinct challenge in her tawny eyes.

Matthew clenched his jaw. The provocative *grande dame* had materialised once more.

Eleanor turned to the innkeeper. 'I shall require a carriage to convey my party to Stockport, where we have rooms bespoken for tonight, if you please.'

Before Fairfax could respond, Lady Rothley swayed, groaning quietly, her hand to her head. Eleanor was instantly at her side, her arm around her aunt's waist.

'Aunt Lucy! Are you all right?'

'A little shaken still, my pet—I feel utterly overcome of a sudden.'

'Come, let us go inside. You need to sit down and rest. Oh, what was I thinking? How could I even *consider* making you travel any further after what you have been through? Only…what are we to do now, with no rooms available?'

Matthew could not resist the hint of desperation in Eleanor's voice.

'Might I suggest you ladies take my room here? It is not ideal, with so many strangers in town, but I am sure you will be safe enough. And I am in no doubt Fairfax will be able to provide a cot somewhere for your maids.' It would mean a longer drive to view the fight tomorrow, but that would be a trivial inconvenience. 'The ladies' carriage was involved in an accident,' he continued, by way of explanation to the innkeeper.

'Of course, sir. If the ladies don't object to sharing, I'm sure we can find a corner for their maids, and any men can bed down above the stables. I dare say they're used to making do.'

'I shall continue on to Stockport today and stay at…the White Lion, was it not?' Matthew said.

Lady Rothley perked up, reminding Matthew of a bird that had spied a juicy worm, with her tiny, delicate frame and her bright, beady eyes. 'That is a splendid notion, Mr Thomas, is it not, my pet? I must confess that the thought of travelling further today quite overset me.'

Eleanor ushered her aunt into the inn. 'I am sorry, Aunt. I hadn't given a thought to how you must feel. You've had such a shock. Well,' she added, 'so have we all. I make no doubt the servants will also welcome the chance to rest here.' She paused on the threshold, turned to Matthew and held out her hand. 'Mr Thomas, we greatly appreciate your assistance today but, please, do not let us detain you any longer. I am sure you have many demands upon your time.'

Anger rumbled through Matthew at her arrogance. What was wrong with the woman? First, she resented him helping out at the roadside and now she was dismissing him—after having sacrificed his bedchamber, no less—when at the very least she could invite him to stay and take some refreshment.

'Thank you so much for your concern,' he replied, ignoring her outstretched hand, 'but, if you care to recall, we have a discussion to continue, and I have every intention of staying until I am satisfied you and your aunt are not in danger.'

Lady Rothley had stopped to listen. She frowned at her niece. 'Really, Eleanor, how can you be so ungracious after all Mr Thomas has done for us?' She smiled at Matthew. 'I am most grateful for your assistance, sir, and I assure you that we shall *both* be delighted to take a dish of tea with you, if you would care to join us?'

Eleanor had reddened at her aunt's rebuke. 'I apologise, Mr Thomas. I was concerned for the time, considering you still have to drive to Stockport. Of course, you must stay and take tea with us, if you have the time.'

Matthew studied her expression. There was contrition there, but she could disguise neither the strain she was under nor the distrust that haunted her eyes. Perhaps, in view of the dark picture painted by her aunt, he should not blame her.

'You have no need to be concerned on my account,' he said, understanding full well the mendacity of her words. 'I have plenty of time to get to Stockport before dark.'

'Very well. Fairfax, we should appreciate some refreshments served, if you would be so kind,' Eleanor ordered.

Fairfax bowed. 'Of course, my lady. Please, follow me.'

They were shown into a small but clean parlour. Matthew waited until Eleanor and her aunt were seated before settling on a small sofa on the opposite side of the fireplace and, before long, two maidservants served them tea with thinly cut bread and butter and rich pound cake.

Eleanor had removed her bonnet, cloak and gloves on entering the parlour and Matthew studied her with appreciation. She was even more attractive than he had first thought: her smooth ivory skin— enhanced by the rosy hue of her cheeks as she was warmed by the flames—invited his touch, and her wide mouth and soft pink lips were ripe for kissing. Her hair was a glossy dark brown, the curls that framed her face glinting as they caught the light from the flames. How would her hair look—and feel—loosened from the restricting hairpins, cascading over her shoulders and down her back? It was a long time since he had been so attracted to a woman. Were it not for her air of superiority, he might say she was his idea of the perfect woman.

It's a shame she is married.

The thought caught him unaware and he tore his gaze from her.

It is not a shame. Even were she not wed, she moves in a very different world to you. You know she would never give you a second glance had circumstances not thrown you together.

Matthew's modest fortune had been built from his own hard work, a touch of luck at the tables—he had won his curricle and pair in a game just the night before—and from trade, that term that was despised by the idle aristocracy. No, the likes of Lady Ashby would never look at the likes of him.

He waited until the servants withdrew before raising the subject on his mind. 'Will you tell me about the fire your aunt spoke of, my lady?'

After some initial reluctance, Eleanor recounted the night of the fire—the smell of the smoke that woke her; the terror of her escape through her window; the mystery of Fretwell's injury and his shadowy assailant. Through it all, her anguish at the damage to her beloved home shone through.

Matthew's fascination with Eleanor marched in step with his mounting concern. Her eyes, framed by thick lashes and strong, dark brows, revealed her every emotion as she warmed to the telling of her tale. They sparkled with impish amusement as Lady Rothley sprinkled the story with a selection of servants' lurid tales, learned through Matilda. They lit up in laughter at some of the more ghoulish speculations that Eleanor had clearly not heard before, her generous mouth widening into a stunning smile that transformed her already attractive face into one of mesmerising loveliness. Glimpses of the real woman were revealed when she forgot to stand on her dignity and Matthew had to keep reminding himself of her earlier arrogance and also that she was married and, therefore, out of bounds.

Her uninhibited and infectious laugh triggered an unexpected surge of loneliness that he swiftly thrust aside. Apart from his business partner, Benedict Poole, he was dependent on no one and no one was dependent on him, and that was exactly how he liked it. His burgeoning desire for Eleanor was as unwelcome as it was unexpected and he forced his thoughts from the direction they were taking to concentrate on her words.

'As for this afternoon,' she was saying, 'you have already heard what happened. A stray shot—surely an accident—hit one of the team, causing the carriage to overturn. It was no more a deliberate attack on me than the fire was, despite my aunt's vivid imaginings. Mark my words—it was a burglar, or someone with a grudge. It must have been.'

He recognised the faint hint of desperation in her final words. Eleanor was nowhere near as confident as she pretended to be. Still, it was none of Matthew's concern. He would go on his way very soon—and, judging by his increasingly salacious thoughts, the sooner, the better—and he would likely never see either of the ladies again.

'I must agree with your aunt that a burglar would be unlikely to set fire to a library,' he said, 'but I also think you may be right that a grudge was the cause. If someone was intent on killing you, surely they would pick less haphazard methods? After all, both the fire and the carriage accident had the potential of injuring, or even killing, many more individuals than you and with no guarantee that you would be amongst the casualties.

'It would appear that, for once, you and I are in agreement,' he added, unable to resist a final teasing comment, biting back his smile at her disgruntled expression.

Chapter Six

Eleanor had begun to relax despite her suspicions about Matthew, initially roused by Fretwell, and her earlier irritation at his relegation of her to the role of helpless female in a crisis. After all, had she not pictured him in the role of a white knight before lamenting she was not the sort of female to arouse protective instincts in a man? And he had proved an easy man to converse with, when he was not deliberately goading her, or flirting, that was. When his blue gaze settled on her in that particular, assessing way he had, her blood heated and her insides fluttered in a way they never had with Donald.

'It would seem that, *for once*, you are right, Mr Thomas,' she retorted. How *did* he manage to ruffle her feathers quite so effortlessly?

He laughed. Their eyes met and Eleanor felt a jolt of pure energy shoot through her. Her cheeks flamed. Flustered—and irritated by her reaction—Eleanor jerked her gaze from his and stared at the flames, saying, 'Goodness, this fire is hot.'

She searched in her reticule for her fan and plied it, grateful for an occupation as she fought to control her inner turmoil. Thankfully, Aunt Lucy appeared not to notice anything amiss, and launched a determined crusade to discover as much information as possible about their rescuer.

Matthew proved adept at evading her questions, clearly relishing their verbal swordplay, and Eleanor viewed her aunt's increasing frustration with quiet enjoyment.

She relaxed back in her chair, allowing her nerves to settle. Without volition, her gaze wandered over Matthew, admiring the breadth of his shoulders and the solid muscle of his legs. She watched as he picked up his cup with a broad hand—no gentleman's soft, well-manicured hand this, but strong and masculine and capable. He drained the contents, his penetrating eyes flicking to her face as he leaned forward to set his cup on the table, his lips still moist from the tea. Desire coiled deep within her as the rumble of his voice enveloped her. She could listen to him for ever. How wonderful would it be to be able to lean on such a man, to share the burden of her life?

Even as that thought flitted into her brain, she suppressed it. She needed no man to lean on. She had spent the three years since her father's death striving to prove that point. Besides, he would end up the same as all the men who had ever shown her any attention—interested only in her fortune.

She dreamt of being swept off her feet, of being wooed by a man who was besotted with her and declared his undying passion for her, but could she ever trust her own judgement?

Donald had fooled her with his eager courtship after they met at James and Ruth's wedding. He was an army officer and had returned to Ashby, shortly afterwards, when he was on leave. Eleanor had believed he was in love with her and, even though his kisses had left her strangely unmoved, she had persuaded herself her love for him would blossom given time.

She studied Matthew and desire flickered deep within her...surely a kiss from a man like Matthew Thomas would not leave her unmoved? She tore her attention from his sensual lips, vaguely scandalised by her outrageous thoughts.

Would she ever know the feel of a real man in her arms?

She blessed the day she had discovered Donald's true intent. She had overheard him discussing her with his sister, Ruth, and their contempt for Eleanor was clear. Donald was interested only in her position and the wealth she would inherit from her ailing father. The following day, to her father's distress, she had refused Donald's offer of marriage and he had returned to his regiment. Sadly, she had heard, he had not survived the war.

Eleanor's father had died the following spring and Eleanor still regretted that he had died worrying over both her future and that of the estate.

The room had fallen silent. Eleanor came back to the present with a guilty start.

'You appear lost in your thoughts,' Matthew said. 'It would seem they are not all pleasant?'

Blushing, Eleanor realised that she had been staring directly at Matthew whilst her mind wandered. Aunt Lucy was dozing by the fire and they were effectively alone together.

'I am sure they would be of no interest to you, Mr Thomas.'

'I think you would be surprised at my interests, my lady,' he replied softly, his blue eyes aglow.

There was admiration in his gaze. Awkwardly, Eleanor gazed down at her hands, entwined in her lap, uncertain how to respond. Her come-out, as well as her experience with Donald, had taught her to be cautious of reading too much into a man's supposed admiration for it seemed, more often than not, that it was disingenuous.

Matthew continued to regard her steadily, waiting for

her reply. Irritation at his persistence clambered over her discomfort.

'Indeed, you are mistaken, sir.' She injected a bright, vacuous note into her voice. 'My thoughts were exceedingly pleasant. I was thinking of all the gowns and hats and shoes and other fripperies I shall buy in London and of all the wonderful parties and balls I shall be invited to. Why—' she fixed him with an arch look '—I dare say I shall never be at home, what with all the shopping and the amusements London has to offer.'

His lips twitched and his eyes crinkled at the corners.

'In other words, your thoughts are none of my business. I shall pry no further. We are all entitled to our secrets, after all. Now, let us return to the innocuous subjects you seem to prefer; do you go to London for the Season every year?'

Eleanor laughed, unaccountably pleased that he had not been fooled by her performance. He was clearly intelligent and she did have some pride. She had no wish for this man to believe she was a brainless ninny, despite her subterfuge.

'I believe I answered that query the first time, sir. But I shall expand upon my previous effort, which was, I admit, a little brusque. This will be the first time I have been to London in seven years.' She faltered momentarily, memories of her first Season all too raw even after all this time, before continuing, 'I am looking forward to it. I have become quite dull at home, you know, and I am more than ready for all the excitement and diversion London can offer.'

She saw his eyes narrow as she stumbled over her words. She cautioned herself to take care. *Intelligent? Oh, yes. And disconcertingly perceptive, to boot.*

'I am most fortunate that Aunt Lucy is accompanying me,' she continued. 'To lend me countenance, she would have me believe. She has not been to town for several years, but she was a notable hostess in her day. I suspect,' she added, smiling, keen to eliminate her slip from his mind, 'she is eager to see if she can still wield the same influence.'

'She appears to be a most redoubtable lady—I have no doubt she will be setting the standards with ease. Will you be joining other family members in town?'

'My cousin James and his wife, Ruth, live in London. James has kindly leased a house on my behalf, however, so we shall not be obliged to reside with them. My family is small in number, I fear. Other than James, there are only my cousins on my mother's side—Lucas and Hugo, Aunt Lucy's sons. Lucas is at Rothley, but I hope Hugo might be in town, for Aunt Lucy's sake.'

'Rothley,' he said. 'I know the name, but I cannot quite place where it is.'

'It's in the county of Northumberland.'

'And a colder, more desolate place you could never imagine,' Aunt Lucy interjected, 'although it's very wildness is extraordinarily beautiful, too, in its way. Exactly what part of the country do *you* hail from, Mr Thomas?'

Chapter Seven

Aunt Lucy—wily lady that she was—had out-manoeuvred Matthew. Eleanor could see his frustrated struggle to avoid answering such a direct question without telling an outright lie. Somehow, she did not think him so dishonourable. Evasive, yes. Secretive, yes. But not out-and-out dishonest.

'Worcestershire, my lady.'

'Ah.' There was a wealth of satisfaction in that one word. 'I believe you said earlier that you are headed there before you return to London. Do you visit family?'

Matthew's eyes widened and he shot a stunned glance at Eleanor. She could not help but smile. He had just re-alised that Aunt Lucy must have heard their every word during the journey to the inn. Eleanor was unsurprised, knowing from experience just how far her aunt would go to hear a juicy morsel of gossip, even if it did involve de-ceiving her only niece by pretending to doze.

'No. I merely plan to visit a few of my youthful haunts, for old times' sake.'

'A beautiful county, Worcestershire. What part of the county did you say?'

'Near the town of Bromsgrove.' Matthew's brows were now low enough to almost conceal his eyes. 'It is many years since I have lived there, however.'

Eleanor intervened before her aunt could continue,

afraid she would poke and pry until Matthew became annoyed. Better to cut straight to the point. 'Forgive my direct speaking, Mr Thomas, but what my aunt is trying to ascertain is whether she might know your family.'

The crease between Matthew's brows deepened as their gazes fused. Eleanor waited for his answer, brows raised. She recognised his irritation with her persistence, but stood her ground.

'I am a merchant,' he said to Aunt Lucy, after a long pause. 'Can you think of any reason why a lady such as yourself should know my family?'

Oh, clever! He blocked that thrust with ease.

'You are clearly well educated,' Eleanor said.

'Indeed. My family were…are…not poor. I went to Harrow.'

A knock at the door announced Fairfax. 'Your luggage and servants have arrived, miladies.'

He disappeared, and Lizzie and Matilda soon appeared at the parlour door. Aunt Lucy rose from her chair, extending her hand to Matthew.

'Mr Thomas, I beg you will excuse me, for I am very tired. I am afraid the events of the day have caught up with me. I have the headache and am exceedingly stiff and sore. I shall go to our bedchamber for a rest now that Matilda is here to assist me. I do hope we shall meet again. Perhaps you will call upon us in Upper Brook Street, once you have returned to town.'

Matthew bowed over her hand. 'I shall be pleased to, my lady, if only to ascertain you have reached your destination without further mishap.'

Then Aunt Lucy turned to Eleanor.

'Eleanor, would you speak to Fairfax and request a light supper be sent up later for the two of us? As the inn is so full, I do not think it would be wise for us to dine downstairs. We should not wish to attract unwarranted attention.

'Mr Thomas, allow me to thank you once again for all your assistance today. I do not know what we should have done without you.'

Looking pale and drawn, Aunt Lucy clung to Matilda's arm as they left the room. Lizzie hovered in the doorway, clearly awaiting Eleanor, who waved her away.

'You go on upstairs, Lizzie, whilst I speak to Fairfax. I promise I shall be up in a trice.'

'You make sure and come upstairs as soon as you have spoken to him, milady,' Lizzie hissed over her shoulder as she turned to go, having cast a suspicious glare at Matthew. 'There are some most undesirable characters a-wandering around this inn.'

She stalked off down the passageway, muttering. Fretwell's suspicions must be contagious.

Eleanor smiled at Matthew, ready to take her leave.

'I regret we appear to have started on the wrong foot, my lady,' Matthew said. 'May we call a truce? I have accepted your aunt's invitation to Upper Brook Street, but I should like to feel that you, too, are happy for me to call.'

Eleanor was aware she had been both snappish and arrogant in many of her responses to Matthew, but she could not help but be flustered by him. He was by turns aggravating and flirtatious and she didn't quite know how to respond to him, other than with a sharp retort or by pokering up. She forced a smile and extended her hand.

'I, for my part, owe you an apology, Mr Thomas, for I did not mean to appear ungrateful for your help this afternoon. I am not always so quarrelsome—I dare say I am too used to ruling the roost and it is increasingly difficult to allow another to make decisions on my behalf.'

'No apology is necessary, I assure you.'

'I should also like to start anew. I shall be delighted to welcome you to our house in Upper Brook Street when you return to town.'

He took her hand in his, but instead of a shake, as she had intended, he carried it to his mouth. Her stomach fluttered as his lips pressed against her bare flesh. He captured her gaze with piercing eyes, setting her pulse skittering.

Heat washed through her and her legs trembled as her body seemed to sway towards him of its own volition. Disconcerted, she took a step back, and then another. She gasped as he followed her, his blue eyes intent.

'Sir... Mr Thomas...?'

Matthew halted and Eleanor saw his jaw tighten before he executed a brief bow. 'I fear I was in danger of forgetting my manners, my lady. I can only beg your forgiveness and hope you won't hold it against me when we meet again.'

What had she done? Although she had scant experience of men, Eleanor was aware, on some deep, primeval level, that when they had locked eyes she had *wanted* him to... what? Touch her? Follow her? *Blood will out.* She had, somehow, enticed him without words and honesty compelled her to admit it, if only to herself. She couldn't censure him when she was equally at fault. She was simply grateful that he was too much the gentleman to accuse her of leading him on.

'As we have only just agreed upon a truce, Mr Thomas, it would be a little poor spirited of me to resume hostilities so soon. It has been a long, trying day, so perhaps we may blame it upon that?'

'You are all generosity. Now, I must be on my way but, with your leave, I shall convey your aunt's request to Fairfax before I depart. And might I suggest you return to your aunt forthwith, before that fierce maid of yours comes in

search of you?' He made an exaggerated pretence of looking behind him, a comical expression of fear on his face.

Eleanor tried, and failed, to swallow a giggle. 'Goodness, I never took you for a coward, Mr Thomas. Lizzie
was only doing her duty as she saw it, with Aunt Lucy too
exhausted to look out for my reputation.'

As she laughed up at Matthew his eyes darkened and
Eleanor saw a powerful emotion swirling in their depths
before he blinked, and it was gone. When he spoke, however, his voice was steady. Had she imagined his response?

'I trust you will spend a comfortable night, my lady,
and I will see you upon my return to town.'

'I shall not say goodbye, then, but *au revoir,* Mr
Thomas, and thank you again for your assistance today.'

'It was my pleasure. Until we meet again.'

He bowed and was gone.

Chapter Eight

Just before dawn the following morning, Matthew was jerked awake from a fitful sleep by a piercing scream. It took a couple of moments for him to register his whereabouts—he was in one of the two rooms bespoken for Eleanor and her aunt at the White Lion in Stockport. He catapulted from his bed as a series of thuds sounded from the next bedchamber. It was dark in his room and he groped his way to the door.

In the passage, the next door but one to Matthew's room had opened and the occupant peered out, holding aloft a candlestick. The wavering flame illuminated the scowling features of an elderly gentleman, clad in his nightcap and gown.

'What's to do?' he grumbled.

Matthew didn't waste time answering, but ran to the door between them and flung it open, vaguely aware of the man hurrying along the passage, quavering, 'That's my Jenny's room!'

The bedchamber was as dark as his and all Matthew could make out was a shapeless, struggling mass on the bed. He darted forward, yelling, 'Bring the light.'

As the elderly man reached the open door, the scene was suddenly revealed: a figure in black, turning in Matthew's direction, eyes glinting through holes in a mask; the flash of a blade; blood, streaking the bed linen in vivid splashes of red; a girl's terrified face, mouth suddenly slackening as her eyes closed.

Matthew grabbed the man, hauling him from the bed. He staggered backwards as the assailant swiftly changed from resistance to flinging himself at Matthew. Stiff fingers jabbed at Matthew's windpipe as a blade burned his arm and the man wriggled free, barging past the man with the candle as he fled the room. Matthew dragged in a painful breath and rushed to the door, but the assailant was already out of sight. The elderly man—presumably Jenny's father—stood frozen, his mouth gaping in horror.

On the verge of giving chase, a moan from the bed stayed Matthew. The victim needed help. He found a candle on the mantelshelf and lit it. He went to Jenny's father, gripping his shoulder, then shaking him hard.

'Sir, you must be strong.' He could hear the sound of people stirring, voices getting louder. 'Find the innkeeper. Tell him there has been an accident and to send for a doctor immediately. And send his wife here, to me.' He pushed the man out into the passage. 'Hurry!'

He crossed to the bed, shrinking inside with the dread of what he might find. Jenny lay motionless. Her face, shoulders and arms were the only parts of her visible. Her arms and hands bore the signs of struggle. Blood seeped from her wounds, but it wasn't pumping out. That was a good sign. Matthew put a finger to her neck, feeling for a pulse. It was there, not as weak as he feared. He lifted the candle, to examine the bedclothes that covered Jenny. The slashes he had feared to see were not there. The blood appeared to have come from Jenny's arms and hands and one long diagonal slash from her left collarbone that had ripped through her nightgown. Matthew grabbed a towel from the washstand to try and stanch the bleeding. Jenny did not stir.

As he worked, Matthew's mind travelled back to India and to his great-uncle, Percy, who had been so kind to a bewildered and resentful youth, unjustly banished from his family and his homeland. Poor Uncle Percy, who had died after being attacked and stabbed during the course of a robbery. Matthew's throat squeezed tight as he relived his futile efforts to save his great-uncle. He prayed Jenny had suffered no injuries other than those he could see.

His thoughts returned to the present as the innkeeper's wife, Mrs Goody, bustled into the room, followed by Jenny's father.

'Lord have mercy, sir,' Mrs Goody gasped, hands clasped at her ample bosom as she halted by the bed. 'Whatever happened?'

'She was attacked. Her hands, arms and upper chest are bleeding, but I do not think she has been stabbed elsewhere.'

'Stabbed? My Jenny? Oh, Jenny, Jenny, my love…' The elderly man cast himself on to his knees by the bed, clutching at Jenny's hand. Her eyelids fluttered.

'Goody's sent for the doctor,' Mrs Goody said. She glanced at Jenny's father, then leaned towards Matthew, lowering her voice. 'Did you examine the girl for more injuries, sir, or…?'

Matthew felt heat flood his cheeks, understanding both her question and her discretion. Her father had enough to worry about.

'No,' he said.

Poor girl. Depending on her position in society, if news of this got out there would always be gossip and innuendo about her innocence. The thought made his blood simmer. *'No,'* he repeated. 'I merely examined the bedcovers and, as they do not appear torn, I took that to mean she was only injured in those areas we can see.'

'Thank you, sir. We will do all we can to protect her. Can I ask you to find Goody and ask him to boil water and send up some clean linen? If you close the door on the way out, I'll check the lass for any further injuries. Oh, to think such an evil thing could happen here.'

On his way to find the innkeeper, Matthew came to a dead stop, his knees suddenly weak. *Dear God!* The realisation robbed him of his breath. Had he not swapped accommodation with Eleanor and her aunt, it could have been one of them in that room tonight. He quelled the wave of nausea that invaded him—there would be time enough for that horror later.

After speaking to Goody, Matthew sped back to the bedchamber, with a bundle of clean cloths, to find Jenny awake. As he entered, her eyes widened and she clutched at her father. Mrs Goody shooed him from the room.

'She's had a terrible fright, sir. It'll take her time to get over it. You go on back to bed. You've done all you can.' Her eyes skimmed him and then she touched his arm. 'You're bleeding. I'll fetch a cloth to bind it.'

Matthew remembered that burning sensation as he had grappled with the attacker. He pulled up the sleeve of his nightshirt. It did not look deep. Mrs Goody soon returned with a strip of linen. She wrung a cloth out in cold water from the washstand.

As she bathed and bound his arm, she said, 'The lass has no other injuries, sir, thank the good Lord. None at all, if you get my meaning. It was a lucky thing for her that you were there.'

Matthew nodded, relieved for poor Jenny. At least she did not have that nightmare to deal with on top of everything else. He pulled on his clothes and sought out the innkeeper again. Goody had already roused some of his ostlers to search for Jenny's attacker and Matthew joined them. How he regretted not chasing the villain immediately but, with Jenny's father in a state of shock and without knowing how severe Jenny's injuries were, he knew he had been right to tend to her first.

A lengthy and thorough search of the area around the White Lion—joined by other local men—proved fruitless. Whoever the culprit was, it seemed he was long gone, or holed up somewhere. Matthew returned to the inn and ate a hearty breakfast, after which Goody beckoned him into a room at the back of the inn. Jenny's father levered himself to his feet as Matthew entered.

'George Tremayne,' he said, in a gruff voice, holding out a trembling hand.

Matthew shook it. 'Matthew Thomas.'

'I must thank you for what you did for my daughter. I don't know what I should do if...' His voice cracked, and he harrumphed noisily, taking a large handkerchief from his pocket and blowing his nose.

'How is Jenny?'

'As well as she can be. Physically, at least. She is still very shaken. The doctor advised her to stay here for a few days' rest, but she doesn't want to spend another night under this roof.'

'Understandable,' Matthew said.

'The magistrate and the constable were here, asking questions,' Mr Tremayne said. 'They want to speak with you.'

Matthew grimaced. 'I don't think I can tell them much to help. The rogue was masked. Do they know how he got in?'

'A window at the back was open. There's a lean-to roof just below. They think he was a thief and Jenny woke up at the wrong time. She doesn't remember much. That's probably for the best.'

'Indeed. Is the magistrate still here?'

'No, but he said he will come back later and asked that you remain here until then.'

Matthew quashed his frustration. The sooner he left, the sooner he could catch up with Eleanor and her party on the road and assure himself of her safety. Had she been the real target? If the attacker had meant to kill, he would know he had failed. And, if he was still in the town, he would soon discover he'd attacked the wrong girl anyway. Eleanor was still very much in danger.

It was mid-morning before the magistrate returned and Matthew could recount his version of events and answer his questions. At first, he seemed disposed to believe Matthew the culprit, until Matthew pointed out—with some vigour—that Mr Tremayne had also seen Jenny's masked attacker. Finally, satisfied Matthew had given all the information he could, the magistrate gave Matthew leave to continue his journey. The interview had seemed to Matthew to last a lifetime and he had fretted throughout. All thought of returning to Ashton to attend the boxing match was forgotten. He was convinced Eleanor was in grave danger and his one thought was to protect her.

The minute he was free to leave, he leapt aboard his curricle—with Henry perched on the rumble seat behind—and whipped up the horses. It was almost noon already. Even though he doubted Eleanor would have set off early—bearing in mind she must arrange a suitable replacement for the damaged carriage first—her party must surely have passed through Stockport already, on their way to the capital.

Matthew drove south, worry gnawing at him as he wondered what further dangers Eleanor might face. He varied the pace, mindful of the need not to overtire his horses, but also needing enough speed to give him some chance of catching up with Eleanor's party. He was conscious of Henry muttering behind his back and, upon hearing his man's sharp intake of breath as they flew past a lumbering farm wagon with mere inches to spare, Matthew shot a quick glance over his shoulder.

'You do know, I s'pose, that this is the wrong road for Ashton?' Henry said, leaning forward to speak into Matthew's ear.

'Indeed.'

'Can I ask where we're headed?'

'That,' Matthew replied, setting his teeth as he narrowly avoided a stagecoach coming in the opposite direction, 'is a very good question. I don't precisely know. But we are following Lady Ashby and her party. They are heading for London. I need to find out where they will stop for the night.'

'You think that attack was connected to them?'

Matthew tamped down the surge of fear as the image of Jenny, lying bloodied in her bed, rose in his mind. Her features rearranged themselves in his imagination until it was Eleanor's face he saw and he knew, deep in his gut, that she might now be dead, had they not swapped accommodation.

'I am certain of it,' he replied. 'We must enquire at the posting inns we pass, to find out if they have changed horses. We can ask if anyone knows where they plan to stop for the night. Whoever was responsible for the accident and the attack clearly knows the route she is taking and could try again.'

'Last night brought it all back, didn't it?' Henry said. 'You aren't responsible. You *weren't* responsible. You can't protect the whole world and everyone in it.'

Matthew clenched his jaw. Henry had been with him since the early days in India, and was a trusted employee, taking on the roles of both servant and groom as required. He knew Henry referred to Uncle Percy's death, but Matthew was still haunted by his insistence on going out that night. If only he had been at home… The guilt had near overwhelmed him at the time. His uncle's death had spurred Matthew's decision to return home. There was no one to anchor him to India now and he and Benedict could run their business equally well from England.

He was driven by the need to protect. It was in his nature, a part of him, but that did not fully explain why the thought of Eleanor being hurt made his stomach clench with such fear. Frustration flooded him as their progress was slowed by the need to enquire for the travellers at every likely-looking inn they passed, and the need to rest his own horses.

'Where on earth can they be?' he bit out, as they drew yet another blank. 'They must have stopped for the night by now.'

'Maybe they just had too much of a head start on us, sir. Now, don't bite my head off, but them cattle are getting weary and you'll be risking their tendons if we carry on much further.'

Matthew knew Henry was right. He cast a worried look at the sun, sinking to the horizon, then straightened in his seat as a milestone proclaimed they were one mile from Leek.

'This must be it,' he muttered. 'They surely can't have gone any further today. They have to be here.'

* * *

Shortly afterwards, they drew up in the yard of the George, situated right in the middle of the small market town, where the first person they saw was Timothy. Leaving Henry to see to the horses, Matthew strode into the inn, breathing easily—it seemed—for the first time that day.

'William Brooke at your service, sir—landlord of this fine hostelry. How may I be of assistance?'

'Good evening, Brooke. I understand Lady Ashby is a guest here tonight? I wish to see her.'

The innkeeper lowered his gaze. 'Lady Ashby, sir? I'm sure I couldn't say. Might I ask who is enquiring?'

Matthew resisted the urge to grab the fool by his neck. Drawing himself up to his full height, he looked down his nose at Brooke. 'My good man,' he announced haughtily, 'I am *Lord* Ashby. Now, please be so good as to conduct me to my wife.'

The innkeeper bowed low, almost wringing his hands in his obsequiousness. 'My humblest apologies, my lord, I wasn't expecting you. Your lady is in the private parlour, if you would please follow me?'

Matthew followed Brooke along a passageway to the rear of the inn. The innkeeper paused outside a closed door and Matthew stayed him before he could announce Matthew's presence.

'Thank you, Brooke, that will be all. If you could see that we are not disturbed, I should be grateful.'

'Very good, my lord.' Brooke backed away, bowing as he retreated.

The fear that had plagued Matthew since before dawn that morning receded only to be replaced by a rush of anger, stoked by Brooke's meek acceptance of his identity.

I could be anybody.

He hauled the door open and stepped inside the room.

There, sitting at her ease on a comfortable sofa, glass of wine in hand, was the object of all his fretting and fears throughout the long day. Relief exploded through him and all his pent-up emotions surged to the fore as he slammed the door shut and crossed the room in three swift strides.

Chapter Nine

Eleanor's eyes flew open, fear seizing her throat as the door crashed shut, startling her from her drowsy thoughts. She barely had time to register his identity before Matthew Thomas was looming over her, taking her glass from her hand and hauling her to her feet. Before she could utter a word, she found herself clasped in a pair of strong arms, her head pressed hard against a broad chest, the sound of his heart thundering in her ear.

'Thank God you are safe.'

As soon as his hold relaxed, she pushed her hands between them, against his chest, leaning back to look into his face.

'Mr Thomas…whatever is wrong? Why are you here?'

He met her gaze with eyes that swirled with anger and fear. What had happened? Why was he so anxious? How had he found her? She gradually became aware of their surroundings. They were entirely alone, in the private parlour she had reserved for use by herself and Aunt Lucy, who was resting in her room. How did he get in? Where was Brooke?

Matthew held her gaze, his ragged breathing loud in the silence of the room. She pushed harder against him and stepped back. Instantly, his gaze sharpened and he gripped her shoulders, preventing her from retreating further, wringing a gasp from her.

'I have been searching for you…following you…trying to catch up with you…*worrying* about you…'

'But…why? I thought you were—'

'You need protection. I—'

'Protection?'

Eleanor, now with her wits fully about her, stiffened. This was about Aunt Lucy's ludicrous idea that the fire and the shooting were somehow connected. For one fleeting, joyful second she had thought maybe he had followed her for her own sake—because he felt something for her. As speedily as the thought arose, she quashed it, inwardly berating herself for being a romantic fool, beguiled by a handsome face and rugged charm. She and Mr Thomas were worlds apart.

'It seems to me the only protection I am in need of is from you.'

Her heart quailed as his eyes flared and he stepped closer. The heat emanating from him surrounded her as his breath fanned her hair, but she was determined not to reveal her rising alarm and stood her ground, glaring up at him as his eyes pierced hers.

'A young girl was attacked—' He stopped abruptly, his voice cracking with emotion, his expression haunted.

'What…? Attacked? But…what has that to do with me?'

'I've been frantic. If anything had happened to you, I—'

'Mr Thomas! You're making no sense. You said someone had been attacked?'

Matthew swiped one hand through his disordered locks and took a hasty turn about the room, returning to stand in front of an increasingly concerned Eleanor.

He hauled in a deep breath, then let it out slowly. 'She was asleep in the room that had been reserved for you. At the inn in Stockport. Luckily, she screamed and fought him off for long enough for help to arrive. Her attacker ran away, but she ended up with several knife wounds.'

'Oh, the poor, poor thing.' Eleanor's stomach churned as the full significance of Matthew's words finally sank in. 'But...you said...in my room? That poor girl was attacked in the bed I would have slept in?'

Her hand rose to her mouth and she felt herself sway. Matthew was by her side instantly, arms around her as she leant gratefully into his solid strength. He helped her to the sofa and sat by her side, holding her hand, rubbing his thumb gently across her knuckles.

'I'm sorry,' she said faintly. 'I am not normally...that is, it was such a shock.'

She raised her gaze to his, only to find his face much closer than she had anticipated.

'For me, too,' he murmured, his blue eyes darkening. 'I can't bear to think...' His voice tailed away as he cradled her cheek and slowly lowered his head.

Eleanor stilled as warm breath feathered her skin. Lips—surprisingly soft and tender—brushed hers...once, twice...then settled, moving enticingly. She leaned into him, feeling his hand in her hair. Pleasure and anticipation spiralled through her as her lips relaxed and she pressed closer. As his tongue probed her mouth, she raised her restless hand to caress his cheek, but her action seemed to return him to his senses. He wrenched his lips from hers and jumped up from the sofa.

'I'm sorry.' Harsh lines bracketed his mouth.

Eleanor tried to gather her wits, to understand what had just happened.

'I shouldn't have done that... I had no intention... It was a mistake,' he said, and then muttered, as if to himself, 'I do not need complications.'

'Complications?'

The word jarred, rousing Eleanor from her dreamlike stupor.

He looked distant and reserved and didn't quite meet her eyes as he said, 'Please forget that ever happened.'

'You regret kissing me?'

Humiliation flooded Eleanor. She had allowed a virtual stranger to kiss her, and had kissed him back, without a murmur of protest. She was her mother's daughter all right. *Blood will out.* Aunt Phyllis's voice—accusatory, censorious—echoed in her head.

'Yes. No!' He turned abruptly from her, raking his hand through his hair once more before facing her again. His eyes met hers, and softened. 'No, I cannot regret it. But I forgot myself. I was frantic with worry, but that is no excuse for my behaviour. You are a lady and I like to suppose myself a gentleman, despite my station in life, yet at the first opportunity I have behaved like the lowest of rogues.'

Complications. The word rankled. He obviously regretted his impulsive embrace. For that is what it had been— an impulse. He had found her alone and taken advantage, stealing a kiss simply because he could. Now, he was shouldering the blame in order to make her feel better and to excuse her shameful conduct in returning his embrace. Furious with herself, Eleanor turned and would have left the room without a further word had Aunt Lucy not chosen that very moment to come in, her bright gaze darting from one to the other before lingering for some time on Eleanor's hot cheeks, triggering another surge of shame.

'Why, Mr Thomas,' Aunt Lucy said at length, her voice icy, 'how very nice to see you again so soon. I had understood you to be heading in a quite different direction from ourselves. Had I been informed of your presence, I should have made sure I came down to greet you immediately.

I am, after all, Eleanor's chaperon. I can see I shall have to keep a wary eye on you, sir—it is so very easy for a woman to lose her reputation, as I am sure you are aware.'

Eleanor cringed inside. Not only did Mr Thomas now have a complete disgust of her wanton response to his advances, but Aunt Lucy's suspicions had also been aroused. She could wonder at neither of them, for she had no less disgust for herself. Gathering her pride, she walked to the door and opened it, standing to one side.

'Mr Thomas is just leaving, Aunt Lucy. He has said all he needs to say.'

She raised her chin, boldly meeting his gaze. He might have crushed her feelings, but she would rather die than reveal her humiliation.

'Oh, no, I'm not,' Matthew retorted, holding her gaze for what seemed an eternity before switching his attention to Aunt Lucy. 'I have brought grave news, Lady Rothley, news that has serious implications for the safety of your niece.'

Eleanor clamped her teeth shut on the remark she longed to fling at his head. How had the mere touch of his lips managed to block the news of the attack from her mind?

'What news do you bring? What implications?' Aunt Lucy sank on to the sofa and beckoned Eleanor to sit by her side. 'Please, Mr Thomas, be seated—' she waved her hand at the chair opposite '—and explain yourself.'

'Last night, a young woman was attacked in the White Lion in Stockport,' he said. 'She was attacked by an intruder wielding a knife as she slept in one of the bedchambers reserved for your party. I occupied the other.'

Aunt Lucy gasped, turning stricken eyes to Eleanor, who took her hand, her fear giving way to annoyance at Matthew's brutal telling of the story.

'It does not mean,' she said, 'that the attack was intended for me. Surely…' she faltered as Matthew focused his hard gaze on her once more '…surely, it must be a—'

'Coincidence?' Matthew interrupted roughly. 'One co-incidence I can believe, but two? So close together? It would now seem beyond doubt there is a pattern. There have been three attempts on your life in the past few weeks. It is time to take this threat seriously. Tell me, can you think of anyone who would wish you ill?'

'Why, no, of course not. I've barely left Ashby Manor in the past seven years.'

The very idea was absurd.

'Forgive me, but…your husband? Could he wish you harm?'

'Husb— But I'm not married, Mr Thomas. Why would you believe that I am?'

'Not married? But, how…? You're a baroness. You must be wed, or…perhaps you're a widow?'

Aunt Lucy put him straight. 'My niece is a peeress in her own right. Unusual, to be sure, but not unheard of.'

Eleanor watched as Matthew digested this information. He looked, at best, not pleased. The implication of his be-lief she was married dealt a further blow to her already fragile self-esteem.

Was that why he kissed me, because I was a safe tar-get? A married woman who might enjoy a flirtation in her husband's absence? And how much more disgust must he feel now, knowing I'm single and yet returned his kiss?

'Hmm, that puts a very different complexion on it.'

'What possible difference does my being unmarried make?' Shame made her sharp with him.

'It makes every difference. There are many reasons to kill or harm another. Were you married, the reasons someone might wish to kill you might be hatred, or pos-sibly jealousy or passion. But now, with greed as part of the equation, it begins to make more sense. May I ask—who is your heir?'

'My cousin, James Weare.'

'Then he must be our prime suspect.'

'James? Never!'

'Greed has driven more than one to kill, my lady. The lure of a peerage, and the power and privilege it bestows, is more than enough, quite apart from any wealth that accompanies it.'

Eleanor was silent, weighing Matthew's words against her knowledge of her cousin and his character. The fear that had plagued her at odd moments over the past few weeks returned to gnaw at her insides and she shuddered, thinking of that poor girl who had been hurt.

That could have been me. But...no! Not James. He couldn't...not the James I know. It's just too horrible. This is nonsense. It must be nonsense.

Eleanor looked at Aunt Lucy and Matthew, both wearing the same troubled expression, and bitter resentment bubbled up inside. How dare he come here and scare her like this, accusing her much-loved cousin of trying to kill her?

She sprang from the sofa to pace the room. 'No, I will not believe it. James and I grew up together at Ashby—we were like brother and sister. It makes no sense. If he had wanted to kill me he could have done so with ease many times. I am convinced the fire and the accident were unrelated.' She rounded on Matthew. 'I will thank you, sir, to keep such wild accusations to yourself.'

Chapter Ten

Eleanor's agitated pacing prompted Matthew to abandon the topic of her cousin's likely guilt rather than antagonise her further.

The news she was unmarried was an unwelcome shock. He was not the kind of man to dally with innocents—although, eyeing her determined stance as the baroness challenged him, innocent hardly seemed an apt description. But also, to his surprise—and equally unwelcome—was a spurt of pleasure that she was unattached. All nonsense, of course. What on earth could he, a lowly merchant without even the backing of his family name, offer a wealthy baroness? His plans for the future were set. He would work hard to build up a successful business and then he would take the greatest satisfaction in repaying his father every last shilling of his debts. He would prove that the son so easily disowned had made a success of his life without his family's backing.

That kiss, though... He clamped down his desire to taste Eleanor's sweet lips again. *Concentrate on the matter in hand, man...surely it's serious enough to warrant your full attention without being waylaid by such thoughts.*

'You are in danger, my lady,' he said. 'That is a fact and, regardless of who might wish you ill, you must take all possible measures to ensure your safety until the culprit is found.'

'Mr Thomas is right.' Lady Rothley went to Eleanor, taking her hands. 'Oh! It doesn't bear thinking about. That could have been *you* attacked in your bed. You could have been murdered.' Her voice quavered. '*Please*, Ellie, do not be stubborn. Surely you must see these happenings cannot all be coincidence? What do you suggest we do, Mr Thomas? Should we return to Ashby? Will that be safer than London?'

'It might be the wisest move.'

Eleanor directed a scathing look at Matthew. 'I'm sorry you are so troubled, Aunt, but I have no intention of returning to Ashby. Besides, Batley, if you remember, was concerned that the house cannot be made secure during the renovations, so we would be no safer there.'

'Who is Batley?'

Eleanor scorched Matthew with an impatient glance. 'He is my bailiff. No, we will not return to the Manor. We shall continue our journey to London. And that,' she added, jabbing her finger in Matthew's direction, 'is not up for negotiation.'

Matthew bit back his instinctive retort. There was no point in quarrelling with Eleanor in the mood she was in. Never had he come across such an opinionated female.

'I can see you are determined to have your way, Eleanor,' Lady Rothley said, 'so I shall not try to dissuade you. But I give you warning—unless you treat this seriously, we shall return to Ashby, whether you like it or not.' At Eleanor's mutinous look, she continued, 'If I leave London, you will have no option other than to accompany me. You could not remain there unchaperoned. Think of the *scandal*.'

Eleanor visibly subsided. Her aunt's emphasis on the

word 'scandal' must have some particular meaning for her. Matthew wondered if she had been embroiled in some sort of scandal in the past. Was that why she was still unmarried?

Lady Rothley returned to the sofa. 'What precautions would *you* advise us to take, Mr Thomas?'

'The servants accompanying you must be put on the alert immediately, as must the whole of your household in town as soon as you arrive,' Matthew said. 'I will escort you for the remainder of your journey and your niece must take care never to go out unaccompanied. And by that—forgive me, Lady Rothley—I mean that she must take someone other than yourself for protection.'

He watched the conflicting emotions chase each other across Eleanor's expressive countenance. He knew she was still mortified by their kiss, but that could not be the only reason she was so determined to hide her fears over the murder. Was it her reluctance to accept her cousin's involvement?

'There is no need for you to inconvenience yourself, Mr Thomas. I am certain you are reading far more into this than you need to. I am grateful for your concern, but I have no desire to cause further delays for you. You should forget all about this little matter and continue with your—'

'*Little matter?*' Matthew exploded to his feet, itching to take hold of Eleanor and give her a good shake. Infuriating woman! 'Have you not taken in a word I've said? You have more need of protection than I supposed, if that is your belief. I will *not* allow you to continue to put yourself in jeopardy—I must and I will escort you tomorrow. What if your cousin should try again?'

Eleanor stared at him incredulously.

'Ellie.' There was a wealth of warning in Lady Rothley's voice. 'Please remember your—'

'*Will...not...allow?* How dare you? You have absolutely no jurisdiction over me, sir. I have known you precisely one day. I have known James *all my life*. I will *never* believe him to be capable of something like this.' She drew herself up to her full height, standing almost nose to nose with him. 'I know him. You don't.'

She held his gaze, her large eyes defiant. If he continued to pursue the matter, might she stubbornly show her defiance by taking needless risks? Short of throwing her over his shoulder and carrying her off to safety—which, he thought with a silent oath, he would be more than happy to do at this moment—he was not sure how else to persuade her.

But...there was one angle they had not yet considered. 'Who else knew the details of your journey? Maybe that will help us to identify the culprit.'

Eleanor stilled, staring at him, her eyes stricken, her rebelliousness dissipating as swiftly as it had arisen. 'James.' Her voice caught and the word came out as a croak. She cleared her throat. 'James knew.'

She slumped on to the sofa, next to her aunt, who clasped her hand.

'He wrote and reserved the rooms for us in order that we would not be stranded for the night.' She looked at her aunt, her tawny eyes huge in her suddenly ashen countenance. 'I still cannot believe it. Not James. Oh, Aunt Lucy. How shall I ever face him?'

'There, there,' Aunt Lucy patted Eleanor's hand, raising worried eyes to Matthew. 'It seems we are indebted to you once again, Mr Thomas. Your offer to escort us tomorrow is gratefully accepted. Although,' she added acerbically, 'do not for a moment imagine that I have forgotten your earlier behaviour, for I have not.'

Matthew merely bowed his head. He could not deny he was at fault there and could think of nothing to say that would not make an awkward situation even worse. When he raised his head, he found Aunt Lucy eyeing him with suspicion.

'I am curious,' she said. 'How did you find us? And how did you come to be in here, alone, with Eleanor? I am certain Brooke would not have conducted you to our private parlour and left you here with Eleanor without so much as a maidservant in attendance.'

Matthew cursed silently as the enormity of the lie he had told Brooke hit him. The innkeeper was certain to let slip his belief that his guest was a distinguished lord and married to Eleanor to boot.

'I was late leaving Stockport because I had to speak to the magistrate before I could leave—'

'Why should the magistrate wish to speak with *you*?' Eleanor asked.

'I told you—I was in the next bedchamber to the girl who was attacked. When she screamed, I went in. I saw him…but he gave me the slip.'

'Then you know what he looks like. Describe him. I shall soon know if it was James.'

'He wore a mask. All I know is that he was shorter than me and of a medium build. There are any number of men who would match that description. By the time I left I was sure you would be well on your way. We—that is, Henry and I—enquired at all the posting inns we passed until we found where you had stopped for the night. Mr Brooke was indeed reluctant to admit you were in residence. I'm afraid I had to resort to a little subterfuge.'

Two pairs of eyes watched him expectantly. He drew a deep breath, bracing himself.

'I told him I was Lord Ashby. Your husband.'

There was a moment of stunned silence, then Eleanor let forth a peal of laughter that made Matthew stare in bewilderment. *What on earth...?* She should be furious... ringing a peal of anger, not laughter, over his head.

'What is so funny?' He sounded so stiff and pompous he almost cringed.

Eleanor gasped for breath, hand flat to her chest, as giggles continued to spill from her lips. Was that a note of hysteria? Matthew glanced at Aunt Lucy, who looked as stunned as he felt.

'Oh... I am so sorry...the look of dread on your face... if only you could have seen it...'

'I shall, of course, ensure that you do not suffer by my hasty and ill-considered actions, Lady Ashby—'

Eleanor sobered at his words. 'Oh, no,' she said. 'Please do not. Really, Mr Thomas, I had begun to think you a man of sense, then you come up with *the* most ridiculous ruse to confound poor Brooke, and then find yourself forced to make amends by making an offer you clearly have no wish to make. Oh, this is just the spur I needed to jolt me out of that horrid fear that was near paralysing me. No doubt it will soon overwhelm me again but, for now, I am happy just to enjoy the joke.'

'Joke?' Indignation stirred. 'You believe an offer from me would be a *joke*?'

She rose to her feet. 'Not in the way you are clearly taking it,' she said, in a placatory tone. 'I promise. I only meant it is a joke in as much as we barely know each other, our stations in life are so different and we have done little but squabble since we met.'

A sudden flush stained her cheeks and she turned from him abruptly. Was she, like him, remembering that kiss? But, other than that omission from her list, she was right.

'Well! My niece might think this a laughing matter, but I can assure you I do not, young man,' Lady Rothley said, as she also stood. 'What were you thinking? Brooke and,

most likely, all his staff, believe you to be Lord Ashby and
are aware that you have spent time alone in this parlour
with my niece. You cannot sustain this masquerade—our
servants will surely let slip that there *is* no Lord Ashby.
And as soon as your trickery is known, Eleanor's reputation will be in tatters. What a tangle.'

She was right. He had acted without thought, driven
by his frantic belief that Eleanor was in danger. Now he
had succeeded in embroiling her in a possible scandal.
That thought brought to mind Eleanor's reaction to Aunt
Lucy's earlier threat of scandal. An odd reaction, almost
as though she feared for her reputation more than most.
And yet she could laugh at this situation. She was certainly a puzzling woman.

'You can say you were with me the whole time, Aunt
Lucy,' Eleanor said. 'And Mr Thomas must find another
inn to stay in tonight.' She met his gaze. She was deadly
serious now, no hint of amusement on her countenance.
'It will not do for you to remain, for you cannot continue
the deception of being my husband. Brooke will say nothing. After all, he cannot claim to be blameless. He failed
to even announce you, which is inexcusable. After all, you
could have been anybody.'

'Precisely,' Matthew growled. 'And if you believe I'm
going to leave you unprotected in this place tonight, you
are way off course. In fact, I believe it is too dangerous
for *you* to remain the night. Knowing he failed last night,
I would not put it past the attacker to strike again. And
as he's clearly familiar with your itinerary, he will know
you are here tonight.'

His words brought a flash of fear to Eleanor's expression. It was regrettable, he thought, as he pictured her
laughing only a few moments ago, but it was surely better
for her to be frightened than to dismiss the very real risks.

'When Brooke allowed me to enter your private parlour, simply on my word that I was your husband, he confirmed my belief that you are completely vulnerable. We must all leave.' He paused, pondering. He had caused this problem. He must find the solution.

'Wait here a minute,' he said. 'I have an idea.'

He went in search of Brooke. 'Please attend us in the parlour as soon as convenient, Brooke,' he said. 'I should like to discuss the security of your establishment and the safety of your guests.'

'Yes, my lord. Immediately, my lord.' Brooke followed Matthew back to the parlour.

As Matthew entered, Eleanor said, 'What do you...?' Her question tailed away as Matthew shook his head, hoping she would interpret his warning and follow his lead. He winked, then rounded on Brooke.

'To begin with, I must tell you that I am *not* Lord Ashby. My name is Matthew Thomas.'

'Not...? But, sir, you gave me to believe... I allowed you...'

'Quite. You believed my claim and you showed me into what was *supposed* to be a private parlour for the use of these ladies. I must inform you—and this is not to be spoken of outside this room—that we already had grave concerns over Lady Ashby's safety.

'Now then, I told that lie in order to see how easy it might be for an intruder to gain access to Lady Ashby whilst she is staying here. I not only tricked you into revealing her whereabouts, but also persuaded you—with little difficulty, I might add—to allow me to enter her private parlour unannounced.

'I must inform you, Brooke, that you have failed my test miserably. Had I harboured evil intentions towards Lady Ashby, there would have been nothing to prevent me carrying out my worst. I am extremely disappointed.

'Lady Rothley happened to be with her niece at the time, but you were not to know that. Anything could have happened and, as a result of your failures, I am afraid we have no alternative but to move to another establishment for the night.'

'No, I beg of you, sir, ladies, please do not leave. A thousand apologies, milady—' Brooke bowed to Eleanor, wringing his hands in his anguish '—for my failures. I can promise you it will not happen again. I shall place guards on each door. You are our only guests tonight and I swear to turn any latecomers away. I shall have a man patrolling all night long. The George will be more secure than the Tower itself, of that you have my word.

'Do please reconsider. My wife has prepared a feast for tonight—it is ready to be served, and it is dark outside and beginning to rain. Surely you would prefer to stay here in the warm than go out in search of other accommodation?

'Besides,' he added, 'if there is someone out there who means you harm, he could attack you more easily outside than if you remain safe and snug in here, especially now I am aware of the danger.'

He looked eagerly from one to the other.

Matthew heaved a sigh, concealing his relief that Brooke had fallen for his ploy. 'Well, if you promise you will put guards on the outer doors—and for the whole night, mind, not just until we retire—we will stay. Although, make no mistake, my man, you are still on trial. If I discover any lapse in attention, it will be the worse for you.'

'Yes, my…sir.' Brooke bowed his way out of the door.

Matthew looked at Eleanor and Lady Rothley. 'Well? Have we come through unscathed?'

Chapter Eleven

'I believe so. Well done,' Eleanor said and smiled at Matthew. 'The poor man didn't know if he was coming or going. I don't think it even crossed his mind to question that Aunt Lucy was in here the whole time.'

Aunt Lucy was not so quick to forgive. 'Let us hope this doesn't get back to Lizzie and Matilda,' she warned, 'for I doubt they will be so easy to deceive.'

Dinner was served at a table set for three in the private parlour. Brooke had not lied when he promised them a feast and they were served with dishes of succulent roast meats, pigeon pie, vegetables and rich sauces, followed by stewed apples, blancmanges, dried fruits and nuts, all accompanied by some very palatable wines.

Conversation at the dinner table was necessarily stilted, with the serving maid and Brooke himself in and out of the room. As the last dishes were cleared away, Eleanor heard Brooke murmur in Matthew's ear, 'Brandy, sir?'

They had eaten in the parlour, so it was impossible for Eleanor and her aunt to leave Matthew to his brandy, as was customary. As he pushed his chair back and stood, presumably to go through to the taproom, Eleanor said, 'If you would care for some brandy, Mr Thomas, please do not feel obliged to leave.'

'No, indeed,' Aunt Lucy said. 'In fact…Brooke, my good man, would you bring two glasses, please? A little tot will help me sleep, I make no doubt. My niece and I shall retire very soon, Mr Thomas, and leave you to enjoy your brandy in peace.'

'Thank you.' Matthew said. 'I doubt I shall be long in following you to bed. It's been a long, eventful day.'

Brooke soon returned with a full decanter and two glasses. After drinking her tot, Aunt Lucy rose to her feet. 'Come, Ellie, it is time for us to retire. Mr Thomas, may we leave you with the task of checking Brooke's security arrangements? We shall see you in the morning. Goodnight.'

'My pleasure,' Matthew said. 'Goodnight, ladies.'

As soon as the door closed behind them, Aunt Lucy said, 'I wonder who our Mr Thomas really is?'

Eleanor paused, her foot on the bottom stair. 'What do you mean: who he really is?'

Aunt Lucy looked back at the parlour door. 'I'm not sure,' she said. 'But there is something…oh, I don't know… something almost *familiar* about him. And, just as I think I'm on the brink of grasping it, it slips away again. Never mind. I am sure it will come to me in time.'

They continued up the stairs to the first landing and Eleanor wished her aunt goodnight at her bedchamber door. Lizzie helped her to undress before leaving and Eleanor climbed into bed, exhausted, ready for a good night's sleep. As soon as her head hit the pillow, however, her mind sprang to life, reliving the fire and the accident, fretting at the attack on that young girl—could it truly be connected to her? Was James responsible? No, she could never believe it of him. Not attempted murder. But the very thought that someone might wish to kill her was too much to bear and she tossed and turned until finally, still wide awake, she decided to go downstairs to see if she could sneak a tot of brandy for herself. If it helped Aunt Lucy to sleep, mayhap it would do the same for her?

Relighting her candle, she found her slippers and wrapped her large woollen shawl around her. Taking up the candlestick, she stepped softly on to the dark landing and crept to the head of the stairs. Stomach churning uneasily, despite Brooke's promise to post two guards at every external door, she tiptoed down the stairs to the parlour. Surely everyone must have retired by now? She could hear nothing but the distant rumble of snores—a comforting sound, confirming there were people within reach should she need them.

She hesitated a moment at the parlour door, listening, before lifting the latch and pushing the door open.

Her heart leapt into her throat.

Matthew stood before the fire, one booted foot on the fender. He had removed his jacket, leaving him clad in shirt, waistcoat and pantaloons, which clung to his buttocks and muscular thighs. His left hand was propped against the mantelshelf as he stared down into the glowing embers and his right cradled a goblet of amber liquid. Eleanor had not thought for one minute he would still be up, for had he not said he would be retiring soon after them? Thank goodness he had not heard the door open. Her fingers tightened, clutching her shawl closer around her. She must leave. Now. She would be foolish to remain.

Still she hesitated. Something about the way he was standing and staring into the fire tugged at her heartstrings. He looked a little…lost, somehow, and the urge to offer comfort was strong. The memory of his kiss set her lips tingling, despite her confusion over his subsequent reaction when he had said he did not want complications. Eleanor bit her lip, considering.

No. She must go. They had tempted fate once already

today. She must not do so again. She stepped back but, before she could close the door, something—a slight noise perhaps, or just the movement—betrayed her. Matthew looked up. She caught a glimpse of loneliness and sorrow before his mask slipped back into place.

She swallowed hard, her nerves in shreds. Why, oh, why, had she lingered? Why did she not retreat the *second* she saw him? It was too late now. She stepped inside the room and closed the door.

'I am sorry to disturb you, Mr Thomas,' she whispered. 'I was unable to sleep and I thought to come down for some brandy, in the hope it might help.'

His voice was low, but she could hear the steel behind his words. 'And so you decided to wander around the inn at the dead of night? Even after everything that's happened?'

'I was careful! Besides, I knew you had inspected the doors and windows, so nobody can get in.'

His jaw firmed. 'You place far too much faith in my abilities.' He lifted his glass to his lips and tipped his head back.

'Why should I not?' Eleanor said. 'I trust you.'

She hesitated. What had she said? That sounded… Matthew was appraising her, brows raised, a knowing smile lurking at the corners of his mouth.

'I mean,' she added quickly, 'I trust your *capabilities*.'

'Oh, no,' he said, 'don't spoil it now. I could get very used to basking in your approval.'

Eleanor felt the blood suffuse her face, her insides squirming at his teasing smile. 'I must go. I bid you goodnight.' She turned to the door.

'Don't go.'

She paused, her hand already on the latch.

Are you going to flee every time a man shows a smidgeon of interest in you? Irritably, she tried to shrug away that insidious voice in her head.

'Stay a moment, please. I'd welcome the company.' There was a hint of a plea in those words.

Her awkwardness receded. He *had* looked desolate. Mayhap she could help. She had come downstairs for brandy... She would not scuttle away as though she had done something wrong. There could be no harm in staying for a minute or two, as long as they weren't seen.

She slowly faced him, then gestured to the decanter that remained where Brooke had left it on the sideboard. 'Would you pour me some brandy, please?'

She crossed the room, hugging her shawl even more tightly around her, as he poured out a measure of the spirit. Her doubts reared up again...*why did I not go when I had the chance?*

Because you want to know, the treacherous voice in her head whispered. *You want to know how it feels when a man desires you.*

Matthew's blue gaze captured hers as he handed her the goblet, their fingers brushing. Eleanor all but snatched the glass from his hand.

'Thank you,' she said, moving swiftly to stand next to the fireplace.

'You are *most* welcome, my lady.'

His deep voice resonated, sending a quiver of excitement darting through her core. *Oh, my.* Warning bells rang loud and clear but she chose to ignore them. Yes, it was scandalous to be here, alone, with Matthew, but she was in control. Nothing would happen. Mayhap she could view this as practice—to help her conquer the hideous embarrassment that had plagued her during her come-out. If she could learn to converse unselfconsciously with the attractive, but undoubtedly unsuitable, Matthew Thomas, might that not stand her in good stead in London, where there would be attractive, *suitable* gentlemen to talk to and dance with?

Eleanor fixed her gaze on the goblet cupped in her hands. She swirled the glowing liquid round the bowl, warming it before lifting it to her lips. She sipped, then coughed at its fiery strength. She was aware, without looking, that Matthew had resumed his stance on the opposite side of the hearth, setting the decanter on the mantelshelf.

Feeling emboldened, she said, 'You know a great deal about me, but I know next to nothing of you. Other than you have a good eye for horseflesh.'

He stared into the dying fire. 'There is nothing much to know and the details are unlikely to interest you.'

'Nevertheless...' She allowed the silence to hang between them. While she waited, she drank again, relishing the warmth as the brandy slid down her throat.

'Since the age of eighteen I have lived and worked overseas. I am a merchant—my world is far removed from the world you inhabit.'

Eleanor raised her brows. He had been more forthcoming in that one sentence than he had since they first met. 'Where did you live?'

'India. I only returned to England a few weeks ago.'

'Do you miss it? Will you go back there?'

He frowned, still gazing into the embers. 'I miss some aspects of it and I may return in the future, who knows? But not to live. England is my home from now on.'

'Why did you go out there in the first place?'

He shrugged. 'I needed to make a living. My great-uncle was an East India merchant, and I went to work with him. When he died, I decided to come home.'

'What about work? How will you make your living now?'

He laughed, softly. 'You ask a lot of questions, my lady,'

he said. 'More brandy?' He proffered the decanter and waited, brows raised.

'Thank you.' Eleanor held her glass out and he poured her another measure of the amber spirit. 'It is very nice. I can understand why Aunt Lucy thought it would help her sleep.'

Matthew watched her sip again at the brandy, eyes crinkling. 'Is this the first time you've tasted brandy?'

'Oh, yes. Now, what was it I said?'

'You asked how I will make my living now I am back in England. I warn you, this is the last question and then it is your turn to be interrogated. I shall make my living the same way I always have—in trade. We import tea, rugs, cloth, porcelain, anything really, from India and, sometimes, China. If there's a market for it, we import it.'

'We?'

'My business partner, Benedict Poole, and I. He is, as we speak, sailing back to England with two more cargoes.

'And that is more than enough about me... You told me you have you not been to London for seven years. Was that your come-out? Why have you never been back?'

The swift change of subject had Eleanor replying before she could consider her words. 'It was my come-out, yes, but I *hated* it.'

'*Hated?* That is a strong reaction to something that is meant to be pleasurable.'

'What do *you* know about come-outs and Seasons?'

'Oh, I hear talk,' he replied. 'I thought it was compulsory for *every* young lady to *adore* their come-out.'

She couldn't help giggling. 'Not me. I was shy and, looking back, too immature.'

'That doesn't explain why you have not been back since. You are far from shy now.'

Heat rose to burn her cheeks as their kiss loomed large

in her thoughts. Matthew's suddenly intense expression suggested he, too, was thinking of it. She gulped her remaining drink, then held out her glass for more, ignoring Matthew's raised brows as he poured a little...a *very* little... brandy into her goblet.

As she opened her mouth to ask for more, Matthew said, 'Why are you so wary of scandal?'

The breath whooshed from Eleanor's lungs. 'What... what do you mean? I am not—'

'Uh-uh.' Matthew shook his head at her, eyes brimming with amusement. 'I answered all your questions... no avoiding the awkward ones.'

'Yes, but—'

'Your aunt gave me the clue. You were full of indignation and she stopped you with that one phrase—"Think of the *scandal*."'

Eleanor forced a light laugh even as she registered— somewhere deep down—that her mind was a touch fuddled. She concentrated fiercely on her words. 'You show me anyone who relishes their own scandal, Mr Thomas. It seems quite reasonable to me that I should not wish to be tainted.'

'Entirely reasonable, yes. But her words and your reaction suggest something more than the normal desire to avoid scandal. As if, maybe, there is something in your past? Come now, how bad can it be? A few stolen kisses?'

Eleanor stiffened. She could hardly blame him for believing such a possibility.

His lips twitched. 'I promise I will not hold your scandal against you.'

'It is not *my* scandal. It was my mother's. And I do not wish to talk about it.' She put her glass on the mantelshelf. 'I am going to bed.'

Matthew caught her hand. 'No, don't go. I didn't mean to offend your sensibilities.' He smiled, ruefully. 'I fear I am out of practice in how to treat a lady. I promise to pry no further.'

His touch sent a tremor racing through her and she snatched her hand from his. For some reason, his assumption that she needed protection from the truth—that her female sensibilities somehow precluded her from facing up to the harsh realities of life—irritated her. She was an independent woman. She flattered herself she was strong. She was capable of facing up to reality. She did not need a man's protection from that.

'My mother left my father and me when I was eleven,' she said. 'She lived openly in London with another man. *That* was the scandal. I never saw her after she left and she died in childbirth a few years later. You asked why I hated my come-out and *that* was why—the whispers, everywhere I went. The eyes that followed my every move. The *gentlemen* who seemed to believe "like mother, like daughter".' The memory of that horrible time choked her voice. She paused; shook her head; huffed a short, bitter laugh. '*This* time I vow I shall be the perfect lady. My behaviour will be beyond reproach and I *will* have vouchers for Almack's. You *see* if I don't.'

She stared belligerently at Matthew.

'I have no doubt you will be a complete success,' he said, soothingly, as he grasped her arm and turned her towards the door. 'Now, however, it is time you went to bed. Come.'

He guided her to the door, his hand at the small of her back. Warm. Comforting. His scent was in her nostrils— musky, male, a hint of citrus. She spun to face him and had to steady herself with a hand on his chest.

'Whoops. That brandy was stronger than I thought.' *And it's loosened your tongue, Eleanor. Take care.* She focused her gaze on Matthew's neckcloth.

Matthew removed her hand from his chest and reached for the door latch.

'Thank you,' she said. 'I must be quiet, mustn't I? Can you imagine what Aunt Lucy would say were she to see us here like this? She would, quite rightly, wash her hands of me.'

She lifted her gaze to his face as she spoke. Swayed towards him. His eyes caressed her, warming her as the brandy had done. He lifted one hand, trailing a long finger down her cheek, before tracing the outline of her lips, which parted as she drew in a shaky breath. She closed her eyes, revelling in the swirl of need burgeoning inside her.

'You are very beautiful, Eleanor,' he murmured. 'So hard to resist.'

Her soul blossomed at his words. She was standing so close she could feel his coat brush the tips of her breasts. Her nipples tingled and tightened and her bones felt like they were melting.

Matthew brushed her lips—hardly even touching them—with his own. 'Goodnight.'

Her hands lifted of their own volition and clutched his lapels. She rose on tiptoe. Her kiss was no fleeting flirtation of the lips, but a warm, moist pressure as she angled her mouth to his. Matthew responded with a groan, his arms enfolding her, pulling her against the full length of his hard body. One splayed hand supported her back and the other cradled her head as he returned the pressure of her lips and increased the intensity of the kiss. Warm, brandy-flavoured lips parted and she opened in response. He captured her breath as his tongue caressed and explored. She followed his lead, surrendering to a deeper, darker, more wanton kiss than she had ever imagined possible. She never wanted that kiss to end.

She threaded her fingers through his hair as he gathered her closer, his hand tracing the curve of her spine to her bottom. She lost track of time. The only reality was in their kiss—a wicked, glorious promise of greater delights to come. She clung ever closer, her hands exploring the width of his shoulders and the long line of his back until she reached his taut buttocks, so very different to the soft roundness of her own.

He gasped into her mouth and, with another groan, tore his lips from hers, taking her by the shoulders and holding her away from him, steadying her as her knees threatened to buckle. Bemused, she studied his features, reading his regret and his resolve.

'I think,' he said, his voice husky with desire, 'you should go. This is not wise. It can never be.'

His words brought her back to reality. Heavens! What was she doing? She searched his eyes, deep blue, swirling with so many complex emotions.

'I should not have stayed,' she whispered. 'It was reckless. You are right. This can never be. We should not be alone together.'

He gave a shaky laugh. 'No, we should not and, as you said, heaven help us if your aunt should discover us. Go on, now. Go. We will forget this ever happened.' His deep tones resonated through her. 'I'll see you in the morning.'

Eleanor returned to her bedchamber as if in a dream, her emotions in turmoil. Thoughts and memories tumbled through her mind. What had she done? Dismay at her disgraceful behaviour clashed with desire; regret with joy; mortification with a guilty longing for more. Confused, she slipped into her dreams.

Chapter Twelve

The following morning Eleanor breakfasted in her bed-chamber.

'She has the headache,' Lady Rothley announced when she joined Matthew at the breakfast table. 'I'm sure it is not to be wondered at, with all these goings-on.'

No, indeed it is not, Matthew thought, with a wry inner smile.

'I am sorry to hear that,' he said. 'I hope she will feel well enough to travel today.'

'Oh, I am sure she will bounce back. My niece is a strong woman. She will not allow a headache to overset her, or her plans.'

That I can well believe.

'I will send a message to the stables to delay our departure for an hour,' Matthew said. 'Hopefully by then she will feel better.'

'That is most thoughtful, Mr Thomas,' Lady Rothley said, beaming as she beckoned to a serving girl, who had just entered the parlour with a plate of freshly cooked eggs.

The maid curtsied. 'Yes, milady?'

'Please ensure a message is taken to Lady Ashby to tell her our departure is delayed until half past ten.'

'And ask Mr Brooke to relay the same message to one of our men, will you?' Matthew added.

'Yes, milady. Yes, sir.' The maid hurried away.

'I very much appreciate your sacrifice, Mr Thomas,' Lady Rothley said, as she nibbled at a slice of toast. 'This will, I am afraid, delay you even further. I cannot tell you how much better I slept for knowing you are to accompany us on the rest of the journey.'

'I am delighted to be of service, my lady.'

If only Lady Rothley knew how close he had come to leaving the inn at first light, urgent with the need to put Eleanor, and the conflicting emotions she aroused in him, out of his mind for good. He had a plan for his life. And that plan most definitely did not include a beautiful, strong-willed baroness who—having blithely informed him how determined she was to prove to society that she was *not* her mother's daughter—had then kissed him. Very thoroughly. And most enjoyably. His blood thrummed at the memory.

'She is not a *bad* girl, Mr Thomas.'

Lady Rothley's attention was on her plate, so she did not notice Matthew's start at her words. Was she a mind-reader? He blanked his expression, lifting his coffee cup to his lips.

'She is so determined to prove that she can succeed without a man to lean on,' she continued, 'she becomes a touch…*overbearing*…at times. You may have noticed.'

Matthew almost choked on his coffee. 'No,' he gasped, battling to contain a near-overwhelming urge to laugh. 'No, I cannot say I have noticed. Not overbearing. A little…*managing*, perhaps.'

'Ah, yes.' Her ladyship's dark eyes twinkled. 'That is much more diplomatic. You have a nice turn of phrase, Mr Thomas. Eleanor works so hard, you see, and has been too isolated since her father died. He wished her to wed before he died, but…well, it did not work out. And her aunt—not me, her Aunt Phyllis, the one who lives with her—well, she has no more sense than a noddycock, filling poor Ellie's head with dire warnings about bankruptcy and how women don't have the brains for business. Well, what would you expect from a spirited girl like Ellie? She's bound to want to prove everyone wrong.'

'Yes. Of course,' Matthew replied, his head reeling.

'Oh, dear. Now I have put you to the blush, Mr Thomas. I should not let my mouth run on so, but all this business… the attacks…and the responsibility of taking Eleanor to London after last time—' She stopped abruptly. 'There I go again. You are too easy to talk to, Mr Thomas, that is the trouble, and I must confess it is a relief to have someone to confide in. One cannot talk to the servants about such matters and, of course, I could never speak so frankly of my worries to Ellie. It helps, too, that you are not part of our world, so I forget to be discreet.'

Matthew stood, his chair scraping across the floor. He did not want to hear any more of Lady Rothley's confidences… he was intrigued enough by Eleanor already, without learning more about her, or having his sympathy stirred.

Although the temptation to abandon Eleanor and her aunt this morning had been powerful, in the end his conscience had won. He could not forget they were in danger. He had given his word that he would escort them to London and he would do so. But he had vowed to avoid being alone with Eleanor for the rest of their journey. He need only be strong for another few days, and then he need never see her again.

'You may rely on my discretion, my lady. Now, if you will excuse me, I must settle my account with Brooke, and speak to my man about the arrangements for the journey.'

Eleanor, meanwhile, was battling not only her pounding head, but also the lowering memory of her scandalous conduct. She had appeared in the parlour, in the dead of night, clad only in her nightgown and a shawl. Would any red-blooded male not have taken advantage of the opportunity she so naively presented? Although…and she had cringed as the full version of events from the night before unfolded in her mind's eye…*she* had kissed *Matthew*. Not the other way around. And the *things* she had told him. She winced at the memory. She did not doubt that the brandy had lowered her inhibitions, but her decision to stay had been before a drop had even touched her lips. What on earth had come over her? All the tenets of her upbringing, all of her innate sense of self-preservation and good old-fashioned common sense, had simply disappeared.

And what must Matthew Thomas think of her? She must take care in her future dealings with him—she must guard both her reputation and her heart, for he was clearly a danger to both. She conjured up a picture of those rugged good looks and the memory of that kiss, and she quivered. Oh, yes, he was a danger to her all right. A danger she would find hard to resist. But resist she must. Aunt Phyllis had only been half-right about the dangers of men and their seductive ways. She had never warned Eleanor of the treachery of a woman's own body, when she was attracted by a man. Why had none of the gentlemen of her acquaintance ever enticed her like this?

Hmmph. It was no good brooding over it. What had happened had happened. She must ensure she was never again alone with Matthew. It would only be for a couple of days and then their paths would never cross again.

In the yard of the George two chaise-and-fours were standing ready for their journey. Aunt Lucy and Eleanor would travel in the first—as yesterday—and Lizzie, Matilda and Timothy would ride in the second. Eleanor looked around. There was no sign of Matthew, or of his

curricle and pair. Perhaps, she thought with a swell of relief, ignoring the sting of disappointment that followed
close on its heels, he had decided against accompanying
them after all.

A footstep behind her, and the waft of tangy citrus, alerted
her to his presence.

'Good morning, my lady. I trust your headache is better?'

Eleanor inclined her head. 'Very much so, Mr Thomas.
Thank you for enquiring.'

So formal. She risked a glance. He held out his hand.

'Allow me to assist you into the chaise.'

She placed her gloved hand in his. Strong fingers closed
over hers and anticipation whispered deep in her belly. She
lifted her chin and climbed the steps into the vehicle, taking her seat next to Aunt Lucy, who was already inside.
She looked to the door, to thank Matthew, and bit back a
gasp as he climbed in behind her.

'Are you not driving yourself?'

She felt her colour rise as Matthew regarded her, one
brow raised. She had not meant to sound so brusque.

'I drove the horses hard yesterday,' he said. 'They will
benefit from a day or two's rest and then Henry will drive
them to London in easy stages. I am afraid, therefore, that
you must endure my presence for the remainder of the
journey to London.'

'How pleasant it will be to have your company, Mr
Thomas.' Aunt Lucy beamed as she nudged Eleanor. 'Will
it not, my pet?'

We will forget this ever happened.

Matthew Thomas had been true to his word, Eleanor
granted him that. Not by a single look, or word, or deed
did he even hint at what had passed between them at the

George. Far from being relieved, Eleanor found herself growing more and more irritated as time passed. When she had vowed never to be alone with Matthew again, she had imagined him contriving circumstances in which they would meet and she would be the strong one, denying him despite his protestations. Instead, he made no effort whatsoever to manoeuvre her into being alone with him. They had not even had the opportunity to exchange a private word.

Not that I want *to be alone with him.*

She simply longed for the chance to spurn him. To prove that kissing him was something she regretted. Deeply.

The following morning, Eleanor paid the reckoning at the White Hart in Loughborough and was about to climb into the post-chaise, when Matthew strode from the inn, a thunderous frown on his face.

'I pay my own way.'

'And a very good morning to you, too, Mr Thomas,' Eleanor said, lifting her chin. Both she and Aunt Lucy had broken their fast in their rooms, so this was their first meeting of the day. His manner did not bode well for a pleasant journey. 'There is no call for you to turn top-lofty. This is my party, my journey. I pay.'

It was the only way she could retain her dignity. The tug of attraction was still strong. The memory of his kiss still set her senses aflame. His assumption of command throughout their first day of travel—overseeing the changes of the horses, arranging refreshments and private parlours to rest in, and checking and organising the security of the inn they stayed in overnight—had lifted the burden of responsibility from Eleanor. And she was both relieved and affronted by it. An inner tussle with her conscience had resulted in her admitting—but only privately

—that, on balance, it was pleasant to have a man to take charge for a change.

She was no longer shy and uncomfortable with him. Mayhap that was because he no longer looked at her in that particular way, his blue eyes penetrating until her innermost thoughts felt exposed to his inspection. And, since that night at the George, he had neither teased her nor flirted with her. His manner had been that of a polite, casual acquaintance. Eleanor had been able to move past the fluster and the blushes, and treat him—on the surface, at least—as the simple travelling companion he was. But the desire to assert her authority was powerful and paying their way was how she chose to salvage her self-esteem. Ultimately, she who pays the piper calls the tune, she thought with satisfaction.

She had known he might object. She had not anticipated such fury. It was rigidly controlled, but fury none the less.

'You may pay for your own accommodation and that of the servants,' he said in a tight, low voice, 'but I will not have you paying for *my* room and board. Here.' He thrust out his hand, opening it to reveal a clutch of coins on his palm. 'Take them.'

'No. You are supplying a service. I will be responsible for your expenses.' Eleanor turned and climbed into the post-chaise.

'By God, you are the most infuriating woman I have ever met.' Matthew leant in the open door, blue eyes blazing. 'I have no need of your charity, *Lady* Ashby.'

Eleanor swallowed hard. 'I do not view it as charity, but as my obligation.'

'I may not have your wealth, but I am not poor. I can pay my way.'

'I did not think for one moment that you couldn't. Tell me—' she locked gazes with him '—if I were a man, could you honestly say we would be having this same discussion?'

Matthew opened his mouth, then closed it again. Inhaled, nostrils flaring. He climbed into the chaise and sat down, leaning back into the corner, eyes narrowed as he regarded her.

'I don't know,' he finally said. A smile tugged at the corners of his mouth. 'I cannot imagine another man accepting he might need my protection. But do not think that means I will accept you paying for my accommodation or my meals on the rest of the journey, for I will not.'

'And if I pay anyway?'

'Then there will be some very lucky innkeepers between here and London, for they will be paid twice over for the one service.'

Hmmph. 'It appears I must concede the point this time.'

'What point might that be, Ellie?' Aunt Lucy asked as Timothy handed her into the post-chaise.

'Mr Thomas is offended that I have settled his account at the inn.'

'I see,' Aunt Lucy said, as she settled on to the seat between them.

She said no more, but it was clear from the sidelong look she bent on Eleanor that she considered her niece to be in the wrong. The journey passed with very little conversation other than passing comments on the scenery or the weather.

At the first stop to change the horses, however, Aunt Lucy returned to the subject as soon as Matthew left the post-chaise.

'I am surprised at you, Ellie. Have you no consideration for a young man's pride?'

'Of course I have.' Eleanor was stung by her aunt's

criticism. What about her own pride? Being kissed by a man—no, *kissing* a man—and then being roundly ignored? 'I meant no slight.' Had she really bruised his pride? Guilt stirred deep inside as she reviewed her actions and their conversation. Although she was determined to prove her capabilities in running her estates, she had always taken care not to flaunt her wealth or her privilege in front of others. Particularly men. She had realised, as she matured, that many men resented her title and her wealth simply because they afforded her that elusive advantage—for a female—of independence.

'The best solution is for you to hand over the travelling purse to Mr Thomas,' Aunt Lucy said, 'and then *he* can settle the accounts and his pride will not suffer.'

'No. Why should I hand over my money to a near stranger? What if—?'

'What if I were to abscond with your funds?' Matthew had appeared at the open door. His eyes glittered. 'Trust me, Lady Ashby, I have no need of your few paltry coins. I have my own business and my own property. It may not match yours, but it is more than sufficient for my needs.'

He climbed in and slammed the door. The vehicle jerked as the horses took the strain and they were on the road again.

'You have property, Mr Thomas? In London?' Aunt Lucy asked.

Eleanor was, for once, grateful for her aunt's insatiable curiosity. She would never have lowered herself to ask the question, but she was dying to know the answer.

'Yes, in Bloomsbury. My great-uncle bequeathed me a small house in his will. As I said, it is enough for me.'

'What was his name?' Aunt Lucy asked. 'Mayhap I knew him.'

'You would not have known him, Lady Rothley. He spent

all of his adult life in India. He was my grandmother's brother—their father was a cloth merchant. They did not move in your circles.'

The conversation was at a close and Eleanor settled down for the remainder of the journey. *Just two more nights, then we shall be in London.* And then…she closed her eyes and concentrated on planning her campaign for full acceptance in society and those all-important vouchers for Almack's, burying deep the ache in her heart at the thought she would never see Matthew Thomas again.

Chapter Thirteen

Matthew gazed broodingly at Eleanor across the dining table on the evening of the following day. It was the last night of their journey. Tomorrow they would be in London. He would deliver Eleanor and her aunt safely to their door, say goodbye and never have to set eyes on the top-lofty, arrogant, beautiful, stubborn woman again. His brain and his body were in complete conflict. He wanted her. Badly. He was not even sure he liked her. But he definitely wanted her. The tension in his muscles whenever she was close could not be denied.

He'd had to steel himself against the hurt in those beautiful, tawny-brown eyes as he had treated her with cool civility during the first day of travel, when he barely trusted himself to even look at her. After that, it had become easier as Eleanor withdrew behind her *grande dame* persona. Matthew had busied himself as much as possible at every stop they made, lest he reveal the desire that burned deep within him every time he came within touching distance of her.

'You still won't be safe.' The words were out there before he could consider them, or where they might lead.

Eleanor lowered her knife and fork and fixed those luminous eyes on him, candlelight highlighting gold flecks he had not noticed before. They drew him in, charging his blood, making him wish the impossible.

A man could drown in such limpid beauty.

Pfftt. Next thing, I'll be reciting poetry. That's what happens when a man spends too long in the company of females. He gets soft.

'Would you care to expand upon that remark, Mr Thomas?'

'I meant to say, how will you keep safe in London? There have been no further incidents, but the closer we get to London, the more traffic there will be, the more people on the streets. How will you distinguish friend from foe?'

Eleanor's eyes narrowed before she returned her attention to her plate and resumed eating. Time suspended as he held his breath. Was she ever going to reply?

'I was thinking the same thing myself,' she said, finally, surprising him. He had expected vehement denial of the risk.

'I shall have to employ extra footmen as guards,' she continued. 'I have Timothy, and there is William, who travelled ahead with the others to prepare the house, but I do not think I can rely on just those two. Not when they have other duties to fulfil as well.'

'Do you truly believe a couple of extra footmen will suffice to protect you?'

She regarded him steadily. 'What action would *you* suggest I take, Mr Thomas?'

Her tone was sweet, at odds with the challenge in her eyes. All day he had been telling himself they would reach London tomorrow and he could walk away. He *should* walk away. It was not his problem, no matter how attracted he was to her. But, deep down, he struggled against the notion of leaving her to her fate. She was still in danger; he would be leaving her unprotected. Yes, she was wealthy enough to hire a small army to guard her, but they would still be hired men, motivated by money. What if her cousin were to bribe one, or more, of them? No, he could never trust hired men to protect her as well as he would.

It is not your problem. There is nothing you can do.

It was true…and yet he could not abandon her.

His dilemma had pounded incessantly at his brain. If he were to stay, how could he protect her? It would mean entering her world. He could not allow Eleanor and Lady Rothley to introduce him as Matthew Thomas, only to have his true identity revealed by someone who happened to remember him and what had happened.

He was the black sheep of his family. He had never felt as though he belonged—the third son, his two older brothers providing the requisite 'heir and spare.' Then Sarah, two years his junior, fêted and spoiled as the only girl until, seven years later, the last of the five siblings—another girl, favoured as the baby of the family, leaving him, smack bang in the middle, with no place to belong.

Yes, he had been a wild youth, up to all and every caper: expelled from Harrow; sent down from Oxford; drinking; gambling deep; huge losses; and affairs, not always discreet, with married women. He understood, looking back, his father's fury. But, no matter how wild and impetuous he had been, Matthew could never forgive his father for believing his own son capable of not only cheating at cards, but also cold-bloodedly attacking and robbing his accuser, Henson, and leaving him for dead.

Neither his father nor Claverley, Matthew's eldest brother, would listen to Matthew's protestations of innocence. *Dishonourable conduct.* Their easy acceptance of his guilt had deeply wounded Matthew. Their sole concern had been to get him out of the country in case Henson died. They had hauled him off to the docks and bought him passage on the first ship to India and to his great-uncle.

He had long ago been cleared of the charge of attacking

and robbing Henson—thanks to Uncle Percy's efforts—but the accusation of cheating still hung over him and the knowledge that his father had discharged so many of Matthew's debts still rankled. On his return to England he had vowed to repay those debts come what may. Other than that, he wanted nothing to do with his family...none of them had ever replied to the letters he had written in those early years of exile and he had given up writing after a while. They had disowned him. He would forget them in return—put them out of his mind.

'Mr Thomas?'

He came back to the present with a start.

'I beg your pardon. I was thinking of my commitments. It so happens that I have some free time at my disposal at the moment. I believe I told you I have two cargoes *en route* from India—'

'No, did you?' Lady Rothley interjected. 'I do not recall that, Mr Thomas. When was it you told us?'

Matthew cursed beneath his breath. He had told Eleanor, that night in the parlour of the George. The night they kissed. He should be more cautious. Her ladyship was much too sharp to fool. 'I apologise,' he said, smoothly, 'I thought I did mention it. Obviously not.'

'No. I cannot remember *anything* about that at all,' Eleanor said, nose in the air as her lips tightened.

Ha! She says the words, but her eyes tell the truth. She remembers that night as clearly as I do.

'To continue, I have a few weeks' respite until the ships are due in dock. I can be available to escort you wherever you wish whilst you are in London—only until we can unmask the culprit, of course.'

'Thank you for your kind offer, Mr Thomas.' Eleanor's words were so sweetly reasonable, with just the right hint of apology, they made Matthew's teeth grind. 'I must decline, however. I have no doubt you will still have some business to attend to and I have no wish to further *complicate* your life.'

She was still flinging that ill-considered remark in his face. Resentment bubbled in his gut.

So bloody superior. Leave her to her fate, man, and get on with your own life.

Being back in London had been hard enough, with the memories it evoked, despite his care in avoiding the fashionable haunts where he might be recognised. His pride dictated he remain incognito until he was in a position to pay back his father—which he would be just as soon as Benedict arrived in port. If he reverted to his family name any earlier, it would be bound to rake up the past.

'Very well, my lady. I shall say no more on the subject.'

The idea was preposterous. Did Matthew really believe he could pass himself off as a gentleman? Guilt nibbled at Eleanor at that ungenerous thought. She was being unfair. He was intelligent, educated; he had presence. Of course he could pass as a gentleman. She had long since stopped viewing him as anything but. He might be a merchant, but no one else would know, only herself and Aunt Lucy.

That presence of his: he exuded raw masculinity—it enticed her, enthralled her, terrified her. Honesty compelled her to admit that her real objection to his protecting her in London was the way her heart leapt every time she saw him.

The way her lips tingled every time she relived their kisses.

The way her blood boiled every time she recalled those words: *I do not need complications.*

How ironic that the only man who had ever made her heart beat faster was the one man she could never have. He might have the wherewithal to fool society for a short time, but she knew the truth. He was a merchant. He might be successful. He might even be wealthy. But she could never, ever, ally herself with a man of his class. *Like mother, like daughter.* It would bring all the old scandal tumbling out of the past, piling on to her head. It would bury her. She could never hold up her head in society again and she would *never* be accepted for Almack's.

Nevertheless, she could see by his scowl that her words had touched a nerve.

She drew breath. 'I meant no offence, Mr Thomas. I am persuaded you would loathe kicking your heels at those interminable society parties. You have had a fortunate escape. Members of the *ton* can be very narrow-minded and are not welcoming to outsiders.'

Matthew's eyes narrowed. 'I quite see that you are doing me a favour.'

Was that bitterness? The urge to soothe his ruffled feelings was strong, but Eleanor forced herself to continue eating. Their mutual attraction was undeniable. But that was all it was. There were no tender feelings there.

Not on his part.

Nor on mine!

They had been thrown into one another's company during the journey, and she had come to rely on him. Too much. Once she made new acquaintances in London, she would lose this dependence on him. It was all false. Not real. She rubbed at her temples and then pushed back her chair.

'It has been a long day. If you will excuse me, I shall retire.'

Chapter Fourteen

Matthew came awake instantly, his eyes wide as he strained to see. He leapt from his bed as he heard the click of the door latch and, as his eyes grew accustomed to the darkness of his bedchamber, he could make out the slowly widening crack as the door inched open. One stride and he hauled it wide. A tall figure stumbled against him. Soft curves, a feminine gasp and the scent of jasmine identified the intruder as Eleanor. Every fibre of every muscle tensed as his arms came around her in reflex.

'What—?'

'Mr Thomas!'

Even in the extremes of arousal, he identified the panic in her whisper.

'What is it?' He gripped her upper arms, moving her away from his rampant body, giving thanks he had chosen to sleep in his nightshirt.

'I thought I heard a noise downstairs. And I saw someone outside, from the landing window.'

'What were you doing on the landing? No, never mind.' Matthew grabbed his jacket from the chair and bundled it into her arms, pushing her towards the bed. 'Stay here, wrap up and don't, whatever you do, make a sound.'

He slipped out on to the landing. At the top of the stairs he paused, straining his ears. Nothing. The window was along the landing, a few feet beyond the door of Eleanor's bedchamber. Silent in his bare feet, he ran along and peered out. Nothing. Then a movement caught his attention. A bulky figure, in the shadows of the outbuildings. The figure moved, split in two, came together again. A flash of pale flesh as skirts were bundled up…and Matthew retreated from the window. That was the last thing he needed…to watch some lovelorn fool of a stable boy tupping his lady love when his own body was crying out for the same relief.

He gritted his teeth, willing his desires back under control. He would check Eleanor's room, then go downstairs to make sure there was no one there, even though it appeared likely one of the maids had slipped outside to meet her lover. Which was all very well, but it had left the inn insecure, despite his impressing on the innkeeper the importance of barring the doors and posting a guard.

Where the hell was that guard? How had the maid got out without alerting him? The quicker he checked Eleanor's room, the sooner he could go downstairs and find out what these fools were about. Galvanised into action, he entered her bedchamber. A quick glance around showed nothing amiss. He crossed to the window and flipped the curtain aside. It faced a different direction to the landing window. All was peaceful. He returned to the door and stepped out on to the landing.

And collided with a soft, familiar body.

'What the…?' For the second time that night, he steeled himself as he forced Eleanor away from him. 'I told you to stay put.'

'You were gone an age. I needed to know what was happening. Have you seen anyone?'

'Yes…no…look, wait in there…' he pushed her through the door into her room '…and I will come to tell you as soon as I've searched downstairs.' He grasped her chin, forced her to look up at him. Her eyes glittered in defiance. *'Stay here.'*

Eleanor huffed a sigh but, thankfully, made no attempt to follow him on to the landing.

Ten minutes later, Matthew knocked softly on Eleanor's door and went in. A solitary candle flickered, illuminating Eleanor, sitting on the bed, his jacket hugged around her shoulders, her hair…her glorious hair…framing her face, flowing over her shoulders…a river of silk. He itched to plunge his hands into those fragrant tresses.

Eleanor bounced to her feet, his jacket gaping. After one glance at the thin nightgown beneath, Matthew riveted his gaze to her face.

'Well? Was there anyone down there?'

'Just one of the maidservants.'

She had breezed in through the back door, bright-eyed and pink of cheek, as he had reached the kitchen. She had halted, momentarily disconcerted, then, with a calculating eye had swayed provocative hips as she approached him. He had declined what she offered, bolted the door, and searched the rest of the ground floor of the inn. The guard was sprawled on one of the settles in the taproom, snoring. Tempted as he had been to wake the fellow, solely in order to knock him senseless again, Matthew resisted. It was two in the morning. The inn was safely locked up again and, in a few hours, they would be gone.

At that moment, it had seemed more important to return to Eleanor…before she decided to follow him again to find out what was happening.

'What was a maid doing up at this time?'

'She said she had forgotten to do something.'

'What?'

'I don't know. I didn't ask.' He wasn't about to tell Eleanor the truth about the maid's night-time wanderings. 'She's back inside now and the doors are all bolted. It is safe.'

Eleanor visibly relaxed. She took a step towards him, into a shaft of moonshine that slid through a gap in the curtains. 'I am sorry I disturbed you,' she said. 'I…I was scared.'

'And yet you came out of your room.' His gaze returned again and again to her bare toes, washed by moonlight, as they peeped from the hem of her nightgown. Blood thrummed through his veins. The after-effects of danger, nothing more, he told himself. 'You could have bolted the door—'

'The door was already bolted.'

'And you considered the wisest course of action was to *unbolt* the door and venture out on to the landing? Have you no…?' He bit his tongue against the diatribe he longed to heap on her head. He did not want an argument now. Not here. Not with her standing there like that. Passion simmered dangerously close to the surface as it was. Anger would fuel an already tense situation. 'Why did you not just shout for help?'

She cast him a scathing look. 'I had no wish to cause a fuss by waking everyone. Aunt Lucy would be petrified and, as for Lizzie and Matilda, they would be in hysterics. Can you imagine?'

He could…but still…

'You have no concept of your own safety, do you?' he growled, closing the gap between them.

Her eyes were large and watchful, glinting as they held his gaze. Her lips firmed. She did not retreat.

'I was completely aware of the risk,' she said. 'The noise I heard was downstairs. I merely peeked out of my door. There was no one there, or I would have screamed.

Loudly. I am not a fool. But neither will I cower in my bed until trouble finds me.'

Her stubborn courage infuriated him; it terrified him; it made his heart swell with an emotion akin to pride. Her breath had quickened, her chest rising and falling. Without volition his gaze lowered to her pebbled nipples, outlined by the thin fabric of her nightgown. Blood surged to his loins. He forced his attention back to her face, his heart hammering.

He could feel her heat. Her breath whispered over the suddenly sensitised skin of his face and neck. An intense feeling of protectiveness washed over him and he raised his hand to caress her cheek—soft and smooth. Her eyelids fluttered down and she drew in a tremulous breath.

'Goodnight, Eleanor,' he whispered. He dropped his hand and forced himself to turn for the door.

'Wait!'

He paused, his hand on the latch, not trusting himself to look round. There was a rustle and his jacket was thrust into his arms.

'It would not do for Lizzie to find this in the morning.'

Matthew opened the door.

'Thank you, Matthew.'

Her words stayed in his mind long after he had climbed into his cold, empty bed. He could not decide whether she was thanking him for what he had done, or for what he had not done.

And she had called him Matthew.

She had long dreamed of falling in love. She would not give up her independence for anything less. What she had never considered was this confused state of mind that accompanied her feelings about Matthew Thomas.

Desire.

Yes, she desired him, and she recognised it and admitted it for what it was, despite her innocence. Was it possible to feel desire without love? Men certainly did.

Think of it the other way round. Could I imagine loving a man without desiring him?

She thought not.

Desire.

The following morning, Eleanor studied Matthew, who was seated on the far side of a dozing Aunt Lucy, from under her lashes. He stared broodingly out of the chaise window at the passing scenery. The bump on his nose was more noticeable in profile. How had it been broken? Fighting? How little she still knew of him.

Last night... In her mind's eye she saw him again, clad only in his nightshirt, the neck open, revealing bronzed, smooth skin. It reached to just above his knees and she had drunk in the sight of his naked calves and feet—muscular, hair-dusted, so very different from her own pale, smooth limbs. She, thank goodness, had been totally covered by her nightgown and, apart from her hair being loose, she had been no more exposed than if she had worn a day dress. Less, in fact, as the fashion now was for a scooped neckline and her nightgown buttoned chastely to her neck.

Matthew moved, shifting round to prop his shoulders into the corner and refolding his arms. He stretched his legs out, crossing them at the ankle, and glanced across to Eleanor. She did not look away, but held his stare as his blue eyes darkened and his jaw firmed. He looked away first.

Desire.

He felt it, too. That fact gave her an inner confidence she had not imagined before they met. Even her own mother had abandoned her...that pain still ran deep. And

Donald…his silken words and treacherous kisses…he had lied without compunction…told her he loved her…and she had believed him because she wanted to, until the truth had smacked her in the face and she could no longer fool herself with the pathetic fantasy of her own making. Being desired by an attractive man like Matthew had salved her inner doubts about her allure as a woman and her self-esteem had blossomed.

It had not taken her long to become comfortable in his presence. It helped that he no longer teased or flirted. She appreciated his restraint, even though she felt she might now enjoy such banter and might even be able to join in the game without fear of ridicule. Trust. She barely knew him, yet she trusted him, not only to protect her against her unknown enemy but, and more importantly, to protect her against herself. Against her desire and her needs. Last night—if he hadn't left when he did, she shuddered to think of the consequences.

Now, she must look to her future. There would be many suitable men in London. She hoped she might meet one who would make her blood sizzle the way Matthew Thomas did. And that he might view her as an alluring woman and not as a walking treasure chest.

'We are almost there,' Matthew said.

The view from the window had gradually changed. Where before there had been fields and woods and heaths and pleasant market towns and small hamlets, they now travelled through a maze of busy, dingy streets, the wheels clattering over endless cobbles.

'It will be a relief not to have to travel again tomorrow,' Aunt Lucy said, stirring and yawning.

'Are you quite well, Aunt? You are very pale.'

'I have the headache, my dear. I shall be quite all right after a lie down.'

* * *

At Upper Brook Street, the servants sent on ahead had readied the house, and it was almost like arriving home, with Pacey, Eleanor's butler, and Mrs Pledger, her house-keeper, at the door to greet them. Matthew supported Aunt Lucy into the hall and then Mrs Pledger and Matilda took over, helping her up the white-marble staircase to settle into her bedchamber.

Eleanor surveyed the bright, welcoming entrance hall. If the rest of the house was of a similar standard, it would be more than adequate for their stay in London. She was resigned to spending the next few months, at least, in London, whilst Ashby Manor was made habitable.

Eleanor smiled at Matthew. 'Would you care for a dish of tea before you leave? Or a glass of wine?'

'Thank you—tea would be most welcome.'

Pacey showed Eleanor and Matthew into a back parlour, decorated in green and gold.

'Please leave the door open, Pacey, and instruct one of the maids to come and sit in here with us,' Eleanor said. She would start as she must go on, with a keen regard for her reputation and those vital vouchers for Almack's. After the butler left, she continued, 'I might not always seem it, but I am grateful for your help, Mr Thomas. And for your company. You have helped make a long, tedious and what might have been a dangerous journey infinitely better.'

'Have you any idea how soon you will be able to appoint new footmen?'

'No. I am sure Pacey will arrange that. There is bound to be a Register Office nearby.'

'Indeed there is, my lady,' Pacey said when asked upon his return to the parlour. 'Shall you require me to appoint additional staff?'

'Yes.' Eleanor told the butler of the happenings on the road.

'Lady Ashby will need two footmen to accompany her whenever she goes out,' Matthew said. 'Plus, you must treat the security of this house as of the utmost importance. External doors must be bolted and ground-floor windows latched at all times, no matter the inconvenience.'

'My lady?'

The butler turned to her for confirmation, allowing Eleanor to accept Matthew's instructions with more grace than she might otherwise have achieved. 'Yes, Pacey. It is as Mr Thomas has said.'

'And strong lads, mind. They need to be stout enough to protect her ladyship.'

'With your leave, my lady, I shall visit the Register Office immediately. The sooner we can appoint the extra staff the better, it would seem.'

Two maids brought in a tea tray and a plate of sandwiches, and one of the maids remained in the room afterwards. A rebellious part of Eleanor regretted her impulse to follow propriety so strictly, but she knew it was the correct thing to do. It forced their conversation on to everyday matters. Eventually, Mr Thomas stood to take his leave. Eleanor rose to her feet, her insides hollowing as she realised she might never see him again.

'I do hope you will call upon us from time to time, to let us know how you go on.'

He bowed. 'Of course.' He reached into his pocket and handed her a sheet of paper upon which he had written an address. 'If you have need of me, send word.'

Eleanor took the sheet with suddenly trembling fingers. 'Thank you,' she said, her voice strangling as her throat swelled. To her dismay, her eyes filled with tears and she hurriedly tried to blink them away. This would never do.

Matthew reached for her hand, and squeezed. He lowered his voice as he asked, 'Are you all right?'

Eleanor hauled in a deep breath. 'Yes. Yes, of course. I am sorry...so foolish of me. I dare say it's the journey... so very exhausting.'

She braved a glance at his face. His blue eyes burned into hers and she could not tear her gaze away.

'Day or night,' he said, 'if ever you have doubts, or you are scared, do not hesitate to send for me. I will get to you as soon as I can.'

Chapter Fifteen

Matthew stood in the shadows of King Street, opposite the house where his life had changed for ever. It looked smaller, somehow, and seedier than he remembered. Or was it the enthusiasm of youth that had coloured the place as glamorous and alluring? The sight of excitable young bucks, in twos and threes, swaggering along the street before lifting the knocker and gaining admittance, was profoundly depressing. *Nothing changes.* Young men…their bravado…seeking thrills…believing themselves up to any and every trick in the book.

If only they knew…

Thud…chest about to explode…king of hearts, fluttering to the floor… Henson, accusing, face dark, fists clenched…*thud, thud*…stammered denial, hands shaking, mouth sucked dry…faces, in and out of vision, disbelieving, sneering…voice hoarse, trying to be heard…needing to be believed…failing…alone…*thud, thud, thud*…anger, fury boiling over, challenging Henson…challenge accepted… men turning from him…no one willing to stand as second.

His breath juddered as he hauled it in and he was aware of sweat coating his brow and upper lip. He reached for his handkerchief, and passed it over his face. So real. He had sworn never to return. Why had he come?

A pair of large, tawny eyes materialised in his mind's

eye. He had handed Eleanor his address as he took his leave of her and, for the first time in days, her outer shell of bravado had cracked. He had glimpsed the frightened girl inside, belying her rejection of his help. He had itched to take her in his arms and soothe away her fears. He would never have that right, but she needed protection and he could not deny that urge deep in his gut, no matter how hard he tried. He must find out who was trying to kill her. It was his duty to keep her safe, even if it meant facing his worst fear.

When he'd arrived from India, nigh on a month ago now, he would have cut his eyes out rather than start probing this old sore. Henson had been stabbed and robbed that same night, before their duel, snatching away Matthew's chance to fight for his honour and to clear his name.

Dishonourable conduct. He could not allow his scandal to taint Eleanor by association, which it would surely do once his true identity became known. He must—somehow—prove his innocence. A lead weight settled in the pit of his stomach as he pictured Eleanor's growing trust of him turn to scorn when she discovered the truth of his exile to India.

He would gain nothing by going inside the house opposite. All these hells were crooked—in favour of the house, of course—but it was not the house that had falsely accused him of cheating all those years ago, nor the house that had believed him responsible for attacking Henson shortly afterwards. The old resentment curdled his stomach. His own father. His own family. They had believed him capable of both charges. They had washed their hands of him. And now, if he was to protect Eleanor, he would—inevitably—be recognised. Remembered. Accused all over again.

Henson.

Where to begin to look? Matthew ran through the names of the men round the table that night—names branded in his memory.

Henson, both Alastairs—Lady Rothley's sons, Silverdale, Hartlebury, Perivale.

He would have to hope some of them were in London for the Season. The older of the two Alastairs, Lucas—now the Marquis of Rothley—was not in town. That was no loss; he and Henson had been thick as thieves. But the younger brother, Hugo…he might be a good place to start.

He must prove his innocence. Deep in his gut, he believed others around that table must know the accusation to be false. They just hadn't spoken up against Henson—older, worldly-wise, a man the young bucks admired and wished to emulate. Maybe now, as more mature and, hopefully, responsible adults, they would take the opportunity to clear their consciences.

Matthew turned abruptly on his heel and strode away.

Three days after their arrival in town, Pacey opened the front door for Eleanor and Matthew was on the doorstep. Rendered temporarily speechless, she was grateful Aunt Lucy took charge.

'Mr Thomas! Why, what a pleasant surprise. How do you do?'

Matthew removed his hat and bowed, his blond hair glinting in the early afternoon sunlight.

'Good afternoon, Lady Rothley.' He bowed and then his blue gaze rested on Eleanor's face and her heart kicked into a gallop. 'Your servant, Lady Ashby. I am very well, thank you. Have I called at an inconvenient time?'

'Yes,' Eleanor said. 'We are—'

'No,' Aunt Lucy said. 'Your timing is perfect. We are

going to call on Eleanor's cousin, James. Would you care to accompany us?'

'Aunt! I don't think… I beg your pardon, Mr Thomas, but—'

'I should be honoured,' Matthew said. 'Are you planning to walk?'

'Yes,' Aunt Lucy said. 'It is not very far, but it will be pleasant to have a gentleman's arm to lean on. Come, Ellie. Peter and William can still accompany us.'

Eleanor straightened her bonnet and sailed past Matthew on to the pavement. She could think of nothing worse than Matthew being present when she and James had their first meeting. Her irritation that James had not even had the courtesy to call on her in the three days since her arrival was bound to reveal itself and she was loath to give Matthew another reason to think ill of her cousin.

Eleanor winced inwardly at the spectacle they must present: it was bad enough having two burly footmen dogging her footsteps wherever they went but, now, to be seen in the company of… Eleanor looked beyond Aunt Lucy to Mr Thomas, strolling nonchalantly along the pavement, cane swinging. A cane? His blue superfine coat was well tailored, his tall hat set at a jaunty angle and—although he still presented a rugged and slightly dangerous appearance—no one would doubt him a gentleman. Mayhap he was wealthier than she had assumed. But he was still a merchant.

'…and we have spent much of our time shopping and with dressmakers,' Aunt Lucy was saying. 'The fire at Ashby destroyed much of Eleanor's clothing, of course, and it is a long time since I came to London. My dresses are sadly outmoded, I fear.'

Eleanor smiled to herself, recalling their argument over Aunt Lucy's need for some new gowns. Suspecting her aunt's funds were limited, Eleanor had refused to give way and eventually Aunt Lucy had conceded that Eleanor might treat her to a couple of new evening gowns. *After all*, Eleanor had argued, *you are only in London on my behalf. It is right and fair that I should bear your expenses.* Pride satisfied, Aunt Lucy had then thrown herself with enthusiasm into their shopping expeditions.

'What had your cousin to say about the carriage accident and the attack on that girl?' Matthew asked as they turned into Hill Street, where James and Ruth lived.

Trust him to settle upon the one topic she had hoped would not arise. Anger at James for not visiting her battled against her anxiety at seeing him again.

'We have not yet spoken,' she replied.

'Very discourteous of him,' Aunt Lucy said. 'Both Eleanor and I are disappointed by his neglect of his familial duty. It's been three days since our arrival and not even a note from him to enquire if the house is satisfactory.'

'I am sure he has good reason, Aunt.' Why she felt obliged to defend James, she did not know, when in reality she thought his conduct indefensible. She glanced behind, reassured by the stoical presence of William and one of the new footmen, Peter.

'No doubt his guilty conscience,' Matthew said.

Eleanor glared at him. 'Mayhap you should not come inside with us, if you are determined to stir the coals. James is hardly likely to attack me in his own house. Even if he is guilty.'

'Please do not desert us now, Mr Thomas. I feel so much safer with you here. I begged Ellie not to call upon James unannounced like this, but she would not listen to me.'

'Why did you not just send him a note and ask him to call on you?' Matthew said. 'Then you would meet him on your territory.'

'I cannot sit at home on tenterhooks waiting and wondering when he might appear. Surely that is understandable?'

'I understand you are impatient, Eleanor. Just like your mama.'

Eleanor stiffened. Just like her mama. That was exactly what no one must think any more. Apprehension had churned her stomach on and off all day, for tonight marked the beginning of her assault on society, at the Barringtons' ball. Aunt Lucy had been busy leaving cards with her old acquaintances and the invitations had started to trickle in.

Their new gowns had been delivered that morning and Eleanor was both looking forward to and dreading the moment she must enter the Barringtons' house and find all those eyes upon her. This time, however, she would not allow the whispers and innuendoes to overset her. She would hold her head high and prove she was not like her mother. At least visiting James gave her something else to worry about.

Aunt Lucy grabbed Eleanor's hand. 'I am sorry, Ellie. I don't know why I said that. I dare say I am nervous at the thought of facing James and what to say to him. I know you are nothing like my silly, selfish sister.' She halted outside a tall, narrow house. 'Look, isn't this James's house?'

'Yes,' Eleanor said, her stomach beginning to churn. 'This is it.'

She inhaled deeply to settle her nerves as Matthew rapped on the door.

'Mr Thomas, I know I do not have to say this, but please do not say anything to provoke James.'

'Me? Provoke?' Matthew's brows shot up.

Eleanor laughed. 'Of course, you would never dream of such behaviour, would you?'

For a long time there was no sound from within but, just as Matthew lifted the brass knocker to rap again, the door opened.

Eleanor stepped forward. 'Be so good as to inform Mr Weare that his cousin, Lady Ashby, is here and begs a few moments of his time.'

The footman stared at her with a doubtful expression and then stood aside. 'Good afternoon, Lady Ashby. I shall inform the master you are here. If you would care to follow me?'

They entered a dim hallway that, despite the good address and smart external appearance of the house, showed signs of wear and neglect. The house smelled in need of a good dose of fresh air, to blast away the stale cooking odours. The footman led them into a small reception room—equally musty and shabby, with heavy, dusty-looking dark green curtains framing the dirty glass of the window. Eleanor stripped off her gloves to await her cousin, trying to conceal her increasing unease.

Within a few short minutes, the door flew open and James appeared. Eleanor went to him, her hands held out in greeting, smiling, genuinely pleased to see him again. One look into those clear grey eyes banished many of her doubts. This was James—her beloved cousin, her childhood playmate.

'James, my dearest cousin, it has been much, much too long. Do please forgive us for calling unannounced, but I could not wait to see you. I do hope we are not putting you out?' She looked him up and down, then added, teasingly, 'You look very well, Cousin, but it seems you might have gained one or two pounds since last I saw you. You remember my aunt, Lady Rothley, do you not?'

'Indeed I do,' James responded, with a brief bow in Aunt Lucy's direction. 'How do you do, Lady Rothley?'

'And this is Mr Thomas.' Eleanor sent Matthew a warning look, which he returned with an innocent lift of his brows. How should she explain his presence? 'He kindly escorted us here.'

'In addition to the two footmen loitering in my hall?' James asked, but nevertheless shook Matthew's hand. 'You are looking very well, Eleanor,' he continued, 'but you should have informed me of your arrival. *I* would have called upon *you*.'

Eleanor frowned, puzzled by his manner. As James entered the room his surprise had been palpable, but there had been no sign of pleasure, and his greeting—although polite—held no warmth. Neither had he reassured her that they were welcome. Indeed, his words held more of a scold than a greeting. There was something about his manner— an edginess—she could not understand. Her doubts began to stir again.

Surely Matthew can't be right about James? No! I will not believe it.

Her stomach started to churn and she clenched her hands, digging her nails into her palms. 'You must have been aware we were to arrive on Saturday.' She squared her shoulders, steeling herself to keep her voice steady. 'It was you, after all, who made the arrangements for the journey. For which, by the by, I thank you.'

James frowned. 'I am sorry, Eleanor. I left the arrangements to my man and I seem to have lost track of the days somewhat.'

It is up to me to bridge this divide between us.

'Well, never mind now. It is not so very far to come. Oh, it is so very good to see you again, James.' Eleanor determinedly quashed her doubts as she clasped his hands again. 'We have become virtual strangers since you left Ashby. I do so wish it could be otherwise.'

James's face darkened at the mention of the Manor. 'There is nothing for me there, Eleanor, as you very well know. We are better off in town.'

Again, an underlying wariness. 'Is there anything amiss, James? You do not seem completely happy to see us and you have not even invited us to take a seat. Have we called at an inconvenient time?'

He had the grace to look ashamed, casting a fleeting glance at the door as he said, 'I'm sorry. I'm afraid I have an appointment in half an hour, one I cannot cancel. May I arrange to call upon you tomorrow instead?'

The door opened and Ruth—a slight woman with wispy, fair hair—entered the room. On seeing Eleanor, she stopped abruptly, her pale face set in its customary peeved expression.

'You did not tell me we were expecting visitors, James,' she said.

'I am sorry, my dear.' He hurried to her side, placing one hand under her elbow. 'Come and say hello to Cousin Eleanor. Her aunt Lady Rothley is here, too. And this is Mr Thomas. I was just explaining to Eleanor about our appointment.'

'I am sure they can have no interest in that,' Ruth said, as James urged her forward.

Reflecting that uncivil behaviour in another did not mean one should forget one's own manners, Eleanor smiled at Ruth, extending her hand.

'Cousin Ruth, how do you do? I hope we find you in good health?'

Ruth touched Eleanor's hand fleetingly. 'I am well enough, thank you.'

She dropped a brief curtsy to Aunt Lucy, 'Lady Rothley,' and nodded unsmilingly at Matthew, 'Mr Thomas.' After a brief pause, she added, 'I am sorry, Cousin Eleanor, but we must leave now if we are not to miss our appointment. I hope you will forgive us.'

Aunt Lucy caught Eleanor's eye and raised an elegant brow.

'There is no need to apologise, Ruth,' Eleanor said. 'We took a chance in calling upon you uninvited and I understand you cannot tarry if you have an appointment. I hope you will both call upon us soon so we can have a proper catch up with all the news.'

Ruth smiled again and inclined her head. 'We shall bid you goodbye, then.' She tugged her arm free from James's grip and moved to stand by the open door, leaving the visitors no choice but to leave.

Chapter Sixteen

'Well! How very peculiar.'

Lady Rothley shook her head as she gazed back at the firmly closed front door. Eleanor tucked her hand through her aunt's arm and turned her in the direction of home and Matthew fell into step beside them. The two footmen followed behind.

'Indeed,' she said. 'I thought James very ill at ease and Ruth looked…unwell.'

Probably the result of being married to a man like James Weare. Matthew was wise enough not to voice that opinion. Eleanor had been so happy to see her cousin again. She would be devastated if he did turn out to be responsible for the attacks. Matthew vowed to keep a sharp eye on Cousin James.

His quest to prove his innocence of cheating had not started well. Not one of the other players in that long-ago game were currently in town and Henson—that lying bastard who had accused him of cheating—had long been in exile, forced abroad by unpaid gambling debts. The irony would have amused Matthew had the matter not become—suddenly—of the utmost importance.

He had discovered, however, that his brother Stephen was in town. Two years Matthew's senior, they had always been closer than either of them had been with their eldest brother, Roger, Viscount Claverley—the heir and their father's son through and through. Stephen would be Matthew's next port of call. He would find out exactly how the rest of the family felt about him. Unanswered letters were one thing; if Stephen rejected him face to face...

He switched his attention back to Eleanor's words.

'I must talk to James on his own when they come to call and try to discover what is wrong. I cannot believe his coolness is solely due to my inheriting the title, although he did react badly to my mention of the Manor. It makes no sense, though—he has always known he would not inherit, even if Ruth did not. I can only think that she has turned him against me.'

'He was not happy at our calling in like that, Ellie.'

'I know, but that does not mean he was behind the fire or the accident.'

'Don't forget injuring that girl,' Matthew said.

Eleanor speared him with a glare. 'In fact,' she continued, her nose firmly in the air, 'if anything, it makes me believe he knows nothing about any of the incidents, for would he not have better concealed his feelings if he were responsible?'

'I was hoping you would tell your cousin about those incidents,' Matthew said. 'I should have liked to see his reaction.'

'There was no time to discuss anything of note. You saw what he was like. Besides, he already knows of the fire.' Eleanor's voice was strained.

Matthew sympathised. He knew how hard it was to accept your own family turning against you.

'I will tell James about them when he calls upon us. Surely he will now come tomorrow? It is not his fault they had a prior engagement today.'

'It will do us no harm to be on our guard with him,

Ellie,' Aunt Lucy said, as they crossed over South Audley Street. 'Mayhap it isn't about the title after all, but the money? Ashby is a wealthy estate and that house of James's looks in sad need of refurbishment. Ruth, I noticed, was dressed in the height of fashion and I'll wager she is a demanding spouse. I almost feel sorry for him—being wed to that sour-faced madam is enough to turn anyone peculiar.'

'I would not argue with that,' Matthew said. 'In fact, I—' He slammed to a halt. Two gentlemen were strolling along the pavement towards them. His heart pounded in his ears.

Stephen.

'Is something wrong, Mr Thomas?' Eleanor asked, stopping and looking back at him.

'I... I beg your pardon, ladies. I have this minute recalled a matter of the utmost urgency. I regret, but I must attend to it right away. You have the footmen for protection and it is not so very far to Upper Brook Street.' Stephen and his companion were getting closer. 'I will call on you very soon, to enquire how you go on. Goodbye.'

He doffed his hat and walked rapidly back the way they had come, angling across the road. He intended to face Stephen. But not here. Not now. Not in front of others and, most particularly, not in front of Eleanor.

'Well! How very abrupt,' Aunt Lucy said. 'I wonder what can have been of such importance?'

'I do not know,' Eleanor said, watching as Matthew paused to speak to a stranger on the other side of the road. He pointed back along South Audley Street, then glanced in Eleanor's direction before disappearing round the corner, back into Hill Street. 'It cannot matter to us,' she continued, determined not to reveal any hint of disappointment. 'Mr Thomas has his business to run, and we, dear Aunt, have a ball to attend.'

They resumed walking and Eleanor recognised, with a lurch of nerves in her stomach, two acquaintances from her come-out. Would they remember her? Would they snub her because of her mother?

Aunt Lucy had no such qualms. 'Lord Derham,' she said, smiling up at the taller man of the two. 'And Mr Damerel...' she nodded her head at the other '...how delightful to see you both.'

The two halted and bowed.

'Good afternoon, Lady Rothley. It is entirely too long since you have graced us with your presence for the Season,' Lord Derham said.

'It is indeed. I am here to chaperon my niece, Lady Ashby. Are you acquainted with his lordship and Mr Damerel, Eleanor, my dear?'

Eleanor smiled at them and dipped a curtsy. 'We have met, Aunt, but—like you—it is some years since I have been in London. I cannot be so bold as to hope the gentlemen might remember me.'

There was an immediate flurry of protest from the two men, with no hint that either recalled her mother's scandal.

'Do you go to the Barringtons' ball tonight?' Mr Damerel asked.

Upon being told they would be there, each gentleman immediately engaged Eleanor's hand for two dances. They parted company and Eleanor and Aunt Lucy continued towards home.

'I am pleased Mr Damerel has engaged me for the first,' Eleanor said. 'It will save me from the lowering prospect of sitting with the chaperons and attempting to look happy.'

The memories of her come-out still had the power to make her shudder. This time, surely, was going to be very different. She had even conversed with the two gentlemen without blushing. But…her surge of confidence dwindled as her self-doubts threatened to overwhelm her again. Mr Damerel and Lord Derham had been pleasant and polite, but they didn't know the real her—her mother had abandoned her; neither her father, before his death, nor Aunt Phyllis seemed to notice her unless it was to criticise; James had completely withdrawn from her; and, as for Donald and any other would-be suitors, they were only ever interested in her fortune.

'Have you heard from Hugo?' she asked, in an attempt to distract her thoughts from her own shortcomings.

'I sent one of the footmen to his lodgings. Evidently he is out of town and no one knows when he is likely to return,' Aunt Lucy replied. 'Really, it is too bad of him…'

Aunt Lucy happily grumbled about her younger son all the way to their front door, distracting Eleanor from her newly resurrected worries about the ball that evening.

Knowing Stephen was in town was one thing, tracking him down quite another. No good revealing himself in a public place—who knew how his brother might react? Matthew pulled the collar of his greatcoat around his ears and settled down to wait outside the house in Jermyn Street, where Stephen had bachelor rooms.

He had called at the house several times since he had seen his brother on South Audley Street, only to be informed Mr Damerel was not home. A coin pressed into the porter's palm had elicited the information that Stephen was expected to return home before going out again that evening.

It was two days since he had first seen Stephen. Two days in which he had not spoken to Eleanor, although he had watched over her from a discreet distance, alert to anyone behaving suspiciously.

He had already decided to revert to his family name even if Stephen rejected him. He had nothing to be ashamed of, but he did not want to reveal his true identity to Eleanor until he knew Stephen's reaction. He wanted to be prepared. If Eleanor rejected him…if she believed he would ruin her efforts to be accepted by the *ton*…then he must continue to protect her from afar, as best he could. He was more determined than ever to roust out whoever had put her in such danger, cousin or not.

The wind gusted, battering his hat and fingering his coat, looking for gaps.

Splat.

Hell, that's all I need.

Splat, splat. Huge raindrops burst on to the pavement, scattering the dust and tapping on the brim of his beaver hat.

Why am I skulking outside in the rain instead of waiting in Stephen's rooms?

He knew why, though. If Stephen had the same valet—Pring—he would recognise Matthew in a flash. He would forewarn Stephen and the news he was back in the country would wing its way to Rushock, the family's estate, and to his father and that he most definitely did not want. When he faced his father again, it would be on his terms.

The clip-clop of hooves on the cobbles grabbed his attention. A curricle drew up outside the house opposite. The gentleman driver leapt down and hurried to the front door whilst his tiger scurried round to climb into the vehicle and drive the horses away.

'Nine o'clock on the nose, Col.'

Stephen's voice. No mistaking it, even after all these years.

'Nine of the clock it is, guv.' The voice floated back as the curricle and pair clattered away.

Stomach on a mission to climb into his throat, Matthew strode across the road.

'Stephen.'

His brother froze on the threshold. He turned. Older, of course, but otherwise unchanged. Tall, rangy build, hawk-like nose—he got that from Father—keen grey eyes.

Ignoring the now-persistent rain, Matthew removed his hat. His brother's only reaction was a blink and the firming of his lips.

'You'd better come in,' he said and opened the door. 'First floor.'

Matthew led the way upstairs, thrusting down the nervous questions crowding his mind. Stephen would do what he would do. The die was now cast. On the landing, Stephen indicated a door.

'Sitting room,' he said. 'I'll tell Pring to bring some wine.'

Matthew shrugged out of his greatcoat and, after a second's hesitation, draped it over a ladderback chair set before a writing desk. The room was masculine—to be expected in this popular area for bachelor lodgings—all dark-green damask, polished wood panelling and leather seats. The fire was lit, as were the candles, dispersing the gloom of the murky late afternoon and Matthew used the poker to stir the coals. At the sound of the door closing, he turned.

Stephen's eyes narrowed. 'Defence or attack, little brother?'

'I doubt I would need a weapon in either case.' Matthew placed the poker back on the hearth.

'That I can believe. You have the look of a man who knows how to handle himself. How long have you been back in England?'

'A month or so.'

'And I owe the pleasure of this visit to…?'

'Courtesy call only.'

'It is usual to leave a card.'

'I have forgotten the niceties. You will have to forgive me.'

Like a pair of dogs, hackles raised, walking stiff-legged around each other.

The door opened and Stephen—who had not yet moved away from it—turned. There was a murmured exchange. When Stephen toed the door shut, he had a tray with a bottle and two glasses in his hands.

'You'd better sit down.' He put the tray on a table by the window and poured two glasses of rich red wine.

Matthew took a chair by the fire. Stephen remained standing.

Never mind—allow him the upper hand for now. My decision to come here; my responsibility to come to the point.

'I intend to make my home in England,' Matthew said. 'I had no intention of making contact with anyone from my past—'

'Not even your family?'

'My family—' Matthew placed his glass on a nearby table '—have made it abundantly clear they want nothing more to do with me.'

Stephen frowned. 'Where have you been?'

'Since I returned?'

'Since you left!' Stephen strode to the window and stared through the glass. His tailored coat clung to the contours of his shoulders and back, revealing every breath he took. They were many and deep. 'We did not know if you were alive or dead.' A crack of emotion in his voice.

'But…Stephen…Father knew. And Claverley. They sent me to India. To Great-Uncle Percy.'

Stephen turned, frowning. 'You'd better tell me all of it.'

Matthew told Stephen about that night. As he talked,

Stephen sat down opposite, his attention never wavering from Matthew's face. When he had finished, Stephen leaned back in his chair, his fingers steepled.

'So, Father sent you off to India. Why did you not write?'

The past had begun to reform into a coherent picture. Father and Claverley had not told the rest of the family where he had gone. He had been bundled on board ship and dismissed from their minds. Disowned.

'I wrote. Many times. No one—none of you—replied.'

Stephen's grey eyes searched Matthew's face.

'They never arrived,' he growled. 'Father must have made sure of it.'

'He was too ashamed to acknowledge I even existed after he disowned me.' Matthew could hear the sharp bitterness in his own voice. 'I did not do those things—cheat, or attack Henson.'

'He did try to clear your name. After you left.'

'I did not leave willingly.'

'I know that now. At the time, it seemed as though you had run away. It seemed like an admission of guilt.'

'You said he tried to clear my name. Did he discover the truth?' Knowing Father had at least tried kindled a tiny glow in his heart.

Stephen rose to pace the room. 'About the cheating, no. About the attack and the robbery, yes.'

'I already have the proof about the attack, thanks to Uncle Percy…although I suppose he and Father must have been in contact about that, which is how he knew. But the cheating…' Matthew had relived that night so many times, wondering what had happened, what he might have done differently. 'I know that extra card did not come from me. I have long thought about it. Henson was next to me and losing deep. He was already on the rocks before that night, according to the gossip. I think he meant to palm that king and he fumbled it. When the card fell on the floor, he immediately accused me. I'd been winning—it was an easy accusation to make stick. Have the other men at the game never said anything about that night?'

Stephen stopped pacing. 'I was never even told who was present that night. Father made certain it was all hushed up and forbade any of us to discuss it—or you—again. You know his views on codes of honour and gentlemanly behaviour. Of course, Claverley would never go against Father's decree, but Mother, Sarah and I—and Caro, now she is older—have talked about you and what had become of you. I've never heard the slightest whisper to suggest the accusation of cheating is common knowledge.'

That news was welcome. When he began to use his family name there would be no immediate scandal to taint Eleanor, unless any of those men returned to London. He would deal with that problem when it arose. He needed to speak to at least one of them, to try to uncover the truth of that night.

'You said you had no intention of making contact with any of us,' Stephen said. 'What changed your mind?'

'I'm a merchant, Stephen. I make my living through trade. This world…the world I grew up in…holds no lure for me.' That wasn't entirely true. Not any more. Eleanor's face materialised in his mind's eye. Was she safe? He needed to get back to her, to make sure. 'And neither would that world accept me. I don't belong any more.'

'You still haven't told me why you are here.'

Matthew leaned forward, under the pretence of stoking the fire. 'I have lived and worked with the name Matthew Thomas since I was eighteen. It is now my intention to revert to my real name. Damerel.'

Matthew Thomas Damerel. His birth name, his family name. He could not move around in society without acknowledging it. He could not protect Eleanor without using it. He could not clear his name without reclaiming it.

'Why?'

Matthew shrugged. 'I will not live my life ashamed of something I did not do. I intend to clear my name. I will find proof.'

Stephen grinned suddenly, and thrust out his hand. 'Welcome home, little brother. Let me know how I can help.'

Chapter Seventeen

Eleanor sat at the table in her first-floor drawing room, writing a guest list for a soirée she was planning. It was difficult to concentrate. Her mind kept wandering to Matthew Thomas. He was annoyingly evasive. It was three days now since he had accompanied them to James's house and, since then, not a word. Although…she tapped the end of her quill pen absently against her cheek…there had been a time or two she had caught sight of him. Or thought she had.

In the distance.

Watching.

As soon as she noticed him, however, he had melted into the crowd and she was left wondering if it was the product of an over-active imagination. Or wishful thinking. Was it his way of ensuring she was safe, despite her rejection of his offer? Did he feel obligated to watch over her? Some masculine notion of honour…having once taken responsibility for her safety, did he feel unable to walk away?

If only he would call. She missed him. He had become a friend. One she could talk to. One she felt comfortable with. Unlike the men who had hovered around her like wasps around a ripe plum when she attended her first ball. Since then, there had been a procession of male callers, presenting her with flowers, reciting poetry, generally making cakes of themselves. She had learnt to bite her tongue, but she found herself wishing Matthew was there to share the joke.

And the others: the prowlers, the dangerous ones, the rakes. She shivered at the memory of some of those looks of dark determination. Thank goodness for Aunt Lucy, who was alert to their wiles and gave them all short shrift. Thoroughly distracted, she gazed from the window, overlooking the street. And frowned. Surely…that man…had she not seen him before? The man in question—medium height, slight build, unremarkable other than a pointed nose—paced slowly past on the opposite pavement. As Eleanor watched, trying to place where she might have seen him, he glanced at the house, perusing the frontage from top to bottom. Then his pace quickened and he soon disappeared from view.

Had he seen her watching him? Who was he? He was dressed like a clerk, in a nondescript brown suit. Where had she seen him before? She searched her memories.

The door opened.

'Mr Thomas has called, my lady.'

Her heart stuttered, then raced.

'Thank you, Pacey. Please show him up and inform Lady Rothley.'

Matthew…an image flashed into Eleanor's mind. The last time she had seen him, before he had disappeared around the corner. He had stopped and spoken to someone: the same man Eleanor had just seen outside.

Matthew followed Pacey up the staircase, mentally rehearsing the words to reveal his true identity to Eleanor. She would not be pleased at being misled. He knew her well enough to know that.

'Good morning, Lady Ashby. I trust you are well?'

He knew she was. He had been watching over her, making certain of it. Timothy, Eleanor's footman, had been most helpful in keeping him informed both about Eleanor's outings and her increasing number of gentlemen callers. He had thrust aside his jealousy; whether he was Matthew Thomas or Matthew Damerel could make no difference to his eligibility. He was a third son, making his living in trade. He was proud of his achievements, but that same pride dictated he was not a suitable match for a wealthy peeress.

'That day we visited James,' Eleanor said.

Matthew felt his brows shoot up. 'No greeting? No enquiry after your visitor's health? Tut-tut, my lady.'

Eleanor flushed. 'I apologise. But this is important.' Her words tumbled out one after the other. 'You spoke to a man, after you left Aunt Lucy and me. Who was he? Have you set him to watching me?'

'What man?' Matthew paused; racked his brains. 'I left you and I walked back to Hill Street. I do not recall speaking to anyone. I had urgent business.'

Avoiding being seen by my brother.

Eleanor crossed the room to scrutinise his face. Her scent enveloped him, her tawny-brown eyes huge—and doubtful—in her dear face. Matthew clenched his fists to keep them by his sides, to stop himself cradling her cheeks and kissing those soft lips.

'It was on the corner of Hill Street. Have you set anyone to watch me? A man in a brown suit with a pointed nose?'

'Who is watching you, Ellie?' Lady Rothley had come in and paled with fright. 'Oh, do not say you have seen the villain who has tried to harm you.'

Eleanor's words had sparked a memory in Matthew. 'I

do recall a man in brown, now you say that, but he was only asking for directions.'

Eleanor bit her lip. 'I am sorry, Aunt. It was nothing. I thought I recognised a passer-by just now. I make no doubt I was mistaken.'

She smiled at her aunt, but it was forced and her eyes were strained. Matthew made a mental note to talk to Eleanor about this again but, for now…the subject was distressing Lady Rothley and he had another, more serious, matter to discuss.

'There is something I need to tell you,' he said. The change of subject would no doubt drive all thoughts of lurking villains from Lady Rothley's head.

As Eleanor and her aunt sat down, Pacey returned.

'Are you at home to Mr Weare, my lady?'

Eleanor leapt to her feet again. 'Why, yes, of course, Pacey. Please show him up.'

Matthew cursed silently. His confession must wait.

She crossed the room to greet her cousin as he came in wearing a sheepish expression. He kissed Eleanor on the cheek. Their family resemblance was strong—James was tall with an abundance of thick dark-brown hair and the same tawny-coloured eyes—and yet he seemed somehow less vital than Eleanor; faded, almost.

'Before you say anything, Eleanor, allow me to apologise once again for the welcome we gave you the other day. It was a somewhat trying day all told.'

'Oh, James, there's no need. I told you that I understood. Is Ruth not with you? Is she still unwell?'

'Yes, I'm afraid so,' he said. 'It's the strain, you know. That appointment on Tuesday was with her doctor. She finds these things intolerable, but I'm afraid they are necessary. He has given her a restorative for her nerves, so she'll soon be her old self again.'

James walked further into the room and started when he became aware of Matthew, shooting him a suspicious look from beneath bunched eyebrows. 'Mr Thomas, isn't it? Good day to you, sir. I didn't expect you to have a visitor this early in the day, Cousin. Please forgive my intrusion.

'Lady Rothley, your servant.' He bowed.

Matthew held James's gaze as he stepped forward and gripped the other man's hand, noting the deep worry lines around his eyes and mouth.

'I had hoped to talk privately with my cousin,' James said pointedly.

'You have had ample opportunity since we called upon you on Tuesday.' It was a provocative statement. Matthew knew very well—thanks to Timothy—that James had not called as promised, but had sent a note to Eleanor instead.

James's jaw tightened. 'Eleanor is well aware that my wife has been unwell since then and that I could not leave her. What exactly is your interest in my cousin, sir?'

'James, really, there is no need for such a challenge. Mr Thomas has called in to assure himself that I am still alive.' Eleanor's voice wobbled, belying her attempted humorous note.

'Alive? What do you mean?'

'It is time you told James what has been happening,' Lady Rothley said.

'I know, Aunt, and I intend to. We had an eventful journey to London, James, and Mr Thomas came to our rescue. He appears to think that places him in a position of obligation to me.'

Matthew watched James closely as he elaborated. 'Your cousin and her aunt had the misfortune to be involved in a carriage accident just outside Ashton. One of the horses was shot and the carriage overturned.'

'Shot? Good God, Eleanor. Are you all right? Was anyone hurt?'

His shock was evident. If James had been involved, he was a convincing actor. But who else could be responsible? It was this man who stood to gain from her death.

'Everyone escaped unscathed, James, please don't worry.'

'And, following that,' Matthew continued, 'a young girl was brutally attacked in the very room that you reserved for Lady Ashby in Stockport. Fortunately—although not for that poor girl—I had insisted that the ladies stay in Ashton overnight as they were already shaken by the accident.'

James blanched and groped blindly for the seat behind him, sinking into it. 'No…' he breathed. 'Oh, my God, Eleanor! And she was in the room I reserved for you, you say? I can't believe it. What a…what a terrible coincidence. But thank goodness you are all right.'

'You believe it to be a coincidence?' Matthew glared at James.

'Mr Thomas…please…' Eleanor said.

'What?' James looked wildly from one to the other. 'What? You believe…you mean…you think *I* had something to do with it?'

'James, of course not. It must have been a coincidence. Mr Thomas has merely taken some wild notion into his head. Of course I don't believe you had any hand in it.' Eleanor looked daggers at Matthew, who was unrepentant.

'You must stop denying the gravity of this, my lady. *You* are the common factor to these incidents. *Someone* attempted to kill you on three occasions. That—' he glared at James '—is no coincidence, and when I find out who—'

'And who, precisely, are you, sir?' James snarled, springing to his feet. 'Matthew Thomas? Where are you from? Can anyone vouch for *you*? It seems to me that you, also, have been a common factor to these events. I, on the other hand, have been right here in London. And I can produce witnesses to prove it. I repeat—where are you from? My cousin is a wealthy lady; do you hope to win her over by scaring her witless? Is that your game?'

Matthew's chest swelled with fury when he recognised the doubt that crept into Eleanor's expression, her original misgivings about him clearly reignited by her cousin's words. Now would be the ideal time to reveal his true identity, but he was damned if he would discuss his past and the reason he used a false name in front of this weasel.

Surely Eleanor can't believe I am involved in some way?

He fought to keep his temper under control but, before he could utter a word, Lady Rothley leapt to his defence.

'That is a preposterous slur, James. I am surprised at you.'

'Any more preposterous than your accusations against me?'

'I have no doubt Mr Thomas can prove he was nowhere near Ashby Manor at the time of the fire. And he drove away the man who attacked that poor girl.'

'He was there? At the time? What does that tell you?' James stared triumphantly at Eleanor. 'Ellie, have some sense, I beg of you. You cannot, surely, believe *me* capable of such a thing? You've known me all your life.'

'I don't believe you did anything, James. How could I? I love you.'

'This attack,' James said slowly, his eyes narrowing as he turned his gaze on to Matthew. 'How did you hear of it, Ellie, if you were in…Ashton, was it, you said?'

'Mr Thomas told us of it,' she replied. 'He caught up

with us on the road—' her gaze flicked to Matthew and a delicate colour stained her cheeks '—and then he escorted us the rest of the way to London, as protection.'

'So you take the word of a complete stranger that a girl was attacked as she slept in the bed you were to occupy?' James said. 'And you do not think it odd that he conveniently appeared after the carriage overturned, and then weaved this Canterbury tale about an attack. You just believed him? Have you heard of it from any other source?'

Matthew had heard enough. He had been scarred enough by false accusations in his time. 'The attempted murder can be verified by the magistrate in Stockport,' he said brusquely, 'and, although I do not know precisely when the fire occurred, I have no doubt I can prove my whereabouts if *you* feel the need for such proof,' he added, looking at Eleanor.

Eleanor avoided his gaze and Matthew's heart sank. Her cousin's insinuations were feeding her doubts. His behaviour when he had caught up with her at Leek could scarcely have reassured her as to his motives. She had been in shock; he had seized the opportunity and kissed her. It was little comfort that he had been so very frantic, thinking she might be lying injured somewhere. The sight of her safe and well had triggered an eruption of such relief that his common sense had deserted him. He had acted on pure instinct.

It was even more lowering to view his actions when she had returned to the parlour later that night. He could find all manner of excuses for his behaviour: he was a little foxed, which lowered his resistance; she had seemed to invite his kiss; he had been vulnerable, thinking of his estranged family and craving company and closeness when she had entered the room. Not one of those excuses was worthy.

'I don't believe Mr Thomas was responsible any more than I think you were, James. I should hope that both Aunt Lucy and I are better judges of character than that.'

Eleanor's declaration penetrated his reflections and his heart lifted.

'Indeed we are.' Lady Rothley's black eyes glittered as she glared at James. 'I sympathise with Eleanor's support for you, James, but I tell you straight that I am not yet convinced of your innocence. Why have you avoided Eleanor these last few years? That alone raises my suspicions. You may rest assured Eleanor will be very well protected from now on.'

At this, James spun to face Eleanor. 'I did not come here to be accused in such a vile manner, Eleanor. I shall be pleased to see you again whilst you are in town, but preferably without your companions.'

'I'll just bet you will,' Matthew growled.

'And as for you, sir. If I find these wild conjectures have been made public, rest assured that I shall come looking for you. And do not doubt that I shall be making my own enquiries.'

He strode from the room without a backward glance.

Eleanor, who had risen to her feet when James left, stared at the door, breasts heaving, eyes brimming.

'I hope you are proud of yourselves,' she said. 'I had hoped to rekindle my friendship with James whilst I was in town, but I fear there is no chance of that now. What on earth made you accuse him so blatantly? Could you not see the shock on his face when you told him about the accident? Was that the expression of a guilty man?'

She rounded on Matthew. 'And you, Mr Thomas. You appear to believe I am unable to take care of myself. Well, might I inform you, I have been taking very good care of myself for three years now and I intend to go on doing so for many years to come. I do not need a man to protect me or to guide me and I shall thank you, sir, to stay out of my affairs in future.'

Her hands were clenched into fists, sparks of fire lighting her tawny eyes. Lady Rothley clucked loudly and rose from her chair to go to Eleanor, taking her arm and leading her to the sofa, where she sat down next to her, taking one of those fists between her two small hands, petting and scolding in equal measures.

'Now, now, Ellie, you must calm down, for you know you don't mean that. I am sorry for accusing James, but I just couldn't help myself. You must not blame us for being protective of you, for it is only because we care.'

Eleanor averted her face. 'I cannot believe James would hurt me. You have both made up your minds and poor James will be guilty in your eyes until the real culprit is discovered,' she said, bitterly.

Matthew ached to take her in his arms and soothe all her troubles away, to murmur in her ear that he understood how it felt to be betrayed by the people who should love you most. Her rigid posture, however, suggested it might not be easy to placate her. He cursed James Weare roundly but silently for driving the wedge of suspicion between them.

'If it helps,' he said, 'I do agree that your cousin appeared genuinely shocked when we told him what had happened. All we are asking is that you take your safety seriously.'

'I do,' Eleanor said. 'I promise I shall stay alert.'

She looked exhausted, never mind alert. This was clearly no time to confess his real identity. He would call back this afternoon and tell her the truth. He dare not leave it longer, for he had agreed to attend the Lexingtons' ball with Stephen that evening and the truth would be out.

'I shall leave you in peace,' he said.

Eleanor held out her hand, raising haunted eyes to his.

He took her hand and, unable to resist, bent to press his lips against her sweet skin. 'I hope to see you again very soon. Farewell.'

Chapter Eighteen

'Her ladyship is in the drawing room,' Pacey said, when Matthew called at Eleanor's house in Upper Brook Street that afternoon. He had delayed his visit until as late in the day as possible, in the hope that Eleanor's usual pack of admirers had been and gone.

'Does her ladyship have any callers with her at present?' he asked the butler as he led the way up the stairs.

'Indeed she does, sir. The door knocker has been busy all afternoon.' The butler's voice rang with satisfaction.

Matthew's heart sank. That meant he must kick his heels, waiting for the chance to speak to Eleanor and her aunt in private. Not a comfortable prospect when he had little hope Eleanor had yet forgiven him for the argument with James that morning. As they reached the top of the stairs, however, Matthew slammed to a halt, sick realisation twisting his stomach.

'Pacey!'

The butler looked round enquiringly.

'My apologies, but I have recalled an urgent matter I must attend to.'

That is becoming a too-familiar excuse—the sooner I reclaim my own name the better. I cannot continue like this. Spending time around the fashionable areas of London was proving riskier than he had anticipated.

'I'm afraid I will not even have time to pay my respects to the ladies,' he continued.

Pacey bowed. 'Very well, sir,' he said, and began to descend the stairs again.

'Do you know if Lady Ashby is to attend Lord and Lady Lexington's ball this evening?' Matthew asked, as Pacey handed him his hat in the hallway. If they weren't, maybe he could risk not speaking to Eleanor until the next day.

'As far as I am aware, sir, their ladyships' only engagement this evening is to dine with Lord and Lady Ely.'

Welcome news indeed.

Back out on Upper Brook Street, Matthew leapt aboard his curricle and drove away, breathing heartfelt thanks that he had seen in time the trap that lay in wait for him in Eleanor's drawing room. He pictured the scene: Pacey entering; announcing Mr Matthew Thomas; faces, studying him, sizing him up; the curiosity about this stranger in their midst.

And then, when he was subsequently introduced as Matthew Damerel at the Lexingtons' ball that evening, the gossip and conjecture as to how they met, and whether she had known his true identity all along, would be bound to encompass Eleanor. It would inevitably harm her campaign to banish the memories of her mother's disgrace and her ambition to gain admittance to Almack's.

The past few minutes had emphasised the precariousness of his position. If he had any sense, he would cry off from the ball tonight, but could he delay any longer, knowing his father would arrive in London very shortly? Pring had recognised Matthew as he had left Stephen's lodgings the previous evening, prompting Matthew to write to his parents and also to his sister, Sarah—now married—to inform them of his return. It was better for the news to come from him than from some interfering busybody. Now, he sensed that the sooner he established his presence in society the better. His father—ever wary of sullying the family name—would not publicly disown Matthew which, in turn, would help protect Eleanor's reputation.

When Matthew had returned to England, he'd had a definite plan. He had never intended to revisit that card game—his reputation and clearing his name hadn't been a priority. Once those next two ships had docked, and their cargoes were sold, he had planned to repay his father and then fade back into anonymity as Matthew Thomas.

But now…his plan had changed. Clearing his name had, suddenly, become urgent because Eleanor was in danger, and he had sworn to protect her and he could no longer do that from a distance.

'Mr Damerel and Mr Matthew Damerel.'

'Oh, my.' Aunt Lucy clutched at Eleanor's forearm with urgent fingers. 'I always thought there was a familiarity about him. He favours his mama, of course, and his brother is his father's son. No wonder I missed the connection when we met Mr Damerel with Derham the other day.'

Eleanor excused herself to the group of ladies she was chatting to, and turned to her aunt. They were at the Lexingtons' ball, their dinner engagement with Lord and Lady Ely having been cancelled.

'I beg your pardon, Aunt, what was that you said?'

Aunt Lucy tugged Eleanor round to face the door. 'Look who is there, talking to our hosts.'

Eleanor perused the knot of guests at the ballroom door. As she spied a familiar shock of dark-blond hair, she gasped.

'It's Matthew… I mean Mr Thomas,' she whispered.

'Mr Damerel, it would now seem,' Aunt Lucy said. 'I wonder… I do seem to recall some scandal, years ago. Oh, tsk. My memory is not what it used to be. I have been buried in the country for far too long.'

Eleanor struggled to make sense of what she saw. Matthew—tall, handsome…elegant, even—in immaculate black evening clothes. *What is he thinking? He will never get away with…but… Stephen Damerel? Has Matthew somehow persuaded him to take part in this charade, or…?* She could not think straight. Matthew was looking around, that keen blue gaze sweeping the throng.

Eleanor turned away. 'Aunt Lucy, I am feeling a little faint. Might we go into the other room and sit quietly for a few moments?'

She struggled to keep her expression neutral as Aunt Lucy peered up at her. 'Of course, my pet. Come, let us slip out of this door.'

They made their way into a room that had been set aside for the older, less lively guests who enjoyed a quiet gossip away from the banter and bustle of the ballroom.

Eleanor sank into a chair with its back to the door.

'Who is he?' she demanded, as her aunt sat opposite her.

'It would seem his name is Matthew Damerel.'

'He was with Mr Damerel, so…are they related?'

'I think they must be brothers…it is coming back to me…there was a third brother…he was a wild youth, expelled from school, a black sheep. Left England under a cloud, although his father—Rushock, you know—hushed it all up. He was ever a stickler—couldn't abide scandal. Disowned the boy, I seem to recall. I wonder if he knows Matthew has returned.'

Eleanor listened with a sinking heart. Anger…hurt…humiliation…she could not sort one emotion from the other…they flooded her and she wanted to sink through the floor and never have to face Matthew again. Her behaviour had been shocking enough…succumbing to the hot looks and honeyed words of a man she believed beneath her station in life. But now…that man was one of her peers. The son of an earl, albeit disgraced. How he must have laughed at her naivety. What a disgust he must feel for her, knowing her to be so lacking in morality that she had encouraged…nay, instigated…such intimacies with a man such as she had believed him to be.

And to think…she had even confessed her desire to be accepted into society and her desire to gain approval to attend Almack's in order to banish the memory of her mother's shameful behaviour.

Oh, how he must have chuckled, to hear my hopes and aspirations, when all the time he had his own shady past to conceal. Scandal, Aunt Lucy said. The very last thing I need.

She wanted to disappear. She wanted to die…to crawl into a dark corner and lick her wounds like an injured animal.

But she wouldn't.

She stood up. 'Come,' she said to Aunt Lucy. 'Mr Th— Mr Matthew Damerel might have made a fool out of both of us, but I will not hide away, afraid to face him.'

'Ellie, my dear. I beg of you, do not do anything you may live to regret.'

Too late for that, dearest Aunt, if you did but know.

Eleanor headed for the ballroom, Aunt Lucy on her heels.

I wonder what he did.

I do not care. He is not a suitable acquaintance for me and that is that.

As they reached the door, Aunt Lucy clutched at Eleanor's arm.

'Do not forget that nobody, other than James and Ruth,

knows we are already acquainted with Matthew Damerel. Just follow my lead when we are introduced.'

Eleanor patted her aunt's hand. 'Do not fret. I am not about to ruin my chances of acceptance by enacting a vulgar scene. I shall be above censure at all times, you may trust me on *that*.'

'Lady Ashby.' A tall, russet-haired gentleman was bowing before her. Lord Derham. 'We meet again. If you are not engaged for this dance, would you do me the honour?'

Eleanor smiled. 'Thank you, my lord. I should be delighted.'

This is more like it. An earl. Tall. Very handsome.

Eleanor gazed into green eyes…eyes that did absolutely nothing for her. No shortened breath. No quickened pulse.

Mayhap I simply prefer blue eyes? It means nothing.

As she skipped down the line of dancers, a figure at the edge of the floor—talking to Aunt Lucy—caught her attention. Her heart squeezed, then lurched, and she missed her step. She hastened to catch up with the music, concentrating fiercely on the steps of the dance until the end.

Lord Derham returned her to Aunt Lucy, still standing with Matthew and his brother.

'My dear, you remember Mr Damerel?' Eleanor could hear the anxious undertones in her aunt's voice.

'Indeed. Good evening, Mr Damerel.'

'And this is his brother, Mr Matthew Damerel.'

Eleanor forced a gracious smile as she nodded her head at both men. She could feel the trace of those ice-blue eyes as they travelled from her head to her toes and back again. *How very impolite!* She tilted her chin and focused on Lord Derham.

Only to find a wide-shouldered figure blocking her view.

'Might I beg your hand for this dance, Lady Ashby?'

Matthew leaned in, lowering his voice. 'As long as you do not consider a third son beneath your touch?'

Had she imagined that hint of a warning? Could James be right? Was he another fortune hunter? After all, what *did* she know of him? She was a fool—she had kissed him, told him her secrets and, in return, he had given her a false name and now she discovered he was hiding a disreputable past. Well, she was wise to him now and this one dance would give her the opportunity to tell him so, and to caution him to keep his distance from her. After that, she would banish him from her life and her thoughts, for the sake of her reputation if nothing else.

'Of course, Mr Damerel.' She stretched her lips in a sweet smile. 'I should be delighted.'

It was a country dance. As soon as the opportunity arose she whispered, 'You lied.'

As he opened his mouth to reply, she carried on. 'No, I do not want to hear your excuses. From now on…' The steps of the dance forced them apart. When they came together again, Eleanor continued, '…you are to leave me alone. I do not want my name associated with yours in any way, shape or form.'

His lips thinned. 'That was not your view when you thought me a humble merchant.'

Oh! How ungentlemanly, to throw that at her, even though it was exactly what she had feared he would think.

'I have my reputation to think of,' she whispered at the next opportunity.

'And you want vouchers for Almack's…and association with the likes of me might spoil your chances?'

The steps of the dance separated them. They came together again. Eleanor hissed, 'Precisely!'

Then, after a brooding silence from Matthew, she said, 'Why didn't you tell me the truth?'

They parted. Came together again. His fingers curled around her gloved palm as he took her hand.

'We cannot talk here. Meet me upstairs. I will tell you everything.'

'No! How can you even ask…what if we were seen?'

So far, her evening engagements had gone well, with only one or two barbed comments about her mother, which she had fended off with ease. She had even exchanged pleasantries with Maria Sefton and Emily Cowper, both patronesses of Almack's, and although there had been no promises made, Eleanor harboured the hope that their approval of her membership would be forthcoming. Her confidence had begun to grow.

'We can be careful—'

'No! Do *not* ask again.'

They finished the dance in tight-lipped silence and relief flooded Eleanor when it ended.

A succession of partners—and supper—came and went. Eleanor was in control of her emotions and her behaviour. Not one person could point an accusing finger at her and say *'Like mother, like daughter'*. It was not so bad—now she was over the initial shock of Matthew's appearance in the ballroom and the fact he had lied to her, even though she could not quite suppress her conjectures over the scandal Aunt Lucy had mentioned. Surely the scandal couldn't have been *too* dreadful, or Matthew's brother would not openly acknowledge him like this.

And then Arabella Beckford appeared. Or, as some kind soul informed her, Arabella, Lady Tame, as she now was—a wealthy widow. Of all the girls who had tormented Eleanor during her come-out, it was Miss Arabella Beckford who had stuck in her memory. The acknowledged beauty of the day, Arabella had been—and still was—

petite and delicate, with golden curls, big blue eyes and pouting rosebud lips. In London for the first time, Eleanor had towered over Arabella, feeling utterly unfeminine—all clumsy angles and awkward silences—and she had suffered many unkind gibes from the other girl.

No wonder, thought Eleanor sourly, as she watched Arabella pouting up at Matthew—gazing at him through fluttering eyelashes—she had hated her come-out. The old feelings of inadequacy washed over her.

Why can I not be feminine, like Arabella? Why would any man prefer a huge lump like me?

Eleanor turned abruptly from the sight of Arabella flirting with Matthew.

'Excuse me, Aunt.'

Aunt Lucy looked round from her engrossing conversation with Sir Horace Todmorden, a dapper gentleman with luxuriant side whiskers. 'Yes, dear?'

'I am just going upstairs to the ladies' retiring room.'

'Shall I come—?'

'No. There is no need. I shall sit in the quiet for a few minutes, to catch my breath. I declare, I am quite out of practice and all this dancing has exhausted me.'

'Very well, my pet.'

Eleanor left the ballroom and climbed the stairs to the retiring room. Finding it blessedly empty, other than the maid on duty, she sat for a short while, relaxing back in a chair, settling her thoughts and emotions.

Anyone but Arabella. Surely Matthew will see through her to the spiteful little cat she has always been? She stifled those thoughts. What did it matter to her who Matthew talked to? Or danced with? Or…?

She stood up, suddenly furious with herself. She was hiding again. If she was not careful, it would become a habit. She would not allow anyone to drive her away this time.

She stepped out of the door to return to the festivities, then froze, sensing a movement in the passageway behind her.

'Eleanor.'

The quietest of whispers, but she would know his voice anywhere. And his scent. His unique maleness, plus the tang of citrus. She spun round to face Matthew Damerel.

'I must talk to you.'

'And I must *not* talk to you.'

He stood by the open door into the next room. He held out his hand, beckoning.

The chatter of female voices impinged on Eleanor's awareness. A quick glance over the gallery rail to the floor below revealed a cluster of young ladies mounting the stairs, presumably on their way to the retiring room.

'Quick. Or we shall be seen.'

Eleanor reached for the handle to the retiring-room door. She would be safe in there.

'I will follow you if you go back inside,' Matthew warned, reaching for her hand. 'Come. Please.'

The voices were louder. Even if she headed for the stairs, the young ladies would see Matthew and wonder... The gossip would spread from mouth to mouth...

Wretch! Scoundrel!

With no choice left, Eleanor swept past Matthew and through the open door.

Chapter Nineteen

'Despicable!'

They were in a small sitting room, furnished in a feminine style. One candle, set into a candlestick on the mantelpiece, flickered, throwing shadows around the room.

'You must allow me to explain.'

'Must I indeed? You could have explained this morning. You could call on me tomorrow to make your excuses. You did not have to…to…blackmail me into coming in here with you.'

'Blackmail? Don't be absurd.'

'Absurd? How dare you? You come into my life—I start to trust you, to rely upon you. You make me—' Eleanor bit her lip, appalled by what she had almost said.

You make me love you.

She gulped, her throat burning with the effort of stifling the hot tears strangling her voice and blurring her vision.

Stupid thing to even think. Just the heat of the moment.

'I think I know you and then I find I do not even know your name. Then you threaten me with exposure if I do not do what you want…and you call *me* absurd for calling it blackmail? What would you call it, Mr Thomas, or Damerel, or whoever you are?'

Her chest heaved. Her outburst had stolen the very breath from her lungs. She hauled in a desperate breath.

'I don't even know who you are.' The cry burst from her, searing her throat.

'Eleanor—'

'And *do not* call me Eleanor. You have no right.'

'No right? By God, what wouldn't I give to have that right? You have no idea…'

The grip on her shoulders tightened and she looked up through her tears into blazing eyes that churned with emotion. His face swam closer. He was going to kiss her. She felt his breath, harsh on her skin, as his lips sought hers.

'No. I cannot. I *must* not.'

Eleanor stumbled as Matthew tore his hands from her and strode to the window. She sank into a chair by the unlit hearth, dropping her face into her hands. What had just happened? He had been about to kiss her; she had *wanted* him to kiss her. It was he who had come to his senses and stopped before his lips touched hers. How could she be so weak-willed, so unprincipled? She gritted her teeth, determined to hide her bruised feelings. If Matthew should even begin to guess how she felt about him her pride would never survive—it was in tatters as it was.

Matthew stared out into the void, battling the urge to sweep her into his arms and to hell with the consequences. But it was the consequences for Eleanor that gave him the strength to control himself. He had set out on this path, and he had no choice now but to continue if he were to protect her from her evil cousin.

'Why are you even here?' he said, his back to her. He had been struck with horror when he caught sight of her—stunning in pale-yellow silk—in the Lexingtons' ballroom. 'Pacey said you were engaged to dine with the Elys tonight.'

'Lord Ely was taken ill so we dined at home.' She sounded dazed. 'Then we came…' Her voice sharpened. 'What are you saying? That you would not be here, announcing yourself as Matthew Damerel, had you known Aunt Lucy and I would be present? What a fine joke you have played on us, sir. I hope we have provided you with plenty of amusement.'

He faced her. 'You are upset with me…with every right… I will explain.'

'Go ahead.' Her voice was icy. 'I suggest you do it quickly, before my aunt comes looking for me.'

Matthew crossed the room to stand by the fireplace. Eleanor sat ramrod straight, hands gripped in her lap. Sitting in judgement. On him. Resentment churned his gut. Who was she, to look down on him? Why hadn't he had the sense to walk away that first day?

'My name is Matthew Thomas Damerel. I am the third son of the Earl of Rushock.'

'So you are not a merchant after all?'

'That part was true. I am a merchant; it is how I earn my living.' He had been proud of his independence. Now it felt as though he was admitting to something shameful. There was no shred of encouragement on her face. Her eyes were unreadable, her lips set in a hard line.

'Why lie about your name?'

'Thomas is my middle name. I've lived as Matthew Thomas since I went to India. My own name is too distinctive and I did not wish to invite speculation about my past.'

'But when you returned to England…surely, with your family here—'

'No!' Matthew scrubbed his hand across his jaw. How could he make her understand? 'That is the point. I am… was…' He stared down into the empty grate. Revealing his past—humbling himself—to Eleanor was harder than he anticipated, particularly in the face of her cold demeanour. But the truth was the only way if he was to regain her trust. 'My father disowned me when I was eighteen. I was rebellious in my youth—heedless of the troubles I left in my wake as I pursued my own pleasures. I was expelled from Harrow, sent down from Oxford, I drank too much, gambled, ran up debts...'

'Not so very different to many young men,' Eleanor said into the silence as he hesitated.

Matthew heaved a frustrated breath. 'No, not so very different. But then, at eighteen, I was falsely accused of something. My father believed my accuser's word against mine. He and Claverley—my eldest brother—decided I must go to my great-uncle in India. I refused, determined to stay and clear my name, but they wouldn't listen.' He fingered the bump on his nose—a constant, bitter reminder of their betrayal. 'Claverley took me by surprise. Knocked me out cold. When I came to, the ship had set sail and I could do nothing about it.'

'What were you accused of?'

'Does it matter?' He was loath to admit the sordid details. 'Will you trust me when I say the accusation was false?'

'Trust you? How can I trust you?' The words burst from Eleanor as she shot to her feet. 'You have lied and made a fool of me.'

'How have I made a fool of you?' He fought to hold the reins of his temper. 'And I did not lie... You are not listening—I have lived as Matthew Thomas for eight years. My use of that name had nothing to do with you.'

'Nothing to do with me?' Her voice rose. 'Even after you *kissed* me?' Her cheeks flushed, but she held his gaze.

'Why,' he growled, 'should I tell you something I had no intention of ever revealing to anyone, ever again?'

'So why have you revealed it now?' She jabbed her finger at him, poking him in the chest. 'Why have you changed your mind?'

She was like a dog worrying at a bone…why could she not just accept what he was saying without challenging him?

'Is it to prove you would be an acceptable match for me by birth? Is that it? Was James right? Are you just another fortune hunter?'

The lid blew off his self-control. *'Fortune hunter?'* The words erupted from his mouth. Yet another false slur! Was it not enough he had been labelled a cheat all these years? 'How dare you? There is no force on earth that would persuade me to court a woman who not only outranks me but has tenfold my wealth.'

Her eyes narrowed and her jaw jutted forward. 'Then why are we here?'

'What do you mean? I told you… I needed you to understand.'

'But why me? Why not…oh, I don't know! Aunt Lucy? Or…or *Arabella Tame*? Why have you singled *me* out for your explanations?'

'Because *they* do not need my protection,' he ground out. 'You do. I cannot leave you vulnerable. Good God, I have never met such a stubborn, infuriating woman. I tried to talk to you downstairs, but, no! You would not listen.' He grabbed her shoulders. 'I *had* to change my name back. How the he—*deuce* can I protect you when I was constantly afraid to show my face in society in case I was recognised? That is the only reason I am reclaiming my true identity. Obligation. And believe me when I say I am beginning to regret embarking on this whole nightmare.'

'Oh!' Eleanor jerked out of his hold. *'Obligation?'* She inhaled, then straightened her shoulders, lifted her chin and shook out the skirts of her ballgown. She raised both hands to smooth down her hair. 'I see. Well, you had no need to bother. I release you from any obligation… I have all the protection I need, thank you, Mr Damerel.'

She didn't quite know how she got there, but Eleanor found herself out in the passageway, heading blindly towards the staircase, the crush of the ballroom awaiting her. As she descended the stairs, her wits began to reassemble. Anger and humiliation still bubbled, tempered only slightly by her guilt at flinging that vile accusation at Matthew.

Moistening dry lips, swallowing convulsively, she fumbled for her dance card to discover the name of her next dance partner. The space was blank and she gave thanks for that small mercy. She walked into the ballroom, head high, feeling as though every eye in the place was on her; as though every person knew what a fool she was; and as though her name was on every lip and it was spoken with scorn.

'Aunt Lucy, I am sorry, I have the headache. Would you mind if we go home?'

Aunt Lucy was still deep in conversation with Sir Horace. 'Oh dear, you do look rather pale, my pet,' she said, worry creasing her forehead. 'Of course we can go. Please do excuse us, Sir Horace. I hope we shall meet again soon.'

A delicate pink tinged Aunt Lucy's cheeks as Sir Horace kissed her hand. 'You can be sure we will, dear lady,' he said.

Chapter Twenty

He had two choices. Again. He could follow his head or his instinct. His head told him to leave her to her fate. She had rejected his offer of help enough times now. And she had insulted him. Those two words…circling in his head, like buzzards…is that what she truly thought of him? Of his reasons for returning to her side again and again? A fortune hunter? Had her cousin succeeded in poisoning her mind against him? No one could blame him for walking away this time.

Or he could harden his soul against those words and follow his instinct, which was to protect her come what may. And that meant he must proffer an olive branch. His temper had got the better of him, but he had not said anything untrue. She was stubborn. And she was infuriating. And there *was* no way on earth his pride would allow him to court her—no matter how his heart leapt at the mere sight of her and no matter how his hands curled into fists every time another man spoke to her, or smiled at her, or took her hand and led her on to the dance floor.

He simply could have said those things more diplomatically.

'You are very quiet,' Stephen commented as he drove his curricle into Hyde Park at five o'clock the following day.

'Sorry,' Matthew replied. 'I was wondering how long it would be before the rest of the family arrive in town.'

It was not a lie; he had been wondering what their response to his letters would be. His family hadn't been uppermost in his mind, though.

He had called at Eleanor's house in Upper Brook Street, determined to make amends for the night before, only to be informed by Pacey that the ladies were walking in the park. A short time later, Stephen had driven past—on *his* way to the park—and taken Matthew up.

'Not long, I should imagine, although I would hazard a guess our father will come on his own at first,' Stephen said. 'How will you play it?'

Matthew shrugged, his gaze skimming the clusters of walkers, searching. 'I'm not sure yet,' he replied absently. 'I suppose it will depend on his attitude. I am looking forward to seeing Mama and the girls, though.'

Not only was Sarah now wed, and a mother, but Caroline was to make her bow to society next spring. Little Caro...all grown up. How strange to find their lives had moved on without him. He had much catching up to do.

His heart gave a sudden lurch; speaking of catching up, there was his quarry. Eleanor, stylishly clad in a peacock-blue walking dress, with ivory spencer and bonnet, was strolling with Lady Rothley, who was leaning on the arm of a slight, very upright gentleman. As Matthew watched, they stopped to speak to another group walking in the opposite direction.

'Hey!' Stephen nudged Matthew. 'You need to clean out your ears, little brother. That's twice I've asked you the same question.'

Matthew tore his attention from Eleanor. 'Sorry. Wool-gathering. What was it?'

'I asked you what had grabbed your attention over there,

but I've worked it out for myself. The Baroness Ashby?
Are you serious?'

Matthew glared at his brother. 'What is that supposed
to mean?'

'Whoa, there. Don't raise your hackles at me.' Stephen
reined his pair to a halt a short distance from the group
that included Eleanor. 'It was no reflection on the lady's
charms. Look, Matt, you've only just arrived in town, so
I'll drop you a hint. Don't set your sights on that particular lady. She's only been in town a week or so herself,
but already she's been declared the Catch of the Season,
despite her age. The deuce knows how she's still single,
with all that wealth…those northerners must be a group
of slowtops not to have fixed their interest with her by
now. And it's not just the money…her husband will have
the right to sit in the Lords on her behalf, you know. The
Betting Book at White's is already filling up with wagers
as to which lucky fellow will breach her defences first.'

'I am well aware of her circumstances,' Matthew growled,
his muscles rigid. 'We met on the road to London.'

Stephen whistled. 'Did you now…you kept that very quiet.
Well, well. Thinking of donning leg shackles, are you?'

'No!' Matthew hauled in a breath. He must tell Stephen the truth, or he would end up drawing his cork. 'My
sole concern is for her safety.' He recounted the circumstances of his meeting with Eleanor and his discovery of
the danger she was in.

'Nasty business,' Stephen said. 'You'll be hard put to
protect her on your own, though. I'll pass the word to
some of the other fellows—only the ones I can trust—
and tell them to keep an eye out for any ne'er-do-wells
sniffing around.'

'Ha! Plenty of them to be found, but not necessarily
ones intent on killing her.'

'Uh-oh…do I detect a sour note, little brother? Seems to me you've developed a soft spot for the lady. It won't do, you know. You'd never stomach a wife that much richer than you, not with that stiff-necked pride of yours.'

Matthew jumped out of the curricle, ignoring his brother's knowing smirk.

Let him think what he pleases.

'I'll see you later,' he said.

'Keep that heart of yours well fenced, Mattie,' Stephen called after him. 'I can see it from here…glowing on your sleeve.'

Stephen's laughter faded as he drove away and Matthew grimaced. Had he really lamented the loss of his brother's banter and company all these years?

Matthew thrust Stephen from his mind as he approached Eleanor, who stood apart from the rest of the group, talking with a fashionably dressed lady whose back was to Matthew. Eleanor's eyes widened momentarily when she saw him and her lips firmed before her gaze slid on past him. Other than that, she gave no sign of recognition.

Matthew reached the pair just in time to hear Eleanor's companion—whom he now recognised as Emily Cowper, one of the influential patronesses of Almack's—saying, 'From what dear Lady Rothley has told me, it seems you had a horrid time of it during your first Season, my dear. Let me take your name to the Committee and see what I can do.'

Here was a fortunate coincidence. Eleanor could hardly cut him dead in front of her ladyship, not without risking that all-important voucher. He smiled at Eleanor and lifted his hat.

'Good afternoon, Lady Ashby. We meet again.'

She managed a wintry smile. 'Good afternoon, Mr Damerel. Have you met Lady Cowper?'

'I have not yet had that honour.'

'Lady Cowper—Mr Matthew Damerel.'

'Charmed, my lady.' Matthew bowed, summoning his most winning smile.

Lady Cowper's cheeks took on a pink hue. 'Goodness me, yet another stranger in our midst—we *are* being spoilt this year. Where have you been hiding yourself all these years, sir?'

'Oh, I was a wicked youth, my lady... I have no doubt you were well protected from the likes of me. Alas, as a third son, I needs must earn a living and have lived in India for several years past.'

'Well, I am pleased to make your acquaintance now, Mr Damerel. You were pointed out to me last night, but you disappeared before I was able to gain an introduction.' She smiled teasingly at him. 'Infamous behaviour, sir.'

'I am mortified, dear lady. Had I but known of your presence, I would most certainly have contrived an introduction. Now we are old friends, however, I shall have no compunction in begging a dance the next time I see you, for I have it on good authority there is no other lady in the *ton* so light on her feet.'

'You, sir, are a shameless flatterer, but I shall look forward to it. Oh! There is Lord Plymstock. Please do excuse me, for I have something I most particularly want to say to him. I shall do what I can for you, Lady Ashby. Goodbye.'

Eleanor watched her leave. 'Well,' she said, without so much as a glance at Matthew. 'I had no idea you could act the flirt so convincingly, sir.'

He lowered his voice. 'I know how much gaining approval for Almack's means to you, Eleanor. It cannot hurt to keep the lady sweet.'

A muscle in her jaw clenched and she lowered her gaze to study the ground.

'I owe you an apology. For the things I said last night,' Matthew said.

'Which things, precisely?' She glanced around, then pierced him with an unforgiving glare. 'Do you mean you do not consider me stubborn? Or infuriating?'

A short laugh burst unbidden from his lips. 'By Jupiter, you get right to the point, don't you? My choice of words was poor. My apology is more for my behaviour than for the things I said. And, more importantly, for not telling you the truth of my identity beforehand—although, in my defence, I did try.'

'You did? Might I suggest you did not try very hard?'

'You may believe that if it makes you feel better, but when I called upon you yesterday morning it was my intention to tell you all. Then your cousin arrived and you were, understandably, upset. I called back later, but you were engaged with callers. And, yes. You are stubborn and infuriating. But I suspect you would say the same about me.'

She caught his eye. 'I might,' she said. 'But not in public,' she added, tilting her nose. 'I have too much care for my reputation. Now, I must return to my aunt.'

Before she could move, Matthew took a stride towards her and crooked his arm.

Eleanor raised a haughty brow. 'I do not think—'

'Lady Cowper is looking. Do you want her to suspect we have quarrelled?'

'My returning to Aunt Lucy will not look as though we have quarrelled.'

'It will when I follow you. She will wonder why we do not walk together.'

'Blackmail again, Mr Damerel?' Despite her words, Eleanor laid rigid fingers on Matthew's sleeve and her two footmen—who had halted at a discreet distance from their mistress—fell into step behind them.

'Do not imagine this means I have forgiven you,' she hissed even as her expression remained serene.

'Oh, I know you have not,' Matthew countered. 'I am curious, though. Why, precisely, *are* you still so angry with me?'

'Oh!' Eleanor halted and stared at him. 'Do you have to ask?'

'Well…yes, I'm afraid I do. You see, I cannot decide if you are still cross over my not telling you my real identity or because of my behaviour last night or because of what happened with James yesterday.'

They resumed their stroll, Eleanor staring straight ahead. Lady Rothley appeared to have finished talking with her friends. She looked round and, seeing Eleanor was with Matthew, she gave a little wave and then walked on ahead, her hand on the upright gentleman's arm.

'And if I say it is all three?' Eleanor asked eventually.

'Then I shall have to humbly apologise for all three,' Matthew said promptly. 'But you will understand that I am reluctant to apologise for something you may not still be angry about—there is only so much humble pie I can manage at one sitting.'

He was encouraged to hear a stifled giggle as Eleanor's fingers tightened on his sleeve. A sidelong glance revealed her lips pursed tight.

'There now, that is better, is it not? Do you think we might be friends again, or should I grovel some more?'

Eleanor almost burst with the effort of not laughing. 'G-grovel? C-correct me if I am mistaken, but I have seen little s-sign of grovelling from you, sir. Cajoling, yes. Grovel-ling? I don't believe so.'

It was difficult to maintain her righteous indignation in the face of Matthew's teasing, but Eleanor was not yet ready to fully forgive him. The truth was that her feelings were much more complex than mere anger. There *was* anger—smouldering still—after his behaviour last night. Her heart quailed when she thought of the implications had they been seen; her reputation would have been ruined for ever. And she was hurt by his lack of trust. Why had he not told her the truth earlier, particularly after she had confided in him about her mother? And then there was the humiliation over those kisses and the lowering realisation that—even last night, when she was so furious—she still would not have rebuffed his kiss.

As for his argument with James—

'Tell me you do not place any credence on your cousin's suspicions,' Matthew said.

She shot him a startled look. How could he know what she had been thinking?

'No,' she said.

'Your eyes tell a different tale,' he said. 'You doubt me and my motives. I can see how you might suspect a sinister agenda after everything that has happened to you, but please believe that I told you the truth last night about my reasons for not using my real name.'

Eleanor hesitated. Her doubts about Matthew, raised by James and fuelled by last night's events, had shaken her to her core, but a restless night had brought some perspective. Should she judge him through James's eyes, or through her own experience? His actions—those times on the journey to London when he had saved her from her own naivety—were surely not those of a fortune hunter? Even last night, it had been Matthew who had stopped before their lips had touched.

'I will admit that yesterday did raise doubts in my mind,' she said, still not ready to completely let him off the hook.

'I can only hope you will not allow those doubts to fester,' he replied. 'I thought I could protect you as Matthew

Thomas, but I was wrong—the risk to your reputation if I was exposed was too great. Believe me when I say that is the *only* reason I have reclaimed my own name now. You remain in danger. I have sworn to protect you, and I hope you will accept my continuing protection and allow me the opportunity to expose your attacker.'

Calmness settled over Eleanor at his words. She could not deny her feeling of vulnerability with only footmen in attendance, but she would not admit that to Matthew.

'Very well,' she said. 'I accept. If only to keep Aunt Lucy happy; she feels much safer when there is a gentleman around.'

'For Aunt Lucy's sake,' Matthew repeated, very slowly.

Eleanor glanced at him, suspecting he was poking fun at her, but he remained straight-faced.

'Very well,' he said. 'I am pleased that is settled. Now, I've been dying to ask…who *is* the gent with the splendid whiskers?'

Eleanor bit back a smile as she looked ahead to Aunt Lucy and her escort. 'They are quite magnificent, are they not? He is Sir Horace Todmorden and I believe he is courting Aunt Lucy. Is that not delightful?'

Chapter Twenty-One

Two days later, Eleanor and Aunt Lucy returned to their house in Upper Brook Street, having enjoyed another pleasant walk in Hyde Park escorted by Matthew and the increasingly attentive Sir Horace Todmorden. Eleanor sensed Pacey's disquiet as soon as he opened the front door. Her normally unflappable butler gave every impression of having to restrain himself from chivvying everyone inside.

'What is it, Pacey? Is there something wrong?'

'There has been An Incident, my lady.' His precise enunciation of those two words spoke volumes.

Eleanor removed her spencer and bonnet and handed them to Lizzie, barely noticing the squirm of apprehension deep in her belly, it had become so familiar.

'You had better come up to the drawing room and tell me what has happened.' She led the way to the room.

'One of the kitchen maids was accosted on her way home from running an errand this morning,' Pacey said.

'This morning? But why did you not tell me earlier?'

'The silly girl was too scared to say anything at first, but Cook finally managed to wheedle it out of her,' Pacey said. 'In the normal course of events, I would not bother you with such a triviality, my lady, but in view of the goings-on I thought I must apprise you of the incident immediately upon your return.'

'Goings-on?' Sir Horace queried. 'What goings-on?'

'I think you had better tell us exactly what happened to the maid, Pacey,' Matthew said.

'Wait!' Eleanor said. 'Before you do...' She turned to Sir Horace. She had no wish to become the subject of gossip, so the fewer people who knew of her misfortunes, the better. 'I am sorry, Sir Horace, but—'

'You must not object to Sir Horace knowing what has happened, Ellie,' Aunt Lucy said, settling into a chair by the fireplace. 'He is most discreet. You must not think he will bandy your business about in the clubs. He was a cavalry officer, you know. He is used to all sorts of dangerous situations. He will be a valuable ally.'

A cavalry officer? Eleanor bit back her cynical retort. Quite what use a cavalry officer might be against her unknown assailant she could not imagine, but Aunt Lucy seemed smitten, and Eleanor had not the heart to deny her.

'Of course,' she said. 'Pray continue, Pacey. Which girl was it? Is she all right?'

'Yes, she is now. Once it was all in the open, she calmed down. It was Agnes, one of the kitchen maids. Cook sent her to the grocer's at Shepherd's Market for some almonds and spices. She noticed a man outside the house and he followed her. Then, on her way home, he began to walk beside her. She wasn't suspicious at first. She said he seemed harmless enough and pestered her about when she had time off and so forth. But then he began to ask about the house, and the routines, and about you, my lady. Agnes got scared and told him to go away and that our household was none of his business. He threatened her then and said if she told anyone about him, he would find her and hurt her.'

'I wish she had told us immediately,' Eleanor said, 'although no doubt the man would have run off as soon as she came indoors. Did she describe him?'

'Yes. She said he was about five and forty, and medium height with mousy brown hair. He was dressed respectably, in a brown suit.'

'A brown suit.' Eleanor's stomach clenched. It sounded like the man she had seen. Who was he? Why was he watching her? Was it he who had tried to kill her and had attacked that poor girl in Stockport.

'Yes,' Pacey said. 'And a pointy nose.'

Eleanor sank on to the sofa. 'Thank you, Pacey. That will be all, but please ensure one of the men accompanies any of the maids if they have to go out on errands, will you? I do not want any of my household put in jeopardy.'

'Pacey,' Matthew said, as the butler walked to the door, 'just to be certain…did Agnes tell him anything about the house or Lady Ashby that might endanger her?'

'She says not, sir. But I cannot be certain she did not let something slip without realising its significance.'

'Very well. Thank you.' When the door closed behind Pacey, Matthew continued, 'Does that sound like the man you saw the other day, El…my lady?'

Eleanor nodded.

'Will someone please tell me what all this is about?' Sir Horace demanded.

'May I tell him everything?' Aunt Lucy asked Eleanor. When Eleanor nodded, Aunt Lucy said, 'Come here and sit by me, Horace, and I shall tell you what has been happening.'

Sir Horace settled into the chair opposite Aunt Lucy and Matthew sat on the sofa next to Eleanor. Their conversation in the park seemed a lifetime ago. All she could feel now was relief that he was here and that he hadn't walked away in the face of her suspicions and doubts.

'Are you all right?' he asked in a low voice.

All right? Would she ever be all right again? All she wanted was to feel safe.

'Yes. I am fine,' she said.

She squirmed under his sceptical blue stare. 'No,' she admitted finally, 'not really.' She bit her lip, thinking. 'Would you do something for me?'

'It depends.'

Hmmph. In her head, his response had been unequivocal. *Anything*, he had said. She might have known he would not simply dance unquestioningly to her tune.

'Well? What is it you want?'

'A pistol,' she said, 'a small one that will fit into my reticule.'

'No.'

Was that unequivocal enough, Eleanor? Her lips curved into a smile despite her best efforts to maintain a straight face. She had—really—expected no other response.

'You do know,' she said, 'that I could simply go out and buy a pistol myself? Or send one of the servants to do so?'

'Do you know how to shoot? Or even how to load a pistol, or to care for it?'

'No. That is why I am asking for your help. I want you to teach me to shoot.'

'Why?'

'Because I do not feel safe!' In her agitation, she swivelled to look at him. 'Because you cannot always be here. Because, sometimes, in the dead of night, I lie awake and I think about what happened to that girl in Stockport.'

A low growl rose from deep in his chest. Heartened, Eleanor pressed on. 'It would be safer, surely, for you to guide me in the choice of pistol. And you will be able to reassure yourself that I am capable. And competent.'

'And bl—*impossible!*'

'That, too,' she said, smiling her satisfaction. 'So you will do it. Excellent. Shall we say tomorrow morning? At eleven?'

The thunderous knocking on his front door continued unabated. Where was Henry? Matthew put down his book and went to answer the door.

'Did you not take the hint?'

'Come in.' Matthew stood aside as his eldest brother, Viscount Claverley, swept past. He indicated the sitting-room door, which opened from the small hallway.

'Go on through.'

Henry appeared, red-faced and breathing hard, from the direction of the cellar steps. 'Sorry, sir. I was—'

'It is quite all right, Henry.'

It wasn't, not really. If Henry had been around to answer the knock at the door, he could have denied Claverley admittance, told him Matthew was from home.

On the other hand, this meeting had to take place at some point. Perhaps it was best to get it over with. At least he would know what he was facing. Judging by the scowl on Claverley's face and his opening salvo, it was not destined to be a warm 'welcome home, brother'.

Matthew followed his brother into the room. 'To what do I owe this honour?'

Claverley rounded on him with a cold glare. Matthew was gratified to see that he now topped his eldest brother by a good couple of inches.

'You were told never to return. Father—'

'Did he send you to tell me that?'

Claverley's mouth snapped shut. Matthew waited. Unless he had changed a great deal, he knew his brother would not lie. It was about the only thing to admire about him—his innate truthfulness.

'No,' he said. 'He does not know I am here.' He looked around the room with a curl of his lip. 'Is this the best you could afford to lease? I knew you would never amount to anything.'

Matthew held his temper in check. Claverley. Same smug, self-serving swine he had always been. Matthew's nose throbbed in an echo of the pain of that lucky punch... he would never forgive Claverley for the cowardly way he had caught Matthew off-guard and knocked him unconscious.

'Why,' he asked, suddenly overcome with curiosity, 'have you always disliked me so much?'

'You have to ask? You are a *cheat*. I despise any dishonesty.'

'Good God, you are *such* a pompous bag of wind. You haven't changed a jot, have you? Did it ever—?' Matthew thrust his face close to his brother's and gained some small satisfaction from the leap of doubt in Claverley's eyes as he recoiled.

Good! Let him wonder what kind of man I have become. Coming into my home and throwing his weight around.

'Did it *ever*,' he repeated, 'occur to you that I wasn't guilty of cheating?'

'You would say that. Father tried everything to prove your innocence. I told him he was wasting his time.'

'And I'll wager you were delighted he could not find that proof, were you not? Why have you always resented me?'

Claverley stiffened. 'I do not have to explain myself to you, Matthew. I have come to tell you to leave. Before Father finds out you have returned. You are not wanted.'

Matthew grinned mirthlessly. 'Not by you,' he said, 'but I knew that, anyway. Besides, my being here is not negotiable. This is my house. Yes,' he said in response to Claverley's look of surprise, 'I own it. Outright.'

'If you are indeed that flush in the pocket, you are in a position to repay Father for the debts you left behind for him to settle.'

'And whose fault was it that I was not here to settle those debts myself? You made damned sure I had no choice.'

'Do you think we should have allowed you stay here and continue to taint the family name?'

'But I had done nothing.'

'You had done plenty, even before that night. Debauchery and profligacy. You were a disgrace to our family.'

Matthew clenched his jaw. 'In your eyes, maybe, but then you always were a sanctimonious bore. You are wasting your breath and my time, brother. I have business interests here in London and I am here to stay.'

Claverley's face darkened. 'Do what you have to do, but don't think Father will forgive you, for I shall do my utmost to make sure he does not.'

He stalked from the room, leaving Matthew staring at the half-open door. Claverley had become even more self-important and self-opinionated in the years Matthew had been away. What was it about some people that their opinion of themselves grew out of all proportion to reality as soon as they were placed in a position of authority—even if that position was simply due to the random chance of being firstborn?

Still, his brother's visit had achieved one thing. For the first time since his return to England, there was a glimmer of hope that his father might forgive Matthew. Surely Claverley would not be so agitated otherwise?

Whether Matthew could forgive his father...well, that was another question.

Chapter Twenty-Two

'This,' said Aunt Lucy, as they wound their way up the magnificent staircase at Beauchamp House in Grosvenor Square, 'is *the* ball of the Season. Everyone who is anyone is invited, and no one—unless they are on their deathbed—refuses.'

'It was good of the duke to send us an invitation,' Eleanor said, as they waited their turn to be greeted by their host—the widowed Duke of Cheriton—and his family.

'It was indeed. Although he could hardly hold the ball of the Season without the Catch of the Season gracing his ballroom with her presence, could he?' Aunt Lucy took great delight in teasing Eleanor about her newly minted title.

Eleanor was saved from replying by the duke himself.

'Indeed I could not,' he said, his deep voice warm with amusement. 'And grace my ballroom you most certainly will.' His silvery-grey gaze skimmed Eleanor in her blue-silk gown, his appreciation clear. He bowed. 'You are both very welcome.' His expression sobered and he leaned towards Eleanor, lowering his voice. 'I have doubled the footmen on duty, Lady Ashby, so you need not fear for your safety in this house.'

'I…' Words failed Eleanor. How did he know?

'And if there is anything I can do to help, you have only

to ask,' he added. 'Now, please allow me to introduce my son, Avon—' the youthful Lord Avon was the spitting image of the duke as he bowed elegantly '—my sister, Cecily, and my brother, Vernon.'

Lady Cecily and Lord Vernon—both unwed, as Aunt Lucy had informed Eleanor in the carriage on their way to the ball—smiled as they greeted Eleanor. They were very alike, with auburn hair and green eyes, in contrast to the duke's dark colouring.

'Most of our guests have arrived by now, Leo, so you won't miss me from the line-up,' Lord Vernon drawled, eyeing Eleanor with as much appreciation as his brother. He stepped forward and crooked his arm. 'Might I escort you into the ballroom, Lady Ashby?'

'Why…yes. Thank you, my lord.'

Eleanor shot a look at Aunt Lucy, who merely raised her brows in response. Lord Vernon Beauchamp's caution in never allowing his name to be linked to any woman was common knowledge, as was his determination never to marry. Was he, like the duke, privy to her personal business?

As they descended the short flight of steps into the glittering ballroom Eleanor frowned as she noticed a seemingly casual, but consistent, movement of the people nearest to her. What was going on? A distinct area of clear space materialised at the foot of the steps. Stationed—really, there was no other word for it—around the perimeter of the clearing were five tall, broad-shouldered gentlemen whom she recognised as some of the most eligible bachelors in the *ton*. Not one of those gentlemen had formed part of her court since her arrival in London—they were the older bachelors, the most pursued and, from Eleanor's observation, the most determined to avoid matrimony. She had danced with some of them, but it was clear none were on the lookout for a wife. They had indulged in a little light flirtation with her—as was to be expected from men of their ilk—but none had subsequently called upon her, or sent her flowers.

So *why* were they now so focused on her? For focused they were. Even as their gazes ceaselessly scanned the other guests, she could *feel* their attention.

'What,' she whispered to Lord Vernon, 'is going on?'

Vernon glanced down at her, eyes crinkling, as he led her deeper into the ballroom. The other men formed a rough circle around them, keeping the other guests at bay.

'We take care of our own. Ah, here comes Damerel. I shall leave you in his capable hands.'

He bowed and sauntered over to speak to another of Eleanor's self-appointed guardians.

'Well! Really!' Eleanor hissed to Aunt Lucy. 'What on *earth* do they think they are doing? And *who*, I should like to know, told them about me? I *knew* we shouldn't have told Sir Horace what has been happening.'

'Ellie, please do not throw such accusations around without good reason,' Aunt Lucy said. 'Why, it could have been…well, it might have been the servants. You know how they gossip between the households. Or Mr Damerel, even. Why do you not ask him?'

'Ask me what?' Matthew said, as he reached Eleanor's side. 'Good evening, ladies. May I say how very charming you both look this evening?'

His eyes lingered on Eleanor's *décolletage*, igniting sparks that flickered along her veins, heating her skin. She curled her fingers against the desire to tug her neckline higher.

'Why, I appear to be the centre of attention of some of the most powerful gentlemen in the *ton*,' she said. 'Please tell me you have not told them of my…my *predicament*.'

'Of course I have not. I...*oh!* Deuce take it! Stephen?'

Stephen Damerel stood chatting with Lord Derham, who also formed one of Eleanor's 'guards', as she had come to think of them. At the sound of his name, Stephen strolled over to Matthew and Eleanor.

'Matthew?' He raised an elegant brow.

'You told your *brother?*' Eleanor hissed. 'What made you think it would be acceptable to me for *anyone* to know my business? And now...*look!*' In her agitation, she swept her arm aloft, indicating the surrounding gentlemen. 'The very last thing I wish is to be the centre of attention like this.'

She glared at Matthew, whose jaw firmed. 'I told Stephen because he was full of conjectures as to why I appeared so interested in you and I needed to nip them in the bud.'

Of course, it would never do for anyone to presume he was interested in her as a woman, would it? She could quite see how embarrassing *that* would be for him.

'And besides...' he lowered his voice and dipped his mouth close to her ear '...how did imagine you could *fail* to be the centre of attention in that dress?'

His breath tickled her neck and his scent surrounded her, sending her senses reeling. She stepped away, intent on clearing her head, and looked accusingly at Stephen Damerel.

'You are in danger. You need protection,' he stated unrepentantly. 'I only told a few of my most trusted friends—it is not common knowledge.'

'What do you imagine could possibly happen to me in the duke's ballroom?'

Stephen shrugged. 'They will be discreet—you need not worry. Look, they are mingling now. They only wanted to ensure your safety until Matthew was here to look after you. They will still keep an eye out, but from a distance. No one will know. If I am honest—' a charming smile lit his face '—we are delighted to be of service. It makes a change to have a purpose to these gatherings.' He bowed and wandered away.

'You will not persuade them otherwise, you know,' Matthew said. 'They see it as their duty to protect a lady in need.'

'I know. Which is why I wished to keep this whole débâcle out of the public eye,' Eleanor said.

'Admit that you will feel more secure, knowing there are several pairs of eyes watching over you instead of just mine,' Matthew said. 'You've been feeling vulnerable ever since we arrived in London, I know you have. You wouldn't have asked me about a pistol if you weren't scared.'

'A pistol?' Sir Horace Todmorden had joined them. 'What is this?'

'Hush,' Eleanor said, glancing at Aunt Lucy whose attention, thankfully, had been claimed by old Lady Ely. 'I asked Mr Damerel to help me purchase a small pistol. For protection.'

'Oh, my dear lady, no. I really cannot condone…what? A young lady such as yourself with a firearm? No, no, no. It is far too dangerous. Why, what if the rogue should disarm you? Where would you be then?'

'No worse off than if I had no weapon,' Eleanor said. 'At least if I buy one, I will sleep better at night. There are no *tonnish* gentlemen around at that time to watch over me,' she added, with an innocent look at Matthew.

His eyes narrowed and he shook his head at her as Sir Horace barked a laugh.

'You've got your hands full there, my lad,' he announced, slapping Matthew on the back.

Eleanor's breath caught in her throat as her cheeks

burned. Were their names already being linked? She must take care not to gain a reputation for being fast if Emily Cowper was to succeed in adding her name to the list for Almack's. She raised her fan and, under cover of cooling her face, glanced around the ballroom. Nobody was paying them attention. Her breathing eased.

'Sir Horace,' she said, 'I think you may be suffering under a misapprehension. I know I may speak freely, with you being such a particular friend of my aunt's. Mr Damerel is just a friend who is kindly helping me through this difficult time. That is all. There is no romantic intention on either side, I assure you.'

'None,' Matthew confirmed. 'I am a merchant who works for his living and, once we unmask the culprit, I shall return to my own life. I should hate for any untoward rumours to circulate. There is Lady Ashby's reputation to consider.'

'Of course. My profound apologies, dear lady. Damerel, pray forgive me. I did not mean to imply…oh, dear me, no… I know you only…but your aunt did express a hope…'

The poor man was mortified. Eleanor smiled at him. 'There is no harm done. I am persuaded you understand the situation now. Let us forget all about it.'

Sir Horace, still beetroot-red, bowed. 'You are most gracious. Now, if you will excuse me…?' He left them to join Aunt Lucy and Lady Ely.

What had Aunt Lucy been saying? For that matter, what did she think? Was she harbouring romantic notions about Eleanor and Matthew? Eleanor's heart fluttered against her ribs. Until yesterday, any future had seemed impossible but…now…might there be hope? They were equals by birth. Might there, possibly, be a chance they could…?

Her thoughts faltered. This was foolish thinking. He was a third son and in trade. Her hopes of living down her mother's scandal would be lost for ever. Besides, there was his pride to consider. *I could never accept a woman who outranks me and has tenfold my wealth.*

No, we can only ever be friends.

'Eleanor?'

Her name caught her whirling thoughts. 'Sorry. Did you say something?'

Matthew was watching her, a frown creasing his brow. 'I was saying, on the subject of your protection, I felt I should warn you that your cousin and his wife are present tonight.'

The news set her stomach roiling. She had not seen James since he had slammed from her house in a temper after realising he was under suspicion. What would he say? How would he react? Here was another reason to regret that others were aware she was in danger for, surely, they could not help but suspect James, the same as both Matthew and Aunt Lucy.

Eleanor licked at suddenly dry lips and Matthew signalled to a passing waiter for a glass of wine. She sipped at it gratefully. 'Thank you for the warning.'

'About that pistol,' Matthew said.

Eleanor raised a brow, encouraged that he had broached the subject voluntarily.

'You need a lady's muff pistol. That will be small enough to carry in a reticule or, as the name implies, conceal in a muff. There is an excellent gunmaker on Shoemaker's Row, in Blackfriars. Richard Fenton. I shall buy you one tomorrow and teach you how to shoot.'

'I understood the gentlemen of the *ton* always patronise Manton's?'

'Ah, but you forget. I am no gentleman of the *ton*. My associates frequent different haunts.'

'Oh!' Eleanor pictured a seedy workshop in a dark alley.

'I am not sure…would it not be safer…? I mean, I hope he is *reputable*.'

Matthew laughed. 'Of course he is reputable. What do you take me for? He is simply not quite as fashionable as Manton or his brother.'

'I see.' Eleanor fidgeted with her fan. 'It was my intention to choose my own pistol.'

'Trust me,' Matthew said. 'I shall find you the perfect pistol. A gunmaker's shop is no place for a lady.'

Chapter Twenty-Three

The musicians, clustered on the balcony, struck a chord. The chatter died and the crowd began the ebb and flow that would result in the dancers remaining in the centre of the floor and the onlookers arranged around the perimeter, some standing, some sitting. Gowns and jewels shimmered as they caught the light from the many chandeliers and Eleanor thought she had never seen so many sumptuous dresses and beautifully coiffured heads before.

'Is it not a magnificent sight?' she said to Aunt Lucy, who had finally escaped the clutches of Lady Ely. 'How I wish I'd had the confidence to enjoy my come-out instead of hiding amongst the chaperons.'

'Do not waste time regretting the past, my pet,' Aunt Lucy replied, squeezing Eleanor's hand. 'You made the right choices, for you, at the time. You are here now. Enjoy the moment. There is not a lady in this ballroom to outshine you, so make the most of it.'

'And I second that,' a deep voice murmured in her ear. 'I believe this first dance is mine?'

Her skin seemed to tighten until it felt too small to contain her flesh and her insides quivered.

Matthew. She glanced at him through her lashes as they took their place in one of the sets. His broad shoulders and square jaw allowed no doubt as to his strength and his masculinity. A glance at the other men in their set failed to flame her senses in the same way. His fingers closed around hers and fire flickered along her veins.

Who would choose smooth urbanity and polished address over Matthew's rugged capability and down-to-earth manner? Probably, she mused, many ladies of the *ton* would value those qualities higher. But not her. She did not want pretty words with no heart behind them. She wanted... Matthew. She might as well admit it. She had wanted him since that first kiss. It had just seemed so impossible.

Now...

She looked up and caught his eye. He looked...

'What is wrong? You look preoccupied.'

'As do you,' he said.

'But I was preoccupied in a happy way,' Eleanor retorted. 'You look precisely the opposite. Why?'

He did not reply.

'If you did not wish to dance, why did you ask me?'

His startled blue gaze bored into her. 'Please do not imagine you know what is going on inside my head.' He fell silent until they were near enough to converse again. 'If you must know,' he continued, 'I had a visit from my eldest brother earlier. I was wondering what reception I might expect from my father when he arrives.'

Eleanor pondered his words. Matthew was adamant he had no wish to accept his rightful place in society but... could reconciliation with his father change his mind? Ideas of how she might help ricocheted around her brain but, if she were to help, it stood to reason she must discover the cause of their estrangement: the reason his father had banished Matthew to India.

They joined hands for the next movement of the dance. She barely noticed, dancing by rote. A swift tug caught her attention.

'What are you plotting? I can see it in your eyes. You are up to something.'

Eleanor tilted her chin. 'I am not. I was thinking about supper.'

She avoided his narrow-eyed study of her face. At the end of the dance, she said, 'May we sit this one out, Mr Damerel? I find I am rather tired.' Matthew had marked her card for the first two.

'After one dance?'

'It is the worry. The thought of meeting James and Ruth has quite overset me.' She ignored Matthew's quiet huff of disbelief. 'I would appreciate finding a quiet corner to rest. To prepare myself.'

'Very well.' Matthew offered his arm and led Eleanor across the floor to where a set of French windows stood ajar. 'Would you care for a breath of fresh air? There are others out there, so we cannot be accused of being un-chaperoned. You cannot afford to take any chances; the patronesses of Almack's are present. I saw Lady Cowper and Lady Jersey earlier.'

Eleanor glimpsed several guests outside on a well-lit, flagged terrace, where they were taking advantage of a cooling breeze. Perfect…enough in number to provide respectability, but few enough to enable them to converse without being overheard.

'Indeed.' Now to wheedle the truth out of Matthew.

They walked slowly to one end of the terrace, which ran the full width of Beauchamp House. Matthew held his tongue—Eleanor would speak her mind soon enough. Until then, he was content to enjoy the peace. As they turned to retrace their steps, Eleanor drew breath.

'Your father,' she said.

'Ah, now we get to it. I *knew* you were up to something.'

'I am *not* up to something. I am…interested. Your

brother Stephen has accepted you back. Why do you imagine your father will not? What did your other brother say?'

And if she thought he was going to tell her about that interview, she was mistaken. 'He was hardly overjoyed to see me.'

'And yet he visited you. Why?'

Matthew shrugged free of her hand on his arm and strode over to the balustrade. He gazed blindly into the dark garden beyond the terrace.

Tenacious.

It described her perfectly.

She's only trying to help.

As if she had heard his thoughts, she said, 'I only wish to understand.'

'I know.'

He turned to look at her. *Gorgeous.* His blood heated instantly. Her glorious dark tresses, piled on to her head, artful ringlets framing her beautiful face. That gown…the colour of a summer sky, over a white satin underdress…the low neckline revealing an enticing glimpse of full breasts and emphasising her fragile collarbones and swan-like neck, adorned by an elegant string of pearls. His hands curled into fists against the urge to reach for her.

She touched one of those fists…a fleeting contact, but enough to trigger that vibrant spark that arced between them whenever they touched. His resolve hardened. He must stay strong. Eleanor might believe her feelings lay hidden, but they shone from her eyes. He must disillusion her—she must understand there was no future for them, for her sake and her standing in society as much as for his pride.

'I was caught cheating at cards,' he said. 'My accuser was then attacked and robbed. That is why my father sent me to India. My accuser was badly injured and Father feared he might die.'

'But you didn't do it.' Her declaration rang with conviction.

'I was long ago cleared of the attack,' he said.

'Why did you not come home, then?'

'I am not wanted here.' Claverley's scornful words had pierced deeper than he realised. *Damn him. And damn everything.* And, in particular, damn his youthful indiscretions… his thoughtless, careless certainty that nothing could touch him. 'Not then. Not now. I have a debt to repay to my father. Once that is discharged, I shall return to my previous existence.'

'You are still bitter about his rejection of you. Is it not time to put that bitterness behind you and think of the future?'

'Am I not justified if I do feel bitter? Would you not feel the same had you been rejected by your…?' Too late, he bit his tongue. 'I'm sorry. I forgot. I should not have said that.'

He saw her swallow. 'It is true my mother left me. I don't think I have ever been bitter about it, though.' She took his arm. 'Come, let us walk and talk. It is easier to speak with honesty when you cannot see the other's face.'

They continued to stroll.

'Mayhap I was never bitter because I still had my father,' she said.

'But it must have affected you.'

'Of course it did. It devastated me. But…but…' From the corner of his eye he saw her shrug in a helpless fashion. 'I thought it was my fault.'

He had to strain to hear her. His heart swelled. He had been eighteen—old enough to rationalise his father's behaviour. Eleanor had been eleven years old. Still a child. No wonder, at times, she doubted herself. No wonder she concealed that inner doubt behind a shell of determined independence. He covered her hand with his and squeezed gently.

'You know now it was not your fault, I hope?'

She inhaled sharply. 'Of course. But we were talking of you and your father.'

Her voice was bright and positive. He bit back a smile. She was the most courageous woman he had ever met.

'May I tell you what I think, without annoying you?'

And here was a first—asking if he wanted her opinion before voicing it. 'Go on.'

'I think you should meet your father with an open heart. Listen to what he says and, more importantly, how he says it. Do not barricade your heart behind a wall of pride.'

That's easy for her to say. 'I will try,' he said.

'Did you prove you did not cheat at cards?'

'Who says I didn't cheat?'

'I say. I know you, Matthew Damerel. You are too honourable to do such a thing.'

A lump formed in his throat and his eyes smarted at her absolute conviction. She believed in him, unquestioningly, when his own father had not.

'Come.' His voice was gruff. 'We must go back inside. I do not want you to catch a chill.'

'Cousin Eleanor, how are you?'

It was some time later when the familiar voice roused Eleanor from her reverie and she turned to see James standing over her, Ruth clinging to his arm. Eleanor's heart faltered. She studied James's face. Could he really be responsible for those attacks? But, if not him, who? And why?

'I am delighted to see you without that guard dog of yours in tow,' he continued.

At least he hadn't noticed her new guardians. Despite her earlier annoyance, the sight of Lord Derham and Lord Vernon Beauchamp, hovering watchfully, eased her apprehension. They had appeared shortly after Matthew—with a wink at Eleanor and a whisper of 'Think of Almack's'—led Lady Cowper on to the dance floor. Eleanor, grateful for a respite from dancing, and for some time to ponder Matthew's earlier revelations, had sunk into a vacant seat next to Aunt Lucy and several of her friends.

Conscious that Aunt Lucy had stopped talking and was looking over in a none-too-friendly fashion, Eleanor rose to her feet, keen to avoid a repeat of the unpleasantness when James had called into Upper Brook Street.

'I am very well, thank you, James, and Mr Damerel— for I must presume that is to whom you refer—is merely a friend concerned with my well-being.'

'Damerel?' James's brow wrinkled. 'I thought he was called Thomas. You don't mean to tell me there are two of them?'

Eleanor inhaled deeply, determined to remain calm. 'He is the son of Lord Rushock,' she said. 'He uses another name for his business.'

She ignored the disdainful curl of James's lip. 'It is delightful to see you both,' she said, including Ruth—who looked pale and anxious—in her smile. 'I was about to take a turn around the room. Would you care to join me?'

They fell into step, with James in the centre, and made their way slowly around the edge of the dance floor.

'Have there been any further incidents?' James asked quietly.

'Yes.' Eleanor told him of the man she had seen outside the house, and the man who had accosted and threatened Agnes, and described him to James.

Rather than further the conversation, James turned

monosyllabic, his arm under Eleanor's hand rigid. What had caused him to clam up? A guilty conscience? Matthew would surely say so if he were here. Eleanor gave up trying to make conversation and spoke across James to Ruth, who clung to her husband's other arm.

'I trust you are fully recovered now, Cousin Ruth.'

Ruth shot a nervous glance at James before replying, 'I am quite well, thank you, Eleanor.'

James nodded approvingly at Ruth, who smiled tremulously. What did that look mean? The tension that simmered between husband and wife was palpable, but Ruth appeared to gain in confidence and proceeded to chat to Eleanor in an unusually friendly manner. She quizzed Eleanor about the forthcoming parties and events to which Eleanor had received invitations and offered advice as to which were likely to be the most enjoyable and which might prove a bore. Eleanor began to wonder if she had misjudged Ruth at their previous meeting. Perhaps Ruth *had* simply been on edge due to her imminent visit to the doctor, as James had claimed?

'James,' Ruth said, fanning herself, 'it is exceedingly hot in here and I do not see any footmen nearby. Would you be so good as to fetch us some wine?'

James hesitated. 'I don't…are you sure you will be all right?'

Eleanor stared in puzzlement. As James met her gaze, his jaw clenched. 'Eleanor?'

'A drink would be most welcome. Thank you.'

'Very well.' He found them two vacant chairs in an alcove. 'Do not move from here,' he said in a warning voice.

Eleanor raised a brow. James caught her look and reddened. 'It is very crowded. I am afraid I will not find you easily,' he said before hurrying away.

As soon as they were alone, Ruth turned to Eleanor and, taking her hand, regarded her earnestly.

'I am pleased to have this opportunity to apologise to you, Cousin Eleanor, for I fear I might have appeared unfriendly when last we met.'

'Think nothing of it, Ruth, for it is quite forgotten.'

Ruth's intensity unnerved Eleanor. She leant so close as she spoke that Eleanor had to force herself not to recoil. She could not help but look around for reassurance that her guardians were in view. They were. She relaxed.

'I was anxious about the appointment with my doctor.'

'Yes. James did explain.'

'Oh, James.' Ruth chewed at her lip, momentarily silent. 'He has changed, Eleanor. I do not know… Oh, it is nothing really.' She swayed closer and Eleanor, despite her best efforts, drew back. Ruth tightened her grip on Eleanor's hand and lowered her voice to a whisper. 'I know I can unburden my heart to you, dearest Eleanor. If only things had been different, we would be sisters now and I know my beloved Donald would urge me to trust you. I know that you love James and will not allow my worries to alter your regard for him, but I have no one else I can talk to.'

Eleanor swallowed hard. Where was James with their wine? What was Ruth implying? She had never liked Eleanor and had blamed her for her brother's death, yet here she was, introducing Donald into the conversation without a blink of emotion or blame.

'It is a sensitive subject—' Ruth continued.

'Then I implore you to say nothing,' Eleanor said, pulling her hands free. 'To be honest, Ruth, if you and James have problems, they should be resolved between the two of you. Do not forget I have loved James from childhood— I am unlikely to take your side in any marital squabble.'

'No, no! You misunderstand me.' Ruth grabbed Eleanor's hands again. 'I do not seek to drive a wedge between you, but I need to talk of this, in case…in case…the worst comes to pass.' She gave a low sob and held a handkerchief to her lips. 'I am sorry. I am a little overwrought.'

'Very well.' Eleanor saw that she was unlikely to escape Ruth's confidences. 'What is the matter?'

'James is desperate for a son. But…but…I have been unable to get with child. Oh, Eleanor, he blames me, I know he does. Our appointment the other day was to determine whether anything can be done to help, but the doctor offered no hope. And now…I am so afraid… What if he should…what if he decides he wants a new wife? Mayhap you can understand the strain I have been under and forgive my unwelcoming attitude?'

'I am so sorry to hear that, Ruth, and of course I forgive you.' Eleanor buried her instinctive dislike for the other woman under her very real sympathy and patted Ruth's hand. The woman was so brittle it felt as though she might shatter into a thousand pieces and there was still a fervent glitter in her eye that made Eleanor uneasy. 'I am always available, if you should feel the need to confide in someone, but I am convinced your worries are without foundation. James is an honourable man. He would never cast you aside.'

'It is not being cast aside that I fear,' Ruth said.

'Then—?'

Ruth turned her head away and Eleanor strained to hear her words. What she said made Eleanor's blood run cold.

'It is James.'

Chapter Twenty-Four

Matthew cursed—with fluent inventiveness—under his breath as he watched a succession of wealthy, handsome, titled men dancing with Eleanor. A lead weight anchored in his chest as yet another of her self-appointed guardians led her from the dance floor. He was reconciled—most of the time—to never being worthy of Eleanor, but it was agony to watch her with these men, any one of whom would be a perfect match for her.

'You're back.'

Matthew whipped round at the sound of that familiar voice. Every muscle tensed and his chest swelled as he drew in a seemingly never-ending breath. Familiar hard grey eyes assessed him and it was as though the last eight years had dissolved, leaving his eighteen-year-old self facing the man whose love and approval he had craved above all else. He held his father's gaze as his brain battled for control of both his body and his speech. The colourful, noisy ballroom receded until there was just Matthew, facing his father.

Breathe out. Now.

He willed his voice into the open. 'You got my letter, then.'

'What are your plans?'

No welcome. No softening of those stern features. No

pleasure in seeing his youngest son—now a man grown—after eight long years.

'I'm back for good.'

Matthew swung away, but…suddenly, Eleanor was by his side, with a swish of satin and the scent of jasmine. She grabbed his arm, pushed him back round to face his father.

'Mr Damerel,' she said. 'Would you do me the honour of introducing us?'

No! The silent roar reverberated around his head. He scanned the nearby guests; curious faces had turned in their direction. His jaw clenched so hard his teeth ached as he looked his father in the eye again. He stilled, momentarily breathless. Was that uncertainty in those familiar grey orbs?

Not out-and-out rejection, then.

Maybe? Possibly? Hopefully?

'Eleanor, Lady Ashby, this is my father, Lord Rushock.'

Eleanor dipped into a curtsy. 'I am delighted to make your acquaintance, my lord. Your son has proved *such* an invaluable support to me over the past few weeks. He is, if I may say, a son of whom any father would be proud.'

Matthew fought his inclination to close his eyes in despair. What on earth was she thinking?

His father inclined his head. 'Good evening, Lady Ashby.'

He said no more. The silence loomed around them, prodding Matthew to say something…anything…to fill that void.

'I am sorry to speak to you of such things in company, but you must know that I intend to pay the debts I owe you.'

A frown creased his father's brow. 'That is not necessary.'

'It is more than necessary to me—it is essential. I…you need not fear I shall ask anything of you, but I should like to see my mother and sisters.'

'I have not told them you are back.'

'You did not tell them where I went. You allowed them… all of them…to believe I would leave without a word. They did not even know if I was alive or dead.' His voice shook; the words near choked him. He swallowed convulsively, and drew strength from Eleanor as she—under cover of her skirts—feathered his hand with warm fingers.

'No doubt Stephen told you that.'

'Why would he not? He was as shocked at your actions as, no doubt, Mama will be. You should know, sir, that I have written to Sarah, so it will do you no good to try to prevent Stephen from telling Mama the truth. Besides—' Matthew gestured at the onlookers '—you know how fast news travels.'

'I did my best for you. If Henson had died—'

'But he did not. And…*I…was…innocent.*'

'But not of cheating.'

Eleanor's gasp soothed the wound to his heart. As did the sudden realisation that his father had the look and the sound of a man who suspected he was in the wrong, but was desperate to justify his actions.

Matthew reached a decision: this should not, *could* not, be resolved in a crowded ballroom.

'I will call on you tomorrow,' he said. 'With the money. And we can discuss how we move on from there.'

His father opened his mouth, then snapped it shut.

'Very well,' he said, after a pause. 'I shall await your visit.'

Matthew watched his father walk away, the tightness in his chest relaxing as his galloping heart eased to a trot.

'I am sorry you had to witness that, my lady,' he said, without looking at Eleanor.

'Are you angry with me?'

She did not sound particularly contrite. More…interested. Was he angry? Yes…and no. He felt a reluctant smile tug at the corners of his mouth.

'What made you imagine it was your business?'

'I was interes—'

'Interested. Yes. I gathered that. Interested; or interfering, depending on your perspective. Or…' he glanced at her, and her expression dispelled the remaining shards of any anger he had felt, '…or a friend, trying to help.'

She smiled. 'Thank you. One question.'

'Go on.'

'How shall you repay your father?'

His spine stiffened. *This*, surely, was a step too far, even for her.

'Do you have enough funds readily available? If not, I can—'

'No!'

She recoiled, a wounded look on her face. 'You do not know what I was going to say.'

'I can guess.' He gripped her arm and steered her into an empty alcove nearby. 'Do not insult me by offering me money. I am no pauper. I can pay my own debts.'

But he couldn't. Not yet. Not until Benedict arrived with those two ships and their cargoes were sold. After that, he would have the wherewithal to pay his debts, invest in further imports and to live comfortably. Until then, however…

'I was only offering a loan,' Eleanor said, in a hurt voice.

Matthew groaned inwardly. He must raise the money somehow. His pride would never allow him to admit to his father he was not yet able to pay his full due, but neither would it allow him to accept money from Eleanor, loan or not. It would have to be the bank. Or, if the bank failed him…he had always thought of moneylenders as the last possible resort but, now, Eleanor had supplanted them.

'I'm sorry,' he said, 'but I will not accept money from you, even as a loan.'

'Very well. I cannot force you to accept, but the offer is there if you have need.'

'Thank you.'

'Lady Ashby? I believe this is our dance?'

Matthew fought the burning jealousy that scorched his gut again as he watched Eleanor walk away on the arm of yet another self-assured, titled and no doubt wealthy member of the St James's set.

His mistake had been to secure her hand for the first two dances. He could not dance with her again without causing gossip. It was bad enough they had spent so much time already in one another's company, although the continued attentions of the cream of society's most eligible bachelors would no doubt preclude any criticism. No one would risk upsetting *them*.

He was now condemned to spend the rest of the evening either watching Eleanor from the edge of the ballroom or dancing with another lady. Neither option particularly appealed. With a muttered oath, he spun on his heel and headed for the card room.

In the hallway he passed two jaded-looking elderly gentlemen, making their slow way to the ballroom. The name 'Baroness Ashby' caught his attention and he slowed.

'I only said that I don't know as *I* should care for a wife who is mistress of her own property,' said the one, as he availed himself of a liberal helping of snuff. 'An independent wife? Goes against the natural order of things, don't you know. How's a man to keep his pride?'

'You'd be too lily-livered to stand up to her, anyway,'

his companion retorted. 'Why, she must be six inches taller than you for a start. Besides, you wouldn't get a look in, old fellow. With her wealth, she can look as high as she pleases for a husband. I doubt she'd settle for a paltry baronet like you, not with all the rich blood in town at the moment.'

They moved out of earshot and Matthew entered the card room with a heavy heart.

'Milady!'

Eleanor jerked awake, heart clambering into her throat, mind groping to identify that voice. Her maid's anxious face was lit by the wavering flame of a candle, the shadows casting her normally unremarkable features into a macabre mask.

'Lizzie. What is it?' Eleanor pushed herself into a sitting position and gathered the bedcovers to her chest. 'You frightened me. What time is it?'

'Nigh on four. Mr Pacey told me to come in here and not to leave the room no matter what.' The urgency in her whisper set Eleanor's scalp prickling. 'Peter's standing guard outside the door.'

'Standing…?' Panic clutched at Eleanor. 'Is everyone all right? Aunt Lucy?'

'Matilda is with her.'

'Tell me.'

'Peter heard a noise in the dining room.' One or other of the footmen were always on duty in the hall during the night. 'He went to look and there was a window open.'

The sound of Lizzie's chattering teeth broke the silence of the night. And it was silent, Eleanor realised. The servants must be searching very quietly.

'Come here and get under the covers, Lizzie,' Eleanor

said, not sure if the maid's violent shivers were from cold or fear or a combination of both.

Lizzie scrambled into the bed. 'Oooh, milady. Everyone is up now and searching for him. Mr Pacey said I was to come to you and I was that pleased…what if *I'd* happened to come across that monster?'

'Surely the maids aren't searching? Why, what if—?'

'Not on their own, milady. They've paired up with the men, to carry the candles. Ooh, milady, the men have all got weapons and everything.'

'Weapons? What weapons? I did not know we had any.'

''Twere Mr Matthew, milady. He made sure there were enough stout clubs for us all to hide under our beds.'

Everyone except me. And, I presume, Aunt Lucy. Hmmph. The sooner I get that pistol the better.

'Just in case, he said. And wasn't it lucky he did that, milady?'

'Indeed. Was Peter certain that window had been closed before?'

'Oh, yes. And Mr Pacey—he always does a last round after everyone has gone to bed.'

Eleanor had the sensation of thousands of ants swarming through her veins. The urge to get up…to take action… battered at her, but she ignored it. She would only make it worse if she left her room. At least in here she was easier to protect. It was difficult, though, as the seconds stretched into minutes. From time to time they heard the muffled thud of a door closing, or the creak of a floorboard, and at each noise Lizzie squeaked and huddled closer, comforting Eleanor and helping her to conceal her own terror.

'Did Peter see anyone?' she asked. Had anyone got inside? Was he, even now, in the house—hiding…biding his time? Or had Peter frightened him off?

'No. There was no one in the room. But he could have gone through into the parlour, couldn't he, milady? Peter came upstairs to wake Mr Pacey. Mr Pacey was very cross. *He* said as how Peter should have stood his ground and shouted. Now, Mr Pacey says, we don't know where he might have gone while Peter—'

A yell followed by the thud of running feet silenced Lizzie, who huddled even closer to Eleanor. Shouts echoed through the house. Doors slammed. Glass shattered. Then silence reigned once more. Eleanor pushed back the bed-covers and swung her feet to the floor. Lizzie grabbed at her, tried to tug her back into bed.

'Milady! No!'

Eleanor patted Lizzie on the shoulder. 'It's all right, Lizzie. I only intend to poke my head out of the door. Peter is outside, after all. I need to know what is happening.'

She wrapped a shawl around her, and approached the door. Despite her conviction that Peter—solid, dependable Peter—was on the other side, she hesitated. What if…? Lizzie was watching wide-eyed from the bed, knuckles white as she clutched the sheet.

'Peter?' she called, low-voiced. 'Are you there?'

'Yes, milady.'

'Is it safe for me to come out?'

The door inched open and Peter's familiar face appeared in the gap. 'I think so, milady. It was Mr Pacey that found him, but he couldn't hold him. Some of the other lads are giving chase.' He sounded disgruntled and Eleanor had to smile. What young man wouldn't yearn for some excitement in an otherwise mundane life?

'Has he left the house?'

'Yes, milady. Agnes came up to tell me and John—it was John was put to guard Lady Rothley. He wouldn't have got to either of you, milady. Not with us here.'

'If you are certain he has gone, you and John may go and help the others if you wish.'

Eleanor shook her head, smiling at the sight, moments later, of the two footmen bounding down the stairs with the eagerness of hounds on the scent.

Chapter Twenty-Five

'I don't think we should, Ellie. Why can we not wait until Mr Damerel is here to escort us?'

'I will not be made a prisoner in my own home, Aunt. We are only going to Hookham's and we will have the men with us.' As a concession to her aunt, Eleanor had agreed that three of the footmen should accompany them to the circulating library this time. 'It is broad daylight. No one would be reckless enough to try and attack me in public.

'Besides, Mr Damerel is not promised to his father until noon, so we shall not see him until mid-afternoon at the earliest.'

'That sounds encouraging,' Aunt Lucy said. 'The more time dear Matthew spends with his father, the more likely they are to resolve their differences.'

Matthew had undertaken to go to Blackfriars to buy a pistol for Eleanor straight after meeting Lord Rushock. Eleanor did not enlighten Aunt Lucy. She still did not know about the pistol, although how Eleanor might contrive to practice shooting without her aunt knowing…mayhap she could enlist Sir Horace to distract her?

Later, as they walked along Bond Street on their way back from the library, Eleanor began to regret her insistence on having her own way.

The pavement was even busier than usual and tension spread its tentacles from Eleanor's stomach to encompass her entire body. People were too close, brushing against her as they weaved around each other. Occasionally a passer-by stepped between her and the two footmen behind her, and her heart would pound and her palms grow clammy. Why hadn't she simply postponed her visit to Hookham's? There were too many people, all hurrying about their daily business: too much jostling, too much noise, too much traffic. The din from the passing wagons, carriages and hackneys—rattling over the cobbles, their drivers losing patience, shouting at their horses and each other alike—was tremendous.

They were often forced into single file, with Aunt Lucy and William ahead of Eleanor and Peter and John behind. A sudden surge in the crowd forced strangers both in front and behind Eleanor, there was an outcry from the middle of the swarming mass of people and then a hard shove knocked Eleanor off her feet. There was a flurry of move-ment as a crew of urchins scuttled past, into the road, dodg-ing the traffic, as a cry of 'Stop, thief!' rang out.

Eleanor landed with a painful bump on her bottom, her heart seized with fright. For one awful moment…she struggled to catch her breath, eyes screwed shut in an at-tempt to pretend it had not happened, knowing it was only by the merest good fortune she had not landed in the road itself, under the iron-clad, dinner-plate-sized hooves of the straining workhorses hauling a coal wagon past at that very moment.

An accident. That's all. Nothing to worry about, just a gang of pickpockets. She forced her lids open, looked in vain for her servants and Aunt Lucy. Nowhere to be seen. Strangers crowded her vision—all craning their necks to see what had happened.

'Allow me.'

Breathless, shaking, Eleanor turned her head to stare up into dark eyes lit with a sardonic gleam.

'Why,' the speaker proclaimed, 'if it ain't my little coz, Eleanor. Well met, my dear.' He smiled, his handsome face lighting up.

She stared at him. Recognition dawned. 'Hugo! It's you.' Her relief was indescribable. At that moment, she could have kissed him.

'It is indeed. And why, may I ask, are you sitting on the pavement in Bond Street? You could have afforded a hackney coach if you were that tired.'

'Do try not to be so ridiculous,' Eleanor retorted. 'That's just like you—always funning. Help me up, Hugo, please; we are providing everyone with quite a spectacle here.'

'You are, you mean,' he said. 'I was simply passing by, mindin' my own business.'

'Are you all right, milady?' She looked up to the welcome sight of William, Peter and John as they shouldered through the onlookers. 'The crowd…it was impossible…'

'I'm fine,' she said. 'Where is her ladyship?'

Peter plunged back into the surrounding throng, presumably to look for Aunt Lucy. Hugo helped Eleanor to her feet and helped her to brush the dust and debris from her clothes.

'*Three* footmen, my dear? I had not realised you were of such consequence.'

Eleanor bit her lip against a bubble of laughter. 'I will explain later,' she said as Aunt Lucy was shepherded through the gathered spectators by Peter.

'Ellie! What happened?' Her frantic gaze was glued to Eleanor's face.

Eleanor looked up. 'I was knocked over,' she said.

'Attacked?' Aunt Lucy shrieked. 'By him?'

'Not attacked, no.' Eleanor told her aunt what had happened.

'Good morning, Mama.'

Aunt Lucy shrieked again, this time a happy sound. 'Hugo. It's you.'

'It is, isn't it,' he agreed, 'as I have already confirmed to Eleanor. I was not aware you were coming to town, Mama.'

'I wrote and told you, Hugo.'

'Ah, did you indeed? That might explain it.'

'Explain what?'

'Why I didn't know, of course, m'dear. Been out of town. Rusticating. Only got back last night.' There was a pause. 'Now I come to think of it, there *was* a pile of letters and suchlike on my desk.'

'And you didn't think it important to look through them this morning?'

A pained expression appeared on Hugo's face. 'I thought they must be bills, m'dear. Far too unpleasant this early in the day. I was just heading to my club. To fortify m'self, you understand. But you still haven't told me what you are doing in town?'

'I came with Eleanor, to lend her countenance, you know, whilst the repairs were carried out.'

'Repairs? And, please do forgive my curiosity, but why would you think Eleanor had been attacked?'

'It's a long story.' Eleanor shivered, her legs suddenly like jelly.

Hugo put his arm around her and gave her a squeeze. 'C'mon, Coz, let's get you home.' He flagged down a passing hackney. 'Your men can walk back.'

Once inside the coach, Hugo eyed Eleanor with concern.

'I am unharmed, Hugo, truly I am.'

'If you say so, m'dear. I shall, however, expect a full account of what has been going on once you're safely home.

Lucas'd have my guts for garters if anything happened to you—or to Mama—on my watch. Besides which, as you may have noticed, she's the only the mother I have.'

He winked at Aunt Lucy, whose cheeks glowed as she beamed. 'You are such a good, kind son.'

Hugo grimaced. 'Hush now, Mama; I do have a reputation to uphold, you know.'

Eleanor let their words wash over her and she breathed a sigh of relief as the carriage drew up in Upper Brook Street.

Matthew paced the drawing-room carpet in Eleanor's house. The news with which Pacey had greeted him when he arrived in Upper Brook Street five minutes before had shaken him to the core and driven his doubts over the wisdom of that bank loan clean from his head.

'Wise move, getting this for her ladyship,' said Sir Horace, turning the dainty muff pistol over in his hands in the light from the window. He had arrived not two minutes before Matthew and was equally as troubled by Pacey's account of the happenings during the early hours of that morning. 'Fine workmanship.

'Pleased to admit I was wrong last night, m'boy. The ladies are more vulnerable than I realised.'

'More than I realised as well,' Matthew admitted, coming to a halt near the older man. 'I thought we had covered all the angles and they were safe in their own home. It seems I was mistaken.'

'But the scoundrel did fail to get anywhere near Lady Ashby,' Sir Horace said. 'No need to blame yourself. The measures you took were effective—it was just a shame it was Pacey who discovered where he was hiding. Had one of those strapping footmen winkled him out, I doubt he would have broken free so easily.'

Matthew resumed his pacing. 'Where are they?' He headed for the door. 'The blazes with what Pacey says, I'm going…'

Voices in the hall alerted him to Eleanor's return. Pacey had sworn they would be home any minute and it seemed he was right. Matthew flung the door wide just as Pacey was about to open it for his mistress. Two quick strides and he was in front of her, searching her dear face, taking her hands, raising them to press relieved lips against sweet-scented skin.

'Well, well. Matthew Damerel, if my eyes do not deceive me.'

Matthew froze. That voice… Eleanor tugged her hands free of his.

'I did not know you two were acquainted,' she said. 'Come, let us go into the drawing room. Pacey, some refreshments, if you please.'

Matthew, speechless, brain scrambling to order his thoughts, stood aside to allow Eleanor past. She was followed by Lord Hugo Alastair and Lady Rothley.

This was his chance. Alastair had been at that game.

'How do you two know each other?' Eleanor asked, after introductions had been made.

She sank into a chair by the fire with a relieved sigh. Lady Rothley settled on to the sofa, with Sir Horace on one side of her and Hugo on the other. Matthew took the other chair. Hugo's dark gaze switched from contemplation of Sir Horace to Matthew.

'You're back,' he said, ignoring Eleanor's question. 'How long has it been?'

'Eight years, give or take.'

'Never mind that,' Lady Rothley said. 'Tell Mr Damerel about your accident, Ellie.'

'Accident?' Matthew recalled the general grubbiness he

had noticed, but not really registered, on Eleanor's primrose walking gown. 'What happened? Are you hurt?'

'I am a little bruised, no more. I was knocked over by some boys. Hugo came to my rescue.'

'Hugo? Pacey said you took three of the men with you. Where were they?'

'It was crowded. It was hard to stay together. I have discovered,' she added, with a rueful smile, 'the disadvantage of being escorted by one's servants. One can hardly walk along Bond Street on a footman's arm, can one? And you were right, Aunt. I should have waited for Mr Damerel to escort us. I only wished to return my book, it was hardly a matter of life and death.'

'Unlike last night,' Lady Rothley said.

'Pacey told us what happened,' Sir Horace said, patting Lady Rothley's hand. 'What a dreadful experience, dear Lady Rothley. You will pleased to hear, Lady Ashby, that Mr Damerel has acquired that pistol on your behalf, so—'

'Pistol?'

Matthew cursed under his breath. Why hadn't he reminded Sir Horace not to talk of the pistol in front of Eleanor's aunt?

'Matters of life and death? Pistols? Would somebody please tell me what, precisely, has been going on?' Hugo said.

Eleanor caught Matthew's eye. He interpreted her silent plea and told Hugo all that had happened since the library at Ashby Manor had been set on fire.

Hugo stirred and rose elegantly to his feet. 'It would appear that, despite my every effort to appear otherwise, I do have a sense of familial duty after all,' he said. 'Mama, Ellie, I shall see you both later.'

'Where are you going?'

'Why, to fetch a change of clothing, of course. I shall

move in until after this villain is caught. As your sole male relative here in town, I am almost honour bound to join the fray, do you not agree? It should not be the responsibility of—' his gaze switched from Matthew to Sir Horace '—random strangers to protect you. However, I find I do have one question before I go—have you any idea who the culprit might be?'

Matthew stood, gritting his teeth against the other man's deliberate provocation, conscious he needed Hugo's co-operation if he were to have any chance of proving his innocence of cheating.

'You have one thing wrong, Alastair—you are not El— Lady Ashby's only male relative in town. James Weare, her other cousin, is our main suspect.'

Hugo's eyes gleamed. 'James Weare—well, I never. I had forgotten he was your cousin—and your rightful heir to boot, if I am not mistaken. The little worm,' he added, softly.

Matthew instantly warmed towards Hugo. He might give the appearance of careless, pleasure-seeking selfishness but with those three last words he had revealed his dangerous core—a good man to have on the spot, protecting Eleanor. But… Matthew's spirits plunged at the realisation that his own indispensability was shrinking by the minute, what with Hugo moving into Eleanor's house and the watchful presence of Stephen's friends by night.

'That reminds me,' he said to Eleanor, 'what did Weare have to say for himself last night?'

Eleanor pulled a face. 'The conversation was…*stilted* is the best description. He did ask if I'd had any other problems, and I told him about the man I saw, and about Agnes. He was uneasy and Ruth seemed timid.' She paused, then continued in a quiet voice, 'James was reluctant to leave

Ruth and me alone. And when he did...' she chewed at her bottom lip, her eyes haunted '... Ruth is scared of him.'

Hugo crossed the room to take Eleanor's hands in his. 'Do not fret, little coz—'twill all be settled before you know it, now that *I* am here,' he said, with a mischievous glint in his dark eyes as he flicked a glance towards Matthew.

Matthew thought if his jaw clenched any harder his teeth might shatter.

Remember. You need him.

Eleanor tilted her head, a sweetly loving smile on her lips as she regarded her cousin. 'Dear Hugo,' she said. 'You have always been such a reliable fellow, has he not, Aunt? I declare, I do not know how I should have managed all these years without such constant, devout attention.'

Lady Rothley laughed as Hugo grinned.

'Minx,' he said and bent to kiss Eleanor's cheek.

'Before you go, Alastair, might I have a word in private?' Matthew said.

Hugo raised a brow. 'Secrets?' he murmured. 'Do tell.' But he followed Matthew to the far end of the room without further demur.

'That card game,' Matthew said, 'the one where Henson accused me of cheating. Do you remember it?'

'I do. And, before you say any more, and because I'm a generous sort of fellow, I do know it was a false accusation.'

A hard ball of anger lodged in Matthew's chest. 'If you knew,' he said, 'why the hell didn't you say so at the time?'

Hugo raised a brow. 'For the very good reason that, at the time, I did *not* know.'

'Then you can prove Mr Damerel was innocent,' Eleanor said. She had joined them, unnoticed. Matthew sighed. He should have known.

'Ellie, my dear, this is not for your ears.' Hugo attempted to usher Eleanor back to the other end of the room, but she held her ground.

One look at the determined set of her mouth persuaded Matthew. If she did not hear what Hugo had to say now, Matthew would only have to repeat their conversation later. 'It is all right, Alastair,' he said. 'Your cousin knows about the game and the accusation, although she did not know you and your brother were present that night.'

'Lucas was there, too?' Eleanor said. 'Why did you not tell me?'

'Lucas. Yes,' Hugo said. 'And, as this appears to be important to my cousin, I will tell you. Luke is your man. He was friends with Henson, until *he* caught Henson cheating. He challenged him and Henson just laughed—congratulated Luke on being the first to catch him out. Luke was furious and then, not long after, they had a huge row. Over some woman, I believe. However, I digress. Luke told me Henson admitted it was he who had cheated that night. He—Henson, I mean—thought it highly amusing that you had taken the blame.'

'Why did he not say something to clear my name?' All that time, he could have been back home, with his family.

Hugo shrugged. 'No one knew where you'd gone. There didn't seem much point.'

That was true. Apart from his father and Claverley not one soul in England had known where he was, or what had happened to him.

'This is wonderful,' Eleanor said. 'Now you can prove your innocence to your father.'

'I shouldn't have to. He should have trusted me.'

'But he did not. And think of your mother and your sisters.'

She was right. Finally, he could hold his head up in the knowledge that nobody could point the finger at him.

'Hugo, will you write down what you have just told us? Or, better still, do you think Lucas would write a letter, setting out the facts?' Eleanor said. 'So that you have written proof, should anyone ever mention it,' she added, to Matthew.

Hugo shrugged. 'I can try,' he said. 'Lucas keeps himself to himself these days, but I shall use my best powers of persuasion. I will fetch my belongings and then, dear cousin, I shall write to my brother.'

'This is so exciting,' Eleanor said after Hugo had left.

She gazed up at Matthew with glowing eyes and Matthew's heart sank. Did she not know him at all?

'You can reconcile with your family,' she continued, 'and take your rightful place in society with no fear of those past lies lurking in the background to sully your name.'

She was all eagerness, her wealth and position giving her the confidence that her vision of the future was a rosy certainty. He knew what she felt for him: it radiated from her eyes whenever she looked at him, even when she was angry with him. And his feelings, also, had grown far beyond the initial attraction and the subsequent lust. But he would not allow those feelings to turn to love. She deserved better than him. She deserved to take her rightful place at the pinnacle of society. It had been her goal in coming to London and she was on the brink of achieving it.

'You forget, my lady,' he said. 'I have neither the desire nor the intention of taking *any* place in society. I have a life of my own and to that I shall return once the danger to you is past. Come, we should rejoin your aunt.'

He hardened his heart against the flash of hurt in her

eyes. He could protect her from her unknown assailant, but he could not protect her from the pain of his snub.

It is for the best. But...if only...

No. Regret was pointless. He had kissed her. Twice. Those kisses burned in his memory. He should have resisted her. He should never have called upon her once they returned to London.

How easy it was to be wise after the event.

Chapter Twenty-Six

Aunt Lucy watched with interest as Eleanor examined the muff pistol purchased by Matthew. Surprisingly, her aunt had raised not a single objection to her having the weapon—a circumstance that made Eleanor even more fearful for her safety. Even Aunt Lucy thought her in enough danger to warrant having a weapon to hand for protection. When would this nightmare end? But…the end of the threat to her life meant the end of her association with Matthew. He had made that abundantly clear. Unconsciously, she sat straighter, lifting her chin. He must never know how his earlier words had plunged ice into her heart.

'I say we should confront that weasel now, Damerel—you and I together. What do you say?' Hugo had returned with a packed valise, his valet in tow, and an eagerness to act.

He was talking about James. The truth tore at her. The truth she could no longer deny.

'We have tried before,' Matthew said. 'He will only deny it and we have no evidence. We must get hold of that fellow who accosted the servant girl. That is the only way we might get evidence.'

Eleanor concentrated on the pistol, its curved walnut grip smooth under her stroking thumb. The pistol blurred and she blinked hard to prevent her tears from spilling.

What a fool she was. Of course Matthew did not care for her. Who would? Her mother hadn't. James didn't—he was prepared to kill her, for goodness' sake.

Why should I care? She was at the pinnacle of her success, fêted as the Catch of the Season and her ultimate ambition was within her grasp—Emily Cowper had dropped her a hint just the other day, saying that her approval for Almack's was all but secure.

'Will you teach me to shoot this?' she asked Hugo, uncaring that she interrupted his quiet discussion with Matthew and Sir Horace.

'I am flattered you should ask, m'dear, but I'm afraid I won't have the time. We've come to the conclusion that, if confronting Weare is not the answer, he must be tailed, at all times. Sir Horace and I are to organise it, as Damerel has so few acquaintances in town. But never fear, I shall be back to escort you this evening and I told Pacey to place me in the next bedchamber to yours, so you may sleep easily tonight.'

Eleanor and Aunt Lucy exchanged startled looks. This brisk-talking, resolute gentleman was nothing like the nonchalant and care-for-nothing Hugo they were familiar with, the man who never stirred himself on anyone else's behalf.

'Besides,' he continued, 'although it pains me to admit this, Damerel was always a far better shot than I. He will teach you.'

Not the news she wanted to hear, but she acquiesced, determined not to reveal any hint of dismay. From now on, she must look upon Matthew as a dear friend. Nothing—and never to be—more.

Hugo and Sir Horace said their goodbyes and left.

'Well, Mr Damerel? Where do you suggest we go to practise? To the park?'

'First, I shall teach you how to care for it and load it. Then…' he hesitated. 'I fear it will be too public in the park—you will not want to attract attention. And you will be very exposed. What about here? Not indoors, but outside in the back yard?'

'It is not very big. Will there be room?'

His lips twitched. 'It'll be big enough for our purposes. This—' he plucked the pistol from Eleanor's hand, leaving a trail of tingles where his skin brushed hers '—is not designed for long distances.'

She tried to bite back her gasp of consternation.

Matthew crouched beside her chair. 'Are you certain you want to do this?' he asked. 'Now Alastair will be here overnight, and Weare will be followed, I doubt you will ever need it.'

He touched her hand. She raised her gaze to his, searching his expression. Compassion and concern: emotions prompted by fondness for a close friend.

'I hope I will never have to use it,' she said, 'but I want to learn. I will feel safer.'

'Very well. I suggest we go outside and begin.'

'Aunt Lucy. Will you come, too?'

'Oh, no, my pet. I can think of nothing worse than all that noise. Take one of the footmen with you—I am sure that will suffice for the proprietaries.'

Outside, Matthew showed Eleanor how to load the gun by unscrewing the short barrel, seating the gunpowder and the ball and carefully screwing the barrel back in place, first ensuring no powder had spilt on to the threads. He showed her the action of the sliding safety catch and explained how to carry the pistol in the half-cocked position to prevent accidental discharge. She repeated the actions several times until she was confident. By then Timothy had joined them, carrying a tightly stuffed sack.

'What is inside it?' Eleanor asked, eyeing the sack with horrified fascination as Timothy placed it on an old stool brought outside from the pantry, the garden wall behind serving to prop the sack upright. That, according to Matthew, represented her attacker. The man she would have to shoot if ever he got close enough to her to threaten her life. She swallowed down the sour bile that flooded into her mouth. She must not flounder at the thought of shooting into a sack. If she could not do this, how could she ever defend herself?

'Old rags and the like, milady. Mrs Pledger gave them to me.'

Matthew stood behind her. Close behind her. Suddenly, it was hard to breathe…his scent and his heat enveloped her as he lifted her arm to demonstrate how she should aim at the target.

'Close your left eye.' His voice in her ear, the rumble of his words vibrating through his chest, through her muslin dress and reverberating through her body, deep into her core. She sucked in a breath, willing her hand not to shake. 'Steady now.' He covered her white-knuckled hand where she gripped the pistol, his fingers gentle; reassuring. 'Relax.'

It was easy for him to say, nigh on impossible to do. She tried to breathe more evenly; tried to relax her arm and fingers.

'Aim for the centre of the sack. Gently now. Squeeze.' His breath tickled her ear, causing a ripple of gooseflesh down her neck. Her arm jerked as she pulled the trigger.

Bang! Smoke puffed from the pistol and Eleanor stifled her scream as the recoil vibrated up her arm. She had braced herself for the noise, but had not realised the power of the kick of such a small weapon. She swallowed hard;

turned to Timothy, who held the powder flask and spare balls; began to reload.

'I will do better this time,' she announced, to no one in particular, and took her stance as Matthew had showed her.

Matthew moved behind her.

'No. I will do this myself.'

She took aim, squeezed—striving to keep the movement smooth—and fired again.

'Yes!'

Matthew's triumphant shout bounced from the surrounding garden walls and Eleanor prised open her eyes, which she had screwed shut—quite without intent—at the moment she fired. A ragged, black-rimmed hole had appeared in the sack. Not in the centre, but at least she had hit the target.

'Well done,' Matthew said. 'Try again.'

She glowed with his praise. Donald had never praised her. He had always found fault.

She practised until the sack was in shreds and her right arm trembled with fatigue.

'That is enough for today,' Matthew said, gesturing to Timothy to clear everything away. 'You must be worn out. Let us go inside.'

Aunt Lucy was nowhere to be seen when they returned to the drawing room. A maid followed them in, bearing a tray laden with a jug of lemonade and a plate of sandwiches.

'Cook said as you would welcome some refreshments, milady.'

'Thank you, Nell, that is most thoughtful. Where is Lady Rothley?'

'She's gone up for a nap, milady. Would you like me to sit in with you?'

'No, that won't be necessary, thank you, but leave the door open on your way out, will you?'

Eleanor sat on the sofa, a glass of lemonade in her hand, whilst Matthew propped one arm along the marble mantelpiece.

'Thank you for teaching me,' Eleanor said.

Matthew sipped at his lemonade. The sweet yet sharp drink reinforced his bittersweet thoughts throughout this long day. What would the future hold for Eleanor? He knew his own future—the days would be filled with running his business. But what of hers? Would she wed? He tamped down the pain such a thought evoked. Maybe she never would marry. She certainly seemed content with her independent life.

'Why have you never wed?'

He hadn't meant to ask the question quite so bluntly, but he did not regret asking it. A memory stirred. Lady Rothley…talk of a betrothal. Or a near betrothal. He racked his brain, trying to recall her exact words, as Eleanor stared pensively into her glass, as though it might provide answers.

'I almost did,' she said eventually. 'Three years ago, just before my father died. I was on the brink of getting betrothed, when I found out…' She paused. 'I was fortunate I discovered his true nature before all the settlements had been agreed. I withdrew my acceptance of his offer.' She looked up, eyes glittering defiance. 'I have never regretted it.'

'And what was his true nature?' He could guess what was coming.

'Avaricious!'

'He was after your wealth.'

'He was. He was quite the expert at hiding his true intentions, though. He intended to live a life of luxury in

London whilst I remained at Ashby, running the estate to fund his pleasures.'

Bitterness surfaced, breaking through that outer shell of confidence she customarily hid behind. No wonder she was so uncertain of her own allure as a woman.

Before he could probe further, she continued, 'It is the reason Ruth never liked me.'

'Ruth?' What did Ruth have to do with it?

'Donald was her brother.'

'Her *brother*?' Whatever he had expected, this was not it. 'Why have you never told me?'

Her brows snapped together. 'Why on earth should I tell you? It's in the past. All finished with.'

'But…could it not be him trying to kill you? Revenge is a motive.'

'No!' Eleanor jumped up from the sofa and crossed the room to the window. She stood rigidly, her arms wrapped around her waist. Matthew set his glass down and followed her.

'He is dead,' she said. 'He was a soldier. He had planned to leave the army but, when I refused to marry him, he had no choice but to return to the military life. He was killed in battle. At Talavera.'

'I am sorry,' Matthew said.

She turned to face him. 'It is in the past, as I said.'

Matthew cleared his throat. He must say this without a single tremor in his voice to betray him.

'You will find someone worthy of you, I am certain.'

Only the slightest flare of her nostrils revealed her emotions. 'I am sure I will,' she said, her voice flat as she stepped to one side and glided past him to gain the centre of the room. 'Thank you once again for obtaining the pistol and teaching me to shoot.'

Her dismissal of him was plain. It was for the best. He must concentrate on finding proof against her cousin.

'It was my pleasure. Are you engaged this evening?'

'No. We were to have gone to the theatre but, after such an eventful night and day, we have decided to stay at home.'

'In that case, I shall see you tomorrow. I hope you will feel safer now, with your pistol and with Alastair staying in the house.'

Her pursed lips stretched into a semblance of a smile. 'I shall indeed. Goodbye, Mr Damerel.'

Chapter Twenty-Seven

It was the night of Eleanor's soirée, several days after the intruder had broken into the house on Upper Brook Street, and there had been no further incidents, to Matthew's relief. If she never had to use that pistol he would be a happy man—it went against his every instinct, to hand over even the smallest part of her protection to her or, indeed, to others. He had found fewer and fewer excuses to call upon her now Hugo was in residence and, although he still escorted her to her evening entertainments, the presence of her 'guardians' meant she was well looked after. His position was fast becoming redundant.

He arrived early at her soirée, hoping to snatch a few moments with Eleanor before her guests arrived. Pacey showed him up the stairs and there she was, her back to him, fiddling with a flower arrangement on a side table set into an arched alcove on the first-floor landing.

As Pacey stepped forward to announce his presence, Matthew stayed him, then crossed the landing to stand behind her.

'Good evening, my lady.'

Eleanor started, then turned to laugh up into Matthew's face, soft lips parted revealing white, even teeth, her eyes glowing, the gold flecks in her irises reflecting the candlelight.

'Goodness, you startled me.'

Matthew's heart turned in his chest. She looked so beautiful, her elegant pale rose gown displaying her womanly curves to perfection. He drank in the vision. How much longer would he be able to do so? How much longer could he remain part of her life?

Eleanor brushed a wisp of hair from her face. Her hands were bare, her gloves lying abandoned on the table behind her.

He sketched a bow. 'My apologies for my early arrival— I thought I would come early in case your cousin showed his face before the appointed time.'

'He is not attending,' Eleanor said, as she led the way into the drawing room, 'and neither is Ruth. I feel…such lightness of spirit. I shall be able to enjoy this evening without the constant apprehension of what James might say or do. I felt obliged to invite them despite my dread of seeing him again.'

The doors between the drawing room and the sitting room beyond had been thrown wide, the furniture removed and the carpets rolled up ready for the dancing. The piano was set at one end of the room, the pianist already there, running his fingers up and down the scales.

'James sent a note round this morning to say he was going out of town on urgent business and Hugo has confirmed he left on the mail coach,' Eleanor continued, as she crossed to the front window, twitched the curtain aside and peered out into the twilit street. She laughed self-mockingly, and shook her head. 'It is foolish, I know, but I cannot help but look outside every so often, in case I see *him*.'

'It is not foolish. You are right to stay alert. Where is Alastair? Is he here?'

'Oh, yes.' She smiled at Matthew over her shoulder,

eyes twinkling. 'He is upstairs, completing his *toilette*. He attends society events rarely and his pride dictates he is not found wanting.'

'He does not enjoy such gatherings, then?'

'No, and judging by what has remained unsaid, I suspect that, in my cousin's case, it is a case of mamas and chaperons beware.' She lowered her voice. 'He leads a reckless life and my uncle did not leave the family fortunes in a robust state. Not many parents would countenance an impoverished second son courting their daughter.' She flushed. 'Oh! That was tactless indeed. I am sorry, I did not mean... I hope I did not cause offence?'

'My shoulders are broader than that, I hope,' Matthew said. Her words might have stung if he had not already inured himself to that truth. 'Besides, Alastair's position as second son is positively charmed compared to mine. A third son is a far more hopeless proposition, would you not say?'

She looked up, laughing again. 'Only if those parents were fixed upon their daughter marrying for position. Or wealth.'

Their gazes fused. Matthew's waistcoat suddenly seemed too tight to draw breath as Eleanor's smile faded and her eyes questioned his. Without volition, he raised his hand to her cheek and trailed his fingers down soft, silken skin to her mouth.

'Eleanor.'

Her eyes widened, darkening as her lips parted. A quick glance to the pianist, who was absorbed by his trilling chords, and Matthew tilted her chin, lowering his head to touch his lips to hers. It felt like home. Where he belonged. With a deep groan, he gathered her to him, backing her through the curtains into the narrow bay beyond, ignoring the clamour of caution in his head.

Her arms snaked around his neck, her fingers threading through his hair as their tongues entwined. The rush of blood to his groin kept his conscience at bay as he plundered her sweet mouth. The press of her body to his, her full breasts squashed against his chest, her unique perfume—jasmine, interwoven with the tantalising scent of feminine arousal—flooded his senses as his hands roamed her voluptuous curves. Lost in the most arousing kiss of his life, he forgot time, place and propriety as Eleanor cupped his face, then slipped questing hands beneath his coat to caress his chest.

As her touch crept lower Matthew reluctantly resurfaced. A stolen kiss was one thing. Any more…

'Eleanor…' A harsh whisper from fevered lips as the enormity of his actions hit him. 'You are…irresistible.'

He could hardly bear to meet her eyes. Instead, he peeked through the slight gap between the curtains. The room was still empty. The pianist beyond was still absorbed in his music.

'Quickly,' he said, leading her back into the room. He stepped back. Examined her. No signs of ravishment, her hair still in place.

It wasn't her hair you were manhandling. Guilt shrouded his thoughts, penetrated deep into his heart. What had he done?

'Matthew…?'

'I am sorry. I had no intention…' He paused. It was not possible. The future. Could he…? Every ounce of his pride rose up to smother his guilt. No. He could not. 'You are so very lovely. But…'

She released him from the hook upon which he squirmed. 'But it can never be?'

He shook his head.

A frown creased her forehead. 'You will make up your

differences with your father and the rest of your family, you will see. You only need the time and the opportunity.'

'And then what?'

He had not meant to sound so harsh, hated the hurt that surfaced in her tawny eyes before she dropped her gaze.

'I will not be a kept man.'

'You have your business interests—'

'They are nothing in comparison.'

'In comparison to what?' she snapped. 'You have worked for what you have, Matthew. How does that make you a lesser being?' She laid her hand on his arm. 'I would never view a gentleman who earns his way in the world as inferior to a gentleman who has inherited his wealth.'

'Then you are the exception to the rule,' Matthew said, 'for that is exactly how society views a man who has to work for a living.'

'Who cares what—?'

'*You* care. You came to London to erase the memory of your mother's scandal, to be accepted for Almack's. You care what society thinks of you. You want a position in society, and you have one. And *I* care what society would think of *me* if...'

His voice had risen. He stepped back and Eleanor's hand slipped from his arm.

'I am sorry,' he said, quieter now. 'I had no intention of raising false expectations. I will not be labelled a fortune hunter on the catch for a rich wife. My honour...'

'Your honour?' Her eyes flashed scorn. 'You speak of honour, yet you think nothing of stealing kisses from a maiden who, by your own admission, you would never wed.'

The bitter words hung in the air between them. Why could she not see how hard this was for him, too? Did she think it gave him pleasure to picture her with another man?

'You should go and find your gloves before your guests arrive.'

Eleanor left the room without another word, back straight, head high.

He had expected nothing less.

Although he had stated his case, Eleanor's words nevertheless came back to him at times during the evening. *I would never view a gentleman who earns his way in the world as inferior to a gentleman who has inherited his wealth.* He believed her. The problem was not with her views on the chasm between them, but with his. And with his pride. He might start with just a tiny feeling of inferiority, but what if it were to grow? What of Eleanor's penchant for having her own way? How long before their disparate circumstances reared up to cause trouble? *He* would never be approved to buy vouchers for Almack's—not that he would want them, but that was hardly the point. Would she grow to resent him and to regret shackling herself to a gentleman who would not be fully accepted everywhere?

She deserved better than him and, in time, she would see it.

On the other hand…love. He could think about her, and them, and all the reasons—very good reasons—why they should stay apart. It was the only outcome that made sense. But then, in his heart… Eleanor. She was so deeply entrenched he could not imagine a day without loving her. He had no interest in any other woman.

Confused, Matthew chatted, and danced, and played cards by rote as Eleanor acted the gracious hostess. He clenched his jaw against the pain of seeing Eleanor with other gentlemen, all more worthy of a wealthy peeress than he.

* * *

When will they get here? How will he react? Will he hate me for interfering?

Eleanor's nerves skittered as she chewed at her lower lip, hoping she had done the right thing. She looked around, seeking Matthew, and her stomach clenched in irritation at the sight of him dancing with yet another pretty miss. He had not danced with her and she could not blame him.

That kiss…she had been swept away by it…swept away by him…until anger had allowed her to gather her wits. She had returned to reality with a painful bump. Matthew was right. It was for the best. She could see it now. It could never work. She was better off without him.

There was a flurry of movement by the door, and Pacey appeared. He caught her eye and beckoned. *Oh, heavens.* Eleanor's heart raced as she walked to the door. Too late for doubts or regrets: the die was cast.

In the hall downstairs, William was divesting a scowling Lord Rushock of his hat and gloves. Eleanor's heart sank at his expression. Stephen had assured her their plan would work. She must trust him to know his own father. But Matthew…that stubborn pride of his…would it allow him to unbend enough to meet his father halfway in this attempt at reconciliation?

Stephen Damerel stood waiting for his father, with an anxious frown that cleared as he caught sight of Eleanor.

'Good evening, Lady Ashby,' he said, with an elegant bow. 'I apologise for our tardy arrival.'

'I am delighted you could both attend.' They exchanged a conspirators' smile. 'Good evening, Lord Rushock. I trust you are well?'

'Harumph!' Rushock's chest expanded. 'Yes, well enough, I suppose, although—'

'Father, you do wish to mend your fences with Matthew, do you not? Think of Mama.'

The older man subsided. 'Yes.'

His brevity surprised Eleanor. He had appeared an inveterate blusterer, but mayhap it was all show.

'Would you like to come through to the parlour?' she said. 'Mr Damerel, if you would be so kind as to—?'

'I'll go and get him.'

'Thank you. Pacey will show you which room.' And Aunt Lucy and Hugo had been primed to forestall any guests who might notice that both Eleanor and Matthew had disappeared.

They waited in silence in the parlour. Eleanor, full of trepidation now the moment was close, was unable to make small talk. Lord Rushock paced the room, hands clasped behind his back.

The door opened to admit first Matthew, then Stephen, who closed it and leaned back against it in a nonchalant manner; only the tight line of his mouth revealed his tension.

'What is the meaning of this?' Matthew's ice-blue gaze speared Eleanor. He turned to leave. 'Let me pass.'

'Not yet, little brother. Not until you and Father have a proper conversation. It is time you thrashed over the past and set it behind you.'

'We've talked. There is nothing left—'

'For your mother's sake, if not mine.' Rushock gripped Matthew's shoulder. 'Please, son.'

Matthew's indrawn breath was audible. 'Very well. Just family.'

It was as though he stabbed her in the heart. It could

not be clearer that she did not belong. Eleanor walked to the door, trying not to show her hurt.

'I will see you later,' she said in a low voice to Stephen as he opened the door to let her pass.

Chapter Twenty-Eight

Matthew searched the room for his hostess. Ah…there! She could not help but stand out, with her burnished curls piled high, topping every other woman in the room by half a head. He strode across the room to where Eleanor stood with Lord Vernon Beauchamp and his sister, Lady Cecily. Her awareness of his approach was exposed by the sudden flush of her cheeks, despite her determined attempt to keep her attention on her companions.

Beauchamp…rake and darling of the *ton*. Resentment scraped at Matthew's insides. It mattered not that Stephen had assured him none of the gentlemen watching over Eleanor was hanging out for a wife…and why Stephen had even thought it necessary to tell him such an irrelevant fact, he did not know…! Grrr! He'd lost his train of thought. All he knew was the sight of Eleanor anywhere near any of these so-called gentlemen *burned* in his gut.

And the memory of her interference scoured his insides even more. How dare she? What business of hers was it if he and his father were estranged? If he had any doubts over not courting her, her interference had consolidated his decision. She always thought she knew best. She was a stubborn, managing tyrant.

And an utter peach.

His anger subsided—a little—as she shot him a wary

glance through her thick lashes. A tremulous smile hovered for an instant on those full lips before she settled her focus back on Beauchamp.

As the conversation ebbed and flowed he thought back to the interview with his father. It had been awkward. Both men—he recognised from a distance—had been wary of offering too much, in case the other rejected that degree of conciliation. Thank God for Stephen and his patience and diplomacy in brokering their deal. For that is what it had reminded Matthew of. A business deal. With sky-high personal stakes. They had left the parlour with a new understanding and, in Matthew, the joy of knowing he would shortly be reconciled with the rest of the family. Claverley would be furious. That made the reward even sweeter.

Gradually, Eleanor's conversation with the Beauchamps drowned out his introspection.

'I am arranging a day out to Richmond next week,' Lady Cecily was saying. 'I do hope you will join us, Eleanor, with your aunt. I will send you an invitation.'

'Thank you, Cecily. I should be delighted.'

'And you, Mr Damerel? Might I persuade you to join our number?'

'If I am still in town, I should be delighted, my lady.'

'Are you planning to leave London?' Was that a hint of panic in Eleanor's question?

He summoned up every last vestige of his resolve. 'I am. As soon as you are in no further danger, my lady, I plan to visit my family.'

'Then you and your father—'

'Have reached an understanding.' He should thank her for her help, but his anger at her unasked-for interference was too raw. It was an uncomfortable clash of feelings and it was simpler not to give vent to either. Maybe when he had calmed down a bit… 'I am very much looking forward to seeing my mother and sisters again.'

Her eyes glittered. 'There is no need to remain in London on my behalf,' she said. 'Hugo is here and I am sure the other gentlemen who have been so kind in watching over me will continue to do so for as long as necessary. Is that not so, my lord?'

'Indeed,' Vernon said, in his rich, cultured voice. 'We are at your service for as long as you need us.'

'So, there is nothing to prevent you going home tomorrow, if you so wish,' Eleanor said, her tone indifferent although the faint crease between her brows told its own tale.

He could not blame her…he was not the only one with pride.

'I will finish what I started,' he said. 'I shall call upon you tomorrow, at two o'clock, if that is convenient, to discuss your protection over the next few days. Alastair, as I understand it, has a long-standing commitment tomorrow so, if you need to go out, I shall be available to escort you in the afternoon.'

Eleanor nodded. 'Very well. I shall see you at two tomorrow. Now, if you will please excuse me, I have guests to attend to.'

A short time later, a heavy hand landed on his shoulder.

'Well, my boy—' his father's voice boomed in his ear '—I am pleased we have buried our differences.' He chuckled. 'We are too alike, that is the truth. Proud. Your mother would say stubborn, too, but I will not admit to that.'

'I am pleased to put the past behind us too, Father,' Matthew said. 'Although I must tell you again that I shall not give up my business interests. Quite apart from that pride you mentioned, I actually enjoy what I do. I could never live an idle life.'

'You won't be idle, my son, not with that estate your grandfather left you.'

His father had earlier told Matthew that his mother's father had bequeathed an estate in Leicestershire to Matthew, subject to his return to England of his own free will.

'It may not enjoy a vast acreage, but your grandfather was able to live very comfortably off the rents,' Lord Rushock continued. 'It's prime hunting country, you know.'

'Despite that, I will continue in trade with my business partner. That was our plan in returning to England.'

'Plans can change.' His father nudged him and nodded in Eleanor's direction, where she was bidding farewell to some of her guests. 'It looks like you're in a fair way to fixing your interest already, you sly young pup—way ahead of the other bucks hanging out for a rich wife. She'd be a good match for you, worth a tidy fortune. She'd not be to everyone's taste, mind, too tall and robust for most, but a pretty enough face, I'll grant you. And that fortune will be more than enough to compensate. It's good to see the years away have given you some good sound common sense.'

Fuming, Matthew clenched his fists. Even his own father thought he would court Eleanor purely for her wealth. No longer thought a cheat, but now labelled as a fortune hunter.

The next day a frustrated Eleanor gazed at the clock in the drawing room, watching the minute hand creep past the six and tick its way up towards the hour again. It was already past half past two.

Where is he?

Hugo was out and Eleanor had declined to accompany Aunt Lucy and Sir Horace on their visit to friends because Matthew was due to call.

The clock struck three; she paced the floor.

Where is he? It would serve him right if I wasn't here when he arrives.

But still she waited, increasingly annoyed—not only at Matthew for his tardiness, but also at herself for staying meekly at home, awaiting his arrival.

She looked at the clock for the umpteenth time. Five past three. She wandered to the window and craned her neck to peer up and down the street below. A discreet cough drew her attention and she turned to see Pacey at the door.

'A message has been delivered for you, my lady.' He held out a folded and sealed sheet of paper.

'Thank you, Pacey.'

She did not recognise the writing so it was not from Matthew. She broke the wax seal and smoothed the single page, which was covered in a cramped and hurried script.

My dearest Cousin Eleanor

   Our recent conversation about my Troubles gave me such comfort and I would beseech you to come to my Aid. I am in such turmoil about your Cousin James. You are the only person I can turn to in my Distress and I must plead with you to come to me without Delay whilst he is from home.

   I shall be at Home all afternoon and I hope and pray that you will attend me here without Delay, for I shall be unable to answer to the Consequences if you do not come.

   Please do not Fail me. It must be Today, before your Cousin returns.
Your Desperate Cousin
Ruth

Eleanor frowned as she finished the letter, then re-read it carefully, wondering what had caused Ruth to write such a hasty and muddled missive. The 'troubles' she wrote of suggested her agitation at her lack of a family. But her insistence that Eleanor attend her before James came home... Could Ruth have discovered something about the attacks?

Eleanor considered her options, eager to hear what Ruth had to tell her. If she waited for Aunt Lucy—out shopping, with Sir Horace as her escort—to return, she would surely insist upon accompanying Eleanor to visit Ruth. Whilst that might be the sensible thing to do, would her aunt's presence prevent Ruth from being completely honest?

Also, the longer she delayed her visit, the more likely it was that James would return whilst she was there. Therefore, the sooner she went to Ruth, the better.

She could send word to one of her 'guardians', but the same objections to Aunt Lucy's presence applied equally to them. Ruth would be unlikely to speak openly in the presence of anyone else, particularly a man.

Which left Eleanor to rely upon her own resources, much as she had done for the past three years.

She would go in the carriage, right to the front door. She had her footmen. She would take her pistol. With James away from home, what possible danger could there be? Her mind conjured up the image of the stranger she had seen watching her. She had not seen him since that time outside the house. And Ruth would be there, after all.

She made up her mind. She *would* go and, if she sensed the slightest threat when the door was opened to her, she would simply refuse to go inside. She rang the bell.

'Pacey, I am going out in fifteen minutes. Can you send for the carriage and ask Lizzie to attend me upstairs, please? And tell three of the footmen—whoever you can spare most easily—they are to accompany me.'

'May I know where to, my lady?'

'To call upon Mrs Weare,' she replied. 'When Lady Roth-

ley returns, please tell her where I have gone and what time.
And tell her not to worry, for I have protection with me.'

Pacey hesitated. 'My lady, should you not wait until—?'

'*Now*, Pacey.' The butler bowed and withdrew.

Eleanor went to her bedchamber to change into her
sprigged-muslin walking dress and to load her pistol. If
James was the culprit, and he returned home unexpectedly,
she would be ready for him. Lizzie helped her into her po-
mona-green spencer and bonnet, and she carefully placed
the pistol into her matching reticule, ignoring Lizzie's gasp
of horror.

'Come, Lizzie, fetch your coat, please. I wish you to attend me on my visit to my cousin's house.'

'Very well, milady.' Lizzie was stiff with disapproval.

As they trod down the stairs to join William, Timothy
and Peter, who were awaiting them in the hallway, Eleanor pushed her qualms aside.

Instead, she chose to focus on her satisfaction that the
decision of whether or not to continue waiting for Matthew had been taken from her hands.

Chapter Twenty-Nine

The same mournful-looking footman from before answered the door in response to William's knock. Timothy assisted Eleanor from the carriage and she approached the entrance. The front door stood wide and, beyond the servant, she could see a maid busy polishing a console table. The hallway seemed brighter, the sweet scent of beeswax a pleasant contrast to the stale cooking odours that had given the house such a musty air on her previous visit.

Reassured that normality reigned, Eleanor called to the coachman, 'We will not be long, Joey. Please walk the horses around if they get restless.'

She stepped across the threshold into the hall.

'Mrs Weare is in her bedchamber, milady,' the footman said, eyeing William, Timothy and Peter askance. 'She has requested that you attend her there.'

'Is your mistress unwell?'

'No, milady. No more than usual.'

'Is Mr Weare at home?'

'No, he has travelled out of town. He is not due back until tonight.'

'Very well. Timothy and Peter, you will wait for me here in the hall. William—' he was the biggest and burliest of the three '—you can wait for me on the upstairs landing. And Lizzie will come with me.' She had already warned the men that, if James were to return, they must come to her immediately.

James's footman frowned, but raised no objection, merely indicating they should follow him. Eleanor relaxed a little as she climbed the stairs with Lizzie, William at their heels, the weight of her pistol providing comfort. Surely, if there was a plot to harm her here, the servants could not behave in such a humdrum manner. James was still away from home and the fact that the footman had raised no objection to William accompanying her upstairs reassured her.

Ruth's bedchamber was on the second floor. Eleanor entered to find a large, bright room, decorated in rose and cream, the tall windows open to allow the sunlight to stream in. The room was far better appointed than the shabby sitting room into which she had been shown on her first visit. Mentally, she shrugged. How James and Ruth chose to decorate their house was none of her concern.

The bedchamber had been arranged in two halves: to the right of the door was a bed, beyond which there was a door, possibly leading to a dressing room or even to James's bedchamber. An elegant chest of drawers and a vanity dresser in matching mahogany were arranged against the wall.

To the left of the door was a sitting area consisting of two bucket chairs, arranged either side of the fireplace. On the long wall opposite Eleanor, set between two of the windows, was an elegant *chaise longue*, upon which Ruth, haggard in top-to-toe black, reclined. Eleanor faltered. Was she in mourning? No, she could not be. Her parents and brother were all long deceased and no one else had died to Eleanor's knowledge. She crossed the room to greet Ruth, aware from the corner of her eye that Lizzie moved to stand near the fireplace.

'Eleanor, my dear, dear cousin, I am so pleased you have come. I have been in such turmoil.'

Ruth did look unwell, her cheeks gaunt, her eyes blazing with a fervency that brought to Eleanor's mind her discomfort when Ruth had confided in her at the Duke of Cheriton's ball.

It is too late to regret coming now, she thought, with a trickle of unease. *Find out what she wants, then leave as soon as you can.*

'Ruth, I hope I find you well? Tell me, what is so urgent that you needs must summon me with such urgency?'

Ruth rose from the *chaise longue* and Eleanor exchanged a nervous look with Lizzie as Ruth circled the room before walking to the window and staring out, her arms folded around her torso, her narrow back and shoulders rigid. 'I told you I was desperate to get with child, did I not?'

'You did.'

Eleanor moved towards Ruth, angling to one side, so she could see Ruth's expression. It was oddly impassive. Eleanor tried to quash her growing fear. Lizzie was here. William was outside the door, with instructions to come in immediately if she called him.

Suddenly, Ruth spun to face Eleanor. 'It was him! James! I found him out. He was putting poison in my food. Poison to prevent my conceiving…to prevent my child inheriting Ashby. But I fooled him. I stopped eating. I am with child, although he does not yet know it.'

Eleanor's mind reeled. Could this be true? She couldn't believe…*poison*? No, not James. She stepped towards Ruth, vaguely aware of Lizzie, now by her side, clutching at her arm, trying to tug her towards the door. She strove to speak calmly, reaching out to touch Ruth, trying to build a rapport with her.

'Listen to me, Ruth, please. James longs for a child, you know he does. He loves you. Why on earth would he prevent you from conceiving?'

'He doesn't want us at Ashby. He *never* wanted us at Ashby.'

Eleanor shook her head, scrambling to make some sense of it all, remembering the attacks on her. Could James really...? Her whirling thoughts skidded to a halt. *Ashby?*

'But... Ruth...your child won't inherit Ashby. It belongs to me, not Ja—' Her blood froze as pieces of the puzzle began to slot into place. *Ruth?* Could Ruth be responsible for...?

'It's not natural.' Ruth snatched her arm away. '*I* should be Lady Ashby, by rights. James tricked me. I didn't know, until it was too late. Even then, we could have stayed there and lived a comfortable life but, no...he insisted we come here and struggle. He never wanted us at Ashby.'

Did she mean the baby? Eleanor eyed Ruth's slender form. She did not look *enceinte*. 'Us? Who do you mean? Who doesn't James want at Ashby?'

'Me and Donald.'

'But...Donald is—'

'Dead! Yes, he's dead. And it's all your fault.' Ruth's eyes glowed with a fanatical light as she spewed out her accusations. 'Ashby could have been Donald's. Why do you think he proposed to you? For your *charms*? You killed my brother and now you're Lady Ashby, and you have all the money and *we*...we have nothing.'

Even though she knew it was untrue, it hurt. 'Donald died in the war, Ruth,' she said.

'He only went back because of you. Why didn't you just marry him? We could all have been happy then. At Ashby. It's your fault Donald is dead. He died horribly. In agony. And it is your fault. You might as well have pulled the trigger yourself.'

Rationally, Eleanor knew Donald's death was not her fault and yet, deep inside, there lingered a splinter of guilt. *If* she had married him, it was true he would still be alive.

She tried again to pacify Ruth, even though she suspected the other woman was beyond reason, ignoring Lizzie's hissed 'Milady!' and shrugging off the increasingly urgent clutch of her fingers.

'Ruth, you cannot know what really happened in the Peninsula. It is a war. Soldiers face injury and death every day. You must not torment yourself with details you cannot possibly know for sure.'

'I know everything! Garrett was there. He was with Donald when he died.'

'Garrett? Who is…?' Eleanor followed Ruth's triumphant gaze as she looked at the second door opposite the fireplace. Eleanor's stomach clenched in fear as she recognised the man she had seen outside her house, turning the key in the lock.

'William! Help!' Eleanor's scream mingled with Lizzie's.

There was a thump against the door Eleanor and Lizzie had entered by, which shook, but held. Ruth must have locked it, unnoticed, during her circuit of the room. The man—Garrett—smiled and walked towards Eleanor, who backed away, skirting around Ruth. At least she could now see them both at once. She pushed at Lizzie, in a silent attempt to tell her to go and unlock the first door, which was now unguarded, but the maid was more intent on staying close to Eleanor.

A gloating smile played around Ruth's lips. '*Now* you will learn the truth,' she spat, 'before you die. My child *will* inherit Ashby and there is nothing you can do to prevent it.'

Eleanor backed until the *chaise longue* prevented further retreat. *Her pistol!* She fumbled in her reticule but, just as her fingers closed around it, Garrett grabbed her, his hands closing hard around her upper arms.

As Eleanor struggled she was aware of Lizzie tugging at Garrett and more loud thumps coming from the locked door. Slowly, relentlessly, Garrett dragged her towards the open window.

She forced herself to look Garrett in the eye. 'You do not have to...you will hang...why would you risk—?'

'You killed my boy,' he snarled.

'Your boy?' Eleanor panted with the effort of resisting him. Surely William would break the door down soon? Garrett's arms were wrapped tight around her, but her pistol was in her hand and, if she got the chance, she would use it without a qualm. She gritted her teeth, struggling harder, aware of Lizzie now grappling with Ruth.

'I brought him and Miss Ruth up from little nippers. They deserved Ashby! Weare tricked her! Miss Ruth was *born* to be a lady.'

Eleanor's head spun and she gasped for breath as she struggled with all her strength to free herself. Although slightly shorter than her, he was immensely strong and slowly, inexorably, they neared the window. Her heart tumbled with fear. If they reached the low sill, one good push and she would fall. Hauling in a deep breath, she braced herself for one more effort to free her right arm and, somehow, use her pistol.

Suddenly, with a loud crash, the first door flew open. Garrett's grip loosened for a second, but that was enough for Eleanor. With all her remaining strength she pulled away from him, then spun around, holding her pistol up with a shaking hand. Garrett's attention was not on her, however, but on the man who had burst through the door.

'No, Eleanor!'

Eleanor's breath seized as Matthew charged at Garrett, who roared with fury, swinging wild punches. Eleanor's heart was in her mouth as she watched Matthew dodge Garrett's flailing arms, until one well-aimed punch to Garrett's jaw saw him slump to the floor, knocked out cold.

'Noooo!' Ruth's shrill cry resounded around the room. Shoving Lizzie aside, she advanced on Eleanor, fingers clawed.

'Ruth! Stop! I beg of you.' James had appeared. He pushed between Ruth and Eleanor, arms out wide in a placatory gesture. His voice gentled. 'Please don't upset yourself, my love—you know what the doctor told you. Come, come with me. I'll get your medicine for you—that will make you feel better.'

Ruth stared past James at Eleanor, eyes crazed, spittle spraying as her words tumbled over each other in frantic speech. 'Help me, cousin! He is trying to poison me. He doesn't want me to have a baby. Now you can see I am telling you the truth.'

Quick as lightning, she dodged around James and ran at Eleanor, who instinctively flung her arms wide and wrapped them tightly around Ruth's frail form. Matthew was by her side in an instant, but his help wasn't needed for, as soon as Ruth felt Eleanor's arms around her, all the fight seemed to leave her and she slumped. James then took his wife, murmuring to her, and led her from the room as Garrett, still on the floor with William standing guard, groaned and stirred.

With a sob, Eleanor turned into Matthew's arms, feeling him remove the pistol from her slack grasp. Legs trembling, she leaned into him, his heart hammering in her ear, drawing comfort from his solid strength, wanting nothing more than to blot out the horror.

'Thank you,' she whispered, once her breathing had

steadied and her legs felt capable of supporting her. She looked up at him. His hold tightened, and he bent his head to feather a kiss on her forehead.

Then she registered the blessed sound of Aunt Lucy's voice, drawing nearer, until, 'Ellie, Ellie, oh, my pet. Here, Mr Damerel, let me take her.' She put her arm around Eleanor and led her from the bedchamber. The maid who had been polishing in the hall showed them into a small parlour and then disappeared with the promise of refreshments.

James and Matthew joined them some time later. Eleanor, although still shaken, went immediately to her cousin.

'James, my dear...'

He heaved a sigh. 'You deserve an explanation, Eleanor. Ruth is ill. Her moods were always up and down, but controllable if she took her medicine. Then Donald was killed and Garrett returned and started putting fanciful notions in her head, and she got worse. One day she would be convinced the entire world conspired against her, the next it would be as if nothing was amiss, and she would go shopping and spend and spend. Nothing else seemed to make her happy. And, gradually, she focused her blame onto you. When she took the potion the doctor made up for her she seemed to improve, but lately...' He shrugged.

'I have just found out that it was Garrett who was responsible for the attack on that girl. I went to Stockport and showed this around.' He held up an artist's likeness of the man. 'There can be no doubt. The Runners have taken him away.'

He gathered Eleanor's hands to his chest. 'Ellie, I don't know what to say. I am so very, very sorry. I should have had Ruth committed long ago. I tried so hard to keep her happy and contented and to give her all she desired, but nothing worked for long. She would sink into the depths of despair at times.' He looked sadly at a portrait of Ruth that hung over the fireplace. 'I have no choice now. I must have her committed. I thought she could stay here, if we were vigilant. And I tried to keep Garrett away, but it seems the servants were too scared of her rages to stand up to her for long. They were meeting in secret.'

'But why was Garrett prepared to kill for Ruth? It doesn't make sense.'

'I thought the same. That's why, when I first knew of the attacks on you, I didn't think of him. But your description, when you spoke to us at Cheriton's ball...I knew then. That is why I was reluctant to leave you and Ruth alone together. And...when I asked him just now...before they took him...oh, dear God! He was their natural father! Ruth and Donald's.'

'Their *father*? But...how?'

'It's a sordid tale. Garrett was bailiff to Ruth's mother's family. They were in love. When she married Mr Aldridge, Garrett went, too, to work for them, and they continued their affair, right under the poor man's nose. It is quite the scandal.'

'I feel sick,' Eleanor said. 'What will happen to Ruth now? Are you truly going to have her committed?'

'I must,' James said. 'This has proved I cannot keep her safe. Nor keep others safe from her torrid imaginings. I see no alternative.'

His face was etched in misery and Eleanor felt her heart go out to him. To think he had been trying to keep Ruth happy and calm all this time—his reluctance to abandon her to a lunatic asylum did him credit. Eleanor longed to help.

'What do you *want*, James?'

He looked puzzled. 'Want? I do not know, but I know

I cannot bear to think of her in one of those places. They are horrifying. Truly horrifying.'

'Then she shall not go to one. Come home to Ashby. Waycroft Farm is empty. The house is good, solid stone and it is isolated. We will make it secure and we will hire people to help care for Ruth. You always loved Waycroft, James. Come, what do you say?'

'You would do that for Ruth, after what she has done?'

'I am doing it for you, my dear.'

'Eleanor…my lady…are you sure this is a good idea?' Eleanor started at the sound of Matthew's voice. She had almost forgotten anyone else was in the room. 'What if someone makes a mistake and Ruth gets out?'

'Mr Damerel is right, my pet. It is too much of a risk.'

'She will not. We will make sure she is kept securely— and comfortably—for as long as necessary. And it will be lovely to have you home, James. You can help me with the estate.'

'Thank you, Ellie. Your generosity…' James grasped her hands '… I do not feel worthy, but I am so very grateful. I will discuss it with Ruth's doctor. He is upstairs with her now.'

Chapter Thirty

'Her ladyship has commanded me to deny her to all callers, sir.' Pacey stood square in the open doorway of Eleanor's house in Upper Brook Street, blocking Matthew's way.

'It is all right, Pacey. I am sure her ladyship will make an exception for Mr Damerel.'

Lady Rothley had appeared behind Pacey, who reluctantly stood aside to allow Matthew to enter.

'Come with me.' Lady Rothley smiled at Matthew. 'Let us see if you are able to lift her mood, for I have never known her so low. One would have thought, with the danger now past, she would be in the best of spirits. But, no... she has hidden herself away and, as you heard, has instructed Pacey to refuse all visitors.'

It was the day after the discovery that Ruth Weare had been behind the attacks on Eleanor. And that final attack would never have happened if Matthew had not been late calling on Eleanor. That there was a good reason for his tardiness did little to assuage his guilt over her ordeal and the distress she must still be suffering. It was only blind luck that he had arrived in time to prevent injury or even death and it would be a long time before he could forgive himself. And now... He pondered Lady Rothley's words as he followed her to the rear of the house; there was nothing he might say to cheer Eleanor up, for he had come to say his farewells.

Eleanor was sitting by the window in the parlour when they entered. She looked over at Matthew, expressionless, her eyes dull.

'I told Pacey no visitors,' she said, in a lacklustre tone, 'but good afternoon, Mr Damerel.' She smiled, humourlessly. 'If you have come to scold me for going to visit Ruth alone, please save your breath.'

'I have not come to scold you.'

'Good. All that remains, then, is for me to thank you for coming so swiftly to my aid. Aunt Lucy told me what happened.'

Matthew had arrived at Eleanor's house just as Sir Horace had set Lady Rothley down from his carriage. Pacey had immediately told them where Eleanor was and Matthew had driven them to Hill Street in his curricle, at breakneck speed.

'Yes, you were quite the hero,' Lady Rothley said. 'Heaven knows what I should have done if you hadn't arrived when you did, with Sir Horace having already driven away and Ellie having taken the carriage.'

Eleanor turned away as Aunt Lucy spoke and was again studying the sky, as she had been when they had come in.

Aunt Lucy nudged Matthew towards Eleanor. 'See what you can do,' she whispered. 'I fear she is still in shock.'

Matthew drew a chair close to Eleanor's and sat down as Aunt Lucy settled herself in a chair by the fireplace.

What to say? How to begin?

'It will take time for you to come to terms with what happened yesterday,' he said.

'Did Aunt Lucy saddle you with the task of cheering me up? I fear 'twill be a thankless task, judging by how

I feel right now.' She glanced at him. 'You have come to say goodbye.'

He should be relieved she had made it easier for him. Perversely, he felt worse.

'Not simply to say goodbye. And it is only temporary, after all. I shall be back in London in a few weeks. It is, after all, my home. And I have my business…' The words dried on his tongue. After the news yesterday, how much longer would he have the business? How long before the bank foreclosed on that loan? He coughed, to clear the blockage from his throat. 'Not simply to say goodbye,' he repeated, 'but to apologise.'

'Apologise? For what?'

He gazed into her eyes. They looked…defeated. His heart lurched, thudding against his ribs. Why could he not cast aside his pride? His troubles would certainly be over then. No sooner had the thought surfaced than he thrust it down with an inner snarl. He would not live off any woman. Especially his wife. It was a man's place to provide for his wife and family.

'If I had arrived on time yesterday—'

'Then we would still not know who was behind the attacks,' she said.

'We would have known as soon as James arrived back from Stockport.'

'It is possible,' she said. 'But it is also possible that you…we…would not have believed him. Suspicion might always have tainted my feelings for him and my memories of him. For that, I am grateful that yesterday happened, if not for the way it happened. James is part of my life again and he will be back at Ashby, where he belongs.'

What need would she have of a husband now? She had proved herself capable of managing the estates since her father died. Now, she would have James by her side.

Although… Matthew almost laughed as the thought occurred. What a reversal of the customary reason for marriage within the *ton*. Her only need for a husband would be to provide an heir for Ashby. James would never, now, have a child with Ruth, which left Eleanor the responsibility of continuing the barony. What man would settle for such a role? Not him. But—and he knew it with a sinking certainty—there would be plenty out there who would. And probably spend their married life resenting it and making their wife suffer.

It was not his concern. Not any longer. He was further from her than ever, after yesterday's news.

'I should like to explain,' Matthew said, raising his voice to include Lady Rothley in the conversation.

Eleanor's chest rose as she inhaled. 'It is unnecessary. It happened. But explain if you must.'

'I told you of the two ships sailing from India?'

'Yes. With your partner aboard one of them.'

His throat ached. Benedict—never again to see his quick grin, or to laugh at one of his dry remarks. 'One of them, the *Venetia*, docked yesterday morning. The other—the *Laura May*—they lost her in a storm off the west coast of Africa.'

Lady Rothley gasped and Eleanor straightened in her chair…the first sign of animation since his arrival. 'Oh, no! I am so sorry. Were there any survivors?'

'No. After the storm, the *Venetia* turned back to search, but found nothing other than some wreckage floating in the sea.' His voice cracked over his final words: 'All hands are believed lost.'

'And…Mr Poole?'

'He was on board the *Laura May*.' Matthew surged to his feet and took a swift turn about the room. 'He is gone.'

The cargo was insured, but that was no compensation.

And he had, maybe recklessly, presumed they would turn a large profit on the load, as they had done in the past, when he had secured his bank loan. His friend was dead and his business floundering.

'I am going to Rushock first thing tomorrow,' he said, halting by the door. 'I shall call on you when I return, but then I shall resume my old life, so our paths are unlikely to cross.'

'Then I trust you will have an uneventful journey,' Eleanor said, rising to her feet, but staying by the window. 'Goodbye, Mr Damerel, and thank you again for all your help.'

Matthew's heart contracted painfully. She had already distanced herself from him. Despite it being for the best, despite it having been his intention when he called this morning, it hurt. Badly. He hated to leave this cold distance between them but he must.

He left the house with a leaden weight suspended in his chest where his heart should have been.

The heart he had left behind.

'Well?' The thrill in Aunt Lucy's voice was plain. 'Is it all you expected it to be?'

It was ten days since Matthew had left London and Eleanor had finally achieved her dream of attending Almack's Assembly Rooms. Emily Cowper, true to her word, had intervened with the other ladies of the Committee and Eleanor's name had been entered on the List, enabling her to purchase a much-coveted voucher.

She gazed around the grand ballroom and put as much excitement into her response as she could muster.

'It is wonderful, Aunt Lucy. I am so pleased to be here.'

Over the past fortnight she had developed a certain skill in hiding her disillusionment and despondency behind a mask of enthusiasm and delight, but still from time to time she had caught Aunt Lucy watching her with a troubled expression, swiftly erased. Nothing had been said—at least, not to her. But she suspected neither Aunt Lucy nor Hugo had fully swallowed her performance. Even James, preoccupied as he was with Ruth's future care and safety, had commented on her 'enforced gaiety'. He had put it down to the trauma of what had happened and she was content for him to believe it.

The reality was that all pleasure had vanished from Eleanor's world since Matthew's final visit. Colours had leached into a uniform drabness; the sweetest sounds were now shrill cacophonies; and the parties and balls that had once been such a delight were now a dead bore. But Eleanor had thrown herself into the round of social pleasure with a smile plastered on lips that were numb and a false eagerness that saw her, night after night, out until the small hours. She groped her way through each day, counting the minutes until her head would touch her pillow and she might be alone with her thoughts. Her eyes burned with the effort of holding on to the tears she refused to shed, and from lack of sleep, but still she accepted each and every invitation that came her way.

Almack's... She danced every dance, her partners forgotten the instant their allotted dance was over...she sipped at the weak orgeat, hiding her grimace of distaste... chewed with dry teeth and tongue at wafer-thin brown bread and butter that tasted of sawdust...*this* had been the pinnacle of her desire. Her goal when she had set out from Ashby all those weeks ago. This cavernous hall, with its small orchestra on a balcony, playing interminable country dances; its gilded columns and enormous mirrors that reflected the light from huge chandeliers; the fluttering young ladies, mainly in their first Season; the gentlemen, resplendent in their black-satin knee breeches, either very much younger than Eleanor, or old enough to be her father.

'Good evening, my dear.' Emily Cowper stood before her. 'I am pleased to welcome you to our evening. I hope you are enjoying your first attendance.'

Eleanor smiled. 'Thank you for adding me to the List, my lady,' she replied, genuinely grateful to Lady Cowper for her help. It was, after all, what she had aspired to. It was hardly Lady Cowper's fault it had come to represent a hollow victory.

'Please, do not mention it,' said her ladyship. 'Now, are there any young gentlemen here with whom you are not acquainted? If so, I shall be happy to perform the introduction. At least here you may rest assured the gentlemen present have all met the approval of the Committee. A lady in your circumstances cannot be too careful, my dear.'

'Thank you, but I believe I am acquainted with everyone.' And not one of them matched up to the man who haunted her dreams.

'Very well. I shall leave you to enjoy the evening.' Lady Cowper tinkled a laugh and made her way back to the dais at the upper end of the room, where the other patronesses were seated, smiling and nodding at various acquaintances.

A young gentleman bowed before her. 'I believe this is our dance, Lady Ashby?'

Eleanor smiled by rote. They had been introduced, but his name quite escaped her. They were all interchangeable. She took the young man's hand and allowed him to lead her on to the dance floor.

'It'll cheer you up, Coz.' Hugo flung himself on to the sofa next to Eleanor and plucked the novel she had been reading from her hands. 'Say you will. It will be just the four of us. Well, to be frank, I had intended just you, Mama and me, but somehow Tidmungen has included himself. Not sure how that happened.'

'Todmorden,' Eleanor said. 'It's Sir Horace *Todmorden*.'

'Well, whoever he is, he's around here a sight too often for my liking.' A scowl marred Hugo's handsome face. 'Damme if I know what Mama sees in him.'

'He is kind to her,' Eleanor said. 'He listens to her opinion and he squires her about. She enjoys the attention.'

'Hmmph. Can't like the fellow, but don't suppose anyone'll listen to me. So, what do you say, Ellie? Is it to be Vauxhall tonight?'

'Very well, then. But I am not in need of cheering up.'

'If you say so,' Hugo said.

That evening, Eleanor gazed around her in awe as they entered the gardens, having chartered a river boat from Westminster to Kennington on the south bank of the Thames. It was magical, lit by thousands of colourful glass lanterns suspended from the trees that lined the gravelled walks, and Eleanor marvelled at the marble statues, the picturesque caves and grottos, the cascades and waterfalls, the canal with its elegant bridges in the Chinese style and the triumphal arches that spanned the South Walk.

By chance, they met with some of Sir Horace's acquaintances and were urged to join them for supper in their box. They feasted on cold chicken and wafer-thin ham, washed down with arrack punch and accompanied by the music of Handel, played by the orchestra. Afterwards, with Aunt Lucy and Sir Horace content to sit and natter with their friends, Eleanor accepted Hugo's suggestion they walk off their supper.

As they strolled, Eleanor noticed ahead of them a group of young bucks loitering at the entrance to a dimly lit side path.

'What is down there?' she asked.

Hugo laughed. 'Nothing suitable for your eyes, Coz. Wait until you've got a husband to stroll down there with. They're no places for unmarried ladies.'

'Well, if that is the case, I...' Eleanor stopped in her tracks. The breath left her lungs with a whoosh. Her heart somersaulted, like the acrobats who had entertained them earlier.

Matthew was strolling towards them, with Arabella Tame on his arm. As Eleanor watched, they halted and Arabella gestured to yet another shadowy side path, laughing up at Matthew. Arabella, with her dainty figure and her porcelain skin, her golden curls and pouting pink lips.

Eleanor turned on her heel, tugging her cousin around with her. 'Hugo. I am sorry. I am not well. Could we return to your mama?'

'What?' Hugo glanced back over his shoulder. When he spoke again, the surprise had left his voice. 'Yes, of course.'

Eleanor swallowed her pain, gathered the cloak of her pride around her and walked away.

Back at their box, Eleanor pleaded the headache and they made their farewells. She looked neither right nor left as they returned to the mooring to take the boat back across the river. She didn't want to see. She didn't want to know. It was enough that he was here. In London. And he had not bothered to call on her.

She could no longer hang on to the fragile thread of hope that had been her only lifeline since Matthew had left London. It could be no clearer. She had no more hope, no more fight. The Arabellas of this world would always win.

It was time for her to go home. James was leaving for Ashby in the morning. She would go, too. There was no point in staying in London, for she had reached one defi-

nite conclusion. It was Matthew she wanted, or no one.
Not one of the men she had met in London roused the feelings that Matthew could, just by looking at her with those
bright blue eyes. If she could not marry the man she loved,
she wanted nothing to do with marriage.

Chapter Thirty-One

Matthew turned on to the Cross Walk at Vauxhall Gardens, with Arabella, Lady Tame, clinging to his arm. Behind them strolled his brother, Stephen, escorting yet another Society beauty.

'Why don't you allow me to show you some of the other walks?' Arabella purred, her fingers tightening on Matthew's sleeve, indicating a dimly lit side turning. Stephen had told Matthew of them—Lover's Walk, Druid's Walk and others—perfect for privacy; for lovers' trysts; a stolen kiss, possibly more.

He looked down into her upturned, laughing face. She was beautiful. There was no doubt about it. Just not for him.

'Perhaps later,' he said, without meaning it.

There was only one woman he longed to hold in his arms. Only one woman whose lips he wanted to taste. And she wasn't petite, with golden curls framing a perfect heart-shaped face.

Eleanor. His heart groaned with the weight of his longing. He tried to push her from his thoughts, but the attempt was as futile now as it had been every day—and night—since he had last seen her. There she was. Constantly. Hovering at the edge of his mind, voicing her opinion, questioning his every move, reminding him she could not be so easily set aside or forgotten.

He had returned to London three days ago, happy to have seen his mother and his sisters, the raw ache that had plagued him for eight years finally soothed. He was back where he belonged. And yet…*this* pain was worse. Jagged. Sharp. A hole ripped in his soul. How many times had he nearly succumbed…swallowed his pride…gone to Eleanor and laid his heart at her feet? But he had resisted. He had to.

For her sake.

He knew, courtesy of Stephen, that she was as popular as ever. And, it seemed, making the most of that popularity. There was no event of note at which Lady Ashby—the Catch of the Season—was not present. She had even, finally, attended that most hallowed of all institutions. Almack's. Nothing emphasised the gulf between them more—he would never be deemed suitable for that temple of the *ton*, tainted by trade as he was.

Eleanor gave little appearance of missing him as he missed her. He knew, though—and better than most—how adept she could be at hiding her true feelings. But what if she was not acting a part? He was aware she had thought herself in love with him. But she was inexperienced. Had it been mere infatuation, fired by those few stolen kisses? Was she, even now, celebrating her lucky escape? He must stay strong. Keep away from her a little longer. Give her time to know her own mind. Her own heart. And then, when he did see her again, pride or no pride, he would tell her the truth of his feelings and beg for her hand, even though it chafed that he must come to her as a supplicant.

He could not support Eleanor—his business would barely scrape by following the loss of the *Laura May. Benedict.* He ached at the reminder of his friend's death. He still could not believe he was gone. It was far easier to imagine him still striding the deck, out there somewhere on the ocean, sailing the waves for ever.

He started. 'I beg your pardon?' He glanced down at Arabella, who pouted.

'I said, shall we rejoin the others?' She indicated the box that Stephen had secured for his birthday celebrations —full of happy, boisterous revellers, it was now two paces behind them.

Matthew felt his cheeks flush. He had been so lost in his thoughts that they had passed it by. 'My apologies, my lady.'

Supper was awaiting them in the box and Matthew did his best to join in the merriment. He felt a stranger amongst these people. They had different interests, different values. And none of them was Eleanor. He counted the hours until he could, without being damned as a killjoy, leave the party and seek his bed to lose himself in his dreams.

'Sir! Mr Damerel, sir!'

Matthew paused, his hand already raised to push open the door of Offley's tavern, where he had arranged to meet Stephen. Henry was hurrying along Henrietta Street, red-faced, waving a letter.

'This just came, sir.' Henry bent over, puffing, his hand on his chest. 'A seaman, sir. Just come into port last night.'

With a hand that shook, Matthew took the letter, moving to one side with an apologetic nod to allow a gentleman to enter the tavern. He gulped as he recognised the bold writing on the outside of the sheet.

Benedict.

He broke the seal and began to read.

A short time later, Stephen pulled out a chair opposite Matthew.

'You have the look of a man for whom life is good,

brother,' he said, as he settled into his seat and gestured to a serving maid to bring him a tankard of ale. 'Finally summoned the courage to nail your colours to the fair Eleanor's mast, have you?'

In a buoyant mood, Matthew ignored his brother's jibe. Stephen had guessed his true feelings for Eleanor and Matthew had not denied them. Eleanor. He had been on the brink of following his heart. This news brought that decision closer, made it easier.

He had long dreamt of the day he might have his own family. Those dreams now danced within his reach, although he would have to swallow a quantity of humble pie before Eleanor might forgive him for his stubborn pride and for failing to understand, sooner, that love was all that mattered. But forgive him she must, whatever it took, for he could not envisage any other woman in the role of his wife and as the mother of his children.

In the meantime...

'I am celebrating,' he said, with a broad smile. 'This...' he waved the letter in Stephen's direction '...is the best of all possible news. Benedict is alive!'

'Where is he?'

'Somewhere in Africa.' Matthew bent his head to the letter, straining his eyes in the dim interior of the tavern. 'Lagos. The *Laura May* was badly damaged in that storm, but she survived. She was blown off course, which is why the *Venetia* couldn't find her when they went back to search. Benedict writes that they carried out basic repairs at sea, then headed for the nearest port. He wrote as soon as he could and handed it to the captain of another ship bound for England, to deliver to me.' Matthew leaned back, relief settling in, supplanting the race of excitement that had sent his blood coursing hot through his veins as he had read the letter.

'That,' said Stephen, raising his tankard, 'is news to celebrate indeed.'

'It is. And what is more,' Matthew said, 'I am now in a position to—'

A silky voice cut in. 'Damerel—your man said I'd find you here. Been lookin' for you all day.'

Lord Hugo Alastair stood over Matthew, who stiffened. This was a time for rejoicing. Hugo's expression did not suggest he sought a friendly chat.

'Congratulations.'

Hugo lifted an enquiring brow.

'You've found me.'

'Mind if I join you?' Hugo sat next to Stephen without waiting for a reply. He retrieved a letter from his pocket and put it on the table. 'Best get the business out of the way first. It came this morning. From Rothley.'

It seemed to be his day for receiving momentous communications, Matthew thought, as he read the words that confirmed it was Henson who had cheated in that long-ago card game.

'Thank you, and I will write to thank your brother also. I'm grateful for your help.' Even as he spoke, he wondered what else was on Hugo's mind.

'Saw my cousin this morning...' Hugo said, then paused. Matthew's fingers tightened on the handle of his tankard. *Eleanor.* 'Just before she left.'

Matthew stilled, his eyes riveted on Hugo. 'Left? Where has she gone?'

'Home. And what I should like to know is—why?'

Gone? Why would she leave London when she was at the pinnacle of her success? With an effort, Matthew kept his expression blank. Any decision about Eleanor was his to make. He would not allow the likes of Hugo Alastair to push him around. Affecting an air of nonchalance, he raised his tankard and took a long swallow, before raising his eyes to look at his brother.

'As I was about to say—'

Stephen's grey eyes narrowed. 'You seem remarkably calm at Alastair's news.'

Matthew forced himself to shrug dismissively. He was good at hiding his feelings. He'd had a lifetime of practice.

'Or,' Stephen continued, 'you are remarkably good at concealing your feelings. I suspect the latter.'

'You may have noticed,' said Hugo, 'that I still await an answer.' His voice hardened. He leaned over the table, dark eyes hard. 'What happened between the two of you, that one glimpse of you at Vauxhall last night was enough to send her fleeing London, once again, in a state of despair?'

Matthew's stomach balled into a hard knot of fury, his eyes boring into Hugo's. 'I hope you are not suggesting what I think you are, Alastair.'

'I shall allow your conscience to provide the answer to that.'

'My conscience is clear.' *Apart from those kisses.* 'I'm sure I couldn't say why the lady left town. I have not seen her since my return from Rushock.'

Hugo sat back. 'Why not?'

Such a simple question. Almost impossible to answer. The tangled threads of reason barely making sense to him, let alone anyone else.

'I see no reason to justify my actions to you. Or to anyone else,' Matthew growled, glaring at Stephen, who was watching with a faint smirk. 'Lady Ashby leaving town has nothing to do with me.'

'My dear fellow, loath as I am to contradict you, my mother—who is, you will have noticed, exceedingly astute—is convinced your failure to even call upon my cousin is precisely the reason she decided to leave so suddenly.'

Matthew shrugged again. There was a protracted silence during which Hugo contemplated Matthew, who tamped down his irritation. He would explain himself to Eleanor. No one else.

After several tense minutes, Hugo sighed, leaning back. 'I find myself in agreement with your brother. I believe you are concealing your true feelings…' He paused, his dark eyes calculating. Then, unexpectedly, he smiled.

'I'm goin' to regret this,' he said. 'Ask anyone and they'll tell you the same. Alastair? A bad lot—cares for nothing and nobody but his own pleasures and doesn't worry who gets hurt in the process. I don't permit interference in my life and I make it a rule not to interfere in anyone else's.'

Matthew exchanged a perplexed look with Stephen. What was Alastair talking about?

'It so happens that my cousin Eleanor is an exception to that rule,' Hugo continued, carefully examining his fingernails. 'I *do* care what happens to her. When I'm forced to watch her tryin' to be brave and pretend her heart's not breaking, then I'm persuaded it is time I intervened.'

His mouth quirked into another brief smile. 'Devil take it, there's something about you, Damerel. Trustworthy—that's what I thought when we first met. And you were good for Ellie, too—she was blooming when I first saw her in town and, when I saw you together, I knew why.

'So, what I fail to understand is—why have you let her go?'

There was a lengthy silence. Hugo studied Matthew and Matthew forced himself to meet that knowing gaze.

'Deny that you love her and I shall leave right now.'

It was like a punch to his gut. It stole his breath. Hiding his feelings was one thing. Baldly denying them…

'I do not deny it. That is…was…precisely the reason why I cannot be part of her life.'

'Is? Was? Pray explain, for I fail to understand.'

'My brother's financial circumstances have vastly improved since yesterday,' Stephen said, 'although, to be blunt, I have always failed to see what difference that should make if you love one another.'

'I had nothing to offer her. She could do much better for herself than an impoverished third son. And I am no fortune hunter.'

Hugo wagged his head at him and Matthew set his teeth.

'Pride?' Hugo said. 'Is that it? You damned fool! You'll allow your pride to ruin both of your lives? No doubt you are congratulating yourself on your honourable behaviour in leaving the way clear for another man, Damerel, but let me tell you something.

'I know Eleanor well enough to know she will only ever marry for love, after the misery of her experience with Aldridge. She will never marry if she doesn't marry you. How can you deny her the chance to have a family?'

Matthew froze as Hugo's words hit him with the force of a lightning strike. Why had he never once considered Eleanor's point of view? Hugo was right. He had made his decision with no reference to her wishes, putting his pride first, denying her any choice over her own future.

'You have left her with no choice and no hope, Damerel.'

Chapter Thirty-Two

Eleanor was roused from her slumber by the liquid, warbling notes of a song thrush, singing its heart out outside her window. She listened, enthralled, caught up in the magic, until cruel reality flooded in, drowning the beauty of the song as the bitter truth of her life surged to the forefront of her mind.

She flung herself over in her bed, dragging the covers over her head as she buried it in the pillow, squeezing her eyes tight shut, in what she knew would be a forlorn attempt to go back to sleep. It was still early and she was in no hurry to face the day, or Aunt Lucy's pitying looks. At least James, who had travelled up to prepare Waycroft Farm for Ruth, was too preoccupied with his own troubles to concern himself with Eleanor's.

Finally, as sleep continued to evade her, she pushed back the covers, eased out of bed and shuffled over to the window to draw back the curtains. The weather was fine, with fluffy white clouds scudding across the cerulean sky, but the weather did nothing to lift her mood. She did not ring for Lizzie, but poured cold water into the basin from the pitcher on her washstand, washed quickly, then pulled on her shift and a lightweight pale-blue sprigged-muslin dress. She dusted a little rouge on her pale cheeks, determined to shield herself from her relatives' critical gazes.

Despite the early hour both Aunt Lucy and James were already at breakfast when Eleanor entered the morning parlour. Two pairs of eyes lifted to view her with concern as she sat at the table. She gritted her teeth. It was James who had suffered the most; why were they worried about her? Thank goodness Aunt Phyllis had declined to return to Ashby Manor until the renovations were complete. At least Eleanor did not have to face her at breakfast.

'Good morning.' She injected a bright note into her voice and plastered a smile on her lips. 'What a beautiful morning.'

'Indeed it is,' Aunt Lucy responded. 'You are up early, my pet. I was sure we would not see you until much later this morning.'

'Why ever not? I am not in the habit of lying abed half the day, as you well know, particularly when there is work to be done.'

'I thought—'

'You had a disturbed night,' James said. 'I heard you.'

Eleanor bit back her sharp retort. Even James had noticed. It seemed, since her return to her beloved Ashby, it had been nigh on impossible to stem the flood of tears she had successfully controlled whilst in London. In London there had still been hope, however slight. Now... Last night, she had cried herself to sleep. Again.

'I am looking forward to consulting with the decorator,' was her only comment as she picked at her breakfast.

By mid-afternoon, Eleanor's temper was teased to breaking point. Aunt Lucy, in her determination to lift Eleanor out of the doldrums, dogged her footsteps with such relentless cheeriness that Eleanor's nerves were in shreds. From viewing the renovations and discussing the decoration of the East Wing to visiting Joker—fully recovered from his fright when Bonny was shot—in the home paddock, Aunt Lucy was by her side.

Eleanor tried to be patient. She knew her aunt had been sad to leave London before the Season was over and also, she suspected, to leave Sir Horace. Aunt Lucy's heart was in the right place but, everywhere Eleanor turned, Aunt Lucy was there—watching her anxiously…taking her arm…patting her hand…attempting to coax a smile—until Eleanor was ready to climb the walls.

Finally, after partaking of tea and cakes in the drawing room, Eleanor headed for the door, announcing that she was going for a walk.

'What a splendid idea,' Aunt Lucy said, struggling to her feet. 'I shall enjoy some more fresh air.'

Eleanor stopped and looked around at her aunt, ready to snap her head off. But she bit her tongue, taking in Aunt Lucy's drawn expression.

'No, you would not,' she said instead. 'Just look at you—you are exhausted.' She took her aunt by the arm and drew her back to the sofa. 'Please, stay here and rest.'

Aunt Lucy sank on to the sofa with a small sigh and Eleanor crouched by her side, taking her hand. 'I know you are worried about me and I appreciate your efforts, but—'

'But you are plagued by the sight of me?' Aunt Lucy's dark eyes twinkled under arched brows.

Eleanor smiled. 'Oh dear; am I that transparent? I do beg your pardon, Aunt, but I truly would enjoy some time on my own. I shall walk around the lake and sit and rest a while in the summerhouse. It is always so peaceful there. I promise I shall be all right on my own. It is perfectly safe, you know, for the lake is in the middle of the estate and quite private.'

The weather was perfect for a walk. Eleanor strolled down the path that led to the lake. She was relieved to be free of the need to constantly school her expression in case anyone suspected she was unhappy. She sighed. Her life stretched before her in a never-ending round of duty and care. Soon, Aunt Phyllis would be home and Aunt Lucy would return to Rothley, and it would be as if the past few months had never happened.

On a whim, she turned and meandered through the woodland that skirted the path. The dappled sunlight filtered through the leaves and she watched, enchanted, as birds darted hither and thither, gathering food in response to the insistent cries of their young, crowded in the nest or, in some cases, perched in rows on branches, beaks gaping, demanding, never satisfied. Her loneliness—her aloneness—intensified.

She even caught sight of a vixen slinking through the undergrowth at the far side of a sunny glade, followed in procession by three cubs. That, too, emphasised her solitude—the whole world was happily playing families, and she was devastated she would never now have that chance. Angrily, she dashed away a lone tear that spilled on to her cheek, chiding herself for her self-pity. She joined another path, rounded a curve, then stopped to admire the stunning vista that lay before her.

It never failed to enchant her. The lake sparkled in the sunlight, gently rippling in the faint breeze. It was studded with water lilies, the bright green pads interspersed with white crown-shaped flowers, with the summerhouse on the far shore, facing south, framed by a wooded backdrop of majestic oaks and beeches, under-planted with silver birches and other smaller trees. Two huge weeping willows grew, one each side of the summerhouse, their dangling fronds sweeping the crystal surface of the water.

She turned on to the path that skirted the lake, passing dense clumps of reed mace—a few early dark brown velvety spikes providing a vivid contrast with the bright yellow of water flag irises in full bloom. She walked slowly, pausing frequently, breathing in deep gulps of fresh air, concentrating on the birdsong and the hum of busy insects, filling her thoughts with her beautiful surroundings, drowning out the painful memories that lay submerged. She watched, smiling, the amusing antics of a family of ducklings, then continued on her way until, eventually, she approached the first of the large willows that stood sentinel over the summerhouse, which it masked from view.

She had one foot on the narrow footbridge that crossed a stream gurgling down into the lake before she saw the figure on the opposite bank.

Matthew.

A torrent of thoughts and emotions cascaded through her mind. Heart and breath alike stalled. Numbly, dumbly, she stood frozen, greedily drinking in the sight. He was as handsome as ever: tall and broad-shouldered, his dark-blond hair reflecting the sun's rays. A muscle bunched in his jaw as he held her gaze. She couldn't read his expression. He was tense, but she could see neither pleasure nor apology in his look. Why was he here? Her stomach churned as she attempted to decipher his mood.

Then fury overwhelmed her. How dare he? How dare he stand there and make her feel all these swirling emotions, and not even try to ease the tension? Abruptly, she turned on her heel and strode back the way she had come. She heard running footsteps behind her and a hand grasped her shoulder, pulling her round to face him.

She wriggled out of his grip. 'Leave me alone!' She turned again, striding away as fast as she could.

He overtook her, stood square in her path.

'Eleanor. Please, wait. Let me explain.'

'There is nothing to explain. My understanding is quite adequate to the task of recognising a lost cause.'

'It was for your own good—you must see that. What can I offer you?'

'Nothing, clearly. And in that case, please let me pass.'

'No. Wait.' He raked one hand through his hair in the dear, familiar gesture that wrenched at her heartstrings. 'This has come out all wrong. Please, give me a minute. Let me tell you why I am here.'

'I *do not care* why you are here. You are nothing to me, apart from the fact you are ruining a perfectly pleasant walk.'

She could hear the tremble in her voice. She was desperate to get away before her emotions overwhelmed her. She *would not* let him see her cry. She clenched her teeth and crossed her arms, pinching the inside of one arm as hard as she could in an attempt to keep the tears at bay.

'Eleanor! Ellie, my dear, my love—do not, I beg of you. I have been such a fool! I have hurt you, I know. I had no intention—'

At those words Eleanor's temper reignited. 'Don't you dare to use those words to me again. Don't you *dare*. I know you had no intention. You told me so—no intention of kissing me, no intention of raising false expectations, no intention of making me fall in love with you, no intention of humiliating me. But you *did*. I thought you c-cared,' she ended, with a sob.

She lifted her fists to pound at his chest.

He caught her hands, gripping tightly so that no matter how she struggled she could not break free.

'I do! Oh, Ellie, I do care for you, more than you know. I *love* you, so very, very much. And I was wrong, when

I said I have nothing to offer you. I allowed my pride to overcome my good sense. You were right. I do have something to offer—something that is more important than all the wealth and all the titles in the world. I have my heart to offer.

'My heart is what I offer you now, my darling Eleanor. My heart and, for what it is worth, every other poor, humble thing that goes with it—my body, my self, my soul.

'All that I am—it is yours, if you will have me.'

Eleanor stilled on hearing his words and her gaze lifted to fuse with his.

'This is not how I envisaged this meeting,' he said, with a tentative, rueful smile. 'I will explain myself properly, I promise, but I need to do this now.' He dropped to one knee, still clasping her hands in his.

Her heart lurched, then accelerated, pounding in her chest until she felt as though it would burst through her ribs.

'Eleanor, would you do me the greatest honour in the world? Will you marry me and make me the happiest man alive?'

He looked up at her steadily, but she could feel the tremor in his hands as he spoke the words and she knew that he spoke from the heart.

'Yes,' she whispered. 'Oh, yes.'

He surged to his feet and caught her into his embrace, lifting her as his mouth claimed hers. She melted against him, rejoicing in his safe, solid strength. She clung closer, winding her arms around his neck, responding to the urgency in his lips. Without breaking the kiss, he swung her into his arms and strode back to the bridge, crossing it to the summerhouse, where he sat on the daybed, settling Eleanor on his lap. His arms wound around her waist, locking tight.

'I am not,' he announced, 'taking the risk of you running off again.'

She tilted her head back to look at him. 'How did you know where I was?' She peppered the words with light kisses feathered along his jaw.

He held her tighter. 'Your aunt told me where to find you.'

'I'm surprised she did not insist on sending someone to chaperon us.'

Matthew nuzzled her neck. 'She was delighted to see me, scolded me for taking so long to come to the point. Besides, she had other things on her mind. Sir Horace travelled up with me.'

'Sir *Horace*? Truly?'

'Truly. We met by chance as we were both hiring a chaise-and-four. He *said* he was coming north to visit relations and suggested we share the cost of posting up here. Your aunt was *exceedingly* happy to see him. She told me you were heading for this summerhouse and how to find it. I arrived here and I waited.'

Eleanor felt his chest vibrate as he laughed.

'I thought it the perfect setting for a proposal to the lady I love more than anything in the whole world.

'I thought it romantic.

'I *thought* to meet you at the doorway, where I would make my apologies and then propose properly. With decorum.'

He looked at her, his blue eyes glinting. 'I might have known you would set your own agenda. I thought I had missed you, you were such a long time. I was on my way to find you when I saw you at the bridge.'

'I was in no hurry. I needed to be on my own.' She paused. There was so much she didn't understand. 'You didn't call on me when you returned to town. I saw you.

At Vauxhall. With Arabella Tame.' Try as she might, she could not disguise her hurt.

'It was Stephen's birthday. There was a group of us there, celebrating. I was not just with Lady Tame.'

He stroked her cheek, kissed her neck, ran the tip of his tongue around her ear. She shivered with desire.

'The Arabellas of this world mean nothing to me,' he murmured. 'Why would I want a self-centred creature like her when I could have my beautiful, intelligent baroness?'

Eleanor tilted her head, sought his lips. Several satisfying minutes later, Matthew said, 'I returned from Rushock a wiser man. When I saw my mother...the truth hit me. I could have been reconciled with my family when I first returned to England. Instead, I allowed my pride to stop me from contacting any of them. I let my pride win and my resentment sour me.

'I realised then that I was also in danger of allowing my pride to ruin any chance of happiness with you. I was in love with you, but baulked at the idea of being dependent upon my wife. Also—although I did not realise it at first—I was letting my concern about what others would think to dictate my actions. I had lived with the taint of "cheat" for a long time and I hated the thought of being labelled a fortune hunter.

'I returned to London with the intention of laying my heart at your feet. But...'

Eleanor stroked his cheek, his bristles rough under her fingertips. 'But...?'

Matthew huffed a self-deprecating laugh. 'I thought I was doing the right thing in not visiting you. You seemed to be happy. You had achieved your ambition of being accepted for Almack's. I thought... I wondered if your feelings for me had changed. I vowed to give you more time to know your heart and I tried to get on with my own life.

'The truth is…my courage failed me. I was afraid to find out that your love for me was mere infatuation.'

Eleanor straightened, eyes flashing indignantly. 'Infatuation? How could you think that, when I all but begged you—?'

'I know! I know… I was a fool. In my own defence, I was on the verge of throwing myself on your mercy the day after you saw me at Vauxhall. Then I received…the letter.'

The suppressed excitement in his voice was contagious. 'Letter? From whom? What did it say?'

'It was from Benedict. My partner.'

'*Benedict?* But he—'

'He is not dead, Ellie. The *Laura May* was damaged in that storm, but they made it into port, in Lagos. Oh, I can't describe my joy on reading his news.'

'That is wonderful indeed. I am so pleased…but…does that mean you have only proposed because you can now match my fortune?'

Matthew threw back his head and laughed. 'Match your fortune? I shall never do that, sweetheart. The profit I will make on that cargo will be a mere pittance next to your wealth, but I *will* have enough to continue in business with Benedict.' He bent a serious look on her. 'You do understand that I must continue my business interests?'

'Of course I understand.'

'And, in the interest of honesty, I should confess I was also on the receiving end of some blunt talk from your cousin Hugo.'

'Hugo? What has Hugo to do with us?'

'He talked some common sense into me.'

'*Hugo* did? Well, I'm sure it must have been for the first time in his life. '

He laughed, then sobered again. 'You do mean it, Eleanor? You will marry me?'

'Of course I will. I want nothing more in the world than to be your wife. But...are *you* certain?'

'More certain than anything...'

'You will not resent me in the future? You promise you won't allow your pride to come between us? '

'I could never resent you, my love. And, yes, I promise. I was a fool. A stubborn fool. Nothing is more important than loving you—and being loved by you. I am a very... lucky...man.' He interspersed his words with kisses. 'And now, my wife-to-be...'

Eleanor, her eyes riveted on his, saw them darken as he spoke, desire swirling in the blue depths. Her core tightened, a delicious longing awakening deep inside.

'...come here.' His finger slid beneath her chin and nudged it higher. He captured her mouth. Eleanor wrapped her arms around his neck as his lips demanded and she gave, moulding herself to him. He eased her back against the sumptuous cushions, his lips never ceasing their hungry demand.

Eleanor revelled in the weight of his body covering hers as his hand cupped her breast, his touch fiery through the fabric of her dress. Two fingers slipped inside her neckline and found her nipple, teasing the swollen bud until she could scarcely breathe.

She clutched fiercely, her fingers tangling in his hair as he traced kisses down her neck to the upper swell of her breasts. She shivered with need, shifting restlessly beneath him...yearning...wanting...*needing*.

He raised his head and looked deep into her eyes.

'I want more,' she whispered. 'I want everything—all of you.'

He brushed her hair from her face, then placed his lips

on hers in a long, soothing kiss as he moved aside and settled Eleanor beside him, cradled in his arms.

'Not yet, my sweet.'

The bitter memory of rejection rose from the depths of
her past to pierce Eleanor's new-found contentment. She
shifted to stare into his face. A frown creased his brows
as his eyes searched hers.

'What?' he said. 'Why do you suddenly look uncertain?
You surely cannot doubt my love for you?' He kissed her,
long and hard and deep. 'I want you so much it hurts and
it takes every ounce of my resolve to say we must wait
until we are wed.'

'Then why *must* we wait?'

A smile hovered as he shook his head. 'You are as impetuous and as impatient as ever.' He dropped a kiss on
her nose. 'Since we met, I have not always behaved as a
gentleman should. As you said yourself, I thought nothing
of stealing kisses from a maiden I thought I could never
wed. It is important to me now to do the right thing.

'Allow me to be the gentleman now, Eleanor. I would
have you walk down the aisle an innocent on our wedding day. You are worth waiting for, my sweetest desire.'

His sincerity shone through every word.

'Then let us wed quickly,' Eleanor said, leaning into
him to capture his sensual mouth in a smouldering kiss.

'Never again,' he groaned, as he tore his lips from hers
some time later, 'never again will I allow you to leave
without a word. I know…' he placed his finger against her
lips, which parted as she began to protest '…yes, I know
very well it was my stupidity that made you leave. I know
it, but it doesn't make it any easier to bear. I allowed my
pride to become more important than our love.

'Never again.'

He lowered his head, caressing her lips with a tenderness that filled Eleanor with joy and wonder. She kissed him in return, and all the passion and the love she had hidden inside for so long poured out as she surrendered her heart.

* * * * *

SAVED BY
SCANDAL'S HEIR

To my wonderful editor, Julia, who first sparked
the idea of rewarding Harriet with her own
Happy-Ever-After.

Chapter One

Mid-February 1812

Harriet, Lady Brierley, paced the lavishly furnished drawing room at Tenterfield Court, mentally rehearsing the words she would say to Sir Malcolm Poole. If she had known the baronet was hovering so close to death, she would never have made the journey from London at this time of year. She had not known, however, and, now she had come all this way into Kent, she might as well ask the questions to which she sought answers. She had come to Tenterfield to find the truth of the past, in order to help her friend Felicity Stanton come to terms with her sister's death…and Harriet was certain that Sir Malcolm held the key to that particular puzzle.

Felicity's older sister, Emma, had been just eighteen—an innocent girl seduced and impregnated, who had seen no way out of her predicament other than to take her own life when the man she'd believed loved her had cruelly abandoned her.

Harriet suppressed her shiver. She could so easily have suffered the same fate. Was that why she had been so quick to come to Tenterfield? The empathy she felt for Felicity's poor sister? *There but for the Grace of God...*

She crossed the room to stand again before the portrait of the baronet, painted in his younger days, although he was still far from being an old man even now. He gazed down at her, devastatingly handsome, with his lean aristocratic features, dark auburn hair and deep green hooded gaze. Harriet shuddered, partly at the knowledge of what this man was—or what he had been, in the past—partly at his resemblance to... Resolutely, she steered her thoughts in a different direction. This trip was bound to resurrect painful memories... She must rise above them...concentrate on—

'Lady Brierley. To what do we owe this pleasure?'

Harriet froze. It could not be. Had she conjured him up in the flesh, just by allowing her thoughts one tiny peek at those memories? Moisture prickled her palms even as her mouth dried. She drew a calming breath, gathered her years of experience in hiding her feelings and turned.

He was framed in the open doorway.

Benedict.

After all this time.

He had the same long, lean legs and wide shoulders, but this was a man, not the youth she'd once known. His chin was just as determined but the high forehead under the familiar fox-red hair now sported faint creases. His lips were set in an uncompromising line and his leaf-green eyes pierced Harriet as he stared into her face, his gaze unwavering. A cat stalking its prey could not be more focused.

Harriet swallowed past the jagged glass that appeared to have lodged in her throat.

'Good afternoon, Mr Poole.' Had those composed

words really come from her lips? She took courage. She had faced worse than this. 'I apologise for calling uninvited. I did not realise your...' What was his relationship to Sir Malcolm again? All she could recall was that he had been Benedict's guardian. 'Sir Malcolm was so very ill. I had hoped for a few words with him.'

'He is my second cousin. I'm the only other Poole left now.'

'I'm sorry.'

The platitude slid readily from her tongue. She wasn't sorry. The world would be well rid of the Pooles. But she would remain polite. Let nothing of her bitterness show. Sir Malcolm had spent his life in pursuit of his own pleasures, a dissolute rake with not a care for the ruined lives he left in his wake. Felicity's poor sister had been just one of his victims. And Benedict had proved himself equally as contemptible, equally as careless of the heartbreak he had left behind. Hardly surprising with Sir Malcolm as his only role model since childhood.

Benedict prowled into the centre of the room, nearing Harriet. The very air seemed to vibrate between them. She stood her ground, although she could not prevent a swift glance at her maid, Janet, who had accompanied her, sitting quietly on a chair near the beautifully carved stone fireplace. Benedict followed her gaze.

At least I am not alone.

'Why are you here?' The words were softly spoken. Benedict's green eyes bored into Harriet's. 'Did you think to wed another wealthy man on his deathbed?'

'Brierley was not on his deathbed! And I had no ch—' Harriet shut her mouth with a snap. She'd endured over seven years with that lecher. Seven years of misery and disgust, empty arms and a broken heart, all because of Benedict Poole.

She had not in a million years thought to meet him here. He had gone overseas—right to the other side of the world. And even that was not far enough away for Harriet. Hatred for this man rose as the long-suppressed memories cascaded through her thoughts.

His lying words. His false promises. All of it.

She concealed any hint of her feelings. He must never know how her heart still ached for what might have been. She braced her shoulders and raised her chin.

'If Sir Malcolm will see me, I should be grateful for a few words with him.'

She glanced at the window—the clouds had blended into a uniform white vista of nothingness and she saw a few snowflakes flutter past. The snow that had threatened all morning as she had travelled deeper into Kent had finally begun to fall.

'I should like to leave before the weather takes a turn for the worse. *If* you would be so kind.'

Benedict bowed, and gestured towards the door. 'Your wish is my desire, my lady,' he said, his words flat and emotionless.

'Thank you.'

She stalked to the door, passing close by him…too close… His scent flooded her senses…triggering such memories, arousing emotions she had never thought to feel again. His unique maleness: familiar, even after eleven long years, spicy, heady…and…brandy. Brandy? This early in the day? He was a Poole through and through. Nothing had changed.

'Come, Janet.'

Harriet swept into the spacious inner hall, from which the magnificent polished oak staircase swept up to the first floor. The evidence of Sir Malcolm's wealth was everywhere, from the exquisitely executed landscapes hanging on the walls to the elegant Chinese porcelain vases and bowls that graced the numerous console tables to the magnificent crystal chandelier that hung over the central circular table complete with its urn of jessamine, lilies and sweet bay. *In February!* For all his wastrel tendencies, Sir Malcolm had clearly not exhausted his vast wealth. And, presumably, Benedict would inherit it all. Plus the title. No wonder he was here, with his cousin at death's door. He deserved none of it, but she would not allow him to sour her. Never again.

They spoke not another word as they climbed the stairs side by side, and walked along the upper landing, Janet on their heels. Harriet told herself she was pleased. She had no wish to exchange forced pleasantries.

They reached a door, which Benedict opened.

'Lady Brierley, to see Sir Malcolm,' he said, before ushering Harriet and Janet through, and closing the door firmly behind them.

It was baking hot in the room, which was not the master bedchamber, as Harriet expected, but much smaller, and decorated—tastelessly, in her opinion—in deep purple and gold. The fire was banked high with coal, blazing out a suffocating heat, and Harriet felt her face begin to glow. With an effort, she refrained from wafting her hand in front of her face. It was so airless and the stench caught in the back of her throat. How could anyone get well in such an atmosphere?

The huge bed dominated the room, the level surface of its purple cover barely disturbed by the wasted form of the man lying there. It was hard to believe this was the same man she had always known as strong and vital. He looked ancient but—she did a quick mental calculation—he could not be much more than eight and forty. Sir Malcolm's face was skeletal, the bloodless skin slack, and yet his eyes were still alert, dominating his shrunken features. Those eyes appraised Harriet with the same cold speculation she remembered from both her childhood and from the times her path had crossed with Sir Malcolm's during her marriage to Brierley. Disgust rippled through her.

'Heard I was dying, did you?' The voice was a dry, cracked whisper. 'Thought you'd have another shot at snaring Benedict's inheritance?'

'I have no interest in your cousin,' Harriet said. 'I am sorry to find you in such circumstances, but I have come on a quite different errand. I did not know you were ill, and I certainly did not know Mr Poole was here, or I would have thought twice about crossing your threshold.'

He croaked a laugh. 'That's as well for you. His opinion hasn't changed since the first time you tried to trap him. Even as a youngster, that boy was no fool. A Poole through and through. He could see straight through you then and he'll see straight through you now. He'll look higher for a wife than Brierley's leftovers, that I can promise.'

Harriet bit her tongue against rising to his provocation. It seemed even the imminent judgement of his maker could not cork Sir Malcolm's vitriol. She cast around for the appropriate words to ask him about Felicity's sister. When she'd decided to come to Tenterfield, she hadn't anticipated trying to persuade Sir Malcolm to tell her the truth on his deathbed.

'Well, girl? What d'you want? I haven't time to waste pandering to the likes of you. Tell me what you want and be gone. You hear, Fletcher?' He addressed the servant standing by the window. 'This *lady* is not to spend a minute more than necessary beneath my roof.'

The man bowed. 'Yes, sir.'

Harriet tamped down her anger. 'I wish to ask you about something that happened in the past. Do you recall Lady Emma Weston? She attended Lord Watchett's house party at the same time as you, in the summer of 1802.'

Sir Malcolm's lids lowered to mask his eyes. 'How do you expect me to remember one chit out of so many?'

'She was Lady Baverstock's daughter. It was the year following Lord Baverstock's death.'

His thin lips parted and Harriet recoiled as his tongue came out to touch his lip. 'Ah. Yes, indeed. The golden angel.'

Nausea churned Harriet's insides. Time had softened the memory of quite how contemptible Sir Malcolm had always been, despite his wealth and his handsome face. He had, however, been irresistibly charming to the young innocents he had targeted, and Harriet quite understood how a naive young girl could fall for his silver-tongued lies. She had been fortunate to be immune from his attempts to seduce her when she was young enough to appeal to his tastes. She had resisted, thinking herself in love with Benedict. Time had proved she was just as naive as poor Lady Emma, whom she was now convinced Sir Malcolm had seduced and impregnated and abandoned. Emma had escaped by taking her own life. Harriet had not been so cowardly—or, mayhap, so brave—when *her* heart had been broken, although…there were times during the years following her marriage to Brierley when suicide had seemed an enticing option.

'So it *was* you,' she said to the man in the bed. 'She wrote to you, after the summer you met. She was in love with you.'

His head twitched to one side. 'I said I met her. I admitted to nothing else.'

But Harriet knew, without a shadow of doubt, that Sir Malcolm was the man who had despoiled Felicity's sister. He had been a rake of the very worst kind; she did not need his confession. She leaned in close, breathing through her mouth to avoid the sour smell emanating from the bed.

'She *killed* herself! You seduced her and abandoned her, and she killed herself because she was carrying *your* child.'

He looked at her, his slitted eyes glinting. 'Best thing for her. One less fatherless brat to worry about. Isn't that so, my *lady*? Although *you* could not even manage that, could you? Lost it, as I recall. Careless of you.'

Harriet reared back, pain ripping at her heart. She must get out. Now. She should never have come. She suddenly realised this trip hadn't just been about Emma but about her, too—an attempt to make sense of the path her life had taken since she had fallen in love with Benedict. And she saw that she and Emma were the same: gullible victims of men who used and abused them and abandoned their responsibilities.

'I hope…' The words dried on her tongue. No, she would offer no comfort to this loathsome man, dying or not. She marched to the door.

Outside, the door firmly shut again, Harriet leaned against the wall, dragging in deep, shuddering breaths. Janet fumbled in her pocket and offered smelling salts. She had been with Harriet since the very early days of Harriet's marriage to Brierley, and had proved herself a loyal and protective friend to the young, bewildered bride. Harriet had long blessed the day the older woman had been appointed as her maid.

She waved the salts away. 'No. I will not faint, I promise you. I am trying to calm my anger,' she said, forcing a smile to set Janet's mind at rest.

She glanced back at the closed bedchamber door. How could such a man have lived with himself all these years? She pushed upright and shook out her skirts, smoothing them.

'Come. Let us go. We must get back to the Rose as soon as we can in case the snow begins to drift.'

She had reserved accommodation at the Rose Inn at Sittingbourne, a bare four miles from Tenterfield Court, on their way through from London. The plan was to stay there the night and return to London the following day, when Harriet would tell Felicity what she had discovered. She must hope the news would not prove too upsetting for her friend, who was now with child herself. Harriet ruthlessly quashed her ripple of envy that Felicity would soon be a mother.

She was thankful there was no sign of Benedict as they descended the stairs and went through the door to the panelled Great Hall with its ancient blackened stone hearths at either end. The butler sent word to the stables for their hired chaise and four to be brought round to the front door, and a maid ran to fetch their travelling cloaks, muffs and hats. It was cold outside and they had prepared well for the journey from London, with blankets and furs piled in the carriage.

'The chaise is outside now, milady,' the butler said. 'Take care, it might be slippery. Cooper here will help you.'

A footman, well wrapped up, stepped forward and

Harriet took one arm whilst Janet took the other. They emerged into a world transformed. The air swirled white and she could barely make out the trees that lined the sweeping carriageway that led from the house to the road. The easterly wind had picked up, gusting at times, and blowing the snow horizontal, stinging Harriet's cheeks. The waiting horses stamped their feet and tossed their heads, blowing cloudy breaths down their nostrils as the hapless post boys hunched on their backs. Harriet hoped they had been given a warming drink in the kitchen; she did not doubt they, like her, would be glad to reach the inn where they were to spend the night.

Harriet clung tightly to the footman's arm, feeling her half boots slide on the stone steps as they descended warily to the waiting chaise. She looked across at Janet at the very same moment the maid released Cooper's arm to hurry down the last few steps, presumably to open the door ready for Harriet.

'Janet! No!'

It was too late. A shriek rose above the howl of the wind as Janet missed her footing on the second to last step. Her feet shot from under her and she fell back onto the steps, one leg bent beneath her.

'Oh, no!' Harriet hurried as best she could to where the maid lay. 'Janet? Are you all right?'

'Yes, milady. I—' Janet screamed as she tried to rise, a high-pitched, sobbing scream. 'Oh, milady! My back! It—aargh! My leg! I can't move it!'

'Oh, good heavens!' *What if it is broken?* Harriet remembered only too well the pain of broken bones, a pain that, in her case, had been numbed by a far greater agony. She thrust those memories back down where they belonged. In the past. 'Can you carry her to the chaise, Cooper?'

The footman bent to lift Janet, but the maid batted him away. 'No! Don't touch me. It hurts!'

Harriet crouched down next to Janet, taking her gloved hand. 'We cannot just leave you here in the snow. You'll freeze to death.'

'I can't bear to move, milady. I can't bear it. And I can't go in that yellow bounder, not the way they drive. I cannot.' Her words ended in a wail.

Now what was she to do? Harriet stared through the driving snow to where the chaise and four still waited. It was barely visible now. The weather was worsening. She must move Janet somehow.

'Allow me.' A hand gripped her shoulder as the deep voice interrupted her inner panic.

Benedict.

Her instinctive urge to shrink from his touch battled against her relief that help was at hand. She glanced round, taking in his hard eyes and tight-lipped mouth, and she clenched her jaw. Janet must be her only concern.

'Thank you,' she said.

Chapter Two

Benedict Poole had returned to the library after escorting Harriet to the bedchamber where the last remaining member of his family, other than himself, lay wasting away. He poured himself another measure of brandy and settled by the fire, broodingly contemplating the woman he had never thought to see again. He gulped a mouthful of the spirit and grimaced. She'd driven him to drink already and she'd been here, what? Half an hour?

A bustle of movement in the Great Hall some time later interrupted his thoughts—the unmistakable sounds of departure. He would not say goodbye. She had not afforded *him* that courtesy, all those years ago.

One last look. That's all.

He crossed to the window and positioned himself to one side, shielded by the curtain, in order that a casual glance would not reveal him. Snow drove horizontally across the front of the house and he was all at once aware of the howl of the wind. He had been so lost in his thoughts he had not even noticed the deterioration in the weather. Three figures, well wrapped against the cold, appeared at the top of the steps, the smallest two clinging on to the arms of the taller central figure, presumably one of the footmen. That was Harriet, huddled in a hooded cloak of deep, rich blue, trimmed with fur. As he watched them gingerly descend the steps, the second woman—Harriet's maid—suddenly let go of the footman's arm and appeared to hurry ahead. Benedict jerked forward, ready to shout a warning even though there was no chance she would hear him, but, before he could utter a sound, the maid's feet shot from under her and she fell.

He didn't stop to think but ran to the door, through the hall and straight out of the front door. The cold air blasted icy spikes against his face as he hurried down the steps, almost slipping in his haste. The maid's leg—it could be broken. She mustn't be moved. Maybe he could straighten it… He had helped more than one ship's surgeon set broken bones during his travels. He thrust aside any nerves, any doubts.

Harriet was crouching by the maid, who was shaking her head, her tearful voice begging no one to touch her. He reached for Harriet, who seemed about to try to pull her maid upright.

'Allow me,' he said.

Harriet turned and gazed up at him, her expression inscrutable, those eyes of hers, once so expressive, guarded. Her nose and cheeks were bright red but her lips, when she spoke, had a bluish tinge. 'Thank you.'

'Go inside and wait,' he said. 'Get yourself warm and dry. We'll deal with your maid.'

'Janet,' she said. 'Her name is Janet. It's her back, as well as her leg. You…you won't hurt her?'

'I can't promise that. We must move her but we must first straighten her leg. Ask Crabtree to bring some brandy and something to bind her leg. He's the butler,' he added as she raised her brows. 'But be careful how you—'

She speared him with a scathing look. 'I am not likely to risk falling, having seen what happened to Janet,' she said.

The panic had melted from her voice, which now dripped contempt. Benedict mentally shrugged. Her moods were none of his concern. Harriet stripped off her cloak and laid it over her stricken maid before picking her way back up the steps.

Benedict glanced at the footman—Cooper, it was, he now saw. 'That leg could be broken. Have you ever helped set a leg before?' he asked.

'I have,' a new voice interposed. One of the post boys had dismounted and had joined Benedict standing over Janet, who was shivering violently. 'I'm used to it,' he added with a grin. 'Always someone breaking somethin' when horses are involved.'

'Tell your mate to take the horses back to the yard and bed them down for the night,' Benedict said. 'The ladies will be going nowhere.'

'Right you are, sir,' the post boy said, signalling to his partner, who waved an acknowledgement before kicking his horse into motion.

Benedict crouched beside the stricken maid.

'Don't touch me!' she shrieked. 'It's my back! I can't stand it!'

'Hush, now,' Benedict said as the maid subsided into sobs. 'We must find out if your leg is broken. It will have to be straightened before we can move you.'

The butler appeared at the top of the steps and gingerly made his way to where Janet lay.

'Ah, Crabtree. Thank you.' Benedict took the glass and held it to Janet's lips. 'Drink.'

Janet shook her head. 'I never touch—'

'*Drink*. It will help dull the pain when we straighten your leg. You need to be moved.'

Benedict tipped the glass up, pinching her chin to force her mouth open. This was no time for niceties. The cold had seeped through his clothes, chilling his flesh already. Janet must be in an even worse case, lying on the snow-blanketed stone steps.

'What are you doing? How is she?'

His head jerked round. Harriet was back, peering over his shoulder at her maid.

'I thought I told you to stay inside.'

'Janet is my responsibility. I can help.'

'If you want to help, go back inside.'

Her stare might have frozen him had he not already been chilled to his core.

'Don't leave me, my lady. Pleeeease.'

Harriet crouched by Benedict's side and gripped Janet's hands. The length of her thigh pressed briefly against his and he was aware she shifted away at the exact same time he did, so they no longer touched. Another footman appeared, carrying lengths of cloth and a wooden board, with the information that the doctor had been sent for.

Benedict pushed Janet's cloak aside and raised her skirt, Harriet's soothing murmur punctuating Janet's whimpers. A close look at the bent leg raised Benedict's hopes. The foot looked twisted, making a broken ankle a distinct possibility, but the leg itself appeared intact. A pink stain in the snow, however, suggested it was cut.

Benedict spoke to Cooper and the post boy. 'If her back is damaged, we must move her carefully.' He directed the men on how to tip Janet sideways, keeping her back as straight as possible whilst he moved her leg from under her, silently blessing the time he had spent with Josiah Buckley, the ship's surgeon, on his recent voyage back to England from India. He might not know how to help Janet, but he did know how not to make things worse.

The next few minutes were hellish. Benedict gritted his teeth and forced himself to continue, gently straightening Janet's leg and then, using a knife proffered by the post boy, cutting off her boot. Another snippet of knowledge gleaned from Buckley—that an injured foot or ankle will swell, making boots hard to remove. Not that the sailors wore footwear aboard the ship, but their discussions had been wide-ranging. Benedict distracted his thoughts from Janet's screams by thinking of that voyage but then the shrieking wind recalled the storm that had almost foundered the ship, and he found his heart racing and hands shaking with the memory. He hesitated, squeezing his eyes shut as he gulped down his fear—*It isn't real. I'm here at Tenterfield, not on board*—then jerked back to full awareness as a gloved hand covered his. He glanced round into familiar violet eyes.

'You're doing well,' she murmured. He focused on her lips: too close…sweetly full…so tempting. 'Do not lose your nerve now.'

Benedict dragged in a jagged breath and the icy air swept other memories into focus with a vicious stab in his temples. Not life-threatening memories such as that storm, but soul-destroying nonetheless. Memories of Harriet and her betrayal. His hand steadied and he continued to cut Janet's boot until it fell apart.

They slid the maid onto the board then and, between them, Benedict and the post boy used lengths of linen to bind her to the plank and keep her still whilst they moved her to a bedchamber. Benedict rose stiffly to his feet as the two footmen lifted the board and carried Janet up the steps and back into the house. Benedict clasped Harriet's elbow, resisting her attempt to tug free, and supported her up the steps and into the hall.

'Why have you dismissed the chaise?' she demanded as soon as the front door closed behind them, shutting out the swirling snowstorm. 'I have accommodation bespoken at the Rose Inn.'

'You will stay here tonight.'

'I most certainly will not!' Her voice rang with outrage. 'Stay overnight at *Tenterfield Court*, with no chaperone?' Harriet marched over to Crabtree, about to mount the stairs in the wake of the footmen carrying Janet. 'Send a man to the stables, if you please, with a message to bring the chaise back round.'

'Your maid cannot travel.'

Harriet pivoted on the spot and glared at Benedict. 'I am well aware Janet must remain here,' she spat. 'I, however, am perfectly fit and well, and I will not stay where I am not welcome.'

'I thought you were concerned for your reputation?' Benedict drawled, the drive to thwart her overriding his eagerness to see her gone. 'Yet you would stay in a public inn without even a maid to lend you countenance? My, my, Lady Brierley. I have to wonder if your reluctance to remain here at Tenterfield owes less to concern over your reputation and more to fear of your own lack of self-control.'

'Oh!' Harriet's eyes flashed and her lips thinned. 'How *dare* you?' She spoke again to Crabtree, waiting patiently at the foot of the staircase, staring discreetly into space, the epitome of an experienced butler. 'Is there a maid who might accompany me to the inn?'

Crabtree's gaze slid past Harriet to mutely question Benedict, who moved his head in a small negative motion.

'I am sorry, my lady,' Crabtree said, 'but with Sir Malcolm so ill and now your maid to care for, I am unable to spare any of my staff. And I am persuaded it would be unwise to venture on even such a short journey in this weather.'

The satisfaction Benedict experienced at frustrating Harriet's plans glowed for only a brief few seconds. Her presence could only reopen old wounds. Why had he been so insistent that she stay?

'Inform me when the doctor arrives,' he bit out over his shoulder as he took the stairs two at a time, silently cursing himself for a fool.

In his bedchamber, he stripped off his wet clothes and shrugged into his banyan, then paced the vast room, his thoughts filled with Harriet.

The announcement of her arrival had nearly floored him. His heart had drummed against his ribs as his palms grew damp. She could not have known—could she?—that he was here, attending his dying cousin. That leap of hope, swiftly banished, had angered and unsettled him. Whatever her reason for visiting Malcolm, he didn't want to know. He was only here himself from a sense of duty to his erstwhile guardian. He had no affection for Sir Malcolm but he was indebted to him for supporting him financially ever since the death of Benedict's parents. Malcolm had ensured Benedict attended the best schools, followed by Cambridge University, and, for that, Benedict owed him some consideration.

He hadn't *needed* to meet with Harriet at all—he could have relegated the task to one of the servants. He *should* have relegated it but, dammit, that would be tantamount to admitting he still cared. Besides—and he might as well be honest with himself—curiosity had got the better of him. He'd wanted to see what she had become, this jade who had so thoughtlessly betrayed him and his heart: who had pledged her love for him and then coldheartedly wed another man for the sake of a title and wealth.

Before facing her, he'd gone to the library to fortify himself with a glass of brandy from the decanter there. *She* hadn't appeared to need any such additional support. He walked into the drawing room to find her cool and elegant, an utterly gorgeous woman, with the same abundance of lustrous moon-pale hair he remembered only too well. His fingers had twitched with the desire to take out her pins and see her tresses tumble over her shoulders again. She was more voluptuous than he remembered, but then she had still been a girl when they had fallen in love. Correction, he thought, with a self-deprecating sneer, when *he* had fallen in love. And those eyes—huge, violet blue, thickly lashed; they were as arresting as ever. He had always thought of them as windows to her soul. He snorted a bitter laugh at his youthful naivety. Now, with the benefit of eleven more years' experience, he could see that those eyes had lied as easily as that soft, sensual mouth with its full pink lips.

Such a pity so perfect an exterior disguised such a mercenary bitch.

Later, before dinner, Benedict visited Malcolm in his bedchamber, as had become his habit in the seven days since his arrival at Tenterfield Court. Malcolm's breathing had grown noticeably harsher in the past week and Benedict was conscious that the air now wheezed in and out of his cousin's lungs faster than ever, as if each breath failed to satisfy the demand for oxygen. He pulled a chair to the side of the bed and sat down. Malcolm's eyes were closed, the thin skin almost translucent. A glance at Fletcher elicited a shake of the valet's head.

Benedict placed his hand over the paper-dry skin of Malcolm's hand where it lay on the coverlet. The flesh was cool to his touch, despite the suffocating heat of the room. Sweat sprung to Benedict's forehead and upper lip, and he felt his neck grow damp beneath the neckcloth he had tied around his neck in deference to his dinner guest.

Damn her! Why did she have to come? And now she would be here all night, a siren song calling to his blood as surely as if she lay in his bed beside him. He forced his thoughts away from Harriet as Malcolm stirred, his lids slitting open as though even that movement was too great an effort for his feeble energy.

'Water.'

Fletcher brought a glass and held it to his master's lips, supporting his head as he sucked in the liquid. As Fletcher lowered his head back to the pillow, Malcolm's eyes fixed on Benedict.

'Going out?'

Benedict fingered his neckcloth self-consciously. Malcolm still had the ability to reduce him to a callow youth with just a single comment. He had been a careless guardian with little interest in Benedict, who had been a mere eight years old when he was orphaned. As Benedict had matured and developed more understanding of the world, Malcolm's behaviour and reputation had caused him nothing but shame. Now, although he found it hard to feel any sorrow at Malcolm's imminent death, he could not help but pity the man his suffering.

'I dressed for dinner before visiting you tonight.' The lie slid smoothly off Benedict's tongue. He kept forgetting that, although Malcolm's body had betrayed him, his mind was a sharp as ever.

'Has that harlot gone?'

'Harlot?'

'The Brierley woman. She's no business here… I told her… Fletcher? Has she gone?'

Fletcher glanced at Benedict, who gave a slight nod of his head. 'Yes, sir,' he said. 'She left the house straight after she saw you.'

'Good. Good riddance. Have nothing to do with her, you hear, boy?'

Benedict bit back his irritation at being addressed in such a way. He was a successful businessman. Yes, he was Sir Malcolm's heir and would inherit both the baronetcy and Tenterfield, but he had no need of the man's support or wealth. Not any longer. He was his own man.

It was strange to think he would soon be master of Tenterfield. When he had arrived a week ago, he had gazed up at the red-brick Jacobean manor house with a sense of disbelief that, soon, this place of so many memories would be his. He already felt the pride of ownership and had vowed to restore both its reputation and that of the Poole family name after the years of damage caused by Sir Malcolm's disgrace.

'I have no intention of having anything to do with her, you can rest assured on that,' Benedict said. Then, curious, he asked, 'What do you have against her? I thought Brierley was a friend of yours.'

'That's got nothing to do with it. I saw what her fickle behaviour did to you. She's not to be trusted.'

Benedict felt his eyes narrow. *Now* Malcolm cared about his feelings? Or perhaps he knew more about Brierley's marriage than he was saying. Had Harriet played Brierley false, too? He shoved his chair back and stood up.

'You should rest,' he said. 'I will see you in the morning.'

He went downstairs, Harriet and the evening to come playing on his mind and churning his gut.

Chapter Three

Crabtree appeared, seemingly from nowhere, to open the drawing room doors for Benedict.

'Has Lady Brierley come downstairs yet?' Benedict asked the butler.

'Not yet, sir.'

Benedict was conscious of a sweep of relief. At least they would not have to make small talk before their meal—that would be strained enough, he was sure.

'Please impress upon the rest of the staff that they must not reveal the presence of either Lady Brierley or her maid to Sir Malcolm,' he said. 'It will only agitate him to no purpose.'

'Indeed I will, sir.' Crabtree bowed.

Benedict entered the room to await his dinner guest. Moodily, he poked at the coals in the grate, stirring them to life, pondering this spectre from a past he had long put behind him. He had been caught on the back foot—his feelings tossed and tumbled like a ship caught in a squall. Surely his reaction to Harriet was merely shock and, like a squall, it would soon pass. After all, what was she to him? She was just somebody he used to know a long time ago, when she was a girl. She must be

all of seven and twenty by now, by God. Her betrayal—
her marriage to Brierley—was ancient history. He was
confident he would soon recover his equilibrium, and
then he could treat her with the same detached courtesy
he would employ towards any unexpected guest. Perhaps he should look upon this unexpected trial in the
light of a rehearsal—an opportunity to put their past
into some sort of reasonable perspective. In the future,
should he happen to see her around town, maybe he
could remember their shared past with dispassion and
not with this angry bitterness that was eating away inside him.

Voices from outside the door roused him from his
thoughts. He turned as Harriet entered the room, his
breath catching in his throat at her stunning beauty. She
wore an elegant lilac gown that accentuated the violet
of her eyes and the fullness of her breasts, despite the
neckline not swooping as low as some of the more daring fashions Benedict had seen. Her blonde hair was
pinned into a smooth chignon, exposing the creamy
skin of her neck and décolletage.

Battening down his visceral reaction, Benedict
bowed.

'Good evening, Mr Poole.'

He straightened. Her gaze was both cool and distant, stoking his resentment. The grand society lady:
graciously poised and certain of her superiority regardless of the circumstances. Had she forgotten her humble beginnings?

'Good evening, my lady.' His voice was smooth and
assured—a stark contrast with his inner turmoil. 'I trust
your bedchamber meets with your approval?'

'Thank you, it does indeed.'

The door opened again, and Crabtree announced

that dinner was served. Benedict gestured for Harriet to precede him to the dining room.

'How is your maid?' Benedict asked, once they were seated and the food had been served. 'Janet, is it not?'

'Janet, yes,' Harriet said. 'I'm afraid her ankle is broken. Dr Green has set the bone and seems optimistic it will heal well. I do hope that is true and she does not end up with pain or a limp. Her back is very painful, too—the doctor cupped her and will examine her again tomorrow, when he visits Sir Malcolm. He did warn me, however, that she should remain in bed until the bruising comes out and he can see if there is any further damage to her back.'

'How long is that likely to take?'

A faint crease appeared between her brows. 'He did not say. A few days at the least, I should imagine, so I am afraid I shall have to impose on your hospitality a little longer.'

A few days? With her *as a house guest?* Benedict clenched his teeth against a sudden urge to laugh. *What a fool!* He was aware Harriet lived in London and since his return to England from India, he had taken care to avoid any risk of bumping into her. His efforts had been in vain; fate, it would appear, did not like to be thwarted.

'She may stay as long as proves necessary,' he said with a shrug of indifference, determined to give her no reason to suspect he could care less how long she stayed.

Harriet studied him for a long moment as she sipped her wine. She then put her glass down and leaned forward, trapping his gaze.

'In order there is no misunderstanding between us, sir, I should clarify that I will not leave Janet here alone. I intend to remain with her until she is fit enough to travel to Brierley Place. It is only eight miles away, and she can remain there until she is able to undertake the journey to London.'

'As you wish,' Benedict said. 'Heaven forfend your maid should be forced to undergo the privations of re-cuperating in *these* miserable surroundings.'

A flush lit Harriet's cheeks. 'The point is that she will be happier surrounded by people she knows,' she said. 'And I shall not hesitate to leave her *there* whilst I return to London.'

'Your maid will be perfectly safe here without your protection,' Benedict said, smarting at yet another re-minder of the past scandals that had tainted both Tenter-field and the Poole name. It would take time to restore the reputation of both but he was determined to do so, and the sooner the better.

Harriet's words prompted another thought: he had forgotten Brierley Place was quite so near. 'I wonder, though, that you did not plan to stay with your family at Brierley Place, rather than at a public inn, after your visit to my cousin. Why?'

Her gaze lowered. 'I wish to return to London as soon as possible, and if I stayed with my stepson and his family they would expect more than an overnight visit.'

Her hand rose to her neck, and she began to twirl a lock of hair that curled loose by her ear. That ach-ingly familiar habit catapulted Benedict back in time. She was hiding something. It was the first reminder of the girl he'd once known. He studied her, wondering what currents were masked by that calm, ladylike ex-terior of hers.

'Besides,' she continued, 'my stepson is always up and down to London in his carriage. He will return

Janet to me as soon as she is well. The carriage will be far more comfortable for her than a hired chaise.'

'Indeed it will,' Benedict said, 'and, with that in mind, I shall arrange to pay off your post boys in the morning.'

'Thank you. I shall, of course, reimburse you.'

'Of course,' he agreed smoothly. 'And, when you are ready to leave, I shall put my carriage at your disposal.'

Her brows rose. '*Your* carriage? Do you not mean Sir Malcolm's?'

Benedict's anger flared in response to that challenge but he battled the urge to vent his feelings, telling himself that anger came from caring, and he did not care.

'I am not so devoid of feeling as to step into my kinsman's shoes whilst he is still alive,' he said, careful to keep his tone neutral. 'I have my own carriage. It is the use of that I offer to you.'

A delicate flush swept up from her chest to tint her cheeks as she turned her attention to her food. 'Of course. I apologise. I should not have cast such aspersions.'

The conversation faltered, and the silence accentuated the lonely wail of the wind outside. The windows rattled with every gust, the wind forcing its way through the gaps in the frames to cause the red velvet curtains to billow into the room from time to time.

'How long have you been here, at Tenterfield?'

Benedict finished chewing and swallowed his food before answering, 'A week. My cousin's solicitor sent for me on the doctor's advice.'

'So there is no hope of a cure?'

'None.'

He read sympathy in those glorious eyes of hers. He had no need of it. She, of all people, should know he had no fondness for Malcolm. He would be no loss to humanity and Benedict would not pretend a grief he did not feel. His predominant emotion was impatience to return to London. His business—importing goods from the Far East—needed his attention and he had matters to discuss with his partner, Matthew Damerel, who was due back in town again shortly.

They finished eating and Benedict stood, saying, 'Serve the brandy in the drawing room, will you please, Crabtree?' He caught Harriet's eye and added, 'Would you care to join me?'

'Thank you.' She rose elegantly to her feet. 'I shall wait for the tea tray and then I shall retire. It has been a somewhat exhausting day.'

Benedict had not proffered his arm to Harriet before dinner but now, mellowed by wine and bolstered by the certainty that he was in control of his temper, he waited for Harriet to round the table and reach him, then crooked his arm. She halted, her gaze fixed on his arm, then raised her eyes to his. She seemed about to speak, but then merely laid her gloved hand on his sleeve and allowed him to lead her from the room.

Every muscle in his arm tensed, even though her touch was feather-light. Her scent, sophisticated, floral and quintessentially feminine, assailed his nostrils and he found himself swallowing hard, trying to ignore the unaccustomed flutter of nerves in his belly. He gritted his teeth. He was a grown man, for God's sake. This ridiculous reaction meant nothing; it was merely the spectre of the past playing games with him. Maybe he should take advantage of the circumstances that had thrown them together like this. Lay her and those ghosts at the same time.

'Would you care for a glass of brandy?' he enquired

when Cooper, the footman, followed them into the drawing room carrying a silver salver, complete with decanter and two glasses.

'Thank you, but I have no taste for spirits. A cup of tea will suffice.'

Cooper handed a glass of brandy to Benedict, then bowed to Harriet. 'I will hurry the maid along with the tea tray, milady.'

She smiled at him. 'Thank you.' She settled on the sofa opposite the hearth and Benedict noticed her shiver.

'Are you cold?' He poked the fire, which had recently been refuelled and was therefore not emitting much heat.

'Not really. It is the sound of that wind.' When he turned to look at her, she was staring towards the window, one hand playing with the pearls at her neck. 'I had forgotten, living in London, quite how desolate it can sound. Like a lost soul, crying into the void.'

'Like a lost *soul*?'

She started, and then laughed a little self-consciously. 'Oh! I do beg your pardon. I had quite forgot…that is…' Her voice tailed away and her cheeks bloomed pink as her lips quirked in a wry smile. 'I did not mean to spout such poetical nonsense. Please do forgive me.'

'There is nothing to forgive. I confess there have been times, usually aboard ship, when the wind has conjured many superstitious imaginings in my own mind. I generally avoided voicing them out loud, however, for fear I might be thought to run mad.'

She laughed, a genuine laugh this time. 'Goodness, sir. You put me quite out of countenance. You imply that I might be thought mad.'

Not mad, but bad. Why did you deceive me, Harriet?
The words pummelled his brain and battered at his

tightly closed lips. It was a question to which he had long yearned for an answer. But he would never ask. What would be the point? She could mouth all the excuses in the world but she could never deny the truth. She simply had not loved him enough. She had broken her pledge of love for the promise of status and riches.

One of the maids came into the room at that moment with the tea tray. Relieved by the interruption, Benedict gestured at her to make the tea and he then crossed to the table to fetch a cup for Harriet. As he handed it to her he took advantage of her distraction in handling the delicate china to study her at close quarters.

Maturity had added to her beauty, not detracted from it. Her thick blonde hair was pinned up, exposing the long, vulnerable line of her neck and that sensitive spot below her ear where he had taken a lovesick youth's delight in kissing her and teasing her with his tongue. With her eyes lowered, he could count every one of the long lashes that swept the peaches and cream of her skin. He committed to memory the faint fan of lines radiating from the outer corner of her eye; they only served to render her more enticing, more beautiful... vulnerable, even.

He was so very close he could even see the soft, fair down that coated her cheek. Against his will, his gaze drifted—sweeping again to her shoulder, where pale skin skimmed delicate bones, and then to her chest, to delight in the flesh that nestled within the neckline of her gown. His pulse leaped in response to the shadowy valley between her breasts and saliva flooded his mouth as he recalled the glory of her naked flesh.

Her scent enveloped him, leading him to wish the impossible...leading him to wish the past had been different.

With a silent oath, Benedict straightened abruptly and moved away to sit in an armchair, dismissing that momentary weakness. He crossed his legs to disguise his growing arousal, furious that he had allowed the fascination of the past to intrude upon the present. It was many years since he had believed a woman's appearance was an indication of her true worth, and he would never forget that, however beautiful Harriet might be on the outside, she was rotten and mercenary to her core.

Bitterness still lurked deep inside him. It was under control for now, but it would not take much for it to break free—for him to fling accusations at her and to demand explanations. He would not visit that time. He must allow those memories to fade away, and only look forward. Never back.

'Do you stay at Brierley Place often?' he asked, needing the ebb and flow of conversation to distract him, afraid of where his fixation with the past might lead.

'No, not often since I was widowed.'

'Does the new Lord Brierley not make you welcome?'

'He is very supportive in many ways.' One hand lifted to toy again with that loose curl by her ear. The repeat of that girlhood habit made him frown.

What is *she hiding?* The thought prompted a desire to dig further; to discover the real woman behind that cool civility. He dismissed that desire with an impatient inner snarl.

'What are your plans, Mr Poole? Will you remain here after...after...?'

'After Sir Malcolm dies?'

She blushed. 'Yes. I am sorry if that was an insensitive question.'

'There is no need to apologise. I have a business to

run, so I shall spend much of my time in London once my cousin's affairs are in order.'

It was a prospect he viewed with little pleasure, but in the week since his arrival at Tenterfield—when he had realised for the first time exactly how little time Malcolm had left—Benedict had come to accept he would have no option but to enter society if he was serious about restoring the family name. He was aware he was unlikely to be welcomed into the top tier, but his title and the vast fortune he would inherit would be enough for many to overlook his links to trade.

He had travelled the world these past eleven years and thought of himself as having permanent wanderlust in his blood, with no urge to put down roots. He never dwelt on the past. The past was done. It couldn't be changed. Since his return to England, however, the time he had spent with Matthew and his new bride, Eleanor, had awoken something deep inside him—the urge for a family to call his own.

Benedict's memories of his early life, before his parents' deaths, were hazy. Seeing Matthew and Eleanor together, however, had gradually recalled those happy years and his plans for his future had changed. He and Matthew already had a trusted agent in India who would arrange shipments to England. There was no necessity for Benedict to return to India if he chose not to.

Silence settled over them as Harriet sipped at her tea and Benedict finished his brandy, then Harriet placed her teacup and saucer on a side table. She rose to her feet and he followed suit.

'I shall retire,' she said. 'It has been a long day. Thank you for your hospitality, Ben… Mr Poole.'

'You are welcome, my lady.'

Their gazes met, her violet eyes dark and unfathomable. Benedict stepped closer. Was it his imagination, or did her lips tremble? He saw the convulsive movement of her throat as she swallowed. Then she straightened and drew in what seemed to be an interminable breath.

'Goodnight.' With a swish of skirts she passed him by and headed for the door.

Benedict moved quickly. 'Allow me,' he said, reaching the door before her.

He grasped the handle but then hesitated. Slowly, his hand slipped from the handle and he turned to face Harriet, his back against the door.

Chapter Four

Harriet had halted a few feet away.

'Please let me pass.'

Her voice was low. She searched his face, her gaze uncertain.

'Harriet…'

'Mr Poole?'

But what could he say that would not risk unleashing all that anger and bitterness that scoured his insides? The past had happened. No amount of wishful thinking could change it and no good could come of stirring up all those raw emotions.

He spoke from the heart, but he spoke only of the present. 'You are a very beautiful woman, Harriet.'

His voice had grown husky; blood surged to his groin; he took a pace towards her and breathed deep of her scent. She was close. So close. He reached out and fingered that errant curl and revelled in the whispered sigh that escaped those full, pink lips. He narrowed still further the gap between them, relishing the flush that suffused her skin. Molten-hot currents burned deep within him, making his skin tighten and his breath grow short.

He opened his fingers and released her curl, lowering his hand to his side.

He would not detain her. Her escape was clear, if she wanted it. She had only to step away—walk around him to the door. She did not. Her eyelids fluttered and lowered as her lips parted. He tilted his head, feathered his lips at the side of her neck, savouring her quiet moan, satisfied by the leap of her pulse as he laved that sensitive spot.

'No,' she whispered. 'Please... I...'

'Tell me to stop, and I will,' he murmured as he licked at her lobe.

He blew gently across the moistened skin and she shuddered, swaying, her full breasts and pebbled nipples pressing into his chest for one brief, glorious moment before she jerked away.

'No!'

Benedict, grown hard with desire, reined in his urge to grab her and kiss her anyway. He forced himself to remain still.

'Why?'

'I do not need to give you a reason.'

Head high, she met his gaze. He recognised the flash of vulnerability in her eyes...and something else. Fear? Of him?

'What are you afraid of?'

With his attention fully upon her, he sensed the shift under her skin as she drew her defences in place. 'I am not afraid.'

He wanted to doubt her. He wanted to believe her lips were saying 'no' when she meant 'yes'. But he could not. She—for whatever reason—really did mean 'no'.

He moved aside and watched as she left the room.

His feet moved of their own volition, following her out the door into the hall to watch as she climbed the stairs.

Who is she? Who has she become?

He had no wish to revisit the past, but he could not help but be intrigued by the present-day Harriet. Her outer shell was well crafted: sophisticated, ladylike, at ease. And yet she had revealed some of her true spirit in that snowstorm, after he dismissed the post-chaise. Benedict suspected her calm exterior concealed hidden turbulence, much as the smooth surface of the ocean might conceal treacherous currents.

He wandered back into the drawing room to stand and stare into the fire, his mind whirling. He wanted to dig deeper, to find out more about her. Curiosity. It was dangerous, but that was no reason to retreat. She would be here for a few days yet—time enough to find out more. Perhaps testing those suspected undercurrents was risky, but he had never yet backed down from a challenge. And he wasn't about to start now.

The following day was grey and cold, the land still dusted white. No more snow had fallen, but the weather did nothing to tempt anyone out of doors. Harriet spent some of her time sitting with Janet, and the rest of the day exploring Tenterfield Court. Despite growing up in the area, she had never set foot inside the house until today and she had not realised its true magnificence.

Sir Malcolm had lived, for the most part, in London. He would descend, with guests, for a few days of wild, disruptive parties—the kind that fuelled horrified gossip in the local community—and then would disappear again for months on end. He avoided all interaction with local society on the rare times he visited on his own and, as his dissolute reputation spread, the people in the surrounding area—including Harriet's father, who was the local vicar—had in turn shunned Sir Malcolm.

Benedict, as his ward, had spent most of the school holidays alone at Tenterfield Court, mixing with the local children, including Harriet. Memories tumbled into her brain. He had been so tall and handsome— someone she'd liked and looked up to—and, as they had grown, so had their feelings. Now, looking back, Harriet knew those feelings to be a lie—the fanciful wishes of a naive young girl and the lustful desires of a boy on the verge of manhood.

As she changed her dress for dinner early that evening, she diverted her thoughts away from those past innocent—and not so innocent—pleasures and into the present. She was a woman grown now: experienced, wise in the ways of men, no longer a believer in love. The love she had once felt for Benedict Poole was no more, but she could not deny he was an extremely attractive man.

How would it feel to lie with him now?

That errant thought shook her. How could she even wonder such a thing after the way he had deserted her? Or was it natural to be curious about this past love of hers? Last night—and her blood heated at the memory—he had woven a spell of such sensuality around her that the temptation to succumb to him had near overwhelmed her. Thank goodness she had come to her senses in time.

A restless night had seen her up early in the morning with a vow to avoid Benedict as much as possible during her enforced stay at Tenterfield Court. Thankfully, Benedict appeared to share her reluctance for another encounter; according to Crabtree, he had spent the entire day holed up in the study with Sir Malcolm's bailiff, and that suited Harriet perfectly. The less time they spent together the less likely she would be to reveal too much. Her pride would never allow him to know how much he had hurt her with his brutal rejection eleven years before.

Her customary calm had already deserted her once since her arrival. That he had been right to dismiss the post-chaise yesterday had not even entered her thoughts, and she had allowed her anger and her resentment of him to show. She must ensure such a lapse did not recur, and she vowed to redouble her efforts to stay in control of her emotions.

She delayed coming downstairs until one of the maids came to tell her that dinner was ready to be served. She headed straight for the dining room, and Benedict joined her a few minutes later.

He strolled in, supremely confident and at ease, starkly handsome in his evening clothes. He gave her a lazy smile. 'Good evening, my lady. I trust you have occupied your time pleasantly today?'

Harriet ignored the tiny flutter of nerves deep in her belly. *Don't allow him to fluster you. Stay in control.* After all, she was well practised in the art of concealing her feelings and opinions. Her late husband had schooled her well.

'Yes, most pleasantly, thank you,' she replied. 'And you, sir?'

He grimaced. 'I have been familiarising myself with the estate accounts,' he said. 'My head is reeling with facts and figures.'

He pulled out a chair for Harriet. As the night before, two facing places had been set, halfway along the long sides of the table. As Harriet sat down, Benedict's hand brushed her upper arm, sending a shiver of awareness dancing across her skin. He rounded the table and sat opposite her.

'Did you gain any experience of agricultural matters whilst you were overseas?' Harriet asked as Crabtree served her a slice of roast beef and a spoonful of glazed onions.

'No. My experience is all in trade. This is all new to me.'

Benedict fixed his green eyes on Harriet. 'Tell me—'

'How long have you been back in England?' Harriet asked hastily, keen to keep the focus of the conversation away from her own life.

'Three months.'

'Was Sir Malcolm's health the reason for your return?' She then took advantage of Benedict's distraction as Crabtree offered him a dish of potatoes in hollandaise sauce to say, 'You mentioned before that you are the only family he has left.'

Benedict captured her gaze and quirked a brow, as if to say, 'I know what you're up to,' and Harriet felt her cheeks heat. He took his time in finishing his mouthful of food before answering her.

'No. I had no idea his health was failing until I landed in England.'

'This food is delicious,' Harriet said, somewhat desperately.

Benedict might be answering her questions, but he was doing nothing to ease the evening ahead with the light, inconsequential conversation that any gentleman accustomed to society would employ. But what else could she expect, she thought irritably, when he had spent half his life in foreign climes? His manners were bound to be rough compared to the gentlemen of the *ton*.

'It is indeed,' he replied. 'Malcolm engaged a French

fellow a few years ago—I suspect he relishes the opportunity to practice his art.'

He sipped his wine, studying Harriet over the rim of his glass as she cast around for another safe subject of conversation—in other words, anything that did not involve their past.

'Do you enjoy the theatre?'

He grinned openly. 'Yes,' he said. 'Now, tell me, what happened to your father? I understand the Reverend Twining has been the pastor here for a number of years past.'

She'd known it was only a matter of time before he started questioning her. Her stomach knotted with guilt, as it always did whenever she thought of her father.

'He died six years ago.'

Oh, Papa! Parson Rowlands, deeply shocked by his only daughter's fall from grace, had barely spoken to Harriet during that dreadful time leading up to her marriage to Brierley. His disappointment in her would have broken her heart had it not already been in pieces after Benedict's rejection. Then, after her marriage, she'd had no opportunity to heal the breach with her father because Brierley had discouraged—most strongly and very effectively—any interaction between Harriet and her parents. The mere thought of her late husband and his despotic ways prompted a swell of nausea and she forced it back down. She pushed her plate away, her appetite gone.

How she regretted that she'd had no chance to reconcile with her father before his death. She gripped her hands tightly together under cover of the table, willing her voice to remain steady as she continued, 'After he died my mother moved to live with her sister in Whitstable.'

There was no security of tenure for the widow of a vicar. The rectory had been needed for the next incumbent. She risked a glance across the table. Benedict looked thoughtful, his green eyes locked onto her face.

'She does not live with you?'

'No.' After Brierley's death Harriet had rekindled her relationship with her mother, but Mrs Rowlands had declined to leave her ailing sister. 'My aunt Jane suffers from ill health. She benefits from the sea air and Mama felt her duty was to stay and care for her.'

'I am sorry to raise what is clearly a painful subject.'

'You were not to know.'

Silence reigned once again. Benedict continued to eat and Harriet fixed her gaze upon her half-eaten plate of congealing food. Her emotions were rubbed raw; everything...*everything*...was this man's fault. How she wished she could just leave the table and return to the privacy of her bedchamber. Good manners, however, dictated she must remain. She must distract herself somehow—her mind was as brittle as ice, ready to splinter into a thousand sharp accusations at the wrong look, the wrong word. She cast around for a topic of conversation.

'You mentioned yesterday that you intend to spend much of your time in London in the future,' she said. 'Is it your intention to take your place in society?'

She prayed the answer would be no. How could she bear it, knowing she might bump into him at any time? How could she endure the constant reminders of all that had happened?

'Yes, it is,' he said. Harriet's heart sank. 'I intend to restore the reputation of the Poole family name after Malcolm's depredations.'

'And how do you intend to do that?' Even to her own ears, the question sounded waspish.

Benedict's lips thinned and he frowned. Then he gestured at Harriet's plate. 'Have you had enough to eat? Might I pass you any fruit or sweetmeats?'

'No. I have had sufficient, thank you.'

Crabtree and the footman in attendance began to clear the dishes.

Benedict waited until they left the room, and then continued, 'To answer your question, I shall do it by example. I am conscious that my cousin made no provision for the future of the title and the estate but I shall not make that mistake. I will not allow the baronetcy to fail, nor do I relish the idea of the Poole estates reverting to the Crown to help fund the profligate lifestyle of Prinny.' He pushed his chair back, then rounded the table to draw her chair out to enable her to stand. 'I need an heir. I shall marry a respectable girl from a good family and have a family.'

His words stabbed at her heart. *An heir! How can he be so cruel?* How could he speak of having a child and not even show a flicker of interest in what had happened eleven years ago? Harriet tamped down her fury and distress as she rose, schooling her expression into one of polite disinterest before facing him.

'I wish you well in your endeavour.'

He stared at her for a long moment before speaking again. 'Perhaps you might help me in my search for a suitable wife?' He searched her face, his eyes intent. 'You must be acquainted with a number of young ladies.'

What does he want from me? Proof of the pain he caused? Tears? Harriet steeled herself to show nothing of what she felt.

With an effort, she raised her brows in a coquettish fashion. 'Perhaps you might furnish me with a list of your specific requirements, sir?'

His laugh sounded forced. 'Oh, I hardly think—'

'But I insist, sir! How else am I to help you?'

She was beyond taking pleasure at his look of discomfort. He had clearly not expected her to react in kind.

'Harriet—'

'Or perhaps you have not yet considered the precise qualities desirable in your wife, sir,' she rushed on. 'That is a mistake, I assure you. Allow me to help.'

She faced him, one arm crossed at her waist, her other elbow propped on it as she tapped one finger to her lips.

'Your bride… Now, let me see… You will require a girl of impeccable breeding. Her father should be no less than a viscount, I would suggest, in order to add to your consequence. She must have a substantial dowry, preferably of land, to increase your estates and wealth. What else?' She tipped her head to one side. 'She should be elegant, obedient, schooled in all the ladylike accomplishments. Oh! And, of course, it goes without saying she must be an *innocent*.'

Without intent, her voice had risen until she spat out the final word and Harriet silently cursed herself for rising to Benedict's bait.

Chapter Five

There was a beat of silence following Harriet's outburst.

'Harriet?' Benedict put his hand on her shoulder, curling gentle fingers around it. 'Why are you so upset?' He crouched slightly to gaze into her face and cradled her cheek with his other palm.

How fickle could one woman's body be? How treacherous? In the midst of her distress, she felt the undeniable melting of her muscles, the tug of need deep, deep inside and the yearning to lean into him and to feel his arms around her. To take his comfort.

She kept her gaze lowered. She could not bear to look at him, lest her weak-willed craving shone from her eyes. Harsh breaths dragged in and out of her lungs, searing her chest. What had she done? What would he think? Her mind whirled, looking for anything to excuse her behaviour.

'It was the memory of Papa. I must be overtired, to allow it to upset me so. I am sorry if I have embarrassed you. Goodnight, sir.'

Harriet jerked away from Benedict and swept from the room with her head averted, blinking rapidly to stem the tears that crowded her eyes. She climbed the stairs on legs that trembled with a need that both shocked and dismayed her.

'Harriet?'

She heard him call her, but she kept going. Then she heard the feet pounding up the stairs behind her. Coming closer, ever closer. Memories—dreadful, heart-wrenching memories—crowded her mind. Her heart beat a frantic tattoo and bile burned its way up her throat.

'No!' The breathy scream forced its way out of her lips as she scurried up the last few stairs, clutching at the banister for support. She reached the top. *Not safe. Not here.* Panic swarmed through her veins.

She stumbled across the landing and then spun round—panting in her distress—her back against the wall, well away from the wide open, threatening head of the stairs.

It's Benedict. You are safe. He would never attack you.

It was his fault. It wouldn't have happened if he had—

Harriet cut off that inner diatribe, but other random thoughts still hurtled around inside her head. She hauled in a deep breath, desperate to calm her terror, desperate to think straight. Benedict paused a few feet from her, his face flushed, his chest rising and falling.

'Harriet? Why did you run? What is it? What are you afraid of? Me?'

Harriet shook her head. She did not want his pity; she did not even want his guilt for what he had put her through. 'I am not afraid.'

'That is what you said last night, too, but your eyes tell a different story,' he growled as he stepped closer.

She flinched and he moved back, frowning. 'What kind of a man do you think I am? I might be my cousin's heir, but I have not inherited his tendencies, you may rest assured of that.'

Harriet swallowed, her pulse steadying. 'I know,' she whispered. 'I never thought you had. But…'

But it was complicated. She *was* afraid. Still. Oh, not in the way she had been afraid on the stairs, hearing those feet thundering up the stairs behind her. Chasing her. *That* had been blind panic. Her current dread, though… Words she could hardly bear to think, let alone speak, crowded into her mouth and she barricaded them behind clenched teeth and pursed lips.

What she feared, almost more, were the memories Benedict had awakened. She was afraid of her own body's treacherous clamour for his embrace. She was terrified of where her weakness might lead.

She wanted him. So much. Even after everything.

But she could never forgive him.

'But…?'

Harriet sucked in a deep, deep breath, noticing Benedict's hot green gaze dip to her décolletage as she did so. That brought her to her senses enough to say, 'But I believe the past should stay in the past. Last night… you would have…*we* would have…if I had…' She swallowed. 'I have no wish to revisit our childish indiscretions,' she said firmly. 'I shall bid you goodnight, Mr Poole, and I trust I shall have no need to rely upon your hospitality for much longer.'

She turned and walked away, another rush of tears blurring her vision. She did not allow herself to think. Like a wounded animal, she craved a dark corner and her instincts led her straight to her bedchamber, where she shut the door behind her. There was no key, no bolt.

Desperate, Harriet grasped hold of the heavy wooden chest set at the foot of the bed and tugged it, inch by inch, until it was set in front of the door. She cared not what the maid might think in the morning, when she came to light the fire. All she wanted was to feel safe but, as she collapsed onto the bed and allowed the hot flood of tears free rein, she acknowledged it was not Benedict she feared.

It was her own weakness that terrified her.

The next morning, Harriet woke late after a restless night. She arose and tugged on the bell rope to summon hot water before crossing to the window and twitching the curtain aside. The day was bright and clear and the snow that had clung tenaciously to the ground throughout the previous day might never have been.

The bedchamber was cosy, courtesy of the fire lit by a chambermaid earlier that morning. Harriet wondered what the kitchen gossips had made of the fact that the maid had to knock on the door and rouse Harriet before she could gain admittance. Together they had dragged the chest back to the foot of the bed, Harriet excusing her odd behaviour by saying she was scared of ghosts. The maid's sceptical look had seemed to say, 'But everyone knows ghosts can travel through doors and walls. A barricaded door is no protection.'

A tap at the door revealed a different maid carrying a pitcher from which steam spiralled.

'I've been sent to help you dress, milady, if you are ready now,' the girl said. She told Harriet her name was Annie. 'Breakfast is set up in the morning room for you.'

'Thank you,' Harriet said, turning to the washstand to wash whilst the maid pulled back the covers to air

the bed and then waited until Harriet was ready to don
her dove-grey carriage dress. 'Is Mr Poole… Has Mr
Poole breakfasted yet?'

Please say yes. She could not face him after last
night. When he had followed her up the stairs, the sound
of his footsteps behind her had brought the terror and
the anguish flooding back. What must he think of her?
Had she managed to misdirect him with her talk of the
past and their childish indiscretions?

And earlier, in the dining room—dear heavens, *how*
she had been tempted, once again, to lose herself in his
embrace, even after her loss of control over his provocation. How she had yearned for him, her body melting
with desire. And that, she had thought, as she'd tossed
and turned in her bed last night, her mind whizzing, was
a near miracle considering how she had grown to abhor
the marital act—she would not dignify it by thinking
of it as making love—with Brierley. As recently as one
year ago, her body might not have responded so readily to Benedict. But then she had set out to erase the
memory of Brierley and his vile ways from her mind
and her heart and…yes…her body. And she had succeeded, when she had, after great consideration and
much soul-searching, taken a lover. And, with his help,
she had overcome her fear.

'Oh, yes, milady. Mr Poole is ever an early riser.
Comes from living in foreign parts, Mr Crab—' The
maid stopped, her hand to her mouth, eyes rounded.
'Beg pardon, milady, if I'm speaking out of turn. My
mum always said I never know when to stop.'

Harriet laughed at the girl, relieved to learn she
would not meet Benedict at the breakfast table. 'That
is quite all right, Annie. Now will you show me to the
morning room, please?'

She had taken breakfast on a tray in her bedchamber yesterday and the house was so vast she had no confidence in finding her way on her own. Before they reached the morning room she had discovered that Mr Poole was once again perusing the estate ledgers with Sir Malcolm's agent in the study.

The morning room was a beautiful sunny room with a view to the east, over lawns that curved away, down into a valley that Harriet remembered from her childhood. In her mind's eye she saw happy, carefree days when the sun seemed to be forever shining and adults and their complicated world and rules barely existed, other than to provide food and shelter. Memories were strange things, she mused. From her adult perspective, she knew her childhood had also consisted of lessons and church, duty and chores, but those untroubled sunny days playing with her friends—and with Benedict— eclipsed all else. She pictured the shallow stream that gurgled along its stony bed at the bottom of the slope, with the choice of a wooden footbridge or stepping stones to cross it. As children, of course, they had always chosen to cross via the stepping stones, jostling and daring each other and, inevitably, someone had ended up with wet feet.

The opposite slope of the valley was wooded and stretched up in a gentle curve until, just beyond the far edge of the wood, a grassy hillock, bare of trees, jutted skywards. At the top of the hillock was the folly, modelled upon a ruined medieval castle complete with tower. Harriet's stomach knotted. Here were memories she had no wish to dwell upon.

She finished her breakfast of toast and coffee and then went upstairs to visit Janet, to see how she fared. Janet was sleepy but out of pain; the housekeeper, Mrs

Charing, had been dosing her with syrup of poppies in accordance with the doctor's instructions.

After sitting with her maid awhile, Harriet decided to leave her to sleep. She would go for a walk, to blow some of the cobwebs from her brain. She wrapped up well in her travelling cloak, pulling the fur-lined hood over her head. It was a beautifully bright day, but there was still a cold easterly wind. Harriet strode out briskly enough to keep herself warm.

Almost without volition, her steps took her along the path to the valley where she had played as a child. The path down the slope was wet and rather slippery, but she negotiated it without mishap, right down into the valley and to the stream, which she crossed, by the bridge this time, as befitted a grown woman. She smiled at the thought of presenting herself back at Tenterfield Court with her half boots waterlogged.

She followed the course of the stream a short distance and then struck off up the lightly wooded far slope of the valley, driven by the urge to see if the folly had changed. Just to look at it from outside, she assured herself, as the slope steepened and her breath shortened.

At the top, she paused to rest, gazing up at the stone walls of the folly tower as they reared into the clear blue sky. The curved walls were broken by a single Gothic-style arched window on each floor. The door—solid oak, massive, punctuated by wrought iron studs—was closed. She wondered if it was now kept locked. It hadn't been, back when she was young. Such memories. On the brink of walking on, she hesitated.

It was a foolish whim; one Harriet regretted the moment she entered the folly and realised she was not alone.

Chapter Six

Harriet could feel Benedict's gaze boring into her as she paused on the threshold, giving her eyes time to adjust to the gloom inside the tower.

'This is the last place I expected to see you.'

Benedict spoke the words, but they could as easily have been spoken by her. The memories evoked by this place swirled around her, almost a physical presence. Did he feel them, too? Was his mind also bursting with images from the past? This had been their trysting place: the place where they could be alone, out of sight of prying eyes or wagging tongues to cry scandal.

Silly, trusting girl—thinking she was in control of her life when, in reality, all control lay with others. See where her trust had led her—to marriage with a man who disgusted her, and to unimaginable heartbreak as a consequence of his temper. She had vowed, after Brierley's death, that she would never pass control over her life to another man.

'I am not one to sit in idleness. I felt in need of fresh air and exercise, after being cooped up indoors yesterday.' Harriet strolled with as much nonchalance as she could muster into the centre of the room. 'And why should I not visit here? It was on my walk and I was curious to see if there were any changes.'

He moved too, giving Harriet a wide berth as he crossed to gaze out of the window. 'For a medieval castle, it is in remarkably good repair,' he said, his tone light and unconcerned. 'But, then, it *is* only several decades old rather than several centuries.'

It had been a source of wonder and imagination when they were children and, with Sir Malcolm so rarely at home, they had played at knights and maidens and dragons and swordfights with other local children. Gradually, though, the other village children visited less and less frequently as the reality of their lives—the need to supplement their parents' income by working—had intruded. But Benedict and Harriet had continued to meet here. And their play had, in time, taken a serious turn.

Her head had been full of love; his, full of lust. It was the way of men. She knew that now.

'I am pleased Sir Malcolm has maintained the estate, despite his…' She hesitated. It was not her place to criticise his kinsman.

'Despite his notorious ways? I have scant respect for Malcolm, as you know, but he was no spendthrift. His proclivities veered more towards the flesh than gambling.'

Harriet suppressed her shudder. Her late husband had been cast from the same mould.

'As you are here, it would be a waste not to go upstairs and admire the view.' Benedict stood aside, indicating the studded door that led to the spiral stairs. The tower was cylindrical, built over four floors, and the view from the top, she remembered, was spectacular.

She said nothing, merely inclined her head, and walked past him to the door. It opened easily. Whoever cared for the estate must take their work seriously, to include greasing the hinges to a door in a folly that served no purpose. She paused.

'I understood you to be in a meeting with Sir Malcolm's agent,' she said.

He huffed a laugh. 'And so you thought yourself safe from encountering me on your walk? I regret disappointing you, my lady, but I, too, felt in dire need of a good dose of cleansing fresh air. Do you need any assistance on the stairs?'

'Thank you, no.'

Harriet lifted her skirts high and climbed the stone stairs to the top floor. Here there were wooden benches, but she resisted the urge to sit and catch her breath. She would continue up to the battlements, admire the view over the Kent countryside and then be on her way.

Being here at the folly brought all those memories flooding back to Harriet. Knowing he still wielded that kind of power over her emotions and her body—despite the best efforts of her brain to stay in control—had kept her awake half the night. She had been oh-so-tempted by him. His lovemaking in their youth had been unpractised, as had hers. Now he, like she, would possess a certain skill. She wondered again how it might feel to lie with him, but did not dwell on the thought. It would surely bring regret. He had blood on his hands. Innocent blood. No matter how she might desire him, she could never forgive him.

She gazed across the landscape, dazzling in the sunlight—seeing it, but barely paying it the attention it deserved, all her senses straining for an awareness of Benedict's whereabouts. After several tense minutes she heard the door that led onto the roof open. She had no need to look to know that Benedict had followed her: the rising hairs on her nape confirmed his presence, and the gooseflesh that skittered across her arms wasn't purely caused by the chill wind. She sensed the gap between them narrowing, until she could hear the quiet sound of his breathing and she could feel the heat of his body warming the air between them and she could smell… *him*. Still familiar, after all this time.

She swallowed. A maelstrom of emotions buffeted her this way and that but she strove to stay calm, to stay in control.

'It is as beautiful as I remember,' she said. 'I count it as fortunate the weather is so good today—it has afforded me the opportunity to see the wonder of the countryside again.' She hugged her cloak around her as a gust of wind attempted to tear it open.

'It is a spectacular sight,' Benedict said, his deep voice close by her ear, raising another shiver. 'But it is very cold up here. Come, you must not catch a chill, or you will be forced to endure even more of my company.'

She could hear the effort he put into that light-hearted remark. His tone did not quite ring true and it forced her—for the first time—to consider how her presence was affecting him. Did he feel guilt over his betrayal? Was there a pang of conscience over the death of the baby, born too soon, who'd never had the chance to draw breath? Was there *any* regret—a tiny speck, even if it was well buried? He had not even mentioned the child, seemed uninterested in whether it was alive or dead. Had he wiped his memory clear of the fact she had ever been with child?

Would that she could so easily forget. Her empty arms still ached, as did her heart, at the knowledge that she would never now experience the joy of motherhood, for never again would she risk marrying and placing such power over herself and her body in any man's hands. And she resented—deeply—the fact that Benedict not only felt no guilt and had experienced none of her grief, but also that he was now poised to become a wealthy powerful man—and marry and have a family— whereas she…she was destined to remain loveless and childless for the rest of her days.

She swung away from the view and sidestepped around Benedict to head for the door but, as on the previous evening, he was there before her.

'Allow me to go first,' he said. 'In case you miss your step.'

At Benedict's words, an image rose to tempt her: that of her stumbling…of him catching her in his arms…of him lifting her chin and lowering his head. Her heart pounded and her breathing quickened as she took especial care in descending the spiral stairs, clutching with gloved fingers at the thick rope that looped from bracket to bracket all the way down. Back on the ground floor without incident, her breathing eased and her racing heart steadied as she straightened her cloak in readiness for the walk back to the house.

'Harriet…'

Her name hung in the air.

Slowly, she raised her eyes to his. She could not read his expression in the dim light that filtered through the window, but she did see the muscle leap in his jaw. The air between them crackled with intensity and her pulse responded with a lurch and a gallop. All moisture seemed to have been sucked from her mouth, and she licked at her dry lips as he moved closer. His gaze fastened on her mouth, sending desire sizzling through her. Pure instinct tilted her head, lifting her lips to his.

Aah. The most delicate of touches. Lip to lip…

sweet, gentle, almost worshipping. Memories of love and laughter and pure joy. They had been so young. A shared future planned. They had followed the instinctive desires of their youthful bodies. She had felt so secure in his love for her. Before…

Harriet switched her thoughts away from the past and into the present. A kiss. Why should they not? It was just a kiss.

She leaned into him, raising her hands to his shoulders, broad and strong. A man's body, reminding her he was no longer a youth. A silent sigh for what might have been echoed through her, and tears sprang to her eyes.

He deepened the kiss, his arms coming around her, moulding her to him as his tongue swept into her mouth and tangled with hers. His groan vibrated through her core and she could feel the steady thump of his heart as he tightened his hold, raising her onto her toes. His arousal pressed against her, and anticipation tugged deep inside her. Her own heart thudded in tandem with his as she explored his shoulders and back. She stroked his neck and threaded her fingers through his hair, knocking his hat to the floor. The thought surfaced that her gloves must go but, before she could act on that thought, he changed, urgency taking control.

Her toes barely scraped the floor as he lifted her higher, and backed her against the wall. She couldn't breathe. Panic mushroomed out of the past, bringing it all back—the pain, the disgust—and she swung her head in denial, wrenching her lips from his, grabbing his hair to jerk his head away. He grunted a protest, seized her wrists and raised her arms, stretching them up, above her head, trapping her between his body and the wall, and tasted her again, invading her with his tongue.

She could not move. She was trapped. A scream built inside. She had learned to submit, but this was not Brierley. He was gone.

Harriet twisted her head to one side. 'No!' She panted with the effort not to scream. 'No!' Louder. More forceful.

Benedict stilled. Raised his head to look at her with dazed eyes. 'What…?'

'Let go of me.'

He released her. Stepped back. Frowned. 'Why?'

Harriet stared at the blurry floor. Wiped her mouth with a shaking hand. 'I cannot. I am—'

'Don't say you're sorry,' he said in a savage voice. 'I don't want to hear your excuses.'

He swung away and slammed through the door, crashing it shut behind him, leaving Harriet alone, trembling with the memories that she had tried so hard to put behind her.

Benedict strode down the hill, away from the tower, his blood pounding with fury and unquenched desire. How weak-willed could a man be? After her rejection— *twice*—still he had left himself wide open for another blow. His brisk pace did little to assuage the urge to lash out and, as he entered the Home Wood, on the path that led back to the house, he snatched a fallen branch from the ground to slash at last season's dried-up undergrowth as he passed.

His instinct was to leave. Return to London. Bury himself in his work and his plans for the future or jump on the nearest ship and seek out new adventures. Anything rather than stay here and suffer any more of her games, leading a man on and then freezing him out.

The house came into view. He slammed to a halt.
Considered. Then changed direction.

He strode into the barn, then slowed so as not to
spook the horses in the stalls. Heads turned enquiringly to watch his progress along the passageway, and
he breathed in the familiar, calming smell of horses,
leather and hay, pausing to pat one or two gleaming
rumps as he passed.

A groom's head popped out from the end stall.
'Morning, sir,' he called. 'Was you going out?'

'Yes.' The question spurred him into a decision.
'Saddle the bay, will you, Tom?'

A long, fast ride would do him the power of good.
It would douse both his temper and his lust and, hopefully, blast away the confusion that had beset him ever
since Harriet had reappeared in his life. He swept his
hand through his hair, realising he had lost his hat somewhere. No matter—his appearance would make no difference where he was going.

It was dark before Benedict returned to Tenterfield
Court, weary and slightly foxed after an afternoon spent
in the Crossways Inn in the village. He left his horse
at the stables and walked towards the house, conscious
that his steps were beginning to lag. He entered through
a side door and met Cooper, the footman, in the passage. He must ask. He had no wish to bump into her
unprepared.

'Where is she?' *Hellfire!* That didn't come out as he
intended. 'Lady Brierley,' he added. 'I'm late. Has she
eaten?' It was past the customary time for dinner in the
country. With any luck she had already gone upstairs,
as keen as him to avoid another encounter.

Cooper frowned. 'She's gone, sir. Lord Brierley came and took her off in his carriage.'

Benedict felt himself sway. *Must've drunk more than I realised.* He inched closer to the wall and propped his shoulders against it.

'When?'

'Soon after her ladyship came back from her walk, sir. His lordship was already here. He'd had her bags packed all ready, and been up to see Sir Malcolm and then, when her ladyship arrived, he dragged her off to his carriage.'

Dragged? The image unsettled him, but it also raised a hope he didn't want to feel. 'Lady Brierley didn't want to leave?'

'No, sir. First she said she wouldn't leave without her maid...'

Ah, of course. Her maid. Janet. She was the cause of Harriet's reluctance. Stupid to imagine it could be anything else. Benedict shook his head, trying to clear it and order his thoughts.

'And then,' Cooper continued, clearly relishing being the one to tell him the story, 'his lordship said Janet must go, too, and the doctor was here and *he* said as how she shouldn't really be moved, and his *lordship* said he wouldn't leave her here in this den of...den of...*something*...'

Iniquity, Benedict thought, his head reeling as his temples began to throb.

'...so we had to carry Janet downstairs and prop up her leg on cushions and all the while his lordship was looking like thunder—'

'Had he come to visit Sir Malcolm?'

'No, sir, but he did go up and pay his respects. He

said something about a letter, sir, and *more* scandal, sir. Just like that. *More* scandal!' Cooper paused for breath.

'And her ladyship was happy to go?'

'Well, yes and no, I should say, sir.'

Benedict bit down the urge to bark, *Get on with it, man.* 'I'm waiting, Cooper.'

'Well, she seemed happy enough to go, but she wanted to go back to London, she said. Only his lordship wouldn't budge, even when her ladyship pleaded with him. He said as how she was to come home with him and explain herself properly if she knew what was good for her.'

What was good for her? She's his stepmother, for God's sake. What the blazes did he mean by that?

'And then he said as how he would stop her allowance if she didn't do what he said.'

'And so she went with him?'

'Yes, sir. But she wasn't happy.'

Benedict told himself it was for the best. He told himself it was a relief, but then why did his throat ache and why had his stomach twisted into knots?

'Thank you, Cooper. That will be all.'

Benedict levered himself away from the wall and headed towards the back stairs on decidedly unsteady legs.

'Please inform Sir Malcolm I am unwell and unable to pay him my usual visit. I am going to bed.' He flung the words over his shoulder at the footman.

'Her ladyship found your hat, sir.' Cooper's words floated up the back stairs after Benedict. 'Mr Crabtree brushed it and put it away.'

His hat! A vague memory surfaced of Harriet dislodging it during that kiss. Benedict stumbled as he reached the top of the stairs and turned in the direction of his bedchamber. He cursed under his breath, praying he would not meet any other servants in his current state.

Never again would he touch the ale at the Crossways. It was clearly tainted.

Chapter Seven

Edward's carriage bowled through the elaborately crafted wrought iron gates that marked the entrance to Brierley Place, and Harriet gazed from the window as the familiar manor house with its mullioned windows and ornate chimneys came into view. It had been her home for more than seven years, but she had left it with no regret when Brierley had died three years ago, and Edward, as the fourth Earl of Brierley, had moved his family in.

The journey—slow in deference to Janet's injuries—had been interminable, the silence heavy with Edward's unspoken fury, punctuated only by the occasional moan of pain that escaped Janet despite the clear effort she made to be quiet, biting at her lip and squeezing her eyes shut. Edward had spent the entire journey glowering at Harriet, arms folded across his barrel-like torso. Clearly he could not wait to rip into her, but Harriet knew he would never do so in front of a servant.

Physically, he was just like his father—no more than medium height, light brown hair, inclined to stoutness—but in his character he was the complete opposite. His chief concern, as ever, was for appearances, and he took himself and his duties with the utmost seriousness since inheriting the earldom. He sat as magistrate in the petty sessions whenever required, and he prided himself on his firm but fair judgement; he attended the House of Lords on a regular basis and spoke—according to the newspaper reports that Harriet had read—with authority and gravity on important matters of state; and he expected his family, including his late father's widow, to behave with the utmost propriety at all times.

If only, Harriet had often thought to herself, *he knew what his father was truly like.* Or perhaps he did know—at least some of it—and, like many men, he believed that what went on between husband and wife was nobody's business but their own.

The lack of conversation had given Harriet time to think…time to remember…time to relive. *That kiss!* Shivers rippled down her spine and spread beneath her skin. It was surely the shock of seeing Benedict in such familiar surroundings that had provoked her into behaving so out of character. She determined to put her entire visit to Tenterfield behind her—going there had been a colossal lack of judgement on her part and she could not wait to return to her familiar, humdrum life. Benedict's intention to take his place in society had been a shock, but it should be easy enough to avoid him—he had been overseas for years and they would be unlikely to have friends in common. And once he married and had a family, the dangerous attraction he had awakened within her would be banished.

But first… She sneaked a peek at Edward, sitting opposite her. He caught her look and scowled. Harriet swallowed. First she must placate Edward.

After Benedict had stormed away from the folly,

Harriet had retrieved his hat from the floor and carried it back to the house, where she was swept up in the whirlwind that was her stepson. He refused to listen to reason. Janet couldn't be moved? Nonsense. If she was able to sit up in bed, she could sit in a carriage for a couple of hours with her leg propped up and well padded. He would instruct the coachman to keep the horses at a walk. Harriet wished to return to London? Certainly. He would put his carriage at her disposal. *After* he had spoken to her about her behaviour, as was his duty as head of the family. And he would do that at Brierley Place. Not in this—Edward had looked around, his top lip curled—not in this den of iniquity.

A footman hurried from Brierley Place, ready to lower the steps of the carriage after it drew to a halt outside the front door.

'Lady Brierley's maid has a broken ankle,' Edward said as he clambered from the carriage. 'Find someone to help you carry her upstairs, will you?'

The footman hurried back to the house, and Edward turned to hand Harriet from the carriage. 'I will see you in my study, madam.' He released her hand as soon as she reached the ground and stomped into the house, leaving Harriet to follow in his wake.

Smithson, the butler, was in the hall, giving orders to more footmen about Janet and the luggage.

'Good afternoon, my lady.' Smithson bowed. He directed a passing maid to take Harriet's cloak, hat and gloves. 'Would you care for tea? Her ladyship is in the drawing room with Lady Katherine. They have asked you to join them on your arrival.'

Thank goodness Fanny and the children were as welcoming as ever, despite Edward's strong but unexplained discouragement of her visits to Brierley since his father's death. Harriet had become used to his frostiness and had merely avoided him as much as possible— she had her own life to lead—but this fury and disdain was something new.

'Thank you, Smithson, but his lordship has asked that I attend him in his study.'

'I will inform her ladyship, my lady. If you would care to follow me?'

For all the world as if I did not know the whereabouts of Brierley's study, Harriet thought, biting back her smile as she followed the butler. Edward insisted on the correct procedure being followed at all times. She was a guest; therefore Smithson must announce her.

'Lady Brierley, my lord.'

Smithson stood aside and Harriet walked past him into Edward's study with a smile of thanks before focusing on Edward, standing before the window, hands behind his back. He maintained his silence until the door closed behind Smithson.

'What the *blazes* were you doing at Tenterfield Court?'

She stared at him a moment. 'May I sit?' Her tone was icy. It did not hurt to remind him that she was a lady and his stepmother and that he was, supposedly, a gentleman.

'Of course.'

Edward tilted his chin to indicate the visitor's chair set in front of his vast mahogany desk and then rounded the desk to stand on the opposite side. Harriet sat with a twinge of disquiet, tucking her feet under the chair and loosely clasping her hands in her lap.

Very formal. I feel like a child about to be scolded.

Edward sat down, then frowned at her, his fingers drumming on the desk. 'Well?'

Harriet blinked, taken aback by the contempt conveyed by that one word. 'Why, I wished to make some enquiries on behalf...' She faltered as his expression blackened. She gripped her hands together and drew a steadying breath. 'On behalf of a friend of mine.'

'A likely tale, madam.'

Harriet stiffened. 'I can assure you I am speaking the truth,' she said with as much calm as she could muster. 'Why would you think otherwise?'

'You stayed for two days and nights. With no chaperone.'

'I had no choice. Janet slipped as we were leaving, and she was unable to travel.'

Edward surged to his feet and leaned towards her, fists propped on the desk, eyes boring into hers. 'But you, madam, were uninjured. *You* were fit enough to travel, were you not?'

'I could hardly stay at a public inn without even my maid to accompany me.'

'You could have come *here*.'

'Of course I could. After all, you have never left me in any doubt about my welcome here, have you, Edward?' She had never been able to bring herself to call him Brierley.

Edward's gaze flickered.

'Besides,' Harriet continued, 'there was a snowstorm. It was not safe to travel. Or am I to understand you would prefer the thought of me trapped overnight in a snowdrift to spending time unchaperoned at Tenterfield Court?'

'If you had heeded my advice the last time we met, you would not have been without a chaperone.'

Edward's bluster had started to fade, as it so often did in the face of calm, considered responses.

'And which advice might that be, Edward?' Harriet smiled sweetly at him.

'To accept my aunt Smallwood as your live-in companion.'

'But I have explained before, Edward, that I do not wish to have a live-in companion.'

'You do not care for your reputation?'

'I did not say that, Edward. Of course I care for my reputation. I would never do—'

'And yet you travel to a place like Tenterfield and remain *two nights*, with no other lady present and…and…'

Edward's chest swelled and Harriet eyed his straining waistcoat buttons with concern. He spun round and stalked over to the window.

'Have you so little pride? Was one rejection not enough?' he ground out, his back to Harriet.

She felt a dropping, curling sensation in her stomach. 'I do not know what you mean. Of whom do you speak?'

He whirled to face her. 'Poole! Of whom do you think I speak? Or have there been others? By God, madam, you are not fit to be a member of this family.'

Sick dread welled up to clog Harriet's throat. Only Sir Malcolm, her late husband and her papa had known. No one else. He could not possibly be talking of Benedict.

'S-Sir Malcolm is gravely—'

'Do me the honour of speaking the truth, now you have been found out. Did you think me unaware of your sordid secret? You may think yourself fortunate I have maintained your lies since my father's death.'

At last, the mystery of why Edward had changed towards her after his father died. Up to that point, he had always been respectful but, since then, he barely seemed to tolerate her, treating her much as an inconvenient liability.

'Fortunate, you say, when you have treated me with nothing but disdain since I was widowed? Why have you maintained those lies, if you have such a disgust of me?'

He cast her a look of contempt. 'I will not risk speculation over a family rift to bring your disgrace to public attention. I will not allow your lax morals to cast a stain upon my family name.'

Hysteria bubbled up and Harriet swallowed it down. He had the temerity to accuse *her* of lax morals? When his father… Anger bit at her insides at the injustice of life. What had she ever done but believe the honeyed lies of Benedict Poole when she'd been barely out of childhood?

'How do you know?'

He sat again behind his desk. His eyes narrowed. 'My father's affairs are now mine to deal with. Surely you realised that?'

'He swore… He would not have kept any papers… There *were* no papers…'

'And yet I do know. How do you imagine I felt, to learn that my own father was deceived into raising another man's bast—?'

'He was *not* deceived! He knew I was… He knew everything. That is the reason I had to marry him! Did you think I—?'

Her words ended on a sob. No matter the truth of her married life, she could not bring herself to tarnish Edward's memory of his father with the reality of the man who had been a monster behind closed doors. Despite his pomposity, she knew he was a good husband to Fanny and a kind, if strict, father to his children. Besides, how could she ever discuss such shameful, intimate matters with *anyone*?

Brierley's voice sounded again in her head. *Now look what you made me do. Go and clean yourself up, you disgusting little whore.* Had it been her fault? Had she, somehow, been responsible for his violence, as he had claimed? *It's your own fault. You asked for it.*

Desperately, she tried to bury those memories and to silence his hated voice. She had sworn never to think of him again. It was Benedict's fault—coming back, bringing all those memories to life again. Her hands were shaking, and again she gripped them together as she forced herself to meet Edward's scathing look.

'At least you lost the baby,' he said, as though he were discussing a matter of no more importance than the loss of a handkerchief. 'That makes it—'

Harriet leaped to her feet and glared at her stepson. 'Don't you *dare* say such a thing!' Edward's words, on top of her already fragile state, were too much. 'How would *you* feel if Fanny had lost Kitty? Or James? Or even little Sophie?'

Edward's jerk of surprise was swiftly controlled. He sat back, his expression impassive. 'That is entirely different. They were conceived and born in wedlock. You, madam, are a disgrace.'

Shocked as much by her own behaviour as by Edward's words, Harriet sank back onto her seat. She must not push Edward too far. Although their relationship teetered ever precariously on the verge of estrangement, she loved Fanny and the children and she would be heartbroken if Edward were to ban her from seeing them. As for Edward's warning at Tenterfield that he would stop her allowance... Surely that must be an empty threat? He had not repeated it, and she was sure he did not have the power to do so. If he did... She concealed her shudder. Her widow's jointure was all she had to survive on. If she lost that, she would lose that which she held most dear—her independence. She would have no choice but to remarry.

Harriet studied her stepson, sitting stolidly in the chair opposite. How a man such as Brierley had spawned such a pompously superior son she could not fathom. It could only, surely, have been the influence of Edward's mother—Brierley had constantly held his first wife up to Harriet as a model of rectitude, an example of a perfect wife. It seemed that Harriet had somehow brought out his basest nature.

Edward shifted in his chair and, when he spoke, his tone was calmer. 'Do you still hanker after that rogue? Is that the truth?'

Harriet swallowed her pain at his words. She had not thought so. And yet...

'I did not know Benedict was at Tenterfield,' she said. 'I did not even know he was in the country. I would never have gone there had I known. I told you, I went on behalf of a friend, to talk to Sir Malcolm.'

A muscle leaped in Edward's jaw, his brows still drawn low. 'Hmph. The deed is done now. We must hope news of your visit alone to that place does not become public knowledge.'

'I was not alone. I had my maid with me.'

'Your maid! You know as well as I that—'

'How did you know I was there?' Harriet interrupted. 'Was it just a coincidence that you came to Tenterfield today?'

'Lady Marstone had it from the doctor,' Edward said, his shoulders slumping. 'She could not wait to tell me when I saw her in Sittingbourne this morning. I believe

I convinced her it would not be in her best interests to spread such gossip around, but I am not certain.'

'Lady Marstone? Oh, no.' Sir Walter Marstone's wife was the worst tattletale in the district, and one of the worst in London, too. 'How on earth did you manage to convince her?'

'Her daughter, Bridget, is about to embark upon her second Season and she is quite desperate to get her married off. I hinted that their invitation to Kitty's come-out ball was in the balance, and that I *might* use my influence to persuade Lady Castlereagh to blacklist Bridget from Almack's.'

Lady Castlereagh was one of the powerful patronesses of Almack's, and it was well known that Edward was a political ally of Lord Castlereagh, whose return to government was rumoured to be imminent, three years after his resignation as secretary of state for war and the colonies, following the disgrace of his duel with foreign secretary George Canning. Harriet smiled at the chagrin Lady Marstone must have felt.

'That was quick thinking, Edward. Thank you.'

'Do not think that absolves you, madam, for it does not. I did that solely to protect my family name. But you…you do not appear to believe you have done anything wrong. Are you truly so lost to all propriety? Did you even stop to consider that Kitty is due to make her come-out this spring? I expect her to make a very good match. Do you not care if you sully her reputation with your scandals?'

'That is unfair. I have created no scandals—'

'What about that house in Cheapside? Oh, yes, madam, do not think I am unaware of your involvement with such women. I tell you now, if you wish to continue to be part of this family I suggest you look to your behaviour and ensure no further whisper of impropriety, past or present, reaches my ears.'

Harriet studied his resolute expression and her heart sank all the way to her toes. She set herself to placate him.

'Of course I wish to remain a part of this family, Edward. You know how much I love Fanny and the children. And as for the house in Cheapside… They are young girls—servants who have been despoiled by their masters and then cast out without a penny. Do you condone such behaviour by those men?'

'Of course not. A gentleman has a moral duty of care towards his inferiors,' Edward said, pompous as ever. 'But that does not make your involvement acceptable. I understand you appeal for donations from amongst your friends—'

'*And* from the *gentlemen* responsible,' Harriet said, her passion rising. 'I write to them to give them an opportunity to contribute, and most do eventually pay up, for fear of the slur on their reputations. You surely agree that a gentleman should take responsibility for his actions by supporting his by-blows—' she ignored Edward's wince at her use of the term '—but I am afraid some do not see it that way initially. They cast these girls, and their babies, aside as though they are less than human. With the money I raise, I offer those girls a roof over their heads and the opportunity to learn a new skill.'

She had set up a sewing room and a small bakery in the house, where the girls who chose not to have their babies fostered out could work together whilst caring for them. It was a cause very dear to Harriet's heart after her own experiences, and also since her late husband had violated two such girls—the youngest barely thirteen years of age—who worked in their household and thus had no choice but to succumb to their master's demands. He'd cast them out without a qualm, and Harriet had been helpless to either stop him or to help those two girls.

'No wonder you are so keen to help these young girls after your own lapse from grace,' Edward said. 'At least you had my father to rescue you.'

'*Rescue* me?' Harriet leaped to her feet. She took a hasty turn about the room, dragging in deep breaths in an attempt to calm herself. She returned to the desk and propped her weight on her fists as she leant across it. 'If you *knew*—'

She was interrupted by a knock.

'Hush!' Edward's eyes flashed a warning as the door opened behind Harriet. She straightened.

'Grandmama!' There was the sound of rushing feet, and Harriet turned to find herself wrapped in a tight embrace. 'Smithson said you had come. I didn't believe him.'

Harriet hugged her step-granddaughter hard before holding her away and looking her up and down. It never failed to amuse her to hear this lovely young woman, just ten years her junior, call her *Grandmama*.

'Well,' she said, smiling at Kitty, now fully as tall as Harriet. 'What have we here, Edward? She has every appearance of a young lady, but that behaviour... Was that not more reminiscent of an impulsive child?'

Both she and Edward had become adept at concealing their differences from the rest of his family.

'Oh, phooey!' Kitty's pale cheeks took on a rosy hue.

'Katherine!' Fanny, Lady Brierley, had come into the study in time to hear her daughter's exclamation. '*Such* a vulgar expression.'

Even as Fanny chastised her daughter Harriet could see the twinkle in her eyes. Harriet embraced Fanny with genuine pleasure.

'It is lovely to see you, my dear,' Harriet said. 'It was *such* a pleasant surprise when Edward arrived and *insisted* on escorting me here for a visit.' Harriet shot a mischievous glance at her stepson, knowing he would not retaliate in front of Fanny and Kitty. 'My maid and I were caught in a snowstorm, you know, and poor Janet slipped and broke her ankle. I do hope she may stay here to recuperate? I fear she is not strong enough to attempt the journey back to London.'

'Of course she must stay,' Fanny cried. 'And you, too, Harriet. We do not see nearly enough of you. We go up to London ourselves next week, to prepare for Kitty's come-out. You can travel back with us.'

The thought of spending time with Fanny and the children was too good to resist, even though she knew Edward would disapprove.

'Thank you, Fanny. That would be perfect.' Harriet closed her eyes to Edward's black scowl.

Chapter Eight

Mid-April 1812

Sir Benedict Poole rested his head against the cushioned backrest of his carriage. He stretched his legs, propping his booted feet on the seat opposite, crossed his arms over his chest and closed his eyes—it would be close to five hours before he reached London. The minute his eyes were shut, however, his thoughts turned inexorably to Harriet and that kiss. Two months ago now... Two long, frustrating months in which he had striven to banish her from his mind, an endeavour that seemed doomed to failure.

Damn her, damn her and damn her thrice!

Since Sir Malcolm's death seven weeks ago Benedict had remained at Tenterfield Court, occupied in dealing with both the legalities and the practicalities of inheriting not only the baronetcy but a wealth he was still scrambling to comprehend. But through all those weeks, like an insistent drumbeat that only he could hear, Harriet called to him.

Now, the closer they got to London, the louder her allure rang out—*Harr-i-et, Harr-i-et, Harr-i-et*—

marking time with the rumble of the coach wheels and horses' hoof beats. She was an itch he could not scratch. He did not want her in his head, and he did not want this battle whenever she stole into his thoughts—the battle between his distrust and his urge to understand. And, underlying it all, his greatest fear—the knowledge that, despite everything, he *still* wanted her.

He wanted to return to normality…whatever that might be. He suspected his life would never be the same again.

The carriage drew up outside the Poole residence in Grosvenor Street just after midday. Benedict stirred, stretched and leaped to the pavement, gazing up with a sense of wonder: this magnificent house now belonged to him. He was proud of the business he had built up with his partner, Matthew Damerel, since he had left England to seek his fortune abroad, but he could never have aspired to wealth and position such as this.

The door was opened from within by a solemn-faced butler with a black armband on his sleeve.

'Good afternoon, Sir Benedict,' he said, bowing. 'Welcome home. I am Reeves.'

'Good afternoon, Reeves, and thank you.'

Following a tour of the house—which was every bit as impressive as he remembered from the few times he had visited in his youth—Benedict settled in his library to read the letters that were piled on his desk. Recognising the bold writing on one sheet, he broke the seal and began to read. It was from Matthew, his business partner, announcing his arrival in town and asking Benedict to call upon him as soon as he arrived.

Benedict leaped to his feet, eager to see both his old friend and Matthew's wife, Eleanor, Lady Ashby, again.

A good dose of business talk was just what he needed to distract him from the fact that Harriet lived a mere few streets away.

'Good afternoon, Sir Benedict.' Matthew and Eleanor's butler stood aside to allow Benedict to enter the hall of their newly leased house in Cavendish Square.

'Good afternoon, Pacey. Is Mr Damerel at home?'

'I shall go and enquire, sir.'

Minutes later, Pacey showed Benedict into the library. Matthew, blue eyes bright with pleasure, strode forward to clasp Benedict's outstretched hand.

'Well, well,' he said, laughing. '*Sir* Benedict. Must I bow to you now? Pacey, brandy, if you please—we must celebrate!'

Benedict grinned and allowed Matthew to usher him to a wing chair by the fire whilst he sat opposite.

Several toasts later, Matthew leaned forward, suddenly serious, his piercing gaze direct. 'I have a proposal to put to you, Ben.'

Benedict sat up, his attention caught. 'Go on.'

'With our new responsibilities, neither you nor I will be in a position to travel far from England in the future, so… I've had Carstairs making enquiries about a ship for us to purchase, and I think he's found just the one. What do you say to establishing a merchant fleet of our own?'

Carstairs was a former customs officer they had employed to manage the London end of their importing business. Benedict felt a stirring of excitement deep in his gut. Although he knew his future must now lie in England, he also knew he would miss the cut and thrust of the business he and Matthew had set up together. His estates and investments might be vast but so, also, was the army of bankers, solicitors, clerks and stewards who had run them on Malcolm's—and now his—behalf.

'I say—' Benedict raised his glass '—it is a first-rate idea. I'll drink to that.'

Their glasses clinked in salute.

'Excellent!' Matthew said. 'We'll go and see Carstairs tomorrow and then we'll see the solicitor and instruct him to draw up a new partnership agreement. And, in the meantime...' He paused and his rugged features softened. 'In the meantime, I have one more announcement to make.' He grinned, stood up and spread his arms wide. 'I am to be a father.'

Benedict surged to his feet and gripped his friend's hand. 'That's splendid news, by God. Congratulations, Matt. How is Eleanor? She is well, I hope?'

Matthew headed for the door, eager as a schoolboy. 'Come and see for yourself,' he said. 'She is in the drawing room. She made me swear I would not allow you to leave without first paying your respects.'

The door to the drawing room was ajar, allowing chattering female voices to drift across the hall as Benedict and Matthew emerged from the library. It was the time of day for the ladies of the *haut ton* to pay visits and Benedict tamped down his sudden attack of nerves. This would be his first venture into polite society. How would he be received? He was conscious of the need to make a good impression from the start if he were to restore the Poole name and overcome his own links to trade. He was fortunate to have Eleanor—a baroness in her own right—and Matthew as friends.

'That sounds like Lady Stanton,' Matthew whispered to Benedict as they approached the door. 'Eleanor only made her acquaintance recently, but they have become bosom bows already.' He lowered his voice still further. 'They have much in common.' He used his hands to mime a swollen belly. 'Not that you can tell yet,' he added with a wink, 'so be discreet.'

Benedict grinned at him, though he was still on edge. 'I won't let on that you've told me,' he said as he followed Matthew into the room.

He heard her voice before he saw her—low, warm, melodic—and his gut clenched. Somehow his feet kept moving and he concentrated on locating Eleanor, with her glossy mahogany locks and her wide welcoming smile, ignoring the clamour of every one of his senses to drink in Harriet, only Harriet.

She was at the edge of his vision: blonde hair sleek in a chignon, poised, controlled, politely smiling as Matthew first greeted the third occupant of the room—a slight, elegantly dressed lady, presumably Lady Stanton—and was then introduced to Harriet by Eleanor.

How could Matthew and Eleanor behave so normally? How could they be unaware of the fire raging out of control in his gut? How could *anyone*? That thought steadied him. Of course no one would know. Not unless he gave himself away, and that he would not do. He stepped forward to greet Eleanor, raising her hand to his lips as he caught her eye and mouthed the word *Congratulations* to her. Her eyes sparkled as her smile widened even more, her excitement clear. She tucked her hand beneath his arm and tugged him round to face the two seated ladies.

'Allow me to introduce my husband's business partner,' Eleanor said. 'Felicity, Lady Stanton—Sir Benedict Poole.'

'Delighted to meet you, my lady.'

Benedict dipped his head and when he raised it he found himself the recipient of a tight smile and a searching stare from a pair of clear amber eyes. He had no time to ponder the meaning of that look, for Eleanor began to introduce Harriet.

Before he could think through the consequences, Benedict said, 'We have met.'

The room seemed to still for a moment, then Harriet inclined her head graciously. 'Indeed we have. How do you do, Sir Benedict?'

Benedict managed to voice a polite reply.

Harriet then focused on Matthew. 'Lady Ashby was telling us of your time in India. Is that where you and Sir Benedict met?'

'It was,' Matthew replied. 'It is quite a coincidence, you two knowing each other.' He studied Benedict, who battled to keep his feelings from showing. 'Did you meet recently, or is it an acquaintance of longer standing?'

Benedict smarted at his friend's innocent tone—a tone completely at odds with the knowing smile that played around his lips.

'We were neighbours in our youth,' he growled.

A devilish glint lit Matthew's eyes as he said, 'Then I shall leave you to renew your acquaintance.'

He sat on the sofa next to Lady Stanton and engaged her in conversation, leaving Benedict no choice but to sit on the only remaining seat—the chair next to Harriet.

A sizzle of awareness sped through his veins, fuelling his anger that Harriet's mere presence could affect him in such a way. Conscious of Eleanor watching from her chair at the far end of the sofa, Benedict thrust aside his shock and focused his mind on his goal—making a good first impression on Lady Stanton, and society in general, with a view to building his own reputation and allowing Malcolm's libertine past to fade in people's memories.

He would not allow Harriet's presence to deflect him from that goal, and he must strive to treat her as he would any other society lady.

'I trust you are well, my lady?' he said.

'Thank you, yes.'

To the others in the room, it would look as though Harriet was giving him her full attention, her head turned in his direction. Only Benedict was able to see that her gaze was fixed on a point somewhere beyond his right ear and that her cheeks were pink. She was, perhaps, not quite as calm as she wanted him to think. Despite his best intentions, he soon found himself trying to penetrate her outer shell of indifference.

He kept his voice to a murmur. 'You left without saying goodbye.'

Just like before. The old anger and betrayal swirled through him.

'I could say the same to you.'

'It is not the same. I came home and you had gone.'

Harriet shifted a little in her chair. 'I could not say goodbye to someone who was not there.'

'You could have written a note.'

'To what purpose?'

'To explain. To tell me why.'

Benedict was no longer sure if he meant two months ago or eleven years ago. Or both.

'It would have changed nothing, and you were no doubt told why. I had no choice.'

'Why Brierley?' His voice had dipped, his whisper fierce.

She stared at him now, her violet eyes narrowed, wary. 'What do you mean?'

He rubbed the back of his neck, aware he was heading into deep waters. *Be careful. Stay in the present.*

'Why did you go with Brierley?'

'I had no choice,' she repeated.

'You do not have to answer to him.'

'Yes, I do. He is the head of the family...*my* family. He was concerned about my reputation.'

'A widow is allowed some licence. As long as she is discreet.'

'*That* is entirely immaterial if the widow has no interest in having such licence in the first place.'

'That is not the impression I got. You enjoyed that kiss.'

'You consider yourself a skilled reader of minds, do you, sir? I—'

Benedict leaned towards Harriet and lowered his voice further. 'I may not be able to read minds, Harriet, but the body speaks a very different language. One to which I am well attuned.'

Harriet's chin tilted. Just a fraction, but he knew he had touched on a nerve. Before he could respond, however, Eleanor rose to her feet, smiling apologetically at Matthew and Felicity, saying, 'Please do forgive me, but I really cannot allow Sir Benedict to monopolise Lady Brierley's attention like this.' She then treated Benedict to one of her most direct looks and continued, 'I know you will forgive me for ousting you from the lady's side, sir, but Lady Brierley and I have only just become acquainted and I am convinced we must discover more about one another, in order that we may determine whether our next meeting will be one of new friends or mere passing acquaintances.'

Benedict had risen from his chair when Eleanor stood up, and now he had no choice but to exchange seats. As a good hostess, Eleanor had clearly recognised the tension between her two guests, and had acted to intervene. Knowing Eleanor, Benedict could foresee some probing questions about that tension. He diverted his thoughts from that awkward conversation to come.

Before he could join Matthew and Lady Stanton, however, the lady rose from the sofa, saying, 'I fear Harriet and I shall outstay our welcome if we remain very much longer—we have been here close on an hour already. My apologies for running away before we have had an opportunity to become properly acquainted, Sir Benedict. I should like to remedy that very soon.'

'As would I, my lady.' Benedict bowed. Had he imagined that slight edge to Lady Stanton's words? He watched as she walked across to speak to Harriet.

'Are you ready to leave now, my dear?'

'Yes, indeed,' Harriet said. 'It was a great pleasure to meet you, Lady Ashby, and you, Mr Damerel.'

'I am delighted to have made your acquaintance, Lady Brierley,' Eleanor said. 'And, please, call me Eleanor. I have heard much about you from Felicity and confess I am intrigued by your charity work. I am very much interested in finding out more about it.'

'That is splendid, for we have need of all the patronage we can muster.' Harriet's voice rang with enthusiasm. 'And the school for orphans that Felicity champions is most worthy, as well.'

Benedict's interest was piqued by Harriet's obvious passion. *What charity work?*

Don't ask her. The less you see of her and the less you know about her the better.

'I am eager to visit both places,' Eleanor said. Then, her eyes on her husband, she added, 'As long as *you* have no objection, my love?'

Benedict bit back a smile. Matthew had told him all about Eleanor's independence as a wealthy peeress in her own right before she'd met him and they'd fallen in love. She was clearly trying her utmost to adapt to taking his opinion into account when making decisions.

Matthew smiled at his wife. 'I have no objection, my dear.'

The love that shone in the look they exchanged stirred both envy and yearning in Benedict's heart, as it had since the moment he had first seen them together. Would he ever find love that special?

More to the point, will *you ever find love you can trust?*

He must believe he would.

'Splendid,' Eleanor said, beaming. 'We will make arrangements soon, Felicity. In the meantime, Harriet, I shall send you an invitation to our musical evening a fortnight today. I do hope you will be able to attend.'

'Thank you. That is most kind.'

'Felicity and Lord Stanton have already accepted, and you will come as well, I hope, Benedict?' Eleanor continued with an eager smile. 'It will be our first ever party since our wedding, so I am praying for it to be a success.'

Benedict's heart sank. It sounded deadly dull to him. He exchanged a look with Matthew, whose glum expression suggested he was no more enamoured at the prospect.

But he was fond of Eleanor, and it behoved him to support Matthew, so... 'I shall look forward to it,' he said with a bow.

'Richard and I are very much looking forward to it, too, Eleanor,' Lady Stanton said. 'And you have reminded me of something I meant to ask Harriet. Are you invited to the Cothams' masquerade ball next week?'

'I have been invited, but it is out of town and—'

'But that is why I am asking, you goose,' Felicity said. 'You shall come with us in our carriage. You cannot miss such an event.'

'It does sound like fun,' Harriet said. 'Thank you.'

'Oh, but how delightful,' Eleanor said, her glowing eyes wide with excitement. 'Matthew and I are attending, too. And Benedict as well, I hope. I happened to mention to Lady Cotham that you were coming up to town, Benedict, and she included you on our invitation. I have plenty of garments you can choose from for your costume—I had so many ideas, I hardly knew which ones to pick for Matthew and me. *Do* say you'll come.'

Benedict grinned at her. 'You try to stop me.'

'Indeed,' Matthew interjected. 'Give this man a chance to dress in some outlandish costume and he is as happy as a sailor in a—'

'*Mat*thew…'

They all laughed at Eleanor's warning and Lady Stanton tucked her arm through Harriet's, saying, 'Come, my dear, it is time we left.'

Unanswered questions swarmed through Benedict's head. This might be as good a chance as any to get some answers.

'I must also be on my way,' he said. 'Were you ladies accompanied by your maids?' He had seen no one waiting in the hall. 'Might I offer to escort you home?' He included Lady Stanton in his glance.

A flush washed Harriet's cheeks and a spark of irritation lit her eyes but he knew she could hardly refuse when he was so obviously a close friend of their host and hostess.

Chapter Nine

Once they were outside in Cavendish Square, Lady Stanton turned to Harriet and smiled. 'I shall see you very soon, my dear,' she said, and embraced her. She then faced Benedict. 'Thank you for your offer, sir.'

Once again, he felt the force of her clear-eyed appraisal, reminding him of the look she had given him when they were first introduced. Why did she appear wary of him? Had Harriet confided something of their past to her friend?

'My home is across the square,' Lady Stanton continued, 'and I have no need of company for that short distance. I venture to hope, however, that you will escort Lady Brierley to *her* home. She has developed a sad habit of walking around town unaccompanied now that her maid is indisposed.'

'Most shocking behaviour,' Benedict agreed gravely, wondering why, if she was chary of him, she would encourage him to escort Harriet. 'I shall be sure to see her safely home.'

It was another question to add to the list for Harriet to answer.

'It was only this once, Felicity, as you well know,'

Harriet said. 'My footman accompanied me to Lady Stanton's house earlier,' she continued, in explanation to Benedict, 'but he had errands to run. And I am not a green girl who needs chaperoning everywhere. It is the middle of the afternoon, for goodness' sake. What possible harm could befall me?'

Benedict bowed. 'I shall escort you nevertheless. It was a pleasure to meet you, Lady Stanton.'

She nodded, unsmiling. 'Likewise, sir.'

Before they parted company, however, a shrill voice accosted them.

'My dear, dear Lady Stanton, how do you do? And, if I am not mistaken, it is Sir Benedict Poole, is it not? And...Lady Brierley.'

The fashionably dressed matron's voice noticeably cooled as she spoke Harriet's name. Benedict saw Lady Stanton bristle and he warmed to her. She was clearly a loyal friend.

'Good afternoon, Lady Marstone,' she said with the slightest of bows, and went to pass by the woman and her younger companion, a slim brunette with a pretty face somewhat spoiled by a petulant expression.

Lady Marstone added hurriedly, 'And of course you know my daughter, Bridget?'

Lady Stanton nodded at the girl. 'Yes,' she said. 'How do you do, Miss Marstone? Now, please do excuse me, but I am expected home.'

She smiled at the group and walked on, crossing the corner of the square, leaving Benedict and Harriet with Lady Marstone and her daughter, neither of whom Benedict could recall having met before.

The lady was eyeing him with an eager light in her eyes.

He bowed. 'My apologies, Lady Marstone, but have we met?'

'Oh, no, no, Sir Benedict, we have never been formally introduced, but I recognise *you*. Why, the whole district is agog with your return. We live not three miles from Tenterfield Court, so we are practically neighbours. So fortuitous, our bumping into you in the street just now—I hope you will forgive me for dispensing with the formalities?

'I recognised you the instant I saw you—*so* like Sir Malcolm...although no doubt of more...less...well, yes...' She faltered, but only momentarily, before charging ahead once again. 'And of course I am already acquainted with dear Lady Stanton and with Lady Brierley so there can be no real impropriety, can there?'

'Quite so.'

'As we are such close neighbours, you will of course attend our ball next month? I shall be sure to send you an invitation.'

'Thank you. I shall consult my diary as soon as I receive it.'

'Oh! Oh, yes of course. But...being such *close* neighbours, surely you must... Well, I shall leave it to you, sir, but dear Bridget was only saying yesterday how wonderful it will be to stand up with a gentleman of your considerable standing.'

Benedict managed to prevent himself frowning as Miss Marstone simpered at him. How had this conversation bounced from a chance meeting to the expectation he would dance with this woman's daughter? He suspected his *considerable standing* owed more to his wealth than to anything else about him. Was this what he must expect from society? The pitfalls in business were as nothing beside the perils of negotiating the hazards of the *ton*. He was encouraged, however, that his wealth appeared to override any scruples over Malcolm's past—at least, as far as Lady Marstone was concerned. Although it remained to be seen whether this particular lady was quite as finicky as others in the *ton* might prove to be.

Without volition, he glanced at Harriet, standing to one side. Her expression was neutral but his look resulted in a slight elevation of her brows. He suspected she was hiding a smile.

She addressed Miss Marstone. 'I do not doubt that Sir Benedict will prove a most accomplished dancer, Miss Marstone. I collect this is your second—'

'*Thank* you, Lady Brierley.' Lady Marstone placed herself firmly between Harriet and her daughter. She then turned her steely gaze back to Benedict. 'We have taken enough of your time, sir. I bid you good day. Come, Bridget.'

Benedict stared after them. 'She was intolerably rude to you. Why did you not give her a set-down?'

Harriet said nothing as she walked across the Square in the direction of Holles Street.

'Harriet?'

Benedict hurried to catch her up and then kept pace with her. How did she remain so composed? He could interpret nothing of what was going through her head from her expression or her demeanour.

'Lady Marstone is the person who informed my stepson that I was at Tenterfield,' she said eventually. 'She clearly believes that I am an unsuitable acquaintance for her daughter. And, if I am honest, I cannot blame her for that. She is being protective. It is what any mother would do.'

Benedict digested the implications of this.

'Is she likely to gossip about it?'

'I hope not. Edward threatened to prevent Bridget gaining approval for Almack's this Season—he is a friend of Lord Castlereagh.' She peeped sideways at him and he saw her lips twitch. 'You do not understand the gravity of such a threat, it is clear. Lady Castlereagh is one of the patronesses of Almack's—the group of ladies who preside over who is and who is not deemed acceptable to attend the assembly on a Wednesday evening during the Season. To have her name added to the approved list is the pinnacle of every young girl's ambition. To be denied that privilege would be enough to cast that same young miss into the depths of despair. The threat should be sufficient to ensure Lady Marstone's discretion.'

She then added, 'Almack's is also popularly known as the marriage mart. You will do well to cultivate one of the patronesses—it will be the perfect place to gain introductions to suitable young ladies on the lookout for a husband.'

There was nary a quiver of emotion in her voice—maybe she *had* been telling the truth, back at Tenterfield Court; maybe it *was* remembering her father, and not Benedict's talk of finding a bride, that had so upset her. He had often wondered about that evening.

'And if I am deemed unsuitable? You will recall I have been in trade all my adult life.'

'Your new status and wealth might overcome *that* particular taint. If not, however, I am acquainted with a lady who undertakes to perform discreet introductions between suitable parties. I shall be happy to introduce you to her if you wish.'

'I should prefer to rely on my own instincts, thank you.'

And his instincts were, at that very moment, clamouring to take Harriet in his arms, despite his bitterness, despite his distrust, despite the deafening clamour of his common sense. The idea that had surfaced at Tenterfield re-emerged. She was a widow. They could be discreet. If he bedded her, he might rid himself once and for all of this nagging feeling of unfinished business. And then, when he took a wife, surely these muddled feelings she had awoken within him would disappear?

'Although,' he added, 'if I *should* need some help in the matter, I seem to recall *you* promising to help me with my search for a spouse.'

'I fear my time is already fully occupied in assisting the needy,' she replied.

Benedict stifled his laugh. *Cleverly done. Needy, eh?* Yes, he was needy, but not in the way Harriet had meant. Or—he sneaked a look at her serene profile— was her double entendre deliberate?

They walked side by side for several minutes in silence. As they reached Oxford Street and waited for a break in the traffic to cross the road, Benedict offered his arm. After a second's hesitation, Harriet laid her gloved hand on his sleeve. Something seemed to settle deep inside him at her touch. It felt right.

'I am curious about your friend, Lady Stanton,' he said, after they crossed and continued on their way towards Hanover Square. 'She seemed almost wary of me. I cannot think why as I have never met her before.'

Harriet remained silent for so long, Benedict feared she was not going to answer him.

'It is not you, personally,' she said eventually, 'but your name that unsettles her. It was on Felicity's behalf I went to Tenterfield Court, to discover the truth about a matter concerning her sister. Felicity has no cause to love the Poole name.'

The Poole name... How many others would be of the same opinion? How many would judge him by the actions of Sir Malcolm?

'That is yet another reminder that I should lose no time in restoring good opinion of my family name,' he said.

'So you said before. Well, you might take heart from Lady Marstone. She showed no sign of disapproval but, on the other hand, she does have a daughter to marry off. A respectable marriage would go a long way to overcoming past scandals, and I am sure Bridget's dowry would add nicely to your wealth.'

'I have no need of more money.' Benedict shuddered inwardly at the thought of Lady Marstone as a mother-in-law.

He sensed Harriet's swift sideways glance, but he kept his gaze fixed ahead.

'Everyone always wants more money,' she said, 'or why would wealthy men baulk at providing for...? Besides, I was talking about land. The Marstone estate is not far from Tenterfield and, from what I have heard, it is not all entailed, so Bridget's portion would be likely to include some of the unentailed land. She only has the one brother. That must be an enticing thought to a bachelor considering marriage.'

'The enticement of more land is entirely immaterial if said bachelor has no interest in adding to his estates.'

Harriet halted, raising her violet-blue eyes to peer searchingly into his. 'Those are, almost, my words to you.' Her fair brows drew together, creating a crease between them. 'What is it you want, Benedict?'

He was vaguely aware of people passing them on both sides, but his vision was filled with only her. What did he want? The answer echoed through him, stronger than ever. He wanted her. Harriet. Fickle and untrustworthy as he knew her to be, still he wanted her.

'Let us keep moving,' he said. 'We are causing an obstruction.'

They walked on. Harriet was silent, awaiting his reply.

'It is obvious we are destined to see each other here in London,' Benedict said. 'What I should like is for us to meet and socialise without the past coming between us.'

'The past? Would that be the distant past or the more recent past? Or, mayhap, both?'

The first time either of them had touched upon that most contentious of subjects—the distant past. And yet that was what it was: distant. Those achingly raw emotions that had haunted him in the days, weeks and months following her betrayal should have no influence on the present. But they did, whipping into a frenzy the two contradictory emotions that had plagued him ever since Harriet's unexpected appearance at Tenterfield—bitterness and yearning.

'I meant the distant past,' he replied, thrusting aside the confusion of his feelings. 'Might we relegate it *to* the past? We both said things, made pledges…but we were so young. I was in the throes of calf love. I know better now. But I still… Harriet…'

Benedict took a quick look around. There was no one nearby. They had just left Hanover Square and were walking down St George Street, approaching the great portico of St George's Church, with its magnificent columns. He tugged Harriet to a stop and clasped her shoulders to turn her to face him. She looked up at him, wide-eyed, soft lips parted on an exclamation of surprise, and he battled the impulse to lower his head and to taste her lush lips there and then.

'Benedict…no… Do not…'

Had she interpreted his longing for more than mere words? He reined in that mad impulse to kiss her here, in the street, but—he *had* to remove this awkwardness between them…this feeling of unfinished business. Should he even contemplate asking her? If she refused him, how would he feel then?

'Harriet…'

Her violet eyes darkened as her pupils grew impossibly large, an involuntary sign of her arousal, whatever words she might say. His body reacted to that silent message, his loins growing heavy with desire.

'What I felt for you in our youth may have been calf love, but that does not stop me wanting you now. You feel the same. I know it. I can *feel* it.' He released her shoulder and traced the fine bone of her jaw with a gentle forefinger.

Dammit! Why not? It would draw a line under the past. Allow us both to move on with our lives.

'We are both adults. Will you—?'

'You! Sir!' A hand grabbed at Benedict's shoulder and wrenched him away from Harriet.

With a curse, Benedict spun round to face a spluttering, puce-faced gentleman about four inches shorter than him. Benedict shrugged the man's hand from his shoulder and thrust his face close to his assailant's. Before he could take further action or utter a word, Harriet was pushing between them, her back to Benedict.

'No! Edward, please. Benedict, no, I implore you.'

Her stepson, Brierley; he was called Edward. Benedict battled for control of his fury as Edward continued his diatribe over Harriet's head.

'You, sir, are a blackguard. I shall see—'

'Edward! No. Please…' There were tears in Harriet's voice and Benedict's heart squeezed.

How dare this pompous oaf upset her? Benedict grasped Harriet by her upper arms. She struggled, resisting his efforts to put her aside, panting with the effort.

'Do not, Benedict. I beg of you. You will only make it worse.'

Benedict released her but continued to glare at Brierley, wanting nothing more than to land his fist squarely on the other man's nose. He forced his clenched hands to remain at his sides.

'You will get into my carriage now, madam, and leave me to deal with this villain, if you know what is good for you.' Brierley grabbed Harriet's arm and pushed her towards a carriage that had drawn up by the kerb.

'*Deal* with me?' Rage roared through Benedict at the sight of Brierley's fingers digging into Harriet's flesh. 'Why, you—'

'*No!* Listen to me! Think of the scandal, Edward. Please. Someone will notice and the tale will be all over town in a trice. For Kitty's sake, if not for mine.'

Chapter Ten

'For *Kitty's* sake? It is a pity you did not consider her before wantonly throwing yourself at this…this no-good *merchant* in full public view.'

Frantic, Harriet scanned their surroundings. Edward's carriage effectively blocked them from the view of most of the street and the pavement on their side of the road was empty. Her relief was short-lived, killed off by one look at her stepson, his face deep red and bulging above his neckcloth. His fingers dug like claws into her upper arm.

'You are hurting her. Let go of her now, or I will not be responsible for my actions.' Benedict's voice was low with menace, his face taut with anger, as he stepped closer.

Edward tightened his grip, wringing a gasp from Harriet. 'I expected nothing more than such low threats from your sort, Poole,' he said with a sneer. 'A public brawl *would* be about your level. Now stand aside. This *lady* will do my bidding as head of the family.'

She had no choice but to go with Edward if she were to prevent the two men coming to blows or, even worse, flinging out a challenge to a duel—and she could not bear to be the cause of such a clash. She submitted to Edward's pull on her arm, turning to the open door of the carriage.

'I shall be all right,' she said to Benedict, looking over her shoulder at him with a silent plea.

'You do not have to go with him,' he said, holding her gaze with deep green eyes that sparked rage. He was bristling with controlled aggression, his jaw tight.

'I must. I—'

'Yes, she does,' Edward cut in as he almost shoved her up the step into the carriage. 'If she values this family, and her independence, she has no choice whatsoever.'

He clambered in behind her and slammed the door before rapping his cane on the roof. The carriage jerked into motion, Edward's bulk blocking Benedict from Harriet's sight.

'I am appalled by your lack of judgement, madam. Not only have you defied my clear instructions that you must have nothing more to do with that scoundrel but you appear to have taken leave of any sense you might once have possessed. I repeat what I said to you before. Was one rejection not enough? The man is a nobody and a merchant.'

'He is a baronet, Edward, hardly a nobody.'

'And where has he come from? Who were his parents? Although—' he cast her a scathing look '—I suppose I can hardly expect *you* to consider such niceties as being of importance.'

'My father was a gentleman, Edward, as was Benedict's.' His gibe against her parentage stung and, now that the immediate danger of the two men coming to blows had passed, Harriet's temper—usually so equable—

began to simmer. 'And I happen to know that Benedict's mother was the granddaughter of an earl.'

'He is in *trade*. If nothing else, consider *my* position.'

'I have done nothing, Edward. I was walking along the road—'

'That is not what I saw,' Edward interrupted furiously, 'and I dare say a good many others also witnessed your disgraceful behaviour. You were nigh on *embracing* in the street. You are not to speak to him again.'

Harriet's stomach lurched as she realised that, although his accusation was a gross exaggeration, he had a point. She *had* allowed her emotions to overcome her common sense, but that did not give Edward the right to control to whom she spoke.

'I am your stepmother, Edward, and a widow. I am perfectly capable of handling Sir Benedict.'

'Ha! You have proved that, have you not, madam? You were *handling* him, were you, when I came upon you just now? You were on the brink of a public show— a scandalous indiscretion. And he—baronet or not— thought nothing of subjecting you to such behaviour. But then, what can you expect from someone brought up under the influence of a libertine such as Sir Malcolm Poole?' His voice softened a touch. 'You might be my stepmother, but you are a female and you need protection. I am older than you and wiser in the ways of the world. You will do as I say.

'Poole is trouble. You are to have nothing more to do with him. Do I make myself clear?'

'And if I refuse?'

He regarded her thoughtfully. 'Then I regret but I shall have no choice but to banish you to Brierley Place for the remainder of the Season. There is an empty cottage on the far side of the estate you could live in.'

Harriet's mind reeled. His prompt response suggested he had it all worked out. 'Banish me? But…why? You cannot—'

'I think you will find that I can,' Edward said. 'Very easily. I shall stop your allowance and lock up the house in Sackville Street. You will have no choice. Your only other option will be to walk the streets.'

'But…Kitty's ball…'

He shrugged. 'The remedy is in your hands. My priority must be my daughter's reputation. I am in the process of negotiating a most advantageous match for her, one that is very important, politically and for the family. I will not allow you to ruin that.'

The carriage halted and Harriet saw her own front door through the window. She had been sure Edward would take her to his own house in Upper Brook Street first.

'I shall leave you to reflect upon what I have said. I shall return tomorrow and you may tell me your decision. Will you comply or will you rebel? Until I am satisfied, you are forbidden to contact either my wife or my daughter.'

Stevens, Harriet's butler, appeared at the carriage door and opened it, helping Harriet to the pavement.

'Tomorrow at two,' Edward barked. The carriage drove away.

Later, glass of wine in hand, Harriet fretted over Edward's demand as she relaxed on the green-and-cream-striped chaise longue in the small sitting room—her boudoir—that adjoined her bedchamber. She should be happy to have nothing to do with Benedict after his treatment of her so why did she hesitate to obey her stepson? Was it pure contrariness that made her baulk at doing as she was told? Was her hesitation solely due to her dislike of being told what to do and how to behave and to whom she might speak?

Her heart and mind still reeled from the shock of meeting Benedict today—he had been the last person she'd expected to see when Felicity had urged her to come and meet her new friend, Lady Ashby. He had walked into Eleanor's drawing room and jolted Harriet out of the dreamlike stupor that had assailed her ever since her visit to Tenterfield Court. Since then, she had gone about her daily routine as if in a daze, as though waiting for an unacknowledged dread to come to pass. And now the worst had happened. Benedict was here. In London. And it would seem that Harriet's life was about to become complicated. On the one hand, she could hardly avoid Benedict completely but, on the other, she must tread with care if she was not to completely antagonise Edward.

When Brierley died she had sworn she would never allow another man to control her, and yet here was Edward, intimidating her in an attempt to bend her to his will.

Can Edward really withhold my allowance? Am I not entitled to a pension, as his father's widow?

Without funds to live on, her only other option would be to remarry—a prospect that filled her with terror, for how could she know, before it was too late, if her spouse would have the same violent tendencies as her late husband? She had never questioned her rights, she realised. She had simply accepted what Edward had told her was her due. Mayhap it was time she found out, for if she did not look after her own interests, who else would?

The memory of Benedict facing up to Edward floated through her thoughts. She suppressed her *hmph—*

maybe she had felt momentarily protected but when, in reality, had he ever put her interests first? She could not deny, however, that meeting Benedict today had again awakened some of her old feelings for him.

Are those feelings real, though, or merely an echo of the past?

What had happened between them—eleven years ago…two months ago…today—was not, none of it, complete. She resented how his return had stirred up long-buried emotions to disturb her peaceful life and yet she yearned for some kind of finality to the whole sorry story of their relationship.

But what good could come of raking over the past? Would it not be better to comply with Edward's wishes and have nothing more to do with Benedict? He was not even interested enough in what had happened to her to ask after their baby. Had she not sworn to never forget— nor forgive—the way he had so cruelly abandoned her?

Edward is right. Why risk yet another rejection? Her mind drifted back over her conversation with Benedict, the conversation Edward had interrupted. What had he been about to say? His deep voice sounded again inside her head.

That does not stop me wanting you now. You feel the same. I know it. We are both adults. Will you—?'

Harriet jerked upright, the heat of anger bubbling through her. *He was about to proposition me!* Or mayhap, she thought, swallowing down a bitter laugh, he had been on the brink of offering her *carte blanche*, which was even worse. He had contemplated setting her up as his mistress in the midst of all his talk of restoring the Poole name and finding a suitable bride to smooth his way in Society.

Hmph! Well, Sir Benedict Poole would find himself

sorely disappointed. She would treat him with the same friendly courtesy she had afforded Stanton after their *affaire* ended when he had married Felicity last year.

Thinking of the Stantons reminded Harriet of the friends she now had in common with Benedict, and she realised it would be impossible to avoid him altogether. She vowed to hide her conflicted feelings about Benedict both from him and from their friends: not only her pain at his treatment of her in the past but also her curiosity about the man he had become and, most important of all, that tiny bud of desire deep inside her that, even now, she could feel stirring into life. She could not bear anyone to guess at her jumble of emotions but at least her marriage to Brierley had taught her the value of strict control.

Exhausted by the thoughts swirling around her brain, Harriet relaxed back against the cushions and closed her eyes, drifting into sleep.

Harriet awoke with a start at the tap on the door. It could only be Stevens—the maids would not knock before entering her boudoir—and that could only mean a visitor.

'Yes?' she called.

The door opened to admit her butler. 'Sir Benedict Poole has called, my lady. Will you see him, or shall I say you are not at home?'

Benedict? Here?

On the brink of denying him, she hesitated, remembering the offer he had been about to make to her. Would this not be the perfect opportunity to remind him that she was a respectable widow who was content with her life? Future meetings, surely, would be less fraught if he knew she was not interested.

Harriet's heart quaked at the thought of Edward finding out about Benedict's visit. *Thank goodness dear old Stevens is loyal. It will be just this once, and then never again.*

'Thank you, Stevens. I will see him. Please show him into the salon and send Janet to me.'

It was time she put an end to this dithering and uncertainty.

Her nerve held until she descended the stairs, her hair tidied and pinned in place and her cheeks tinted with a dusting of rouge. In the hall, she hesitated. Stevens, about to open the salon door, paused and waited for her. Harriet drew in a steadying breath and smoothed her suddenly moist hands down the skirt of her pink sprigged muslin gown. She nodded to Stevens.

Benedict stood by the fireplace, tall and handsome. She steeled her heart.

'You should not have come here.'

'I wanted to make sure you were all right.'

It is a pity you didn't feel that way eleven years ago. The memory of his callous behaviour gave her strength.

'Edward is not a violent man. He blusters his way through his anger. I can cope with him.'

'And will you obey him?'

Obey. That word. 'I will do as he asks as it happens to be my natural inclination, too. As I said before, I have no wish to revisit our youthful indiscretions.'

Benedict crossed the room towards her, as lithe and graceful as a panther. Harriet stood her ground, holding his gaze.

'That is not the impression you gave earlier,' he growled.

'Then, you must learn to interpret a woman's behaviour with more accuracy,' Harriet said, lifting her shoulders in a shrug. 'Especially as you intend to look for a wife.'

He was close now. She could smell his cologne, subtle and spicy, feel his heat.

'What did he mean when he said, "If you value your independence"? It sounded very like a threat to me.'

'As I said, it is all bluster. He cannot withhold my allowance. There is no reason for you to be concerned,' she said, with a silent prayer she was right.

I shall make certain. I shall visit the solicitor tomorrow.

'But I am concerned.'

His voice had grown husky, triggering a tug of need deep inside her.

'There is no need. I have managed perfectly well these past eleven years without your concern. I am unlikely to disintegrate now that you have returned.

'However, our conversation earlier was unfinished,' she continued. 'I asked you what it is you want. Your reply was that you wanted us to be able to meet and socialise without the past coming between us. That is what I want, too. As we both want the same thing, our meetings henceforth will be that of casual acquaintances.'

'But…'

Harriet inhaled, and raised her chin. '*If* you are about to suggest some kind of liaison, sir, then I would urge you to resist the temptation to do so, for I shall only refuse and it can only cause more tension and discomfiture between us. I am a respectable widow and I guard my reputation with care, not because my stepson demands it but because *I* wish it.'

Benedict stiffened, his jaw muscles bunching as his brows lowered. He bowed. 'Pardon me for taking up your valuable time.'

Harriet waited until he had gone, then sat numbly on the sofa. She should be relieved. His reaction proved he was, once again, only interested in bedding her. She'd had a lucky escape.

Long-suppressed despair stirred, deep down inside the hollow shell she presented to the outside world. It welled up, invading her constricted throat, stinging her nose and eyes.

She. Would. Not. Cry.

Never again. Not over him. She slapped her hands over her eyes, rubbing furiously as she swallowed down the swell of misery.

Hide your feelings. Don't give in. He'll hurt you all over again.

Gradually, she brought her emotions under control. She stood, smoothed her hair back and crossed the room to the door. It was done. Look to the future.

But my baby... She paused, shuddering. Why did he have to return, bringing all those unwanted memories with him? She could still feel the fragile weight of her daughter in her arms before she had been whisked away, never to be spoken of again, as though she had never existed.

Harriet squeezed her eyes shut, swallowing down her pain. Only when she was certain she could maintain her poise in the face of her servants did she leave the salon and climb the stairs to prepare for the dinner and ball she was due to attend that evening.

Chapter Eleven

'I do not understand.' It was the following day, and Harriet gazed at Mr Drake, the Brierley family solicitor, with dawning horror. 'My stepson… Lord Brierley… I… *Surely* he cannot stop paying my allowance?'

The little man sighed and shuffled the papers on his desk. 'I am sorry, my lady, but I fear he can, if he so chooses.'

'You say there was a sum of money invested in funds at the time of my marriage—was the income not meant for my use? Is that not how it usually works?'

'Usually, yes, but there was an additional condition stated in this particular deed and Lord Brierley, as the primary beneficiary, has the right to withhold the dividends if he so chooses.'

'The primary beneficiary? Please explain.'

The solicitor's cheeks turned the colour of brick. He cleared his throat. 'I recall these were not the usual circumstances.' He selected a scroll and unrolled it, smoothing it flat. 'This is the deed in question—it is not a standard form of settlement deed but I was present at the meeting where the details were agreed and I can assure you your father raised no objection.'

Harriet's stomach churned. How humiliating, to sit here in the full knowledge that this man knew about her sordid past. 'Pray continue,' she said, gripping her reticule tightly on her lap.

She listened as Mr Drake explained that Harriet's father, desperate to get his pregnant daughter a husband, had agreed she would forgo her dower rights over the Brierley estates, which were entailed for Edward, Brierley's eldest son by his first marriage. The sum of ten thousand pounds was settled on her as compensation, with the income intended to provide her with pin money during her marriage, and a jointure in the event she was widowed.

Pin money? Brierley had never paid her as much as a farthing. If she had needed anything, she'd had to go to him and ask. And there would always be conditions attached.

Always.

Harriet tamped down her disgust at those memories—her reluctance to ask him; her despair when she had no choice—and concentrated as Mr Drake continued to explain how her late husband had reserved the right to withhold the income from the funds—which was to be paid to Harriet, for life, through him and his successors in title—if Harriet did anything to bring the Brierley name into disrepute. A condition, Mr Drake said, that Lord Brierley insisted upon in view of—here he gave a delicate cough—Harriet's proved loose morals.

'And my house in Sackville Street?' A part of her thought, *Why ask? You know the answer.* But she needed to hear it spelled out in all its gruesome reality.

'It belongs to his lordship.' Sympathy gleamed in the little man's eyes. 'I am afraid he is correct. He can shut it up anytime he pleases. At least, from what you have said, he would offer you a cottage on the estate. You would not be homeless.'

Scant comfort. Harriet's world tilted on its axis. Nothing was as it seemed. She had—stupidly, blindly— believed she was safe. She had congratulated herself on being an independent widow. But now... Brierley was still controlling her from beyond the grave, she realised with a shudder that vibrated through her very bones. Her security and her much-valued independence had been a complete illusion. Edward could stop her allowance anytime he chose, and she would have no recourse whatsoever. What would her options be then? Sick despair rolled through her. Marriage. That would be her only option—to put herself, once more, at the mercy of a man.

'Why was I never informed of either the allowance or that condition?' Her throat had thickened and she had to strain to speak those words without breaking down in front of the solicitor.

Drake shrugged as he re-rolled the deed and placed it with the other documents at one side of his desk. 'I suggest you speak to Lord Brierley, my lady. It was he who made the decision not to apprise you of them after his father's death.'

Edward... The clock on the mantelshelf read half past twelve. Edward had said he would call at two for her decision.

'Thank you for your time, Mr Drake. Good day to you.'

Harriet stood and blindly headed to the door of Drake's office. How stupid had she been? How blind? Why had she never questioned any of this?

You were only sixteen. It was Papa's responsibility to get you a just settlement.

Her father had let her down, yes, but she was a girl no longer. She should have asked. She should have questioned her position instead of merely trusting the existing state of affairs. Had she learned nothing? She was as naive now as that sixteen-year-old who had succumbed to a handsome youth's charms. As she walked through the outer office she could feel the curious gazes of the clerks burning into her, and she imagined what they must know about her, how they must despise her and laugh at her—a brainless female without a clue as to the ways of the world. She reached the door and stumbled into the street, where she stopped and sucked in several deep breaths.

Her mind would not stop spinning. She could not hold a single steady thought. Could not...could not... She felt her knees sag. Her vision greyed, and then turned black.

'Congratulations, partner.' Benedict clapped Matthew Damerel on the back as they emerged from the offices of Granville and Pettifer in the city.

They had spent a productive morning, first viewing the ship that they intended to purchase—the first of many, they hoped—and, second, instructing their solicitor to draft a partnership agreement for their new business venture.

'Let us go to the club and have a drink to celebrate,' Matthew said. 'I—' His mouth snapped shut.

Benedict turned to see what had caught Matthew's attention, and his insides turned a somersault. Harriet. Pale and trembling, standing on the pavement's edge, looking for all the world... He darted forward and caught her as her legs gave way. Her eyelids fluttered as a soft sigh escaped her lips.

'That is Lady Brierley,' Matthew said, peering under the rim of her bonnet. 'I wonder what—'

'I'll take her home,' Benedict interrupted. He hailed a passing hackney. 'I'll see you later at White's, Matt. We will celebrate then.'

'Shall I come with—?'

'No need,' Benedict said as he swung Harriet into his arms and carried her up the steps into the carriage.

'Do you know where she lives?'

'I know.' Benedict smarted as he caught Matthew's raised brow. 'I escorted her home from your house yesterday, if you recall.'

'Ah...yesterday. Of course. How *could* I forget?'

Matthew's knowing smirk provoked a swell of irritation in Benedict. 'Sackville Street,' he shouted to the driver, then slammed the door, leaving a laughing Matthew standing on the pavement.

Benedict kept his arm around Harriet and manoeuvred her so that she leaned against him and he could steady her against the sway of the hackney. She felt frail. She looked so vulnerable. A wave of protectiveness swept through him, leaving his resolve to stay away from her floundering in its wake.

He studied her... In comparison to her bloom when she had called at Tenterfield Court, she almost looked like a different woman. How had he missed the signs of strain when he had seen her yesterday? Was it, somehow, his fault for reappearing in her life and causing problems with that damned prig of a stepson of hers? Or... He recalled that she had come from a solicitor's office. Perhaps something had happened there to upset her?

The hackney turned into Sackville Street, and Benedict banged his cane against the roof as they reached

Harriet's house. He tossed the driver a coin and carried Harriet to her front door, ignoring the curious stares of the few passers-by in the street. Harriet began to stir as he knocked on the door. The footman who opened it blanched when he saw his mistress cradled in a stranger's arms.

'What happened?' He flung the door wide and ushered Benedict through, shutting it quickly behind him.

'Send for her ladyship's maid immediately.' Benedict flung the words over his shoulder as he strode into the salon, where he carefully laid Harriet on the sofa, then perched on the edge, by her side, facing her.

Within minutes Harriet's butler, followed more slowly by a hobbling Janet, joined him. Janet reached into her pocket, withdrew a small bottle, removed the stopper and waved the bottle under Harriet's nose.

Benedict rubbed Harriet's hand as she coughed, thrashing her head from side to side, dislodging her bonnet. Janet bent to untie the ribbons and remove it.

'Steady,' he whispered, stroking her hair back from her forehead. 'You're safe. You're at home.'

Her lids slowly lifted to reveal eyes of violet blue, dazed and confused.

'What…?'

'Hush. It's all right.' Benedict glanced round at the butler. 'Stevens, I think her ladyship would appreciate some tea.'

'Yes, sir.' Stevens hurried from the room.

Harriet's eyes widened. 'What are *you* doing here?'

'You fainted in the street. In Gray's Inn. I brought you home. What the blazes were you doing in a place like that, without even a maid or a footman in attendance?'

'I… Gray's…? Oh!' She hauled in a ragged breath.

'*Oh!*' She struggled to sit and Benedict gently pushed her back. 'The solicitor… He told me… He *owns* me,' she continued disjointedly. 'He controls *everything*.'

'He…? Who owns you, Harry? The solicitor? You are making no sense.'

'Edward!' Her lips quivered as she clutched at Benedict's hand, despair in her eyes. 'Don't you see? *Everything*. And he can take it away at any time.'

'Edward? You told me his threats were all bluster.'

'I was wr—' Harriet stiffened, then struggled to a sitting position. 'What time is it?'

'It is half past one. Why?'

She almost threw his hand aside. 'You must not be here! You must go, before Edward comes. If he finds you here, he will stop my—'

She stilled, catching her lower lip in her teeth. Then, before his eyes, her expression blanked and she was the serene society lady he had encountered at Matthew's house the day before.

'I must apologise,' she said blandly. 'I am not quite myself. Thank you for seeing me home. I shall be quite all right now.'

Benedict felt his eyes narrow as he held Harriet's gaze. 'Tell me. Let me help.'

'Help? Why, sir, I have no need of help. It is merely an inconsequential family matter that I foolishly allowed to overcome me. Now I can think more clearly, I can see I have overreacted.'

Her tone was overly bright and, even as he watched, her hand crept up to play with a lock of her hair. 'Janet. Please show Sir Benedict out.'

He had forgotten the maid was present. He stood—now was not the time to probe deeper and, really, why should he care? She had made it clear yesterday that she viewed him as nothing more than a casual acquaintance. Any issues between Harriet and Brierley were entirely of her own making. He had offered his help and she had refused.

Despite those harsh thoughts, however, he found himself handing her his card and saying, 'You know where I am if you have need of me. I hope you will soon recover from your…from your *inconsequential family matter*. Good day to you.'

He bowed, thrusting aside the voice in his head that insisted Harriet was in trouble. Outside, he walked a short way down the street then, just as he was about to turn the corner into Piccadilly, he hesitated. Cursing beneath his breath, he looked back along Sackville Street. What was she hiding? And what was she scared of? Was Brierley, in some way, misusing her? But then, why would she defend him? It made little sense. That was twice—no, three times now—he had seen her afraid. He propped his shoulders against some railings and settled down to wait, his attention fixed on Harriet's house. He did not have long to wait. A carriage drew up at the kerb and a familiar stout figure trod up the steps to Harriet's front door.

Brierley.

Benedict roundly castigated himself for a fool, but he could not help himself—for all her betrayal of him, he still felt a sense of responsibility towards her. He *wanted* to protect her. He vowed to keep a close eye on Brierley. The man had taken an instant dislike to him for some reason that Benedict couldn't quite fathom. Was it merely that Harriet had been forced to stay unchaperoned at Tenterfield? That made no sense—the snowstorm had hardly been his fault. It hadn't helped that Brierley had caught that intimate moment between

himself and Harriet in St George Street, but even that
could not explain the extreme threat of cutting off his
support of his stepmother. Besides, he recalled Cooper,
the footman, telling him that Brierley had threatened
the same thing when he had collected Harriet from
Tenterfield Court.

With a muttered oath, Benedict spun on his heel,
crossed over Piccadilly and headed in the direction of
St James's Street.

Harriet turned Benedict's card over and over in her
hands.

*Why is it always me who suffers? He left me without
a backward glance eleven years ago, never caring what
might become of me or our baby, and now he is back
and stirring up trouble for me whilst he struts around,
guilt-free, with a new title and untold wealth.*

A maid came in with the tea tray, snapping her from
her resentful thoughts. She thrust the card into her reticule and stood up to remove the spencer she still wore,
handing both to Janet, who tidied and re-pinned Harriet's hair before taking her discarded outer clothing
upstairs, leaving Harriet to settle on the sofa with her
cup of tea to await Edward.

As the clock struck two, Stevens opened the salon
door and announced Lord Brierley. Harriet placed her
cup in her saucer and put them on the table, taking deep
breaths as she strove to remain calm. She had made her
decision or, rather, she had accepted that she had no
choice. Being under Edward's control was surely pref-
erable to another marriage, where the control would
be of an entirely different kind. She stood to greet her
stepson.

Edward strode into the salon, halted and bowed. 'Good afternoon.'

'Good afternoon, Edward. Thank you for being so prompt,' Harriet said. 'Stevens, a glass of Madeira for his lordship, if you please.' Her stepson's scowling expression prompted her to add, 'And bring a glass for me, too.' She might need a little fortification.

She sat again on the sofa and settled her skirts around her. Edward took a chair.

'Well, madam?'

'Goodness, Edward, you do come straight to the point. Are you in so much haste? Might we wait until Stevens has served our drinks?'

'You have reached a decision?'

Harriet inclined her head, watching Edward carefully. He did not quite meet her eyes and was fidgeting with his watch chain—something he often did when agitated.

'Good. Then we will wait until Stevens returns,' he said.

Their Madeira was served and Stevens left the salon, closing the door behind him. Harriet braced herself, but Edward now appeared content to take his time, sipping at his wine as he studied her over the rim of his glass. His hesitation, rather than providing reassurance, shook her. Had he already decided to do his worst, whatever her answer might be? The fear that thought generated strengthened her confidence that she had made the right decision. She did not want to be cast adrift from Fanny and the children. They were her family, and she loved them all dearly. She was also now more certain than ever that she did not want to be forced to marry again simply in order to survive.

'I have decided I will comply with your wishes, Edward,' she said, unable to bear the silence a moment longer.

His relief was apparent and it made her wonder whether he regretted issuing such a drastic ultimatum to her in the first place. He might be stuffy and pompous, but he was not a cruel man. Unlike his father. Harriet did not believe he would take pleasure in either cutting her off from the family or in casting her into penury.

'Very well, madam. I am pleased you have come to your senses.'

'There is one difficulty I must draw to your attention, however,' Harriet continued.

'Difficulty?'

'Indeed, sir. You decreed yesterday that I must have nothing more to do with Sir Benedict Poole, that I must not even speak to him.'

'I did.'

'It occurs to me that it is inevitable our paths will cross from time to time. We have friends in common and—'

'Which friends?'

'Lord and Lady Stanton, for a start.' Harriet carefully hid her satisfaction. She knew Edward would never risk upsetting the Earl of Stanton. He was a member of a powerful clique of the aristocracy.

'Hmph! Continue,' Edward said.

'It would be rude if, on those occasions, I failed to even acknowledge Sir Benedict,' Harriet went on. 'And it would surely start people wondering why I never speak to him. That would not meet with your approval—it would surely cause that speculation you are so keen to avoid.'

'Hmm. Indeed. Very well. I shall concede that you may treat Poole as you might any casual acquaintance, for the sake of good manners.' He heaved himself to his feet. 'But be under no illusion, madam. If I hear of any further indiscretions on your part, it will be the worst for you.'

'And I may still visit Fanny and the children? And come to Kitty's ball?'

Edward hesitated, frowning at her.

'Come now, Edward. How shall you explain my absence to Fanny?'

'Very well. But make sure you heed my warning.'

Edward marched from the room, leaving Harriet unsure whether to laugh or to cry. At least she had wrung the concession from him that she might at least speak to Benedict without the risk of Edward's harsh penalties. That should at least make life less fraught.

A casual acquaintance. That should prove no problem at all.

Chapter Twelve

Benedict felt the stares burning into him as he followed the footman through the hall and into the morning room at White's. Speculative whispers faded into silence as he came within earshot. He ignored the blatant curiosity as he walked past several members—sitting in small groups or alone with their rustling newspapers or simply dozing, a glass of brandy by their side—to join Matthew, seated by one of the windows that overlooked the street, a glass of red wine in hand.

'Another glass for Sir Benedict,' Matthew said, half rising and reaching across to shake Benedict's hand. 'How is Lady Brierley?'

'She is fine,' Benedict said tersely. The speculative gleam in Matthew's blue eyes did nothing to placate Benedict's exasperation with Harriet and her secrets, and neither did the fresh wave of muttering from the other members when they heard his name mentioned. He sat down, saying, 'I seem to be attracting some interest.'

Matthew glanced round. 'Indeed,' he said with a quirk of his lips. 'For some, you will be the highlight of their day—a titbit to take home to their wives. Al-

though, seeing who has just followed you in, I doubt
you will remain the highlight for long.'

Benedict looked up to see a tall man with dark brown
hair framed in the open doorway. He skimmed the oc-
cupants of the room, then turned and disappeared. The
low murmur of conversation swept away the silence that
had greeted the newcomer's appearance at the door.

'Who was that?'

'Stanton,' Matthew replied. 'Lady Stanton's husband.'

'Why would he cause such attention?' Benedict could
understand a stranger such as himself causing ripples,
but not someone like Stanton.

'A rumour is going the rounds,' Matthew said.
'There were whispers last summer that he was seeing
someone—a widow—but no one could ascertain the
truth of it. Then he married in September and the rumours died down. But someone has started them up
again, and there is a rush to discover who she is and
whether she is still under his protection. There's all kinds
of gossip, including—you might be interested to hear—
speculation that it was your friend, Lady Brierley.'

Matthew's words hit as effectively as a physical blow,
but Benedict quelled the anger that surged through him,
determined to give his friend no cause to question his
reaction. Was Stanton the reason Harriet had been so
quick to forestall his suggestion they become lovers?

'Hmph,' he grunted. 'Have these people nothing better to do with their time?'

Matthew grinned. 'No. That is the point. For many,
their interest is solely in what their friends and neighbours are up to, and if they can embellish the tale, so
much the better. Plus, according to Ellie, there is a certain amount of jealousy amongst some ladies that a

woman such as Felicity succeeded in snaring Stanton where all their efforts had failed. They, no doubt, are relishing their chance to stir the coals. Still—' his piercing eyes lingered on the empty doorway '—I find it hard to believe Stanton has a mistress. I've never seen a man more besotted with his wife.'

Benedict choked on his wine. He eyed Matthew, who was staring at him, clearly perplexed by his reaction. 'Have you taken a look in the mirror lately, Matt?' Benedict shook his head slowly at his friend. 'I'd wager that you'd see one there.'

As Matthew continued to stare blankly at him, he clarified. 'The only husband more besotted with his wife than *Stanton* happens to be you, you numbskull.'

Matthew smiled, his hard features softening, and Benedict felt again the solitude of his own life. He had not known love since his parents had died. He had watched Eleanor and Matthew together, and he was envious. He yearned to be the centre of someone else's universe, and to feel the same way about her. Harriet's face materialised in his mind's eye. Once he had believed that was what they shared. He had been wrong. That had not been love. Infatuation, lust, call it what you would, it was not love. He would be more careful this time.

'In fact,' he continued, 'your blissful contentment with married life has persuaded me it is time to take the plunge myself and find a wife. As soon as possible.'

Matthew frowned. 'Not every marriage is as happy as mine, Ben. It can take time to adjust to it. You'd be wise to get settled into your new life before marrying. Or have you already met someone?' He paused, then said, 'A certain widow, perhaps?'

Benedict clamped his lips against an angry retort and carefully kept his tone unconcerned.

'Not a widow, no,' he said. 'I have every intention of restoring the name of Poole to a place of pride. I am aware my trade connections will count against me, but marriage to a suitable well-bred girl will surely help. You saw the reaction when I came in here—I have the disadvantage of resembling my cousin, so my identity was guessed at the minute I set foot inside the door. I thought I might ask Eleanor for some introductions.'

Matthew's lips firmed in disapproval. 'I still think you should not rush into it, but if you are determined to go ahead, I am sure she will be pleased to help.'

'I did not expect to see you out and about this evening.'

The quietly spoken words prompted a lurch in Harriet's stomach, followed by a skip of her heart. Had she suspected Benedict would be here, she would not have come to the Barringtons' rout, not so soon after Edward's ultimatum. There was no point in going looking for trouble. She swallowed her regretful sigh at the sight of him, so tall and handsome in his beautifully tailored evening coat, his auburn hair burnished in the candlelight, and then chided herself for her inconsistency. It was no good deciding at one minute that she was happy to play by Edward's rules and treat Benedict as a mere acquaintance and the next minute hanker after him purely because she could not have him.

'I was overcome by the stuffiness of the solicitor's office today, that was all,' she said. 'Now, if you will excuse me, I—'

Benedict grasped her arm above the elbow, his fingers warm against her bare skin. Everything inside her clenched tight at his touch, and her heart beat faster.

'Not so fast,' he hissed. Then he raised his voice. 'Allow me to escort you to a chair and to procure you a glass of wine.'

He tugged her to his side, then crooked his elbow. A few nearby guests had turned to stare. Harriet raised her chin and placed her hand on Benedict's arm.

'Why?' Her voice shook despite her best efforts to control it. 'You will make things worse.'

'Worse? How so?'

They left the salon, which had been stripped of virtually every stick of furniture in order to accommodate the Barringtons' guests. As they passed through the hall, Benedict asked a footman where they might sit and they followed him to a smaller room where chairs were clustered in random groups. There were a few other guests in here, taking the opportunity to rest, but it was quiet compared to the babble of conversation in the salon.

Harriet sank onto a chair as Benedict asked the footman to bring them some wine. He pulled another chair round so he faced her. His intense scrutiny unnerved her but she was careful to show no sign, concentrating on breathing steadily and reciting a poem in her head. She had learned the trick in the early days of her marriage, in order to prevent reactions that might provoke her husband.

'How will I make things worse?'

'This!' Harriet gestured to the room. 'It is so *particular*. It is not how casual acquaintances behave.'

'I saw Brierley come to your house after I left. Is he still threatening you? I take it from what you said earlier that he is able to stop your allowance if he sees fit?'

'That is not your concern—my life is nothing to do with you.'

'We used to be friends. If you are in trouble… If there is anything I can do…'

'*Trouble?*' She laughed, battening down the anger and bitterness that roiled her stomach. She had been in trouble since the minute he had decided she was only good for sowing his wild oats. It was a little late for him to develop a conscience now. She eyed him, envying the simplicity of his life. *He* could marry, secure in the knowledge that he would be the one in control. If *she* was forced to marry again, if Edward carried out his threats, she would be completely at the whim of her husband. 'My only trouble will arise from being seen with you.'

The footman brought two glasses of wine and Harriet sipped gratefully, grasping at this distraction from her negative thoughts and emotions.

'Why has your stepson taken me in such dislike?'

'I do not know. I suggest you ask him.'

His hand—large and warm—enclosed hers, where she had been fiddling with a tendril of hair, left to curl loose by her ear. She snatched her hand free.

'Stop it! What if someone should see?'

'What are you hiding?'

'Nothing.'

'Do you already have a lover? Is that the reason for your stepson's threats?'

She stiffened, aghast. 'I *beg* your pardon?'

'Oh, don't look at me with such innocent indignation.' He leaned towards her, lowering his voice. 'After all, you did not scruple to sleep with me when you were still a virgin. Why should you quibble over the suggestion of a lover here and there now you are a widow?'

Harriet shot to her feet. As quickly as she moved, however, Benedict's fingers encircled her wrist. Twist as she might, she could not break free of his grip.

'Why were you afraid of me, in the folly? Were you scared your lover would find out?'

'I do *not* have a lover,' she said through gritted teeth.

'I hear differently.' His rage was palpable. 'Why did you not tell me you already had a protector when you rejected me?'

She froze. *What has he heard?* But it was nonsense; she had only ever had the one lover, and that had ended months since.

'It is nonsense,' she said, out loud for his benefit. 'How could I tell you about something that does not exist?'

'But something terrified you, that day at the folly,' he went on relentlessly.

Why will you not just let it be? 'You are wrong. Your memory is wrong. I changed my mind.'

'What about the evening before? You ran up those stairs as if the devil himself was on your heels.'

He was...in the past. And, just like that, all of her fight drained away. Times like that were hard to forget. Her knees trembled and she sank once again onto the chair. Benedict released her wrist.

'I was upset about my father, and also that you thought I would be so readily available, just because I am a widow.'

He cast a look of scepticism at her. 'And yet you kissed me at the folly.'

'I was confused.'

'Hmph.'

Benedict said no more, but his anger dissipated before her eyes, and she hoped that would be an end to his questions. She wished it was an end to her worries, but it seemed as though they might still be amassing. Fears gnawed away inside her until she felt near overwhelmed.

What had Benedict heard about her? Lately, her life appeared to consist of disaster after disaster, and now— Had news of her *affaire* with Stanton somehow got out? What if Edward were to hear of it?

Her vision swam. She would *not* give way to tears. She reached inside her reticule and found her fan. She opened and plied it in front of her glowing face and then picked up her glass to sip at her wine. Resentment simmered inside her, both at Benedict's unjustified interrogation of her—what business of his was *any* of her life?—and at the unfairness that dictated that *she* should suffer all the penalties of their young love and that he had emerged scot-free. The most wretched and terrifying time of her life had been a mere bump on his road to success and riches.

By the time she was composed enough to glance at Benedict, he had ceased studying her and was gazing around the room. *No doubt selecting the prettiest young ladies to make up to.* She followed his gaze and choked back a sarcastic laugh. He would not find any matrimonial candidates in *here*. There was not one person present under the age of at least fifty.

It serves him right for bullying me into coming in here with him.

He looked round then, as if she had spoken her words aloud.

'I am sorry you feel unable to confide in me, Harry,' he said. 'Whatever happened between us, you do know I would always protect you, don't you?'

A painful lump swelled in her throat. Why was he

making this so hard? All she ever wanted was to feel
safe and secure. She conjured up again the memory of
Benedict standing up to Edward. He had made her feel
safe then, protected and cared for. Except it was not
real. It was an illusion. Besides, she didn't want him
to be nice. She *wanted* to hate him. Her entire predicament was his fault. *Deep breaths. Take care.* She forced
a careless shrug.

'You are imagining dramas where there are none. I
am not hiding anything.'

'Yet you will not tell me why your stepson is prepared to resort to blackmail to keep you from associ-
ating with me.'

'Blackmail? I should hardly call it that.'

Although it was blackmail, wasn't it? And Edward
had the power over her to force her to obey his wishes.
Nausea clogged her throat. Power. All men used it,
to keep women compliant. And Benedict—perhaps
unconsciously—was using his power as a man to persuade her to confide in him. Well, she wouldn't do it.

'Edward is worried about my reputation, in case it
harms his daughter's come-out,' she said. 'Any father
would do the same and I do not blame him. He wishes
to ensure that no scandal attaches to *any* member of
his family. He was upset to find me at a place such as
Tenterfield Court.'

'Scandal?' Benedict's growl was menacing. 'There
is no scandal attached to *my* name. I'd better have a few
words with that stepson of yours.'

Harriet swallowed. An argument between Edward
and Benedict could only exacerbate matters. She drew
on all her years of learning how to calm a fraught situation. At least with Benedict she need not fear raised
fists or forced, unwanted intimacies.

'It will take time for people to forget the link between the Poole name and Sir Malcolm's behaviour,' she said soothingly. 'Edward is conservative. He doesn't like change. Give him time. Once Kitty is out, he will relax. He is in the throes of negotiating an advantageous match for her, one that is very important for both the family and for him politically.'

She raised her gaze to Benedict's, forcing herself to maintain eye contact. 'You have formed an entirely mistaken impression of my relationship with my stepson. That is no doubt my fault. When you saw me this morning I was upset with myself and my failure to ever ascertain my legal right to the allowance Edward pays me. Realising my own naivety was not pleasant, but it makes no difference whatsoever to my position and I most certainly have no need of protection from my own stepson.'

'Then, why say I will make things worse?'

'I have no wish for my name to be linked to yours for the reasons I have stated. It is acceptable for us to converse in the company of others, but you must understand that a *tête-à-tête* such as this will only raise speculation and, possibly, expectations. *That* will help neither of our causes. You wish to find a bride, do you not? Having our names bandied about together will not help.

'We were friends once, long ago, but we are different people now. I no longer know you, and you no longer know me or the person I have become. I fully understand you might gravitate towards me, as a familiar face in a sea of strangers— '

'*Familiar?* You think I suffer from *bashfulness*?'

'Are Lady Ashby and Mr Damerel present tonight?'

'No, but—'

'It is only natural you must feel your lack of acquaintance,' Harriet said, meeting Benedict's darkening expression with a kind smile, 'but you will soon find your feet, I promise. In the meantime, might I introduce you to anyone?' She couldn't resist adding, 'A suitable young lady, perhaps?'

His eyes narrowed. Then he smiled back at her, but his smile did not reach his eyes. He stood up. 'Thank you for your kind consideration, my lady, but I flatter myself I am capable of arranging my own affairs.' He proffered his arm. 'Might I escort you back to the salon?'

Harriet stood and shook out her blue silk skirts before smiling and accepting his arm. 'Thank you, sir. I am so glad we had this little chat. I think we understand one another more clearly now, do you not agree?'

Chapter Thirteen

Benedict kept his answering growl hidden deep in his chest.

Infuriating…patronising…contradictory…*witch*.

They reached the salon and Harriet immediately left his side, heading towards a knot of people standing by one of the open windows. The salon was stiflingly hot, crammed with people, all of whom appeared to be talking at once. The room echoed with voices. How did these people tolerate it? Where was the pleasure in standing around in groups, shouting at each other and struggling to make sense of the conversation? A glance around showed not one familiar face and Benedict found himself wondering if Harriet had a point: had part of his reason for seeking her out been simply that he knew her?

He had become reacquainted with several old school and university friends since his return from India, but he could see none of them in this crowd. He wended his way past various knots of people until he caught sight of a face he did recognise. He hesitated. Did he really want to encourage Miss Marstone's attentions? He deliberated a second too long; Miss Marstone caught sight of him and her eyes lit up as she glided in his direction.

'Sir Benedict! We meet again.'

She halted in front of him, standing too close for his liking. Her flowery perfume, heady and strong, wafted over him.

He bowed. 'Good evening, Miss Marstone. We do indeed. Are you here with your mother?'

'Oh, yes. She is around somewhere.' She raised her fan and fluttered it before her face. 'I declare, it is exceedingly hot in here with all these people, is it not? It is enough to make one feel quite faint.' Above her fan, she watched him through her lashes.

For his part, Benedict eyed Miss Marstone and decided she looked far too robust to swoon on him, but he nevertheless proffered his arm, saying, 'May I escort you across to the window, Miss Marstone? I am sure you will find it cooler over there.' He gestured to the window next to the one where Harriet appeared to be holding court in the centre of a group. He recognised Lady Stanton and, by her side, his large hand at the small of her back, the tall man Matthew had pointed out as Lord Stanton.

Benedict tore his attention away from that group and focused on the girl by his side.

'Such a gentlemanly gesture.' Miss Marstone dimpled up at him as she took his arm. 'Tell me, sir, is it hard to adjust to London society after spending so many years abroad?'

'There are many English people who live in India, Miss Marstone. I did socialise with them in addition to the natives.'

'Oh, yes, but they are *merchants*, surely? Oh…not that there is anything *wrong* with such people, oh, good heavens, no. But in London you can mix with the elite in society. You must, I feel certain, acknowledge the superiority of the company found here to that found anywhere. *This* is the pinnacle of civilisation.'

Benedict bit back his retort. She was young and innocent. She only knew what she had been taught and, with a mother like Lady Marstone, she surely could be forgiven her prejudices.

'I was, and still am, a merchant,' he reminded her.

'Oh, yes, I know. But you are a gentleman as well… a baronet. That makes all the difference.'

The difference to what? Are all young ladies as openly covetous of a title, as Harriet had once been?

He must hope not, or his search for a bride would consist of much biting of his tongue. Such superiority was not an admirable trait in Benedict's book. His head began to ache.

'And,' Miss Marstone added, 'you need no longer work, now you are a property owner.'

The inference being that it was socially acceptable for a gentleman to make his money from land, but not from trade.

Why her words, and the sentiment behind them, rankled he did not know. He knew full well that being in trade was deemed an unsuitable occupation for a gentleman of the *ton*, but he had not been prepared for it to be pointed out to him in quite such a brazen manner.

'Yes, I have property,' he said, 'but I happen to enjoy working, so I intend to continue to run my trading business. In fact,' he added, hoping to puncture her innate conviction that her view of the world was the only correct one, 'my partner and I have just purchased a ship so that we can increase our business interests.'

'Oh! Oh…yes…well…but…your partner?' Her white brow wrinkled, then she drew in a deep breath, and her lips were smiling again. 'Mr Damerel is your partner, is he not? Mama told me all about him, and I make no doubt if that kind of work is suitable for Lady Ashby then *I* can have no objection to it.'

Benedict gave up, but made a mental note not to get trapped in Miss Marstone's company again, or he was likely to say something he regretted.

They had reached the window where there was, indeed, a fresher feel to the air. Miss Marstone released his arm and propped her hands on the low sill as she leaned forward to draw in a deep breath.

Perhaps not so innocent after all, Benedict mused, eyeing the bottom thrust provocatively in his direction.

'Do you need rescuing?'

At the exact time those quiet words reached his ears, Miss Marstone straightened and turned to him, her smile dying on her lips as she saw Harriet.

Laughter bubbled beneath Harriet's cheery, 'Good evening, Miss Marstone. How do you do?'

'I am very well, thank you, Lady Brierley.' Miss Marstone moved to stand beside Benedict and linked her arm through his in a proprietorial manner that made him stiffen. 'Sir Benedict and I were just enjoying a breath of fresh air. There is an uncomfortable *closeness* in the room tonight, do you not agree?'

'Oh, indeed,' Harriet replied. 'Almost suffocating, one might say. I wonder, sir, that you do not propose a walk on the terrace to allow Miss Marstone to cool off. She is looking somewhat flushed.'

Benedict felt Miss Marstone's fingers tighten on his sleeve. He frowned at Harriet, who returned his glare with one of limpid innocence. What the hell was she playing at? One minute she could not wait to get away from him, then she was all false sympathy, concerned that he was *shy*, for God's sake, and *now* she was affability itself. Her changes were mercurial and he did not understand her.

He resisted the urge to massage his temples and smiled at her instead. 'What a very thoughtful suggestion, Lady Brierley.' He peered through the open window. There were several people outside, taking the opportunity to cool off. 'Would you care to take a turn around the terrace, Miss Marstone?'

He did not miss the triumphant smile she directed at Harriet. Harriet, irritatingly, merely smiled graciously, seemingly unconcerned.

'Thank you, sir. I should like that very much,' Miss Marstone said.

Later that evening, Benedict strolled up the dark path towards the terrace. The crowds at the rout party had begun to dwindle and the evening air had cooled significantly, driving everyone else indoors. Benedict had taken advantage of the peace of the garden—large by the standards of most London town houses—and had escaped the throng to soothe his aching head and to mull over the young ladies to whom he had been introduced. Not one of them stood out as someone he would particularly care to share his life with. But it was early days, and he had only just begun looking for a bride, so there was no need to despair.

As he placed one foot on the bottom step up to the terrace, quiet voices reached his ears. Harriet... That was Harriet's voice—with a man. His temple began to throb again. Who was he? Taking care to tread silently, he moved up a couple more steps, keeping to the shadow at the side of the flight. There... A couple in the shadows, standing close, face-to-face. There was an intimacy about their stance that set Benedict's heart

racing with the urge to charge up those steps and haul
the man away from Harriet.

'We must hope Brierley doesn't get wind of these
other rumours, as well.' A stranger's voice, deep and
rich.

'Heavens, yes.' Harriet's reply was heartfelt. 'I cannot believe…after all this time…' There was a pause.
'Stanton…about Felicity… Are you sure? I mean, we
have never spoken about—'

'Hush, Harry. It is all sorted. There is no need for
you to fret. Your friendship means the world to Felicity. She will not jeopardise—'

Something pushed against Benedict's leg and he
jerked it back. His foot slipped over the edge of his
step to the one below with a loud scraping noise. He
glanced down to see a pale-coloured cat slinking away
down the steps, no doubt startled away by his reaction.

'Shh! I heard something.'

Hell and damnation. There was nothing for it; he
must brazen it out. Benedict strolled up the remaining
steps, making no attempt to conceal himself as he silently cursed the cat. He reached the terrace, rounded
a pillar topped with a stone urn and saw that the man
with Harriet was the Earl of Stanton, her best friend's
husband.

Bloody hellfire.

Harriet's alarmed expression eased. 'Sir Benedict!
It is you. You startled me.'

Benedict's mind whirled with the implications of
the snatches of conversation he had heard. That their
talk was clandestine could not be denied. Why else had
they been standing out here, alone, in the dark? Were
the rumours they had been discussing the same ones
that Matthew had told him about?

Although he had nigh on accused Harriet of having a lover, he had not really believed it, but now— Were Harriet and Stanton involved? A hard ball of anger barrelled through his chest.

Virtuous widow indeed.

Harriet and Stanton were staring at him, awaiting his reply.

'My apologies for startling you, Lady Brierley. I felt the need to clear my head.' He eyed Stanton, who returned his glare with a hard stare and bunched brows.

'I understand you are an old...*acquaintance* of Lady Brierley's,' Stanton said. He thrust out his hand. 'Stanton.'

Benedict shook the proffered hand. 'I prefer to think of myself as a friend,' he said. 'A very *good* friend.'

Stanton turned from Benedict and took Harriet's arm. 'Come. Felicity will be wondering where we are.'

Benedict stepped sideways, blocking their path. 'Not so fast.'

Stanton appeared to grow taller and broader as he sized Benedict up. He manoeuvred Harriet so that he stood between her and Benedict, his hand clamped around her wrist.

'Is there a problem, Poole?' Stanton's voice was deathly quiet.

Benedict felt his rage grow. If this buffoon thought he could intimidate him, he was way off course. 'There is. Go inside, Harriet. I want a private word with *his lordship.*'

'Do not,' she said. 'Please.' She twisted free of Stanton's grip and tugged at him, her obvious familiarity with the earl doing nothing to calm Benedict's anger. 'There is no need for this. I do not want a scandal.'

'If you do not want scandal, what the blazes are you doing out here in the dark with a married man?'

'And why is that any of your business?' Stanton snarled. 'Harry. Go indoors. Now.'

'No! I will not leave you two here like this. This is madness. There is nothing—'

'Richard. There you are.' Lady Stanton was suddenly in their midst, chattering away, linking arms with her husband. 'I trust you managed to sort out that little misunderstanding between Harriet and me? Oh, you are here, too, Sir Benedict. Now then…what *will* you make of all this? *Such* a foolish thing… I did tell you, Harriet, not to pay attention to such silly talk. It is a good job, is it not—' she turned guileless eyes to Benedict '—that we ladies have you gentlemen to talk some sense into us when we are all ready to fly at each other, fluffing our feathers?'

She smiled and her rather ordinary features were transformed. Benedict felt his anger abate. Had he misinterpreted that conversation? Lady Stanton seemed relaxed about her husband and Harriet being out here together. He had at first wondered at the pairing of the handsome earl and his lady, but he now began to see the qualities that had attracted Stanton to his wife as she deftly defused the situation. Stanton, too, had relaxed his combative stance and was watching his wife with adoring eyes.

'It is all settled now, Felicity, dear,' Harriet said. 'There is nothing more to resolve, apart from asking these two to shake hands. Sir Benedict has done his own fair share of jumping to conclusions, when he discovered Stanton and me talking in the dark.'

'Really, sir? You have no need for suspicions in *that* direction, I assure you.'

Lady Stanton's voice rang with confidence and Benedict was left feeling rather foolish.

'And the rumours you were discussing?' He could not shake the impression he was being misled, but he could not for the life of him work out why. If there was something between Harriet and Stanton, his wife would not be out here trying to smooth things over.

'Oh, that was just silly talk by somebody who passed on some scurrilous gossip to Harriet,' Lady Stanton said. 'I am exceedingly fortunate to have Richard to rely on, for he sorted it all out in a trice. He would make an excellent diplomat.'

'He would indeed,' Harriet said warmly. 'Now, will you two please shake hands? It is chilly out here and I am feeling the cold.' She slipped her arm through Benedict's and nudged him round to face Stanton.

'I apologise for jumping to conclusions,' Benedict said, holding out a reluctant hand.

Stanton's jaw remained set, but he took Benedict's hand and shook, for the second time that evening. 'Accepted,' he said. 'It was—perhaps—an easy mistake to make.'

'There,' Harriet said. 'Now we are all friends again.' She squeezed Benedict's arm. 'Relax,' she whispered. 'And thank you—I do realise you were trying to protect me but, trust me, it was not needed.'

Trust her? He looked into her violet eyes, reading nothing there but calm friendliness, knowing that underneath lurked secrets and unanswered questions. No, he did not trust her but the Stantons clearly did, so he would keep his own counsel.

They went back inside the house, but as Benedict began to take his leave of Harriet, she stayed him.

'Do not go. Please, Benedict. Not yet. I have something I wish to say.'

Benedict? Against his better judgement, he waited, suspicion niggling away deep inside. What *was* she up to?

Harriet's smooth forehead bunched in a frown. 'You were right, what you said earlier. We *were* friends and, despite Edward, I would like to be friends again. I do not like this feeling of being on edge whenever we meet. Might we start again, do you think?'

He would not refuse. How could he, when he wanted the same thing? But this change in her attitude to him had been prompted by something other than feeling uncomfortable in his presence.

'I would like that,' he said, but he silently reserved judgement.

She was up to something and, when she played her hand, he would be ready for her.

Chapter Fourteen

Harriet studied her reflection in the long mirror on her bedchamber wall. A stranger stared back at her.

'Tie on the mask, please, Janet.'

The black mask, decorated with silver stars and crescent moons, covered her face from above her eyebrows to the tip of her nose, from which point it swept out to follow the curve of her cheeks and then round to her ears, leaving just her mouth and jawline exposed. She felt the weight and worry of the past few days melt away. Tonight, she was not Harriet, Lady Brierley, widow, but Diana, Roman goddess of the hunt and of the moon, and she could relax and enjoy herself without wondering, every time anyone looked at her, whether they had guessed that it was she who had been Stanton's lover last year. The rumours had continued to build day by day and she knew it was only a matter of time before the truth was out in the open. What Edward would choose to do then was anyone's guess.

'Ooh, milady, even I can't tell it's you,' Janet said, grinning from ear to ear.

Harriet smiled at her maid. 'Thanks to you and your hard work, Janet,' she said. 'You have worked a miracle.

I shall have to cultivate a foreign accent, so no one can discover me by my voice.'

She touched the delicate silvery gauze headdress—like the mask, also enhanced with beautifully embroidered crescent moons and stars—that disguised her distinctive silver-blonde hair. Pinned securely in place, she was confident it would not be dislodged by dancing.

What costume will Benedict wear? Shall I recognise him? She must pray she would, for her plan depended upon it.

She had not seen him since the evening of the Barringtons' rout, where the sight of him in private conversation with Bridget Marstone had provoked such a white-hot spike of jealousy within her that she had been unable to stick to her resolution—made only minutes before—to avoid him for the rest of that evening. Now her resolve was for the opposite, and she shivered in excitement at the thought of seeing him again, and at what she was planning.

At the rout, the seed of an idea had taken root in her brain, and in the days since then, its tendrils had infiltrated her thoughts until it was all she could think of: if the worse should come to the worst, and she was forced to look for a husband, well...

Benedict wants a wife. Why should it not be me?

She knew he was not violent, and he had already shown by his reactions when they met at Tenterfield Court that he would not force himself on her. *He* would never punish her for a wrong look or a wrong word.

Her instinct to dismiss the idea as being unfair to Benedict had been drowned by a surge of resentful entitlement.

He owes me!

Her predicament was his fault. Actions had consequences, and his refusal to marry her when she'd conceived his child had resulted in her disastrous marriage, which in turn had driven her to take a lover to vanquish her terrible memories of her husband.

The consequences of Benedict's return, their past relationship and her *affaire* with Stanton had now combined until it threatened to leave Harriet destitute, with no income and no means of support unless she married again.

Besides, he owes it to me. He owes me peace of mind... He owes me respectability... He owes me a baby.

If you are still able to have a baby. She shook the errant thought away, determined to allow nothing to spoil the evening ahead. It was true she had not conceived during her marriage to Brierley, and she had counted that a blessing, but surely God could not be so cruel to deny her a child if she remarried.

She focused on her image in the mirror, spinning this way and that to examine her appearance from all angles. Her dress consisted of a length of fine silver muslin draped around her figure and caught at the waist with a woven silver-coloured belt, knotted to allow the ends to dangle free. A silver brooch, fashioned in the shape of a bow and arrows, pinned the fabric at one shoulder and, daringly, left the other shoulder bare, preventing the wearing of her shift. The fabric flowed over the roundness of her hips and bottom before spilling to the floor in shimmering waves. A silver-coloured quiver containing three 'arrows'—made from slender canes to represent the shafts, with white feathers stuck on the end to represent the fletching—was slung diagonally across her back, secured in place by a fine silver chain. The effect of that chain passing between her breasts, emphasising each full mound, was deliciously provocative.

Did she dare carry out her plan to seduce Benedict?

What if he shrugs his shoulders to the fact he has compromised you? He walked away from you before, and you were with child then.

He is older now. Surely he will be more responsible. Besides, I'll seduce him so thoroughly, he won't be able to resist me.

You know this is wrong. You are not being fair to Benedict.

She thrust aside her niggling conscience. What choice did she have? Anyway, when had Benedict been fair to her… When had *life* been fair? But that thought prompted the memory of all the servants she had given shelter to in the house in Cheapside. She pictured their innocent babies, and she felt ashamed. In comparison, life had been very fair to her. Those servant girls were, however, another reason why she must do something drastic to protect her future. The charity relied on donations. If it came out that she had been Stanton's lover, and Edward cut her off from the family, then those donations would surely trickle to a halt.

'Lord Stanton's carriage has pulled up outside, milady. Are you ready?'

Janet's voice jerked Harriet from her reflections. 'Yes. I am ready.'

The masquerade ball was a private party to celebrate the birthday of Lady Cotham, at her country house, north of Paddington village. A full moon lit the way, as did the coach lamps on the procession of carriages leaving London on the Edgware road. At Cotham Manor they were required to produce their invitations to prove they were invited guests. In the well-lit hall, Harriet got her first proper look at Richard and Felicity, resplendent in their costumes as a medieval nobleman and his lady. Studying the guests arriving at the same time as them, Harriet marvelled at the inventiveness of some costumes and realised that, as much as she had embraced the knowledge that she would be hard to recognise, she was less keen that she was unable to put a name to many of the other masked revellers. Anonymous eyes glittered through masks and she felt a shiver of apprehension descend her spine.

Thank goodness she was with the Stantons and had not ventured here alone.

There was no formal announcement of their arrival. Lady Cotham had decreed nothing should spoil the fun of guessing the identities of her guests and, to that end, the only people whose costumes were known were Lord and Lady Cotham themselves. His lordship was Henry VIII—a role perfectly suited to his ever-expanding waistline—and her ladyship had let it be known that *she* was Boudicca, and that she would not be amused by any other warrior queens of ancient Britain who might presume to turn up.

The ballroom was already crammed with people clad in colourful and sometimes bizarre costumes, resulting in a great deal of hilarity as everyone circulated, making wild guesses. Stanton disappeared into the throng to procure three glasses of punch, leaving Harriet and Felicity by a window with strict instructions not to move.

'It is disconcerting not to instantly recognise the person to whom one is speaking,' Felicity whispered to Harriet.

'Indeed it is.'

Felicity threaded her arm through Harriet's and a nervy sensation stirred deep inside her as she realised it wasn't just her being prudish—Felicity was wary, too.

Somehow, behind the anonymity of their masks, people
had shed their inhibitions. Manners took second place
to innuendo and—in some cases—out-and-out sugges-
tive remarks, none of which were appropriate comments
a gentleman should make to a lady. And, already, she
had witnessed a passionate kiss and a sultan squeezing
the ample breast of a giggling shepherdess. The atmosphere was reminiscent of some of the parties she and
Brierley had attended when they were first wed, after
she had lost her baby. Without volition, Harriet tensed,
squeezing Felicity's hand against her ribs.

'I am certain there is nothing to worry about, Harriet,' Felicity said. 'We will look after you, and I make
no doubt Richard will insist we leave if it gets too dis-
orderly.'

Stanton reappeared, carrying, with some difficulty,
three glasses of muddy-looking liquid. 'It's madness,'
he grumbled. 'It's impossible to tell who is who.' He
handed a glass to each of the women and sipped cau-
tiously at his own. His lips turned down in a grimace.

'Is it horrid?' Harriet said.

'It certainly packs a punch,' Stanton replied, making them laugh as they, in turn, tried the punch. It was
undoubtedly fiery, burning Harriet's throat as she swallowed, but the after-effect was a lovely warm glow.

'You had better not imbibe too freely,' Stanton continued with a grin. 'I can't cope with two tipsy women
on the journey home.'

Felicity had taken one sip, coughed and then passed
her glass back to Stanton. 'You need not worry about
my state of mind, my love,' she said, 'for I'm afraid I
cannot stomach this. Do you think—?'

'I'll find you some lemonade,' Stanton said immediately, and disappeared once more.

He was soon back with a glass of lemonade for Felicity.

'It's no wonder everyone is so merry, with the strength of this stuff,' he said, gazing around at the revellers. 'Can't understand what Cotham was thinking,' he added in a mutter. 'He must have realised such a gathering would descend into chaos. But then, he always was somewhat buffleheaded.'

'He may not have realised what might happen,' Felicity said. 'After all, we did not guess, did we? Do you want to go home, Richard?'

He slipped one arm around her waist and dropped a kiss on her nose. 'I want to keep you and our baby safe,' he said.

The familiar stab of envy pierced Harriet, despite her love for her friend. Silently, she scolded herself, aware that if she did not strive to overcome her jealousy, she would struggle to properly rejoice with Felicity and Richard when the baby was born. Their friendship was far too precious for her to risk losing it because they had been blessed and she had not. *Maybe, if my plan with Benedict works...* Resolutely, she diverted those thoughts, stifling that same whisper of conscience that she was being manipulative and unfair.

'We cannot go home yet anyway,' Stanton continued, raising his voice to compete with the musicians, who had begun to play. 'Carriages are still arriving and it's chaotic out there. Besides, my man will never forgive me if we leave before he's had a chance to brag about his exploits with the other coachmen. And whilst we're here, we may as well have a dance. At least I shall avoid the accusation of being hopelessly unfashionable by dancing with my own wife. We'll give it an hour or so, and then I'll order the carriage round. Our hosts won't be too insulted if we make our escape then.'

'Felicity! Is that you?' A statuesque flower seller, her burnished mahogany hair threaded with flowers and carrying a basket filled with fresh blooms, appeared, followed by a powerfully built, scowling Roman centurion. 'I am relieved you told me what you would be wearing or I might never have found you.'

Harriet recognised Eleanor's voice.

'Yes, it is me,' Felicity said, 'and this is Harriet—she came with us in our carriage.'

Greetings were exchanged all round and, while the two men had a comfortable grouch about the masquerade shaping up to be an unsuitable place for the ladies, Eleanor said, 'It's a pleasure to see you again, Harriet. What a beautiful costume—I should never have known it was you had Felicity not said.'

She lowered her voice, continuing, 'Matthew is being most disagreeable, complaining about the *tone* of the party, but I must confess I have been happily diverted in trying to guess who is who. Benedict came with us, too, but heaven knows where he has disappeared to. He's gone off to find himself a mermaid, no doubt.' She laughed, adding, 'He has come as a pirate.'

So Benedict *was* here. Harriet skimmed the crowd of revellers closest to them, but could see no pirate. She sipped at her punch, watching the guests, the conversation between Felicity and Eleanor washing over her. Babies. Again. Could they talk of nothing else? She instantly castigated herself for her meanness. If she were in their shoes, would she not be the same? Excited, and wanting to speak of it every chance she got? She realised, with a lurch of guilt, that Felicity had not mentioned her baby, unless Eleanor was present, for a few weeks. Had she somehow guessed that Harriet was envious? Tears of self-pity prickled at Harriet's eyes and she drank some more punch, scanning the crowd again until—there he was.

Benedict: tall, lean and unbearably sexy, clad in an open-necked white shirt with full sleeves that billowed between shoulder and cuff; a red waistcoat, fastened by laces; loose-fitting calf-length striped trousers with a wide ragged hem and black shoes sporting large silver buckles. To complete his costume a red patterned sash was tied at his waist and a cocked hat completely covered his auburn hair. As with most guests, a mask covered his upper face, but she knew him in an instant by the line of his jaw and the curve of his sensual lips. He moved amongst the crowds, at his ease, a smiling bow here, a laughing shake of his head there.

As she watched, a buxom milkmaid clutched at his arm, up on tiptoe as she said something. He bent to listen to her, sliding his arm around her waist, then cocked his head to whisper in her ear. Jealous resentment squeezed Harriet's chest, making it hard to breathe, as he led the milkmaid into a set forming in the centre of the room.

Life is so easy for him. Why should he not pay a price for what he did?

She glanced at her companions. They were all preoccupied, taking no notice of her. She could not afford for Benedict to see her with his friends, for then he would guess her identity, so she slipped away and wended her way through the throng, fending off the clumsy advances that each man she passed appeared to feel obliged to make. In escaping her friends she had also lost sight of Benedict so she made her way to the side of the room, reaching the relative safety of a wall to await the end of the dance.

She gazed around, vulnerable and on edge. There must be over a hundred people here and, although the collection of invitations at the door was intended to prevent any uninvited guests from gaining access, the glazed doors along one side of the ballroom all stood open, making the house freely accessible from the garden. At that moment a chimney sweep and a Turkish sultan staggered in through the doors, arm in arm, and kissed passionately before disappearing into the crowd. Was one of them a lady? Or was…? Harriet swallowed, feeling suddenly very naive and very uncomfortable.

This was foolish. She must return to the Stantons. On the brink of plunging back through the crowd, she saw him again, walking from the dance floor, his erstwhile partner nowhere in sight. His gaze passed over her, halted and returned. She felt stripped bare by his perusal, but there was no spark of recognition in his eyes, and that gave her the courage to smile at him, hoping he might ask her to dance. He smiled in response, and moved on. To talk to Queen Elizabeth. Harriet felt the smile freeze on her lips. This was not going to plan. She should forget the whole thing straight away and return to the Stantons.

She had no sooner left the relative safety of the wall than a hand caught hers from behind. She whirled round, tugging her hand free as the Turk she had seen earlier swayed towards her, lips puckered.

'Come here, my little arch…archer…archer*ess*,' he slurred.

'No!' she gasped. 'I must go. My husband is—'

'Her husband is here, and is not amused,' interposed a deep voice.

The sultan took one look at the tall, dangerous-looking, stubble-jawed pirate who stood protectively by Harriet and staggered back into the crowd without a protest. A nervy sensation fluttered in Harriet's stomach. Should she? Shouldn't she? She gathered her courage in both hands. It was only a dance. For now. She need not commit to following her entire plan.

She remembered to disguise her voice, speaking with what she hoped was a passable Italian accent. 'Thank you, *signor*. Would you—?'

'You are very welcome,' Benedict said, cutting across her intended invitation to dance. 'I suggest you go and find your real husband if you do not wish to attract further unwanted advances.'

He melted back into the crowd. Indignation fired Harriet's blood. Did he not find her in the slightest bit alluring? She followed his path through the other guests, and was in time to see him disappear through the open garden door. Before she could talk herself out of it, she followed.

Chapter Fifteen

Outside, Benedict had crossed the deserted stone-flagged terrace and stood, tall and erect, at the top of a flight of steps that led down into a garden, criss-crossed by paths lit by flaming torches.

Harriet crossed the terrace to stand behind him. 'But why did you flee, *signor*?' Her voice low and husky, she slid one hand across his lower back. 'Are you pirates not bold adventurers, taking risks and facing danger as you seize and conquer?'

He tensed, then turned and smiled, slowly and sensuously, as he perused her once again from head to toe, lingering over her breasts, softly outlined by the silky fabric of her dress.

'I was curious to see if you might follow,' he said. 'And now that we are here, allow me to hazard a guess.' His gaze roamed over her again, and then he leaned towards her. He pushed her gauze headdress aside and put his lips to her ear. 'If I am correct, you will owe me a forfeit.'

Shivers danced across her skin. Would he recognise her? 'What is this forfeit, *signor*?'

'Why, one that allows me to worship you, of course,'

he breathed. 'What else would a poor pirate do when he meets the goddess of his dreams?'

His finger trailed from her neck to her shoulder and stroked the bare skin of her arm, barely touching her, raising gooseflesh in its wake. He circled the sensitive skin of her inner elbow and repeated the motion on her inner wrist, before taking her hand and raising it to his lips.

'The goddess of my dreams... Diana, goddess of the moon.' He fingered her headdress and she tensed, ready to whisk out of reach if he attempted to remove it. 'Tell me I am right.'

Harriet forgot to breathe, mesmerised by the magnetism of his eyes, glowing behind his mask. He moved closer, one arm encircling her waist, pulling her hard against him.

'Tell me I'm right.' Demanding now, staring down at her, so close she could feel the thunder of his heart as well as her own. They were in full view of anyone who ventured onto the terrace, but she found she did not care. No one would know her. She relaxed. She would enjoy this moment and her forfeit.

'Diana the huntress,' she said, lifting her chin, 'as well as goddess of the moon.'

'Diana the beautiful, a female deity of unfathomable depths and hidden talents.' His lips quirked. 'And were you hunting me, Diana?' His head dipped and he feathered kisses along the scant inch of skin between the top of her mask and the line of silver stars that edged her headdress. 'Was I your prey?' His lips moved on to her ear and he traced its rim with his warm tongue. 'Do you intend to slay me now that you have me in your power by moonlight?'

His lips were on her neck, tickling as he laved the

sensitive spot beneath her ear. Before she knew it she was arching back over his rock-solid forearm, her entire throat exposed to the magic weaved by those lips. She clutched at his sleeves, aware of the weight of Diana's quiver as it swung free beneath her, the silver chain that crossed between her breasts taking its weight. He kissed and nibbled at her neck, then drifted down to her neckline. She gasped as he pushed aside the taut chain and probed the valley between her breasts with his tongue, desire sizzling through her.

Raucous laughter burst from the ballroom and Benedict lifted his head to look back towards the house. Still arched over his arm, exposed to his view and to his touch, a feeling of defencelessness stole through Harriet and she battled to stop the memories of Brierley encroaching on this moment. She could not upright herself without Benedict's help and was completely at his mercy, and yet she was not afraid. And even if she *could* stand upright, she feared her legs—weak and boneless after so simple a caress—would never support her. But she had no urge to move. She wanted his hot kisses and caresses. She needed him to heal her invisible wounds. She yearned for his loving.

She ran her hands along the length of his arms and kneaded his hard biceps. Benedict's eyes glittered as his attention returned to her and a smile hovered around his lips.

'You wanted danger, my sweet goddess,' he whispered. 'You shall have it.'

He watched her intently as, slowly, he cupped her breast, rubbing her nipple with his thumb, then squeezing and kneading until moisture slicked between her thighs and her breath grew ragged.

'My goddess,' he whispered, his voice hoarse with

need, then dipped his head to nip her aching nipple through the fine muslin of her gown, sending a lightning bolt streaking straight to her core. 'No corsets to contain such abundance—only the purest and silkiest of fabric permitted to caress her soft, moonlit skin.'

His arm tightened and he took her lips in a slow, drugging kiss that stole her breath. He slid his lips from hers to seek her ear.

'Will you follow, me, Diana?'

'Where?' she whispered. She would follow him anywhere. She vibrated with need.

'Wherever I choose,' he said. 'Will you follow my scent, hunt me down and slay me with the abundance and bounty of your charms?'

He caressed her breast once more, and her nipple ached for the touch of his lips. His hand slid lower, to her stomach; lower, to stroke her thigh through the sheer muslin. One finger pressed, a firm but fleeting touch between her legs, and scorching desire seared her veins.

'Yes,' she breathed.

He seized her lips again and then straightened, bringing her with him, holding her against the length of his hard frame until the strength returned to her legs. He stepped back then, and stared at her, a hint of a smile once again playing around his mouth. She absorbed his gaze, her blood racing. He backed away, down the steps towards the garden, one step at a time. He reached with one hand, long fingers beckoning, but when she went to take his hand, he backed down another step, always just out of reach.

Harriet stopped, uncertain what game he was playing. Did he want her, or did he not? Had he somehow guessed it was her?

He laughed up at her, teeth gleaming white as they

caught the light from a lamp set on the terrace balustrade. 'What about your husband, goddess of my
dreams?'

He does not know me. Emboldened, she descended
another step. 'He…is beyond caring.' He was always
beyond caring.

'Then, come, Diana—huntress, goddess of the moon,
temptress and siren. Follow me of your own free will
and together we will taste the ambrosia of the gods.'

He was at the base of the flight now, disappearing along a path flanked by rows of low-trimmed box.
Harriet followed him, the lure of making love with
Benedict—even if it turned out to be only this one
time—too tempting to resist. He waited for her at a
square stone-flagged area edged by taller hedges, with
a raised circular pool at its centre, a place at which four
paths converged.

'Look,' he whispered, glancing over his shoulder as
Harriet entered the square. 'She is beautiful, is she not?
She is almost real.'

As if in a dream, Harriet crossed the square to stand
by his side and they both stared into the dark, silent
pool. The moon was mirrored in the water, the surface
of which was so still the image seemed unlike a reflection, but real and solid, as if it had tumbled out of the
sky and into the cold water where it waited, patiently,
for the time it could rise again.

Benedict slid his palm to her cheek and nudged her
to face him. He cradled her face, gazing deep into her
eyes, his thumb tracing her lower lip. She felt a sigh
escape her as he gathered her to him and claimed her
lips, then his knees dipped and he scooped her up as
though she were a baby, as though she weighed next to
nothing. Eyes closed, she felt him move purposefully

away from the pool. She stroked his jaw, his stubble grazing her palm as she pressed her mouth closer to his, her tongue probing at his lips, which parted at her prompt. She wound her arms around his neck as she melted into their kiss.

Even with eyes shut Harriet knew they were now under cover, shielded from the silver gaze of the moon and prying eyes. The noise of the ball had faded to a distant drone. She kissed Benedict fervently as he bent forward at the waist, and then he was sitting with Harriet on his knee, reclining against his arm, immersed once again in his kiss whilst his free hand roamed her body, stroking and caressing and exploring.

It wasn't enough.

She squirmed around, lips still locked to his, revelling in the hard length of his erection beneath her bottom. She pressed against it, trying to ease the ache that had been building deep inside her since the moment he had reappeared in her life.

Still not enough.

She straddled his lap—the hard surface upon which he sat unforgiving to her knees—and moulded her torso to his, cradling his face in her palms. His hands, large and hard-skinned but gentle, were beneath her skirts, skimming up her bare legs to her thighs...*there.* With an inner sigh, she tilted her hips to ease his access. Her need climbed.

It still wasn't enough.

She eased her upper body away, grabbed at the laces that tied his waistcoat, pushing it from his shoulders. She tore her lips from his to trace urgent kisses down the column of his neck to the open neck of his shirt, swirling his coarse chest hair with her tongue. Sliding back along his thighs, she reached for the fall of his trousers.

The buttons were the work of a few seconds, and she reached to set his erection free. Gripping his hard length, she bent her head. A loud groan reverberated in the night. Strong hands gripped her waist and lifted her, setting her on her feet, standing where she had just been kneeling.

She gasped, clutching at his head and sending his hat flying as she threaded her fingers through his hair. She cracked open her eyelids as Benedict snapped the chain holding her quiver and arrows and flung it aside. She could just make out they were on a bench inside a plant-festooned arbour with a thatched roof. Then all thought dissolved as a hand cupped each globe of her bottom, tilting her pelvis. Her knees trembled with the effort of keeping her upright as his hot tongue explored her moist folds, returning again and again to tease the swollen bud where frantic need burgeoned until finally overwhelming her in a starburst of ecstasy.

Her legs were made of rope. Her knees were jelly. She sank to his lap, panting, her head on his shoulder, clinging tight. But he had not finished and, as her breathing steadied and slowed, he again took hold of her by her waist and he stood up, setting her on the ground before the bench. He was bending her over, sliding her skirts up to her hips. The cool night air momentarily washed over her hot skin, then he was behind her, large hands on her hips.

Her flailing hands found the back of the bench and she gripped as her legs were forced wide, and then he entered her slowly, pushing, pushing until he was buried to the hilt and he filled her completely. He stilled. A groan whispered into the night. She waited, holding her breath, anticipating, impatient. She twitched her hips, and then he was moving with hard, powerful strokes.

She braced her arms to withstand his onslaught, relishing every inch of him as she spiralled higher, racing for the moon and the stars and beyond.

As Harriet reached her second climax, Benedict abruptly withdrew to spill his seed. She slumped forward, panting, her head on her arms, knees propped against the bench seat, preventing them from buckling, every inch of her replete. Her thundering heart slowed and steadied as she drifted in a glorious haze of satiation.

Oh, how wonderful he had made her feel.

Reality intruded and Harriet's nerves began to flutter to life once more as the enormity of her deception pricked at her conscience. Would he propose when he discovered her identity? And yet…her confidence shattered as she suddenly saw, with hopeless certainty, that the only person she had deceived was herself. The plan she had agonised over was useless. How had she failed to see the flaws? Why should any man, offered sex so overtly, feel any obligation to the woman concerned? She was no virgin, and Benedict had even had the presence of mind to withdraw before his climax, ensuring that, this time at least, there would be no unwanted consequences.

Benedict. Where is he?

She peered back over her shoulder. Where had he gone? Hurriedly, she pushed herself upright and straightened her dress. Heavens, what if someone else had come and seen her there, her skirts bunched up, fully exposed? She blushed with the shame of it, and yet…there had been something gloriously wanton about the way he had taken her: controlling her and satisfying his need. But he had ensured her pleasure first—totally the opposite of the way her late husband had behaved and how he had made her feel despite, on the face of it, the acts being similar.

Had Benedict taken his pleasure and deserted her without a second thought, or would he return? Should she wait and reveal her identity, or should she melt into the moonlight? She had abandoned any hope of teasing a proposal from him. Perhaps she had not wanted to see the flaws in her plan. Perhaps, if she was brutally honest, she had wanted an excuse to have sex with him again.

A noise alerted her a split second before a large shape appeared, silhouetted against the moonlit gardens outside the arbour. A lurch of fear gave way to relief. Benedict took her in his arms and kissed her, his lips soothing, caressing, and hope surged again, flooding her with anticipation. Would her sudden doubts prove fruitless? Did he still harbour feelings for her? Might he…possibly…offer for her after all? Her blood raced as she kissed him back, pouring her whole heart into it.

He lifted his lips from hers. 'Did you miss me?'

'Oh, yes.' She had missed him forever.

'I needed to make sure we were alone,' he said. 'I want to see you.'

Her heart rose to fill her throat. She gazed up at him, then raised her hand. She traced his lips with her finger, then slid it under the lower edge of his mask. 'And I, you.'

He clasped her wrist with gentle fingers, removing her hand from his face. 'Not that.' His voice was rough. 'Not your face. Not yet. Let us not destroy this magic yet. I want to see…'

His voice faded as he unfastened the brooch that secured her dress at her shoulder. He withdrew the pin and the fabric slipped down her naked breasts to pool at her waist, where it was held in place by the tie at her waist. With neither shift nor corset beneath her gown, her breasts were bared to him, and she revelled in the swell of his chest as he drew breath, and the way he moistened his lips as though he longed to feast. Her nipples hardened as he raised his hands almost reverently and cupped each mound, weighing them. His head dipped and he suckled first one, then the other, a deep groan rumbling in his chest.

Harriet stood still. Proud. Her head high.

As he pulled at her nipple with warm lips, his hands reached for the belt tied at her waist and loosened it. Then he put his hands to her shoulders and rotated her.

'Do not move,' he whispered in her ear, touching the tip of his tongue to her lobe, and she quivered as heady anticipation near overwhelmed her. *Again?* Her pulse quickened; her breath shortened. The belt was swiftly drawn away and her dress fell to the ground. She stepped clear, pushing it aside with her foot. He then set to work on the ribbons that fastened her petticoat at her waist, warm lips feathering the nape of her neck. Instead of allowing it to drop to the ground, he gathered her petticoat from the hem, baring her legs and her bottom.

'Lift your arms.'

She obeyed. His fingers brushed against her skin as he lifted the garment over her head and her raised arms.

'Hush. Don't move. Keep your arms like that.'

He reached around and cupped her breasts, squeezing, as he kissed and nibbled her neck and shoulder. Her legs trembled and the heat at the apex of her thighs flamed. Desperate need swept through her body again and she moaned.

'Hush.'

He swept his hands down the sides of her body, skimming the indent of her waist and the curve of her hips before returning to lightly settle at her waist.

'Turn to me now.'

His hands fell away. Harriet sucked in a deep breath and turned to face Benedict, her arms still above her head. She felt no shame. She felt no embarrassment. She felt…strong. His jaw was tight. His lips set in a firm line. He took his time, his hot gaze drifting over every inch of her exposed flesh, sparking trails of fiery need wherever it alighted, setting her pulse racing anew. Then he came to her, wrapped her in his embrace and kissed her, sensually and thoroughly.

She returned his kiss eagerly but, all too soon, he lifted his lips from hers, saying, 'I shall help you dress. You will never manage that gown by yourself.'

She was soon fully clothed and stood silently whilst Benedict straightened her headdress, awkwardness flooding her. Ought she to reveal herself, before it was too late? She dithered, unsure if it would serve any useful purpose. It had been a foolish idea, and she had not fully thought through the consequences. And she realised belatedly that he might—quite rightly—be angry with her for tricking him.

He did not speak, but she felt his fingers on the ribbons of her mask, and it loosened. She did not move, but she felt her muscles stiffen. He took the mask from her face and stepped back, the mask dangling from one finger.

There was no sharp intake of breath. No sudden tensing of his lean frame. No questioning lift of his brows.

'You knew,' she said.

'I did.' He paused, then touched her chin and traced

the line of her jaw with one finger. 'And you knew, too.' He reached up and tore his own mask off. 'We both did.'

Harriet licked at suddenly parched lips. What would he do now? Was there any way to encourage him to propose? Did she have the nerve?

He leaned towards her and took her lips in a slow, thorough kiss but, other than where their mouths joined, he did not touch her. Harriet's arms lifted of their own accord to wrap around his neck, but he caught her wrists before she even touched him and gently forced her arms down to her sides.

He took his mouth from hers and stepped back, his eyes glinting with reflected moonlight. 'As the goddess of my dreams, you are perfection,' he said, his voice a deep rasp. 'But you are a mortal being, Harriet. With a mortal's weaknesses and desires. As am I. And we do not have the power to change the past.'

He bowed and walked away from her.

Chapter Sixteen

Harriet opened the letter that had just been hand delivered. It was the evening after the masquerade ball and she had neither seen nor spoken to a soul, other than her servants, since the Stantons had brought her home in the early hours. The letter bore Stanton's seal and was addressed to Harriet in Felicity's handwriting.

Dearest Harriet,

I trust your headache is much improved—I missed your company in the Park today. Eleanor and I have planned a jaunt to Richmond tomorrow! Do say you will come—it won't be the same without you. We shall travel in our carriage and the men have agreed to escort us on horseback. We leave at ten o'clock, and will drive round to collect you unless you tell me you cannot come.

Be forewarned, though, that I shall expect an unassailable excuse if you refuse!

Your friend,
Felicity Stanton

PS: I shall arrange enough food for everyone, so there will be no need for you to bring anything.

Harriet folded the letter and sighed. *The men...* Did Felicity mean just Stanton and Mr Damerel, or was Benedict included? How could she face Benedict after last night when, by the time she had followed him from the arbour and re-entered the ballroom, he had vanished? But, then again, how could she not?

The longer she left it, the more difficult it would become.

They were not even halfway to Richmond Park before Harriet deeply regretted her decision to accept Felicity's invitation. The party consisted of two carriages that conveyed those ladies who chose not to ride, plus several gentlemen and ladies on horseback, Benedict amongst them. She had thought seeing Benedict in company with others would ease the awkwardness of the situation. Instead, for her, it had heightened her discomfort. She noted, however—whenever his horse ranged within sight of the carriage window—that it appeared to affect him not one jot. He had greeted her pleasantly, with not even a flicker of awareness of what so recently had passed between them, and had ridden for much of the journey in company with Barbara Barrington and one of her daughters.

Flames of jealousy had licked through Harriet's veins until she was on fire with the need to jump out of the carriage and confront him. But of course she could not. She would not. She must just swallow her disappointment and her hurt and continue with her life as she had always done. Then Felicity and Eleanor started to talk—again—about children. And, once again, Harriet had battened down her anguish, smiling and nodding in the appropriate places in the conversation. The journey seemed to last for six hours, let alone two.

Servants had been sent ahead of the main party and, by the time they arrived, had set out chairs, rugs and blankets and were ready to serve refreshing drinks and snacks. The sun beat down from a cloudless sky and most of the ladies settled in the shade, under the spreading branches of three huge oaks, whilst the gentlemen dismounted, handed their horses to the care of the three grooms who had also ridden ahead, discarded their jackets in deference to the heat and threw themselves down onto blankets.

Harriet had always loved the easy, informal atmosphere of picnicking but was quite unable to relax today, particularly with Benedict in her direct line of sight, sprawled at his ease next to Matthew and Eleanor. At least, now that there were others within hearing, Felicity and Eleanor had ceased to chatter about babies but for Harriet the damage had been done—the memory of her daughter and her despair at her loss were firmly centre stage amongst the countless issues that buzzed unendingly through her thoughts.

She sipped her lemonade and tried to join in the general chat, her eyes burning with the effort of stemming her tears. Benedict's occasional deep rumble vibrated through her until every nerve in her body felt as tightly strung as a piano wire. Her gaze kept wandering to him, despite her efforts to concentrate on others. His chiselled jaw, clean shaven today…those broad shoulders… his trim waist and those long, lean legs encased in skin-tight buckskin and highly polished top boots.

'Are you all right, Harry?'

Harriet jumped at the quiet question. Stanton had

moved to sit next to her without her even noticing. She felt a flush rise from her neck to heat her face.

'Yes, of course I am,' she replied, a little sharper than she intended. She *would* be all right, as long as nobody offered her any sympathy.

'Hmm, if you say so. Would you like some more lemonade?'

'Yes. No. Thank you, but I think, if you will excuse me, I shall take a short walk. Sitting in the carriage for so long has turned me into a fidget.' She smiled at him, determined to allay any concerns he had about her.

'Would you like some company?'

'I think that would be a bad idea, in view of those rumours,' Harriet said, keeping her voice low in case anyone should overhear. 'Have you heard any more?'

'No, but no one is likely to say anything to my face, are they? Don't fret about them, my dear. They will soon die down.'

Stanton's contented gaze was on Felicity as he spoke. Clearly the rumours gave him no cause for concern, but then *he* had no need to worry—a man of his power and connections could not be harmed by rumour and innuendo. Unlike Harriet. She longed to believe him but she knew the workings of the *ton*. People wanted to winkle out the truth, and some people would not rest until they did.

Harriet bent her knees, ready to stand up, and Stanton rose smoothly to his feet and offered his hand to help. Once upright, Harriet shook out her skirts and then, about to thank him, she caught the significant look that passed between Lady Fenton and Barbara Barrington. The meaning of that look was simple to interpret, their interpretation of Stanton's gentlemanly gesture all too clear. If she had been Felicity or Eleanor, no one would think twice about him assisting her but, because she was a widow and therefore always viewed with some suspicion by married ladies, they would happily think the worst of her, despite her best efforts to keep scandal from her door.

'Thank you,' she murmured to Stanton, careful not to meet his gaze in case he recognised her distress.

'If you will not allow me to escort you, please ensure you do not wander out of sight,' Stanton said. 'Better still, take a maid with you.'

'I shall only walk down to the brook,' Harriet said. It was only about two hundred yards away. 'I promise I shall not go out of sight.'

She opened her parasol, angling it to shade her head from the sun, and walked down the slope towards the stream, feeling the tears come, helpless to stop them. Despite her friends—and she knew how lucky she was to have them—and despite Fanny and the children, she had never felt more alone in her life. She had no one to confide in. No one, apart from Janet and Edward, even knew about her baby. And even if they did know, surely they would think her mad for still grieving when so many babies and children tragically died in infancy. Her baby hadn't even taken one breath.

She had always prided herself on her self-control and yet lately it appeared to have deserted her. She sniffed, then reached into her reticule for a handkerchief, blew her nose and dabbed at her face, sucking in deep, calming breaths. She must tuck those horrid memories away again and be happy for her friends and their families. And she must continue to hold her head high, or those blasted rumours would keep gaining momentum, Edward would eventually hear them, and then being childless would be the least of her worries. She was sure she hadn't imagined that exchanged look between Lady Fenton and Barbara Barrington when Stanton had singled her out. Sick apprehension churned her stomach. All she could do was continue to ignore the gossip and hope people soon moved on to the next *on dit*.

And as for Benedict... A self-deprecating laugh huffed from her lips. How foolish and how naive she had been to think he might provide the answer to her prayers. He had not done so in the past and he appeared disinclined to do so now. The trouble was...she still wanted him. How would she bear it when he found a wife? But yet again, bear it she must. She hauled in a shaky breath, crouched down on the bank, dabbled her fingers in the cool, clear water of the brook and then patted her face with her wet hand.

There. That is better. I must stop all this self-pity. I shall return—

A shadow fell across her and she looked round and up, startled but not scared, for she was still in sight of the rest of the party. Benedict. Somehow she had known it would be. She straightened, and he cupped her elbow to steady her as she did so.

'This is a pleasant spot, is it not?' he said. 'It is most refreshing to get out of London. I had an urge to explore. As did you, I see.'

'Indeed.' She gestured in the direction of the picnic party, avoiding his gaze. 'I must return to the others.'

'Harriet...?' Benedict nudged her chin up with one finger. His eyes grew intent as they explored her face. He frowned. 'Have you been crying?'

'I... No! Why should I cry?' Something akin to panic coursed through her. He must not guess how vulnerable she felt. She could not cope with probing questions right now. 'If my eyes are red it is because they watered in the sunlight.'

Benedict rubbed at his jaw, glancing back to the trees where the others rested and then down at Harriet's open parasol, lying on the bank where she had placed it when she'd crouched to reach the water.

'Is it because of what happened the other night?'

'No! Why should something so trivial cause me to cry?'

She could not bear for him to think she was upset over him. She tilted her chin and started to walk back to the oaks.

She's lying. She has to be lying. Trivial indeed.

As Benedict watched Harriet walk away she paused, glancing back over her shoulder.

'Well?' she said. 'Are you going to offer me your arm up the hill?'

He retrieved her parasol—white with a blue ribbon trim to match her muslin dress and her bonnet—caught up with her and proffered his arm. Her eyes, their violet colour accentuated in the sunlight, exuded nonchalance and her brows were raised in haughty entitlement. But the still-pink tip of her nose and her puffy lids told their own story, and his gut clenched at the thought of her going off on her own to cry but he quelled his natural sympathy. Her tears could only, surely, be that her plan to shame him into offering for her had not worked. He understood enough about her situation to know that if Brierley carried out his threat to stop her allowance she would have no choice but to remarry. And he also understood that he would prove a familiar and convenient choice for that role.

She had wanted nothing to do with him—they would

be casual acquaintances, she had said—until those rumours had begun to circulate in earnest.

He could see it with absolute clarity, looking back. She knew there was a risk Brierley would hear the stories sooner or later so she had considered her options and seen Benedict as her best bet. He could pinpoint the moment her attitude had changed—at the Barringtons' rout party, after he had challenged her about having a lover and had then come across her and Stanton out on the terrace. He had suspected at the time that she was up to something. And he had been right.

Then…at the masquerade…*she* had pursued *him*. He had known her at first glance, and he knew she had recognised him. She had deliberately pursued him and allowed herself to be thoroughly seduced. His anger and his jealousy had driven him to ignore his conscience and take what she had offered, after which, no doubt, she fully expected him to make an honest woman of her. She had been mistaken. He was not so green, nor so soft, as to fall for her game. He had taken her and then he had walked away, vowing to have nothing more to do with her.

His every instinct had rebelled against being used in such a way and even though, having tasted her again, he still wanted her—desperately—he could never, ever trust her. She had married for riches before, and now she had targeted him for his wealth. Whilst he knew his wealth would be a lure for any girl he courted, with Harriet those old wounds ran too deep. He could not live every day for the rest of his life with the knowledge that he was only good enough for her now that he had wealth. Her betrayal would eat away at him and they would never be content together.

'Why are you upset, if it is not about the other night? Is it Brierley? Has he threatened you again?'

'I have not seen Edward. He is out of town on business and not due back until Kitty's ball next week.'

'That doesn't answer my question.'

Her lips firmed and she remained silent, her nose in the air, face averted.

Anger made him rash. 'Did you expect me to offer for you? Was that your plan? It would never work, you know.'

He regretted the words the instant he had spoken them but by then it was too late. High colour washed over Harriet's cheekbones and her eyes flashed.

'You flatter yourself, sir.' She spoke the words through gritted teeth, her voice low as it vibrated with fury. 'It meant nothing, and I harbour no inclinations in *that* direction, I promise you. Why did you follow me today if you have such a low opinion of me? It was clearly not from concern as to my well-being. If it was your intention to humiliate me with your insinuations and accusations, you may rest assured you have succeeded admirably.'

She snatched her hand from his arm but revealed no further hint of agitation as she walked away. She settled onto a blanket, next to a few other ladies who had already begun to eat their picnic luncheon, exchanging a few words with those nearest to her. Was it his imagination, or did that woman dressed in green—he racked his brain…Lady Fenton, that was it—twist her shoulders to casually exclude Harriet from her conversation? Were those rumours about Harriet and Stanton—true or not—the cause?

Benedict crossed to the other side of the group and sat down next to Matthew and Eleanor, where he could keep a surreptitious eye on Harriet.

'Harriet looks very charming today, does she not,

Benedict?' Eleanor said as soon as the maids serving their food had moved out of earshot.

'Indeed she does,' he said. Harriet always looked charming to him, but he wasn't fool enough to say that to Eleanor.

'You have known one another a long time,' Eleanor continued. 'Were you *close* friends when you were young?'

'Ellie…' Matthew's voice held a wealth of warning.

Benedict switched his attention to his friend's wife— and narrowed his eyes as he took in her wide-eyed, innocent expression.

'We played together when we were children,' he said, as repressively as he could.

Eleanor smiled, a knowing sort of smile that set Benedict's teeth on edge. He picked up a portion of pie from his plate and bit viciously into it, pretending he could not hear Matthew chiding Eleanor for being inquisitive.

He was careful not to watch Harriet overtly but, as he ate and drank, he pondered her final diatribe. Why *had* he followed her down to the brook? He had known nothing good could come of any private exchange; his anger, his pain at being so cynically used and his sheer need were all too raw. The conclusions he had come to did nothing to vindicate him. She was right. He *had* wanted to provoke a reaction from her. When she had walked away from the picnic group on her own, he had seen his chance and he had taken it.

He had succeeded in humiliating her and he was ashamed, vowing to avoid being alone with her in future. Nothing good could come of it and—if those rumours about Stanton were beginning to grow claws—he would be wise to keep his distance if he was serious about finding a suitable wife.

Chapter Seventeen

The following Wednesday, Harriet walked along Pall Mall with Fanny and Kitty, heading for Harding, Howell and Company, the linen draper. It was the day before Kitty's come-out ball and Harriet's step-granddaughter bubbled with anticipation. Harriet tried her best to share in the excitement, but found it hard to garner much enthusiasm for anything. Her worst fears had come to pass—since the day of the picnic, her name was being linked more and more with the Earl of Stanton's and, increasingly, she intercepted sidelong glances and walked in on whispered conversations that were suddenly cut short. Edward was still out of town on business and so had not yet heard the rumours, and Fanny had said nothing, although could she really fail to be aware of them? Edward was due to return home this evening and Harriet was by now convinced it was only a matter of time before he carried out his threat. Her nerves were in shreds as a result.

'Oh, I cannot wait until tomorrow,' Kitty said, oblivious to her mother's attempts to shush her. 'Papa said someone of *particular consequence* is to lead me out in my very first dance. Do *you* know who he might be,

Grandmama? Mama knows, but she will not tell me. It is to be a surprise.'

'Well, if it is to be a surprise, Kitty, I could hardly tell you, even if I did know,' Harriet said. 'Or it would no longer be a surprise and your papa would, quite rightly, be very cross with me.'

'Papa is *always* cross,' Kitty said, swinging her reticule.

'Katherine!' Fanny caught hold of her daughter's arm. 'Do stop throwing your arms around. You are supposed to be a young lady, not a child of seven. And do not speak of your papa in such a way. It is most unbecoming. He has much on his mind.'

Fanny's gaze flicked to Harriet's face, and Harriet felt a blush build from her neck. How much had Edward confided in Fanny about Harriet's visit to Tenterfield Court? She appeared as warm as ever when she was with Harriet but what, deep down, was she thinking?

'Your mama is right, Kitty. If you are not to sully your reputation, your behaviour must be exemplary at all times.' She felt her cheeks begin to burn, half her mind on her own behaviour and those dratted rumours. She felt a hypocrite, but she still needed to help guide young Kitty. 'There is nothing more likely to set tongues wagging than inappropriate behaviour in a young lady,' she went on, 'or, for that matter, unbecomingly forthright opinions.'

Kitty subsided but soon perked up when she spied her particular friend, Lady Olivia Beauchamp, perusing the display in the draper's window.

'May I go and speak with Olivia, Mama?'

'Of course,' Fanny said. As soon as Kitty was out of earshot, Fanny whispered, 'It is Lord Wincott. He and Edward have come to an agreement—Kitty and his lordship are to be betrothed before the end of the Season.'

Harriet's heart sank. 'Wincott? But…is he not rather *old* for Kitty?'

Fanny stiffened. 'He is but two and thirty,' she said. 'I should not call that old.'

Harriet had thought him older. 'He is a little staid, surely, for a girl as lively as Kitty. Is she happy with the match?'

'She does not know yet. We thought it best for them to get to know each other slowly. But it is a splendid match. He is a most moral, God-fearing man and you cannot argue with his consequence. He is wealthy, titled and his estates run alongside the land I brought to Edward as my dowry, so they can form part of the marriage settlement. That is where Edward is now, touring the estates with Wincott. And, politically, the alliance between the Brierleys and the Wincotts will be advantageous. Kitty will be thrilled when Wincott leads her out for her first dance. A marquess, no less! That is quite a coup for a seventeen-year-old.'

Harriet realised there was nothing she could say, no influence she could bring to bear. She would end up alienating Fanny, and that was the last risk she felt able to take. Poor Kitty—so open and loving, married to a pompous prig like Wincott. He was a man of a similar stamp as Edward—no doubt that was why both Edward and Fanny deemed it a good match. Harriet swallowed her indignation on behalf of Kitty. It was said that girls were happiest with men who reminded them of their fathers, so perhaps she was worrying over nothing. Fanny had stopped talking and was watching Harriet expectantly. What had she said? Harriet thought rapidly— something about Kitty's first dance.

'I am sure she will be proud to be led out by his lordship,' Harriet said, keen to smooth Fanny's ruffled pride, 'for not only does he have a most impressive title, but he is also a delightfully elegant dancer, I recall. In fact, I wonder if I might persuade him to stand up with me—a lady cannot help but show to advantage with such an accomplished partner and, as a grandmother, I fear I need all the help I can get.'

'Oh, Harriet, what nonsense—you always look beautiful, on or off the dance floor.'

'At the risk of a set-down, I second that,' interposed an amused voice. 'And if he, whoever he is, is fool enough to pass you over as a partner, then I shall be delighted to stand in his stead.'

Harriet spun on her heel. Benedict was right behind her. She could not quite meet his eyes as she tried to quash her surge of embarrassment triggered by their first meeting since the picnic, when they had not exchanged another word after their quarrel. His final words to her still stung—what a fool she had been to even hope he would contemplate marrying an impoverished widow when he might have his pick of wellborn innocents. Since then she had tried to banish him from her thoughts but it had proved nigh on impossible.

'I think you will find, sir, that you are not invited,' she said tartly.

He grinned at her, his eyes glinting. 'And a very good afternoon to you, too, Lady Brierley. Please accept my abject apologies for eavesdropping and for having the audacity to interrupt your conversation.'

He bowed before glancing enquiringly at Fanny. Harriet gritted her teeth; of all the bad luck, bumping into Benedict when she was out with Fanny and Kitty. What if one of them mentioned it to Edward? Her nerves wound a little tighter and she glared at Benedict, trying to convey a warning with her eyes even as her heart pounded at the mere sight of him. His gaze flickered in her direction before he turned his attention back to Fanny.

Harriet sighed, recognising she had no choice. 'Sir Benedict Poole, might I introduce you to my stepdaughter-in-law, Frances, Lady Brierley.'

'Honoured, my lady.' Benedict bowed to Fanny.

'Sir Benedict! It is a pleasure to make your acquaintance. Why, we are almost neighbours. Of course you must come to Kitty's ball, sir—I have no doubt Brierley was unaware of your presence in town or he would have made sure your name was on the list.'

'Fanny, I do not think Edward—'

'I shall send you an invitation as soon as I return home, sir, for the ball is tomorrow night, and single gentlemen are always most welcome. I do so hope you are free?'

Harriet fixed Benedict with a look that she was sure contained the direst warning she could muster, but he studiously ignored her, his lips curving in a smile as he said, 'Oh, yes. I am free. Thank you, my lady.'

'Fanny...' Harriet seethed with a mix of anger and fear. Once Edward returned home and got wind of those rumours, Benedict's presence at Kitty's ball could only make matters worse. 'Perhaps you should not. Not without Edward—'

'Oh, Edward leaves all those decisions to me, my dear. There is no need to worry. We have plenty of room. Now, let us continue our shopping, for I simply must find some ribbon to trim my puce bonnet.'

They took their leave of Benedict. There was no help for it; all she could now do was try to avoid Benedict at the ball. Although whether even that would prove enough when Edward heard those rumours... Sick dread swirled her stomach. She was effectively trapped. Sooner or later, Edward's axe would fall and, in the meantime, she had no choice but to continue her life with a smile upon her face.

The time for Kitty's debut into society arrived. Elegant in her white gown, her dark hair fashioned in the Grecian style and threaded through with pearls, she was the belle of the ball as the Marquess of Wincott led her onto the ballroom floor into the top position for the first dance. Harriet's heart swelled with love and pride and Fanny, standing by Harriet's side, had tears in her eyes.

Edward's greeting had been noticeably chilly when Harriet had arrived earlier, and she was already halfway convinced that he was merely biding his time, waiting until Kitty's ball was over before confronting Harriet over the gossip.

Benedict had not yet arrived, to her relief. She prayed he would see sense and stay away—he must know Edward would not welcome him and that his presence would stir up trouble for Harriet. Or was that his intention? Did he want to punish her for the masquerade? Well, he need not think she had forgiven him for what he had said at the picnic, even though it was the truth. To accuse her so bluntly was inexcusable—definitely not the behaviour expected of a gentleman.

I'm better off without him!

Oh, but she could not help but feel a fool, knowing that Benedict was fully aware of her pathetic and sordid plan.

How he must have laughed at me!

She kept an eye on the late arrivals—constantly

checking to see if Benedict appeared, her nerves all on edge—as Lord Wincott, slender and elegant in his evening clothes, bowed to Kitty and the rest of the dancers began to take their places in the set. As the dance progressed, a movement in the guests standing nearby diverted Harriet's attention from Kitty, and she turned to see Felicity and Eleanor both smiling at her.

'Harriet! Where have you been since we went to Richmond?' Felicity said. 'Have you been away?'

'No, but I have been busy helping my stepdaughter prepare for tonight.'

It was a white lie. She had not been involved at all with the preparations for Kitty's come-out ball, apart from yesterday's shopping trip with Fanny and Kitty, but had hidden away at home, feeling a fool, consumed with embarrassment that Benedict had guessed why she had seduced him at the masquerade and sick with worry over her future.

'Lady Katherine looks stunning,' Felicity said, watching as Kitty and Wincott performed their steps. 'And the room is beautifully decorated. Does it feel strange, seeing another family living here, when it used to be your home? I do not mean to pry, but I do sometimes wonder how Richard's mother must feel, to see me installed as mistress at Fernley Park whilst she lives at the Dower House.'

Harriet gazed around the ballroom—the walls had been draped with swags of silver gauze and palest pink silk and large vases of artfully arranged pink flowers and delicate ferny foliage adorned the side tables placed at intervals along the long wall opposite the tall, imposing windows. The house had never looked so fine when Harriet had been mistress here.

'No,' she said. It was the truth. This had never been

her home. And she had never, in reality, been mistress here. 'I prefer my little house in Sackville Street, if I am honest.'

'I can understand that,' Eleanor said. 'If anything happened to Matthew…why, I can imagine how painful it would be to continue living in the house where we had lived together. Even though Ashby Manor was my childhood home, I'm sure the ghosts would haunt me every day.'

As they haunt me, Harriet thought, barely controlling her shiver. At least Eleanor would have happy memories to sustain her. A hand touched her arm. It was Felicity, her amber eyes full of understanding. It had remained an unspoken agreement between Harriet and Felicity that they would never talk about the past, but she knew Stanton must have explained something of Harriet's marriage to Brierley. Felicity had managed to convey, without words, both her sympathy and her acceptance of what had gone before.

Harriet knew how fortunate she was to have Felicity for a friend and she was uncomfortably aware that, were she a true friend in return, she would be delighted that Felicity was with child, not jealous. She looked at the other two women. Felicity was positively glowing, as was Eleanor. Harriet buried her twinge of regret; she remembered all too well that bloom: the glossy hair, the clear skin, the shining eyes—even though hers had been diminished by Benedict's desertion and the nightmare of her marriage to Brierley.

'You are both looking so beautiful,' she said on impulse. 'And so radiantly happy.'

Felicity blushed. 'Thank you, Harriet, but beautiful is hardly—'

'Now then, Felicity Joy,' came a deep voice from

behind Harriet. 'Do I hear you denigrating yourself again? Come, my *beautiful* wife, dance with me while we still can.'

Harriet watched Stanton whisk Felicity onto the ballroom floor, where sets were now forming for a country reel. She knew what his words meant—Felicity had already confided in her that they would leave town before her pregnancy began to show, and that must surely be soon. But... She turned anxiously to Eleanor.

'Do you think it is safe, Felicity taking part in such an energetic dance in her condition?'

Eleanor tore her attention from the couples on the floor. 'Trust her to know what she is capable of,' she said. 'It is an odd thing. Everyone seems determined to protect us and wrap us up safely and yet—and I know I speak for Felicity as well—we have never felt so alive.'

'I remember the feeling,' Harriet replied. Although no one had protected her. Her throat thickened.

'You?' Eleanor's voice rose in astonishment.

Harriet cursed her unthinking comment. No one knew, apart from her immediate family. She searched for words to divert Eleanor, but none would come.

'I do beg your pardon,' Eleanor carried on, 'but I had no idea... That is, I had not realised... Oh, heavens, here I go making things worse. I shall just say what I was going to say in the first instance. I did not know you had ever had a child, Harriet.'

Harriet felt the other woman's gaze on her and she averted her face, her eyes suddenly moist. She felt Eleanor take her hand. 'I'm sorry,' she said. 'Matthew always tells me I must think before I speak, and now I have upset you and I truly had no notion of doing so.'

Harriet shook her head. 'It is quite all right,' she said.

A glass of wine was thrust into her hand and she took a grateful sip.

'Would you care to sit somewhere quiet?' Eleanor asked. 'I am sorry—our excitement must bring it all back to you. It is odd, is it not, that something so natural and everyday as procreation should become so utterly absorbing when it is happening to you. And, of course,' she added, glancing around at the people close to them, 'a subject *never* to be mentioned in polite company.' She smiled her wide, infectious smile. 'I believe it is safe to say both Felicity and I have abjectly failed in *that* endeavour!'

Harriet dragged in a deep breath and tried to force a smile in return, grateful to Eleanor for trying to smooth over her emotional reaction. She read nothing but sympathy and contrition in the other woman's open, honest expression.

'I am fine now, thank you, Eleanor. And please do not think I am not delighted for you both, for I am. I... I lost my baby before she was born. But it was a long time ago now. You caught me at a vulnerable moment, with the excitement of Kitty's come-out and realising my daughter would never...never...'

Eleanor slipped her arm around Harriet's waist and guided her to a chair at the side of the ballroom. 'Come,' she whispered. 'Drink your wine, and then dance the night away. Keep yourself so busy you will have no time to remember.'

Harriet pushed down her misery. This was not like her. She never dwelt on the past. She looked forward, not back.

Until Benedict came back into your life.

Angrily, she dismissed that voice. She would not disintegrate into a feeble, weeping woman, particularly not in front of a strong lady like Eleanor. A strong, *kind* lady, she realised. She had reserved judgement about this new friend of Felicity's at first, but now she could see her true qualities. Many other women would have pried and poked and then rushed to spread the latest *on dit* amongst their acquaintances. Harriet recalled the whispers of scandal that had followed Eleanor when she had come to London the previous spring, and she knew she could trust the other woman not to gossip about her.

A figure appeared before her. Mr Stephen Damerel—Matthew's brother—begging her hand for the next dance, which was just forming. On the brink of refusing him, she hesitated. She could not spend her life skulking in a corner. Benedict had not appeared—perhaps, with luck, he would stay away.

She smiled at Eleanor. 'Thank you. You are right. I shall make sure to enjoy myself,' she said as she accepted Mr Damerel.

He whisked her into the dance, closely followed by three other partners. As the last of the three led her from the floor, Richard, Lord Stanton, was bowing before her. Harriet laughed up at him, her hand to her chest.

'I need a chance to catch my breath, Stanton.' She dare not risk fuelling the gossip by dancing with him. 'If you care to procure me a glass of wine, you may consider your duty done and return to your wife.'

'It is not duty, and you know that very well, Harry.'

'Maybe not.' She lowered her voice. 'It cannot be wise for us to be seen together like this, not with these rumours. They have me in such a fever of apprehension—who could have started them? Nobody knew about us. We were so discreet.'

Stanton snorted. 'My loose-tongued cousin, that's who. He confessed all last night.'

'Charles? But…but why would he do such a thing? I thought he was my friend, and I know he would not wish to harm you or Felicity.'

'Oh, he didn't mean any harm, but you know Charles—he *never* means any harm, but he just cannot help himself at times. It seems he overheard someone expressing surprise at my choice of bride and—in an attempt to defend Felicity and before he knew what was happening—he managed to let slip that I'd had a close liaison with a very comely widow up until our wedding.' He sighed. 'You know what people are like, Harry. Once the rumour hatched it soon sprouted wings and now a load of nonsense is being passed around as fact. All we can do is ride it out. There'll soon be another scandal to take its place.'

'But my name is already being linked to yours.'

'Don't worry. No one can prove it. We did nothing wrong. And if anyone is ill-bred enough to ask outright…why, we shall simply deny it. If Felicity does not object, why should anyone else?'

Harriet bit her lip. She was tempted to confide in Stanton about Edward and his threats but pride forced her to keep quiet. It was her problem and she must deal with it. Although heaven knew how, now it was clear Benedict—who had finally arrived—would never offer for her. Every time she caught sight of him, he appeared to be glowering in her direction. Was it his intention to punish her for her ill-judged attempt to seduce him into making an offer? If so, he was succeeding. What a complete fool she had been.

She sipped at her wine, quietly despairing as she pondered her future.

Chapter Eighteen

She hadn't stopped dancing since he arrived, other than when she had been with Stanton, in what appeared to be yet another intimate conversation.

Benedict strolled moodily around the edge of the ballroom, trying, unsuccessfully for the most part, to keep his attention from wandering to Harriet too often. She sparkled. She was radiant. Her smile brightened the entire room. He *hated* the fortunate fellows who were the recipients of that glorious smile.

Begrudged them.

Deeply.

You're supposed to be searching for a wife.

Hmph! He'd already cast his eye over the young ladies at the ball. There wasn't one of them could hold a candle to Harriet.

She betrayed you. She didn't love you enough to wait for you. How could you ever trust her? And don't forget Stanton.

Whenever he thought of Harriet with the earl the sharp claws of jealousy raked at his insides until he was ready to roar his rage. The gossip claiming it was Harriet who had been Stanton's mistress was more widespread than ever. Yet when *he* had been about to suggest a similar arrangement she had not even allowed him to speak. Once again, Harriet had chosen another man in preference to him, until she had seen him as the answer to her predicament. Well, he had seen through her game. He had taken what she offered, and he had walked away.

Except…except…it hadn't quite worked out as he had planned. His desire for her was stronger than ever and he feared it was likely to continue to plague him until such time as he wed. Then, surely, his focus would be on his own family and he could pack her back inside the box in his mind where she had lain undisturbed for so many years.

So what was he doing here?

He raked suddenly nervous fingers through his hair, the thought that it needed cutting randomly flitting through his mind. Why *was* he here? Was he so weak-willed that a week without seeing her or speaking to her was too much for him? He had spotted her in the street and, before he could question his motives or think through the consequences, he had inveigled an invitation to the ball tonight, despite knowing Brierley would object.

He glanced around but saw no sign of his host. He had deliberately come late, not wishing to stand in line to be greeted by the Brierleys and their daughter and thus afford Brierley an opportunity to refuse him entry. He had timed his arrival after the dancing had started, when the butler's stentorian announcement of his name had struggled to be heard above the music and the babble of conversation. Since then, he had taken care not to wander too close to his host. If Brierley tried to have him thrown out, Benedict was not sure he would be able to control his temper—which teetered on a knife-edge these days—and that would not bode well for his goal of overcoming Sir Malcolm's legacy of scandal.

'Sir Benedict, I am delighted you were able to come.'

Benedict closed his eyes briefly as he recognised the voice of his hostess. Perhaps Brierley would not… but no. One glance at Lady Brierley revealed a glowering Lord Brierley behind her. So much for his manoeuvrings to avoid the man.

Brierley barrelled forward. 'You were not invited, sir.'

Benedict held tight to the reins of his temper.

'Brierley, do not say so. *I* invited Sir Benedict.' Lady Brierley raised her anxious gaze to her husband.

Brierley's focus remained on Benedict. 'When did you do so? And where?'

'Why—' his lady faltered '—it was yesterday. When Kitty and I were out shopping.'

'Yesterday…when you were with my stepmother?'

'Why, yes, she is an old friend of—' Lady Brierley's eyes sharpened. She drew herself up to her full height and said, 'It makes no matter, sir, for the deed is now done. I did not know… If you had only confided in me… but there. It is of no use now. Come, we have our duties as hosts to attend to—will you spoil your own daughter's come-out by quarrelling with a guest?'

Benedict held his breath, hoping he was not about to witness a full-blown marital dispute, but Brierley—after a quick glance around the ballroom—said, 'Very well. I can see I have no choice.' He glared at Benedict. 'Enjoy the ball, sir. Come, my dear, we must not neglect our other guests.'

Benedict watched the man scan the dancers as they walked away. When the dance came to an end, Brierley headed straight for Harriet, took her arm and spoke quickly into her ear. Harriet gave no sign of what he said, but her gaze roamed the room until it settled briefly on Benedict. She replied to her stepson, a pink tinge colouring her cheeks, who then walked away from her. Her partner had already disappeared, and Harriet made her way across the ballroom to Benedict.

'So you came.' Her voice was low with accusation.

Benedict forced a careless shrug as he faced her. 'I was invited,' he said. 'It struck me as being the perfect place to meet suitable young ladies.'

'So it is. I wish you luck.'

'I am surprised you can risk being seen speaking to me.'

Her eyes glittered as she stared up at him. She looked so beautiful—almost edible in shimmering rose-pink silk clinging provocatively to her lush curves—that he itched to take her in his arms there and then and hang the consequences. Except that would hardly help his quest for the perfect society bride. It was funny how he kept losing sight of that fact—or it would be if he could find anything vaguely amusing these days.

'Edward already knows you are here. The damage is done. I came to beg you to leave—it is unfair on Kitty to court trouble on the biggest night of her life.'

Anger smouldered deep inside him. 'I am not interested in courting trouble,' he growled. 'I am simply eager to secure my future.'

'Then, I suggest you begin by engaging at least *one* of the young ladies present to dance,' Harriet spat. 'For it seems to me that every time I see you, you are staring at *me*. Or perhaps it is your intention to cause strife between my stepson and me?'

'You flatter yourself, madam,' he said, and bowed before stalking off.

His insides churned—in turmoil, as they always were in Harriet's presence. He needed to catch his breath and calm the battle between desire and distrust raging deep within his heart. He gritted his teeth and kept walking. He had a mission to accomplish: the search for a bride. And, however much he might desire Harriet, he would never ask her to marry him.

One betrayal was enough.

As he strolled around the perimeter of the ballroom, he caught sight of Miss Marstone standing with her mother and several other young ladies. He stifled a sigh. He must start somewhere and, as he was already acquainted with Lady Marstone, she would be bound to introduce him to the other girls. Pasting a smile on his face, he joined the group.

'Good evening, Sir Benedict, how gallant of you to join us, for I was beginning to wonder where all the young gentlemen were hiding.' Lady Marstone was positively beaming. 'Of course, you are already acquainted with my Bridget, are you not?'

Miss Marstone smiled up at him through her lashes: a far too seductive smile for an innocent young lady. Benedict wondered how innocent she actually was. He should know how easy it was to seduce such a girl—

Hell and damnation! Why does she keep invading my thoughts? Then he hesitated, thinking back over the words that had run unbidden through his mind. *He* had seduced *Harriet*. She was a year younger than he; she had barely known what was happening until it was too late—how had he never thought of what had happened from her point of view before?

Because you were too busy being bitter that she betrayed you by marrying Brierley.

And she *had* betrayed him, there was no denying it.

They had pledged their love, but she had been seduced all over again—not by lovemaking but by wealth and a title, according to Malcolm. She hadn't been prepared to wait until Benedict inherited; she had wanted instant riches and the easy life they would bring her. Well... He came to with a start, finding himself the focus of several pairs of eyes watching him curiously.

'I do beg your pardon,' he said, smiling his most charming smile. 'I was overcome with the enormity of so much beauty and elegance in one place.' He cringed inwardly at those words—which elicited a trill of giggles—but it was expected that gentlemen should charm and flatter the ladies of the *ton*, and he was now part of this world. A surge of homesickness for the simplicity of his former life swept through him. He ignored it and continued, 'Good evening, Lady Marstone, Miss Marstone. Would you do me the honour of introducing me to the other young ladies?'

Lady Marstone began the introductions and Benedict soon became aware of the irritable looks Miss Marstone was shooting at the other girls. Still mindful of the importance of keeping mother and daughter happy to prevent Harriet's stay at Tenterfield becoming public knowledge, he asked Miss Marstone to dance as soon as the introductions were complete. She smiled graciously, but he did not miss her darting triumphal glance at her friends.

During the movements of the dance where they could not converse, Benedict's thoughts turned inexorably to Harriet, and to her view of their past. They had never spoken of it. She had never told him why she had wed Brierley. Had it been a love match? The man had been old enough to be her father. More than old enough, in fact, for Edward was actually several years older than

both Harriet and Benedict. What had driven her to accept his offer? It could only, surely, have been greed,
as Malcolm had said.

Had he not suspected that was the very reason she
had pursued him at the masquerade—because of his
new position? With his wealth and status, no number of
threats from Brierley could hold sway. She would have
that comfortable, secure life she craved but…if that
was truly the case, would she not have been friendlier
from the start? And why did she appear to have given
up so easily?

'I declare, sir, you have such a look of contemplation
upon your face I would swear you have forgotten I am
here.' It was said with a pout and a coquettish look that
set his teeth on edge.

'Of course I have not forgotten you, Miss Marstone,'
he replied smoothly. 'How could I? I am merely concentrating on the steps. I should hate to tread on your toes.'

'Oh, la, sir. You dance very respectably for a…for
a…'

'For a novice?' he suggested.

Her eyes flashed with relief. 'Precisely. Tell me, sir,
have you made plans for supper? Oh!' She giggled art-
lessly. 'Mama *would* be shocked at my boldness, but I
already feel as though you and I are old friends and can
be *quite* comfortable with one another.'

'I thought a gentleman was honour bound to escort
his partner for the supper dance into supper?' He knew
quite well that was the custom.

'But I do not have a partner for that dance, sir, and
as we have only so far had this one dance…'

He ignored her dangling invitation with relief as the
dance dictated a change in partner. Were all young girls
this shameless, or had he just been unlucky in meeting

this one? He made a mental note to scrawl his name on some other girls' dance cards before they all filled up. And the first dance he must secure was the supper dance.

As they swapped partners again, he said, 'I regret that I am already engaged for the supper dance. Perhaps a little later in the evening?'

'Perhaps,' she replied with a toss of her dark curls.

After barely half a minute of silence, she said, 'Do you like to walk in the park, sir?'

'On occasion.'

'I *love* to walk. I should walk every day, if only Mama was strong enough.'

'Mayhap she should take the carriage,' Benedict said.

'She does, but it is hardly the same, to sit in the carriage next to my mother whilst everyone else is enjoying fresh air and exercise.' Miss Marstone sighed. 'She will only allow me to walk with my friends if there is a gentleman present. Perhaps, if we should happen to meet in the park, you might offer me your arm?'

'Perhaps.'

Making a mental note to avoid the park at all costs, Benedict led Miss Marstone back to her mother at the end of the dance and then quickly took his leave, determined to secure partners for the dances to come.

After dancing with a few young ladies and successfully engaging to partner several more, he found himself standing next to Harriet during a brief lull in the music.

She immediately turned and began to walk away, but he wrapped his fingers around her wrist, saying, 'I want to talk to you.'

Her violet eyes met his warily. 'What about?'

'Brierley.'

'Edward? What has he done?'

'Not Edward. His father.'

Her skin blanched. 'I do not wish to discuss him.' He had to strain to hear her words.

'Harriet—'

'I must go. I am promised to Mr Damerel for this dance… Ah, here he comes now.' The relief in her voice was palpable.

Benedict watched his friend lead Harriet into the dance.

'Sir Benedict?' A timid voice spoke by his side.

'Ah…' He racked his brain. 'Lady Susan, is it not?'

Lady Susan was his partner for this dance. Fair haired, pretty and shy, she had been the only one of Bridget Marstone's friends he had been in the slightest taken with. He smiled, determined to put her at her ease. 'I was just coming to find you,' he said, holding out his hand. 'Come, let us show the rest of them how it's done.'

When the dance ended he returned Lady Susan to her chaperone, then looked around. On the far side of the room he spied a familiar tall figure with a pair of wide shoulders topped by a head of dark blond hair— Matthew, with Harriet by his side. Benedict started across the dance floor, his way hindered by couples forming sets ready for the next dance. He lost sight of Matthew and Harriet for a moment and then, the next time he saw them, Matthew was standing alone. He scanned the surrounding people and caught a glimpse of Harriet slipping out of the room.

He forced his way through the rest of the throng, only to be waylaid by Miss Marstone, a coquettish smile on her face.

'Do I detect that you lack a partner for this dance, Sir Benedict?'

Swallowing an oath, Benedict halted. 'You do, Miss

Marstone,' he replied, keeping a wary eye on Matthew whilst Miss Marstone, in turn, gazed at Benedict. She raised a questioning brow. *Damn.* Only a blind man would not interpret that look. 'I find myself in need of a rest,' he said, hoping she would accept his excuse. He indicated his knee. 'An old injury is playing up.'

'An injury! How fascinating.' She linked her arm through his. 'You must tell me all about it.'

'Another time.' Benedict untangled his arm from hers. Matthew had begun to move away. If he was not quick, he would lose him in the crowd. 'My apologies, Miss Marstone, but I simply must find a quiet chair and rest this leg.'

He bowed and strode away, only remembering at the last minute to mime a limp for the lady's benefit. He caught up with Matthew and tapped him on the shoulder.

'Where has Lady Brierley disappeared to?'

Matthew cocked his head to one side, giving Benedict a quizzical look. 'You appear fascinated by Lady B,' he said. He then grinned. 'Not that I can blame you. She *is* a beauty, and a widow, too, by God.'

Benedict battened down his anger. *No one* should be looking at Harriet in that way, but in particular not a man who was already happily married and setting up his nursery.

Matthew held up both hands, palms facing Benedict, fingers spread. '*Pax*, old chap. She pleaded tiredness and has gone to find a quiet spot to rest,' he said, laughing openly now, his blue eyes gently mocking. Then his expression swiftly sobered. 'What is it, Ellie? You are looking pale.'

Eleanor had joined them. Benedict thrust aside his frustration at the interruption. She did look washed out.

'I am tired, Matthew,' she said. 'Would you mind—?'

Matthew wrapped his arm around her waist. 'We are going home. Now. No arguments.'

Eleanor included Benedict in her answering smile. 'He always imagines I am going to argue,' she said. 'I cannot think why. Yes, please, I would like to go home. Goodnight, Benedict.'

'Goodnight,' Benedict said. 'I hope you feel better in the morning.'

As Matthew and Eleanor turned to go, Matthew paused. 'I believe she mentioned the library,' he said over his shoulder. 'She used to live here, you know, so she knows her way around.'

Benedict nodded his thanks and followed them out of the ballroom into the hall. A footman carrying a tray of empty glasses hurried past. Benedict caught him by the arm and only by some nifty juggling of the precariously tilting tray did the servant avert disaster.

'Which is the library?' He bit the question out, not even apologising to the poor man.

'That door there, sir,' the footman replied, jerking his head towards a door on the opposite side of the hall. He then hurried away, heading towards the rear of the house.

The library was large and imposing, lined with floor-to-ceiling shelves of books. The wall opposite the door was punctuated by three heavily curtained windows that presumably overlooked the street outside. A cursory glance revealed an empty room. Benedict frowned. There were two high wing-backed chairs flanking the unlit fireplace, but they were unoccupied.

He moved towards the table in the centre of the room. Perhaps she had changed her mind and gone elsewhere in the house. He needed to talk to her. Now. He would find out, once and for all, why she had thrown away the love they had shared for an old man like Brierley. And he would find out what lay behind her fear. A gap in the curtains covering the middle window caught his eye.

He strode across the room and wrenched the curtains apart. There, curled up on an upholstered window seat, was Harriet.

Chapter Nineteen

The sudden movement of the curtains jolted Harriet from her musings. Her heart leaped into her throat and she shot to her feet, bringing her hard up against a muscled chest. Benedict, bringing with him the familiar spicy, musky scent that was uniquely him.

'I want answers,' he said.

Her pulse raced. She did not want to answer his questions. Her life was none of his business; it was nobody's business. She wanted no interrogations, no intrusions and she wanted no pity, particularly not Benedict's. All she wanted was to feel safe.

'You should not be here,' she said. She made to push past him. 'I must go.'

'No.'

He grabbed her wrist and hauled her hard against him, then wrapped his arms around her, trapping her. Harriet gasped, wriggling in an attempt to break free.

'Stand still,' he gritted out. 'I need to know—'

She had leaned back against his arms to look up into his face. As their eyes locked, he stilled and fell silent. Harriet's mouth dried at the intensity of his stare. She licked her lips in an attempt to moisten them, and his gaze lowered to her mouth. Her heart lurched and her breathing grew ragged with her rising awareness of his arousal as it pressed against the softness of her belly. The familiar need pulsed at her core, and she felt her body prepare for lovemaking.

She swallowed, aghast at the speed with which she responded to him. Was that really all it took to arouse her? Just the thought of his kiss? The tears that never seemed far away these days threatened to surface, and her pride rebelled against allowing him to see just how vulnerable she was to his allure. She could not break free of his encircling arms and she *would not* talk to him about Brierley. But, oh, how she craved his kiss. How she needed *something* to distract her from her fears over the future, if only for a short time. That need overrode all caution and stifled all the very good reasons why this was akin to playing with fire.

She stood stock-still as he traced her neckline with one finger. She searched his eyes, one hand on his chest, aware of the hard, fast beat of his heart as she played with his top waistcoat button until it slipped free and moved down to the next one, and the next.

'Benedict...?'

She rose on tiptoe, craving the touch of his lips. She brushed her lips over his with a feather-light touch. With a harsh groan that sounded as though it was ripped from him, his arms tightened and he took her mouth, his lips moving over hers as his tongue plunged inside, tangling with hers. She slid her arms beneath his coat, around the curve of his ribcage and then drifted lower, stroking, until her hands cupped the firm muscle of his buttocks. Heat radiated from him in waves.

I want him. Here. Now.
I cannot. I must not.

She did not push him away, despite the voice of caution in her head. She ignored it, pressed closer and wrapped her arms around his neck, melting into their kiss as she weaved her fingers through his hair.

They heard the noise at the same time and they sprang apart as the door started to open. They exchanged a look and Harriet nearly recoiled at the accusation in Benedict's eyes. *He* had followed *her*, not the other way round, although she couldn't deny she had instigated that kiss, to distract him from his questions and her from her fate. And it had worked: his waistcoat hung open rakishly and his auburn hair was ruffled.

'Hide!' Benedict whispered, pushing her back onto the padded seat.

Willingly, she thought, still smarting over that look. He dragged the curtains closed, and she was once again secreted behind the curtains where she had imagined nobody would find her. Her lips felt bruised and swollen and an errant lock of hair feathered her neck where a hairpin had been dislodged. She fumbled around for her lost pin, but could not find it, so had to be content to tuck her curl behind another pin and hope it would stay in place until she could properly repair the damage.

She heard the sound of the library door clicking shut.

'What the devil are you doing here?' It was Benedict's voice, harsh with anger. 'You should not be here... The risk to your reputation if we are seen—'

'Don't be cross with me, Benedict.' A female voice—seductive and cajoling—interrupted him.

Benedict?

Harriet inched the curtains apart and applied one eye to the gap. Bridget Marstone was pouting at Benedict. *The little cat.* Harriet knew exactly what she was up to.

'I am tired,' Miss Marstone said with a pout as she

glided towards Benedict. 'I was looking for somewhere quiet to rest.'

She stopped directly in front of him and laid one hand on his chest. On his shirtfront, inside the waistcoat that Harriet had recently unbuttoned. Possessiveness spiralled up from the depths of Harriet's being, shocking her with its intensity.

How dare she?

Benedict stepped back, the door crashed open and all hell broke loose.

Miss Marstone launched herself at Benedict—flinging her arms around his neck and pulling at him as she strove to plant her lips on his—a split second before Lady Marstone, Fanny and Edward crowded into the room.

'I told you! Unhand her, you rogue! You villain!' Lady Marstone clasped her hands to her bosom. 'My baby! My innocent girl! You shall pay for this, sir!'

Benedict untangled Miss Marstone's arms from around his neck and put her from him.

'You have ruined my darling girl.'

As Lady Marstone crossed the room to clasp her daughter in a maternal hug, Harriet interpreted their exchanged look of conspiracy. Heedless of the consequences, she swept from her hiding place and stalked into the centre of the room.

Everyone's attention was fixed on Lady Marstone, who was still in full flow.

'You enticed my poor, innocent Bridget in here to have your wicked— *Oh!* What is *she* doing here?' Her voice rose to a shriek as she glared at Harriet. 'Hussy!'

Miss Marstone took one look at Harriet and burst into tears whilst Edward's expression changed from irritation to utter fury.

'That is what I should like to know,' he snarled. 'What the devil are you doing in here with *him*?'

Harriet raised her brows. 'And with Miss Marstone, Edward. Do not, I beg of you, forget Miss Marstone.'

'As if we could,' Benedict muttered.

Harriet bit hard on her lip to silence her inappropriate urge to giggle.

'You may rest assured, Lady Marstone, that there was no impropriety,' she said, savouring the flash of fury in that lady's eyes. She was more convinced than ever that the entire farce had been a scheme dreamed up by Lady Marstone and her daughter to entrap Benedict. 'I was here the entire time and can vouch for that.'

'I know what I saw when I walked in,' Lady Marstone said. 'That wretch had my poor, innocent Bridget *in his arms*. As for you, sir—I expect you to make amends. And I warn you, if you refuse to act as the gentleman you purport to be, I swear you will never hold your head up in society again.'

'Do your worst,' Benedict said. 'What you saw was your *poor*, *innocent* daughter flinging herself at me. I tell you straight, madam, I have no interest in your daughter and I will not be making her an offer of any kind. If you wish to create a scandal, I would suggest your daughter will emerge the loser. Not I.'

'You have not heard the last of this,' Lady Marstone hissed, her glare encompassing both Harriet and Benedict. 'Out of the goodness of my heart and my respect for his lordship I have kept my mouth shut about your disgraceful behaviour in staying unchaperoned at Tenterfield Court, but no more, *my lady*. And, from what I hear, that is not the only proof of your immorality. My heart weeps for poor Lady Stanton—only recently wed and yet cruelly deceived by her husband and her supposed friend. Utterly disgraceful!'

She ushered her weeping daughter from the room.

There was a beat of silence after they left, then Edward strutted across the room to face Harriet. 'You have not explained what you were doing in here with Poole.'

'I was doing nothing,' Harriet said, her insides knotting as she realised the risk she had taken in protecting Benedict. She could not regret it, though. She couldn't bear to think of him trapped into a marriage with that devious cat. 'Edward, Fanny…please, you must believe me. I came here alone. I—'

'You hoped Poole would follow you,' Edward snarled. 'I saw you with my own eyes, whispering together. You *planned* this liaison. In my house, on Kitty's special night.' He grabbed Harriet's shoulders, shaking her, and she felt locks of hair again brush her neck and shoulders.

'Hold hard there, Brierley!' Benedict shoved Edward away from Harriet. 'Don't you—'

'*Do not* tell me to "hold hard" in my own house,' Edward said through clenched teeth before glaring again at Harriet. 'I warned you but you went your own way, as usual. And now you must pay the penalty. You, madam, are no longer welcome here. Go.'

Harriet's heart pounded at the implacable look in Edward's eyes.

'Fanny…?' Her appeal was met with a helpless shrug.

'Brierley—' Harriet could hear the effort Benedict made to keep his voice level even as anger flashed in his eyes '—you are making a mistake. It was *I* who followed Lady Brierley into the library. She had no idea I would follow her.'

'That is almost as bad,' Edward said. 'I think we

all know what the outcome of that particular meeting would have been, had Miss Marstone not appeared.'

'I resent that,' Harriet cried. 'How dare you assume—'

'It's a natural assumption, given your past and—' his eyes raked her '—given your slovenly appearance.'

Benedict growled deep in his chest and started towards Edward, his fists clenched. Harriet grabbed at his arm, tugging him back.

Edward stood his ground, saying, 'And that just proves my point. You, sir, are no gentleman. You deserve each other. I shall attend you tomorrow, madam. I suggest you make arrangements to vacate the house in Sackville Street forthwith. I have no doubt one of your lovers will come to your aid and accommodate you, as you do them.'

He marched to the door and flung it open. Harriet stole a glance at Benedict, who was rigid with fury, his hands clenched into fists.

'Do not,' she whispered. 'Please. You will make things worse.'

'So you keep telling me. Oh, very well, but only because you ask. Otherwise…' He shot a look of disgust at Edward.

Harriet swallowed, straightened her spine and walked to the door. As she moved into the hall, Edward caught up with her and gripped her elbow.

'Fetch Lady Brierley's cloak,' he said to a passing maid. 'She is leaving.'

Am I such an undesirable character I must be escorted from the premises?

Harriet contained her bitter laugh and blinked hard to hold scalding tears at bay.

'Grandmama!' Kitty, flushed and happy, emerged from the ballroom, Lord Wincott by her side. 'Papa!

There you all are. I wondered where you were… Where are you… Surely you are not leaving already, Grandmama? It is early yet.'

Harriet bit the inside of her cheek, sucked in a deep breath and said shakily, 'I am so sorry, sweetie. I am not feeling well, so I must go home. But I have had a wonderful time and you…and you…are so very beautiful…'

Her voice failed her. She felt a hand squeeze hers briefly. Fanny. Her heart lifted a little. Perhaps all was not yet lost. Kitty threw her arms around Harriet and hugged her hard. 'I hope you will feel better soon, and I shall tell you all about what you have missed.'

'Thank you, darling. I'd like that. Never forget I love you,' she ended in a whisper.

Her cloak was placed around her shoulders. Harriet hesitated. She had travelled here with the Stantons in their carriage, as she did not have one of her own.

'Allow me to escort you home.' It was Benedict. 'My carriage, please,' he ordered.

Her instinct was to fling his offer in his face.

Why did he have to follow me? It has made everything a thousand times worse.

She had made everything a thousand times worse as well, by distracting him. She could not sidestep her share of blame. She read the righteous expression on Edward's face at Benedict's words but she was beyond caring now what he thought. She must get home somehow. She had much to think about; she had her life to organise. Edward was throwing her out of her home, and he would stop her allowance. She had nothing. She glanced at Benedict's set profile as they waited in silence. Did he imagine, now she had reached such a pass, she would fall into his arms? Allow him to support her as his mistress until he tired of her again?

Yes, she shared the blame for what had happened tonight, but most of the rest was of Benedict's doing, even her *affaire* with Stanton. His rejection of her and their baby had triggered a chain of events until she'd arrived at this point.

Childless. Homeless. Penniless.

Scorned by her family.

Her hard-won reputation in tatters.

The carriage arrived and Harriet allowed herself to be handed into it. Benedict climbed in behind her and sat by her side.

'Why did you have to follow me?' She could not hide her bitterness. 'See now what has happened.'

'If you had talked to me earlier, I would not have had to try to get you alone. I should not worry about it. It will soon blow over.'

She stared at him, incredulous. *'Blow over?* If you truly believe that, you know nothing of the machinations of the *ton*. Do not think Lady Marstone will tell the exact truth, either about tonight or about my stay at Tenterfield Court. She will embellish as much as she can, blackening both our names in the process.'

He did not speak again until they drew up in Sackville Street.

'Why did you marry Brierley?'

Fury sizzled through her. *Why?* His face was dimly visible, his expression noncommittal.

'You *know* why.'

The black-hearted *wretch*. How could he ask such a thing? Her hand itched to slap him, but at the same time she shrank from the idea of even touching him. She climbed hurriedly from the carriage, thankful that Stevens was already waiting to help her out.

'Harriet!'

She ignored him. 'No one is to be admitted to the house tonight, Stevens. Is that clear?' she said as she heard the unmistakable sound of Benedict descending from the carriage behind her. She half ran to her open front door—*not yours for much longer*—Stevens puffing behind.

'I need answers, and I will not rest until I get them,' Benedict shouted. 'Why did—?' His words were cut short as Stevens shut the door behind them.

Now what?

Harriet's mind spun, but she could find no solution. Should she wait until Edward turned up tomorrow, in the hope he might have mellowed? Or should she retain what dignity she still possessed and leave of her own accord? She did not have the luxury of that option, she realised. Her only resort would be to move into the house in Cheapside, or to go to her mother and aunt in Whitstable. Neither option appealed, and both were only short-term answers to a dilemma that needed a long-term solution.

Marriage. Her stomach knotted. There was no one she could trust enough to put her life in their hands.

'Milady? Are you quite well?'

Stevens's question shook her from her thoughts. She was standing in her hall, her cloak still around her shoulders.

'I'm sorry, Stevens,' she said. 'I am quite all right.'

And the servants. What would happen to them? They would all lose their jobs... Sick despair rolled through her from her head to her toes. Accompanied by a wave of guilt. She'd thought she could handle Edward. She'd been wrong, and she had jeopardised her entire household's future.

'I shall retire now, and I suggest you do the same.'

There had been no thunderous knocking at the door, such as she had feared. Benedict had clearly washed his hands of her, too. As she climbed into bed, misery engulfed her and she turned onto her side, curled into a ball and wept.

Chapter Twenty

Edward slammed out of Harriet's salon as the clock struck noon the following day. She stared at the door in a daze. Far from softening his attitude to her, he had grown more implacable overnight. He had been unmoving. Kitty's future was in the balance and Edward was determined the match with Lord Wincott should go ahead for political, financial and social reasons. Wincott had already expressed his disquiet about Harriet's charity, believing such charitable work was tantamount to encouraging immoral behaviour in the serving classes. Now, unless Edward dealt once and for all with the connection between his family and Harriet—before the sordid story of her behaviour became common knowledge—he feared Wincott would never come up to scratch.

'And does Kitty have a say in who she weds?' Harriet had asked. That had been a mistake. Edward had exploded in righteous indignation that she should have the temerity to question a system of arranged marriages that had proved advantageous for the aristocracy for centuries.

'My marriage was arranged,' Edward said, his face

darkening, 'as was yours, madam. What would have become of you without my father rescuing you as he did?'

Harriet had been beyond caution—her temper had been teased to breaking point, and all her pleading and cajoling had got her nowhere. '*Rescuing* me? You simply do not see what you do not wish to see, do you, Edward? Your father was a tyrant. You ask what I would be without him rescuing me. I would be a *mother*. I would have a daughter, and no amount of money in this world can ever make up for her loss.'

'That is hardly my father's fault.'

Harriet had paced the room in her agitation. 'Oh, yes, it is!' She'd struggled to speak, her throat had been so tight. 'He pushed me down the stairs. He *laughed* when I lost my baby. He gloated it would save him money and that my "swollen belly" would no longer interfere with his pleasures.'

'There is no talking to you if you are set on inventing stories to blacken my father's name,' Edward had said, but some of his bluster had abated. He'd marched to the door. 'One week to pack up and to leave. One week, madam.' And he had gone.

What was she to do? Where could she go? She would not allow Edward to banish her to the isolated cottage on the Brierley estate that he had offered. With no horse or carriage, she would effectively be cut off from the outside world, completely dependent on Edward and Fanny.

The door opened and Stevens came in. 'Will you see Lady Stanton, my lady? She arrived just after his lordship. She has been waiting in the drawing room.'

Harriet scrubbed her hands over her face. 'I don't know,' she said. 'I can't… I can't even *think* straight. I—'

What was she saying? She should not speak like this

in front of Stevens. Before she could refuse to see Felicity, however, Stevens said, 'Her ladyship was most insistent, my lady. She—'

'She will not be denied.' Felicity's voice sounded from the doorway. 'Do not blame Stevens, for he did his best to put me off, but I simply must speak to you, Harriet.' She crossed the room to sit next to Harriet and take her hand. 'Thank you, Stevens, that will be all.'

Harriet held her emotions in check until Stevens closed the door behind him, and then a huge wave of exhaustion, misery and hopelessness swept over her.

Later, after she had wept out her despair in Felicity's arms, she sat up.

'I must look frightful,' she said. 'I am so sorry. I do not know what came over me, but I am better now. I was just tired and... Why did you come?'

'After you left last night, there was talk. I was worried about you.'

'Talk?' *Dear God, already?* Her stomach twisted. There truly was no going back; her reputation was in tatters. It was only a matter of time before the tattle mongers remembered her humble beginnings and shook their heads in their superior conviction that blood was everything.

'Yes, about you and Sir Benedict,' Felicity said. 'That awful Marstone woman was spreading all kinds of malicious gossip. We tried to stop her, but not even your stepson could silence her. Oh, Harriet, I am so very sorry.'

'You have nothing to be sorry for, Felicity.'

'Oh, but I do. You went to Tenterfield Court for *me*. If you had not—'

'If I had not, then all this would have blown up in some other way,' Harriet said miserably.

'Do you want to tell me about it?'

Harriet unburdened her heart, telling Felicity all about her youthful love for Benedict, her fall from grace and Benedict's rejection of her. And she told her something of her marriage to Brierley—glossing over the worst of his violence and his part in the loss of her baby daughter—triggering a fresh paroxysm of grief as Felicity squeezed her hands, her own eyes glinting with tears.

'No wonder you made such an effort to help me find out who was responsible for Emma's plight,' Felicity said. 'And as for *Sir Benedict Poole*—his treatment of you was appalling. Now I wish I *had* allowed Richard to call him out!'

Her friend sounded so fierce, a laugh gurgled from Harriet's swollen throat. 'That would solve nothing.'

'No, but it would make *me* feel better,' Felicity declared, her small hands clenched into fists.

'What am I to do?' Harriet asked in despair. 'Edward has all but disowned me. I am to l-l-leave this place. He has stopped my allowance—'

'Can he do that?' Felicity said.

'Yes. I talked to the solicitor and he c-confirmed it. I have nothing. And now I do not even have my reputation.'

'Well, as to the first, you are always welcome to stay with us,' Felicity said.

'I could not possibly.'

Felicity fixed Harriet with a stern gaze. 'If you are feeling awkward because of what happened between you and Richard, then please do not.'

The knot in Harriet's stomach tightened further. Although she was aware Felicity knew of their *affaire*, it had never been mentioned between them. 'How…how can you speak of it so calmly? You should be spitting fire at me, and yet you have remained my friend, and you are here when I need you.' She could not imagine she would be so magnanimous in the same circumstances.

A rueful smile lit Felicity's face. 'I lived through my father's and my stepfather's infidelities,' she said. 'Had your liaison with Richard taken place after our marriage, I could never forgive either of you for that, although I know many wives do accept their husband's *affaires*. But to take against you for something that happened before I was even betrothed to Richard…? No, that would be unfair, although I confess I found it hard at first to forgive you both for not telling me the truth as soon as you and I became friends.'

'I'm sorry.' Harriet hung her head.

'Oh, it was not your fault, I am aware of that. My penitent husband admitted you had advised him to tell me the truth, but that he thought it best to say nothing and hope I would never find out. And even that I cannot be angry about, for it finally forced Richard and me to be honest with one another, and our marriage is happier and stronger as a result. So, I repeat, I will not see you on the streets. You are welcome to stay with us if the worse comes to the worst.

'We *can* do something about your reputation, however. You have done nothing wrong, and you are not to skulk in here as though you have.' She stood up. 'Get some rest, and I shall collect you at four thirty. Put on your best carriage dress, for you and I are going to dazzle them all in the park.'

Harriet's heart sank. 'Felicity, no. I cannot. I—'

'You can and you must,' Felicity said gently before

stooping to kiss Harriet's cheek. 'You will not go down without a fight. I shall not let you.'

It was worse than Harriet feared.

Felicity had driven to Sackville Street in her phaeton and pair, her groom perched behind. Harriet had dressed in her best blue carriage dress and matching bonnet and sat by Felicity as she expertly drove to the park and steered the vehicle onto the carriageway.

As usual at that time of day, the park was thronged with walkers, riders and people taking the air in their open-topped carriages. They were people Harriet had come to know over the past eleven years since her marriage to Brierley. Most had been friendly enough towards her, even though Harriet had mostly kept herself to herself after Brierley's death, finding it hard to fully trust others—the legacy of her marriage, she supposed. Others, however, had merely tolerated the vicar's daughter who had become a countess by marriage. And some—since she had begun her crusade to protect vulnerable maidservants—had given her the cold shoulder. They were no loss—she had no desire to socialise with such people in any case. But now... today...her ears were burning, as was her face, as one after the other turned from her.

Snatches of conversation as they passed reverberated as loudly as a town crier's announcements to Harriet in her sensitive state.

'Her own granddaughter's ball...'

'Shameless...'

'Low breeding, my dear...'

'Tenterfield Court...'

'On his deathbed...'

'No shame...'

'No gentleman...'

'Miss Marstone...'

'Lucky escape...'

'Felicity,' she said, as they bowled along the drive, 'please take me home. I cannot bear this.'

Felicity, however, slowed her ponies to a walk and pointed with her whip to three gentlemen trotting towards them on horseback. Harriet's heart quailed, but then rallied as she recognised Stanton as one of the three. He, at least—surely—would not cut her.

'You are not running away,' Felicity said fiercely. 'You have done nothing wrong.' She turned her attention to her ponies, who tossed their heads, sending their identical flaxen manes rippling on their necks, as the three huge horses were reined in alongside the phaeton. 'Whoa, Spice. Steady, Nutmeg.'

Harriet saw, with a nervous lurch of her stomach, that the other two men were the Duke of Cheriton—one of the most powerful noblemen in the *ton* and, she knew, Felicity's former guardian—and his younger brother, Lord Vernon Beauchamp.

'Good afternoon, Cousin Leo, Cousin Vernon,' Felicity said. 'You are both acquainted with Lady Brierley, I think.'

All three men doffed their hats. Stanton smiled at Harriet, his chocolate-brown eyes warm.

'Don't look so petrified, Harry,' he said. 'You do know that, whatever happens, Felicity and I will always stand by you. And, in the meantime, His Grace has expressed a wish to promenade. So—' Stanton swung elegantly from the back of his huge dapple-grey gelding and strode to the side of the phaeton, holding out his hand to Felicity '—if you ladies would care to join us,

I can think of no more pleasurable way to spend the next half an hour.'

He then addressed the groom perched on the phaeton. 'Dalton, please hold Gambit—' he proffered his horse's reins '—and her ladyship's ponies, whilst we take a short stroll.'

In the meantime the duke, suave and elegant as always, had also dismounted. He tossed his black's reins to his brother, who tipped his hat, smiled and said, 'I'd better keep these two on the move or war is likely to break out. See you back here shortly,' and nudged his horse into a walk.

Harriet absorbed all this manoeuvring with an inner *Hmph.* That the whole encounter had been planned by Felicity she did not doubt, but she was grateful for the effort. Whether it would do any good or not was anybody's guess, although—she looked into the duke's silver-grey eyes as he handed her from the phaeton— if anyone could sway public opinion, it was the Duke of Cheriton.

Hope filtered into her heart. No one would dare to snub her whilst the duke and the Earl of Stanton championed her.

They began to stroll.

'So when are you going to tell me what happened after I left last night, you dog?' Matthew said as he relaxed back in a chair in the coffee lounge at White's late that afternoon. 'There's a new bet in the Book, that Sir B— P— will make a significant announcement before the week is out. Don't tell me you've found yourself a bride already? That's quick work, even for you.'

'Why must it be about a woman? It could refer to the imminent murder of my business partner.'

'Hah! You wouldn't last five minutes without me to prop you up. Seriously, though, I should warn you— you're unfamiliar with the ways of the *ton*. If you are raising expectations enough to be noticed, you will be expected to make an offer. If you don't, then the parents of decent young ladies will warn them against you and your reputation will suffer. I presume you're still serious about restoring the Poole name?'

'Oh, I'm serious, all right. And no, I have not raised any expectations.'

'So what does the wager mean? Come on, old boy, if there's some inside information you can give me, I might have a flutter myself.'

He really didn't want to discuss it but he'd barely slept, wondering what damage had been done to Harriet's wider reputation. Brierley's black opinion of his stepmother was already, he feared, a lost cause.

'What about a widow's reputation?' he asked.

Matthew tilted his head, a knowing smile lurking in his eyes. 'The Lady Brierley again? What *have* you been up to, old chap? And what is the story between you two? Eleanor has been badgering me to find out ever since you met at our house the other week, and *particularly* after your reluctance to discuss the subject at the picnic. She is convinced you two have *history*.'

Benedict ignored Matthew's questions. The past was no one's business but his. But he needed to know what might now happen. 'A widow's reputation is not as vital as an unmarried girl's, is it?'

'Vital in what context?'

Benedict told Matthew what had happened after Matthew and Eleanor had left Kitty's ball.

Matthew whistled through his teeth. 'And Lady Marstone came in with both the Brierleys, you say? She was setting you up, old chap.'

'I know.' Benedict clenched his jaw as he realised his friend was trying not to laugh. 'It is not funny.'

'It wouldn't have been had you ended up shackled to Bridget Marstone,' Matthew said. 'Seriously…I would have had to reconsider our partnership. And to think of having Lady M as a mother-in-law! Thank God for Harriet, eh? So what is the problem? There were enough witnesses to confirm you were never alone with Miss Marstone.'

'Yes,' Benedict said, 'but none to swear how long I was alone with *Harriet*. When Lady Marstone realised I was not about to make an offer for her daughter, she made threats. I'm not concerned about me, but for Harriet.'

He had no choice, he realised, but to confide in Matthew about Harriet's visit to Tenterfield Court.

Matthew straightened in his chair, frowning and suddenly serious, and Benedict found himself thinking that he preferred his friend's mocking banter, irritating as it was at times.

'What did Brierley do last night?'

'He made Harriet leave. I took her home in my carriage.'

'Bloody fool. Brierley, I mean,' he added. 'He missed a perfect opportunity to smooth things over by putting on a united front with Harriet.'

Benedict sighed. 'I think he's moved way beyond wanting to smooth things over. He's set on throwing Harriet out of her home and stopping her allowance. I need to know how her reputation will suffer, Matt. Brierley is more concerned with securing an offer from

Wincott for his daughter than with the damage his actions will do to his stepmother.'

'Self-righteous fool! When you consider what his father was like—'

'His father?'

'He's the reason Harriet set up her charity,' Matthew said. 'Eleanor was full of it after she heard about it. Brierley got two of his servants with child and then dismissed them. Harriet helps other girls in a similar situation—it's sickening to realise how many *gentlemen* feel perfectly justified in washing their hands of those girls and their children. Harriet works hard to persuade the men responsible to pay up and support their by-blows, making her somewhat unpopular in some quarters.'

Benedict felt sick. Harriet might have betrayed him, but she was a decent, caring woman, and his thoughtless action was hurting her. 'And they will no doubt happily spread scurrilous rumours about her if they hear about last night.'

'Oh, yes,' Matthew said. 'They will be in their element. From what I've heard, there have been a few who have tried to discredit her in the past, but she has always taken care to guard her reputation.'

'And I suppose, there I have my answer,' Benedict said slowly. 'Her reputation will suffer because, until now, it's always been spotless.'

Matthew smiled in sympathy. 'It looks that way.'

What would Harriet's answer be? Despite her manoeuvrings at the masquerade, she still might throw his offer back in his face, but at least he would have tried to make things right. He must accept responsibility. What was happening to her was his fault—if he had not followed her, she would not be in this predicament.

Chapter Twenty-One

Benedict rapped on Harriet's front door. Stevens answered it almost immediately.

'Is her ladyship in?'

Benedict went to step over the threshold. Stevens moved to block his way. Benedict scowled at the man.

'Has her ladyship told you to bar my entry?' He was in no mood to be denied; his decision was made and the sooner he asked the question and she accepted, the sooner the damage he had caused could be repaired.

'Her ladyship is not at home, sir,' Stevens said.

Benedict eyed the man, trying to decide if he was telling the truth or if he was merely obeying instructions. If the potential scandal was as bad as he now feared, where would she go? It was far more likely she was hiding away at home.

There was a clatter of hooves in the street behind him. A phaeton and pair, driven by Felicity, Lady Stanton, had turned into Sackville Street, and there she was.

Head high, facing the world. His Harriet.

Your Harriet? Since when? She's never been yours. She will be now. The reply instantly soothed his agitation and he knew, suddenly, he had made the right decision. He wanted Harriet and if this was the only way he could have her, then so be it.

He barely noticed the three gentlemen riding behind the phaeton until they reined to a halt outside the house. Stanton and two of his cronies—although whether it was quite the thing to call a duke and his brother cronies was another matter. He had never formally met either man, although he knew them by sight, and he now found himself the target of hard looks from the three men. Stanton spoke to the duke's brother and swung from the saddle. He strode over to where Benedict waited on the doorstep.

'What the devil are you about, coming here?'

Benedict locked eyes with him. 'I'll go where I please.'

'You've done more than enough—'

'This has nothing to do with you,' Benedict snarled. 'It is between—'

There was a flurry of skirts and Harriet and Felicity joined them, Felicity linking arms with her husband.

'Thank you, Stanton, for all you've done,' Harriet said. She raised her voice and called to the duke and his brother, 'And thank you both, too. I'm very grateful.' She turned cool violet eyes on Benedict. 'Did you have something to say to me?'

'Yes. But not here. Inside.'

She stared. 'Have you learned nothing of the ways of this world? If I allow you inside my house now, do you not realise that all our efforts to repair the damage of last night will have been for nothing?'

Benedict was aware that Stanton had shrugged free of Felicity's restraint and had ushered her away from the door before coming back to stand next to Harriet. He still did not know for certain if those rumours about the earl and Harriet were true or false. If they were, would Felicity and Harriet be such friends? It was yet another question for Harriet to answer.

In the meantime, the duke had dismounted and stood beside Felicity, one hand around her upper arm.

Keeping her out of harm's way. Benedict felt his eyes narrow and his blood began to pound through his veins. He had faced many situations like this in his life—men bristling with menace, protecting their own, whether it was their women, their possessions or merely a jug of ale. A brawl, or even heated words, would do nothing to help his cause but, God help him, he would not back down from these dandies. Although—looking again at their stances and their expressions—*dandies* was no more accurate a description than *cronies*.

He concentrated on Harriet. 'I have come to repair the damage,' he said. 'To make things right. I wish to speak to you. In *private*.'

Sudden understanding flashed in her eyes and a myriad of expressions crossed her face, so fleeting he hardly had time to interpret them, and then she blinked and was again unreadable. She locked eyes with him, probing, and he tried to convey his deepest feelings by expression alone. He must have succeeded, for she released a tiny sigh, turned to the others and said, 'Thank you so much for all you have done for me today. It will be all right now, I assure you.'

'We can come in and wait in the hall,' Felicity said, clearly reluctant to trust Benedict. 'At least, that way, the proprieties will be observed if Sir Benedict is... If he does not...um...' Her voice tailed away as her cheeks flamed.

Benedict pushed past Stanton and crossed the pavement to stand in front of Felicity. 'You have my word,' he said softly. 'I will make things right. Thank you for caring.'

Amber eyes searched his. 'Very well,' she said eventually. She glanced up at the duke. 'Would you help me into my phaeton please, Cousin Leo?'

Cousin? That explained a lot. Harriet did move in exalted circles these days. He felt a tremor of unease. What if she would not accept him? He was but a lowly trader compared to these men.

You are a baronet, now, don't forget, and rich, too.

Oh, yes! Wealthy and a title. How could she refuse? She married for the same before, don't forget.

He dismissed his sudden uncertainties as he walked back to stand by Harriet, ignoring the large form of Stanton, still hovering protectively by her side.

'Well?' He'd stated his case. He would not beg.

She nodded and said, 'Come inside.'

About to follow her across the threshold, Benedict turned to Stanton and thrust out his hand. They would have to learn to get along, with Harriet and Felicity such fast friends.

'Thank you for looking after her,' he said. 'It's good to know she has friends to rely on when her own family are so quick to believe the worst.'

Stanton gave him a hard stare as he gripped his hand.

'You make sure *you* look after her,' he said. 'Or you will be hearing from me. I will not have my wife upset. Do we understand one another?'

'We do.' Benedict followed Harriet inside the house.

'Thank you, Stevens,' Harriet said as she handed him her bonnet. 'Please come this way, Sir Benedict.'

She led him into the salon where he had taken her after she had fainted in the street. It seemed like a lifetime ago, not just two weeks. How had his life taken such an unexpected turn? From being set on marrying a virtuous girl of impeccable breeding, here he was on the verge of offering for a…for a… His thought process stalled. And then he realised.

It simply did not matter what Harriet was or was not. He loved *her*. He had always loved her. And now, more than ever, having seen her vulnerability, he knew it was his destiny to be the man to protect her. The sight of Stanton taking that role—the role that destiny dictated was Benedict's—had made his blood boil.

She had crossed the room to stand by the window, waiting for him to speak. Cool, calm, composed. Hands clasped loosely before her. The perfect lady.

Except now he knew the passion that ran deep below that unruffled exterior. Despite his intention of keeping his distance from her after the night of the masquerade, he had been unable to. And his need had triggered last night's disaster—his need to see her, to speak with her, to learn everything about her, had driven him into following her into the library.

He still did not entirely trust her. He still suspected there was something she was hiding but those questions could wait. He had a lifetime to learn the truth. The way she had responded to his kisses and caresses last night reassured him that, whatever else she felt for him, she felt the same desire he did. He could not wait to make her his wife.

He crossed the room to stand in front of her. She tilted her head to look deep into his eyes.

'Will you marry me?' He should speak of his love but, somehow, the words would not form. This felt vulnerable enough—he could not expose himself further by admitting his love for her. His heart beat faster as she held his gaze, her huge eyes solemn. His entire body was rigid with urgency, his skin stretched so tight it felt it might split if he made a sudden move. He realised he was holding his breath.

'Thank you. Yes.'

No outburst of joy. Barely a glimmer of a smile.

What do you expect, when you have told her nothing of what you feel?

What is he thinking? He looks so stern. Has he only asked me because of last night, or does he have some feeling for me other than lust?

What does it matter? Your problems are solved, and you know you will always be safe in a marriage to Benedict.

She ignored the uneasy thought that she was being unfair in accepting his proposal. She had—eventually—got the result she had planned for on the night of the masquerade. Security. Safety. Maybe even a child, if God saw willing to grant her that blessing. Her heart skipped a beat at the thought. A baby! How she yearned for a baby of her own. Resolutely, she cast aside her guilt.

Benedict *owed* her.

And she loved him. Even though that love was layered under years of anger and resentment, it had survived. Would she ever dare to open her heart to Benedict and admit her love? She shrank from that thought. What if he rejected it? He could still do so, even within a marriage. She could not imagine risking such heartache ever again.

An awkward silence ensued, though their gazes remained fused. He reached out and took a pin from her hair, dropping it to the floor. His eyes never wavered from hers as he felt for another pin and removed it.

And another, until her hair was falling loose around her shoulders. She did not move. Waiting, her heart racing as anticipation spiralled up through her entire body.

He lifted her heavy tresses, weighing them in the palms of his hands, much as he had weighed her breasts on the night of the masquerade. Then he threaded the fingers of one hand through her hair to cup her head.

'Harry...'

The groan came from deep within him. Tormented. Heartfelt.

At last. Her bones were melting. Her blood on fire.

He pulled her to him, against his chest, and his lips crushed down on hers. She moulded her body to his hard, lean frame, winding her arms around his neck, clinging to him, returning his passion.

At least we have this.

'We will wed as soon as possible,' Benedict said some time later. 'I shall consult my solicitor tomorrow and have the settlement drawn up. You will never again be beholden to Brierley.'

A wave of such relief swept through Harriet at Benedict's words she felt she might cry. She blinked several times and swallowed hard before she dared to answer him. 'Thank you. That means more to me than you know.'

He had been standing by the fireplace, but now he came to her and sat by her side, placing his hand over hers where it lay in her lap. 'Tell me,' he urged.

She turned her hand palm up and laced her fingers through his. She forced a light laugh. 'Oh, it was merely a figure of speech. I have to say I am looking forward to telling Edward our news. And to seeing Lady Marstone's face—she made sure everyone believed you would never stoop to taking on a humbly born, penniless widow.'

His fingers tightened around hers. 'She was wrong,' he said gruffly. 'You are more of a lady than she will ever be.'

'May we go and see Edward now? Together?'

'Of course,' he said, but he made no effort to move. His head bent, he watched the interplay of their entwined fingers. 'Do you miss him?'

'Edward?'

'No. Brierley.'

Harriet pulled her hand from Benedict's and stood up. 'No,' she said. 'Come, let us go now before it gets too late.'

They took a hackney to Upper Brook Street. Harriet sneaked a look at Benedict as he stared out of the window, his jaw set. He did not have the look of a man joyously anticipating his forthcoming nuptials. Was he thinking about the coming interview with Edward, or was it their betrothal and all that it meant that was on his mind? She tried to ignore those ever-present pangs of conscience.

Edward received them in his study, standing squarely in front of the hearth. He did not offer them a seat.

'Well?'

'We have come, as a courtesy, to tell you that we are betrothed,' Benedict said. 'The wedding will take place as soon as the banns have been read.'

'I am pleased you are finally making an honest woman of her, Poole,' Edward said.

Harriet felt Benedict stiffen by her side. Well, he deserved that gibe—if he had taken responsibility for his actions years ago, a great deal of heartache might have been avoided. But she had no wish for the two men to be constantly at odds with each other. Edward and his family would still be a part of her life. She slipped her hand into Benedict's and squeezed.

'I trust you will do the decent thing and allow Harriet to remain in her home until our marriage,' Benedict said. 'After all, a continued crusade against your own stepmother can only reflect badly on you.'

Edward scowled. 'There was never a crusade,' he said. 'I had my duty as head of this family not to allow my stepmother to scandalise society with her behaviour. Thankfully, that responsibility will lie with you henceforth. I dare say you will be more equal to the task than I.'

Harriet bit back her retort and lightly tugged at Benedict's hand in a silent attempt to prevent him reacting as she feared he might.

'You may as well come to the drawing room and tell Fanny and Katherine,' Edward added grudgingly. 'Wincott is there, too. I make no doubt *he* will be relieved that scandal has been averted.'

'Lord Wincott? Has he made his offer for Kitty?'

'No.' Edward led the way from his study to the drawing room. 'We have agreed to give her time to enjoy some of her first Season before he offers, although he very nearly backed out after the deplorable goings-on last night.' He halted and faced them both. 'He was utterly horrified by your behaviour.'

'I am sure Lord Wincott is as mindful of the advantages of the match as you are, Edward.' Harriet chose her words carefully. Wincott was, in her opinion, a pompous ass—a bit like Edward himself—and that was no doubt why Edward thought he would make a good husband for Kitty, but Harriet worried about her lively granddaughter being tied to such a dull spouse. 'Lord

Wincott should count himself fortunate to win a bride with so many fine qualities. And the political alliance will benefit him as well as you, so do not be too quick in thinking all the benefits flow in your direction. He will gain, as well.'

For the first time since their arrival, Edward's face softened. 'I had forgotten quite how perceptive you can be at times,' he said. He heaved a sigh, then held his hand out to Benedict. 'I suppose I must welcome you to the family.'

'Edward is not a bad man,' Harriet said some time later, as Benedict's carriage conveyed them back to Sackville Street. 'He is merely inflexible in his views.'

A sarcastic laugh escaped Benedict. 'Inflexible? How I didn't plant my fist in his smug face, I do not know. Or in Wincott's. Patronising poltroon. God help the country, with men like that at the helm.'

'I am pleased you did not,' Harriet said. She had seen the effort Benedict had made to remain polite and agreeable. 'At least you must allow that both Fanny and Kitty are delightful.'

A rumble of acquiescence sounded deep in Benedict's throat. 'Although how in hell they have remained so with that stepson of yours as husband and father, God only knows,' he said. 'Poor Kitty has my sympathy. She'll be going from the control of one pompous windbag straight to another.'

Harriet shivered at the reminder of the control a husband exercised over his wife.

'What is it? Are you cold?'

'No, indeed.'

How could she feel the chill when he sat so close by her side, his heat warming her even through their clothes? He put his arm around her shoulder anyway and she snuggled closer. Maybe, in time, she would learn to forgive him for the past but, in the meantime, she felt safe and she felt secure, and if she could not have her independence that, surely, was the next best thing.

'We have not discussed tonight yet,' Benedict said.

Heady, sensual anticipation swirled at Harriet's core. 'Tonight?'

'Yes. I thought we should show our faces somewhere, even if it is only the theatre.' He nuzzled her ear, whispering, 'We need not stay until the end as long as we allow ourselves to be seen.'

The swell of passion deep inside her burst to the surface, heating her skin. *Heavens!* Was she really that shallow? It seemed he was not the only one consumed with lust. Then reality—plans already made—intruded into her thoughts.

'But it is Matthew and Eleanor's musical evening tonight, and we have both promised to attend.' She shifted on the seat and stared at him. 'You surely had not forgotten?'

Benedict coughed, and then cleared his throat. 'I may have done.' He glanced down at Harriet with a twinkle in his eye—the first sign of humour since he had proposed. 'Be warned, however, that I shall never admit to it if you let on to Eleanor. She is one lady I don't want to get on the wrong side of.'

'She is forthright in her views, certainly, but she has a kind heart,' Harriet said, recalling Eleanor's compassion at Kitty's ball. 'And she has had her share of troubles.'

She recalled the whispers when Eleanor had spent the Season in London the year before—her first visit in several years. They hadn't been acquainted then, but Harriet remembered the rumours about Eleanor's mother having caused a scandal when Eleanor was young, and then—although Harriet had never learned the full story—someone had tried to kill Eleanor.

'Yes. Matthew has told me what happened last year,' Benedict said. 'They are fortunate to have found each other.'

'Indeed.' Harriet conjured up a mental picture of Matthew and Eleanor: a couple very much in love. Could she and Benedict ever be half so happy and content? 'I might not have known Eleanor long, but I like her very much and should not like to offend her by not attending tonight.'

'Then I shall sacrifice my personal preference for spending most of the evening in bed with you, my dear, and I shall escort you to the musical evening. I warn you, though. I am not a lover of music, unless it is a sea shanty or an impromptu tune played in an alehouse somewhere. I did not think Matthew was, either. Strange how marriage can change a man.'

His voice had grown thoughtful. Harriet stole a look at him. All trace of good humour had once again vanished. 'Are you regretting—?'

'Not at all.' His response was blunt and immediate, and Harriet chose to believe him.

Chapter Twenty-Two

The Poole family solicitor was standing at the window of Benedict's study when he entered it the following morning.

'Mr Swain, thank you for coming. Please, take a seat.'

Benedict indicated the visitor's chair and settled into his own chair on the opposite side of his desk. Mr Swain approached the chair, bent slightly to examine the seat and then, very gingerly, he swept his coat-tails aside and perched on the edge. Benedict bit his lip. He had only met Swain once before, and this action only confirmed the opinion he had formed on that occasion.

'Laurence informs me that you are the man I need to speak to with regard to drawing up a marriage settlement.'

Swain straightened, placing long-fingered hands on the rim of the desk. 'Laurence,' he said. 'I have not seen him for a while. How is he?'

Benedict stifled his sigh. This promised to be a lengthy meeting. He was used to commercial transactions: an offer, a counter-offer, brisk negotiation, a handshake.

'Laurence is very well and is kept inordinately busy

answering all my inane questions about the estates and
Sir Malcolm's investments,' he said of the young man
who had been Malcolm's secretary and whom he had
inherited, along with the rest of Malcolm's retainers
and advisers—including old-fashioned, fastidious solicitors, he thought, eyeing his visitor.

'Good, good,' said Swain. He shifted back a little in
the chair and regarded Benedict through his spectacles.
'Marriage settlement, you say. Well, well. And who is
the lucky lady, might one enquire?'

'Harriet, Lady Brierley. She is the widow of the Earl
of Brierley. The third earl, that is.'

Swain was back on the edge of his seat. 'The widow
Brierley?' There was a pause. 'Good heavens.'

Benedict felt his brows draw together in a frown as
Swain removed his spectacles, took a handkerchief from
his pocket and began to polish vigorously. He then replaced his spectacles and looked up. Benedict curbed
his desire to urge the man to get on with it.

'Now, this will take some planning but…yes, yes, it
can be done with very little additional expense to you,
sir.' A smile of satisfaction revealed long teeth. 'Yes,
very little additional—'

'What do you mean by "additional expense"?'

'Well, of course, the *current* settlement will cease
and the capital will revert to you, but that is all to the
good, for it would not serve our purpose at all. Indeed no. Not with the dividends being paid through
his lordship—'

'Whoa! Hold on. You've lost me, Swain. What current settlement? Which dividends and, for that matter,
which "his lordship"?'

'Why, the present Lord Brierley, of course. You are
joint trustees.' Swain regarded Benedict with an avun-

cular smile. 'It is quite all right, sir. No need to worry your head about it—no one expects you to be *au fait* with the entirety of Sir Malcolm's business. Not yet. Shall we discuss figures? Would you think the same amount sufficient? Or would you wish to increase it? It is not over generous for a man with your wealth, but then the lady will have you to settle her major expenses once you are wed, so it will only be in the nature of pin money. And there must, of course, be provision made for any children.'

Benedict stared at Swain, his mind whirling as he tried to piece together the fragments of information the solicitor had scattered through the conversation.

'Let me understand this,' he said slowly. 'Are you telling me that there exists an investment, made—presumably—by my cousin, and that the income from that investment is paid to Lady Brierley?'

Caution crept through Swain's expression. 'That is the gist of it, yes.'

'Why?'

'I beg your pardon, sir. Why what?'

'How did it come about? Why would Sir Malcolm invest *any* money on behalf of someone he barely knew?'

'Well, I… As I recall…the money was settled on her at the time of her marriage. Her father was the minister at the local church, you know, and your cousin—second cousin, I should say—agreed to provide a dowry as her own father could not.'

It made no sense. Malcolm had not had an altruistic bone in his body. Why would he provide a dowry for Harriet?

'The settlement was subject to certain conditions set by Lord Brierley, as I recall,' Swain continued, 'and, although I cannot bring them all to mind, I do remember that the dividends were not to be paid direct to Lady Brierley but to go to her through her husband and now, of course, through the present Lord Brierley. Unusual condition, but his late lordship insisted upon it, and Sir Malcolm did not seem disposed to argue against it. And the Reverend… Yes, I forget his name now… Lady Brierley's father just seemed grateful someone was providing a dowry at all.'

That made even less sense. Malcolm had provided the dowry and yet *Brierley* had dictated the terms? Benedict was loath to question Swain further until he had thought through the implications of this news.

'You said the current investment will revert to me? Presumably that will be because her ladyship is remarrying?'

Swain beamed. 'Yes, yes, that is a standard condition in these deeds, of course, if there is no issue from the union. The capital will revert to you, as Sir Malcolm's successor, and you will be able to reinvest that sum—ten thousand pounds, if my memory serves me correctly, *most* generous of Sir Malcolm—for her ladyship when you marry. Quite a neat solution, all told. Was there anything else, Sir Benedict, or should you like me to proceed with drafting the new deed of settlement?'

Benedict thought quickly. He had intended to settle a large enough sum on Harriet in order that if anything should happen to him she would have financial security. He must also make suitable provision for any daughters or younger sons. Now he hesitated. Had this information changed anything? His thoughts were too random to come to a sensible conclusion. Why had Harriet not told him? But…Brierley had stopped her allowance, and had threatened to do so more than once. If she had known there was money settled on her, would she not have used that to argue her case?

Then he realised. Other than the need to satisfy his own curiosity, it did not matter for, whatever the truth, it would not change the fact that he and Harriet were to marry.

He stood up. 'Thank you for attending me, Mr Swain, and yes, please do get on with drawing up a new deed. I shall instruct you later as to the amounts as I intend also to include a house for her ladyship's use if she should survive me. I will summon you again if I have any further questions.'

He actually had a thousand more questions swarming through his brain, but he doubted the solicitor could answer the question that was uppermost in his mind: the burning question of *why* Malcolm had provided a dowry for the local vicar's daughter.

'Very good, sir.' Swain stood up and brushed both hands over the seat of his trousers.

Swain left and Benedict sat back, hands laced behind his head. The myriad doubts that had hovered beneath the surface of his conscious mind now untangled themselves, fighting their way free of the restraint of his longing to simply trust her.

Why had Malcolm paid Harriet's dowry? Many reasons came to him, and most were dismissed. The few possibilities remaining were the ones he liked least. And the thought that floated to the surface time after time churned his gut with anger, jealousy and despair. He knew Malcolm had a taste for young girls. Had Harriet succumbed to him? Had she, once he had returned to Cambridge after that last glorious summer they had spent together, become embroiled in his cousin's sordid sex games? She was a passionate woman. That was undeniable. Had that passion, once he had awakened it, driven her to seek excitement?

He was loath to believe it. It did not tally with her reputation as a virtuous widow, but who knew what really went on in another's life? And her behaviour at the masquerade... If he had not been there, would she have targeted some other man to flirt with? Or more?

Growling an oath, he shoved his chair back and stood. It was time to ask Harriet.

During the journey to Sackville Street his thoughts turned to the future and what this marriage between himself and Harriet would be like. Last night, at the musical evening, he had watched Matthew and Eleanor—besotted with one another, gloriously happy—and the same envy he had felt before had infused him. Could he and Harriet ever be that happy? Or would their shared past always be a barrier between them? He could only hope not.

Stevens showed Benedict into Harriet's salon, and she came to him, hands outstretched, smiling.

'This is a pleasant surprise. I did not expect you to call this morning.' Then she hesitated, her hands falling to her sides. 'What is it? What is wrong?'

'I have a question, and I want to know the truth.'

She stilled. Not a single muscle in her face so much as twitched but, somehow, her expression blanked. Her guard was raised.

'What is your question?'

'It is about your allowance—the one that Brierley pays you.'

Her fair brows drew together into a puzzled frown. 'What about it?'

'Why did you not tell me my cousin settled a sum of money on you when you married Brierley?'

'I…I do not know what you mean.' She sank onto the sofa behind her, staring up at him, her eyes huge in her pale face. 'Your cousin? Do you mean Sir Malcolm? What sum of money? Who told you that?' She sounded genuinely perplexed.

'My solicitor, when I consulted him today about drawing up our marriage settlement. He told me that when you married Brierley, Sir Malcolm provided your dowry.'

'I want to know why.'

Harriet tried desperately to take in what Benedict was telling her. What did it mean? Sir *Malcolm* had provided a dowry? For her? But…

'No. I had no dowry. My father was poor. He could not pay a dowry.'

She was uncomfortably aware that Benedict was watching her closely. Too closely, his green eyes narrow. He was suspicious, but of what? What had *he* to be suspicious of? *He* was the one who had abandoned *her*. She remembered as if it were yesterday the agonising pain when her father had told her of his interview with Sir Malcolm and Benedict, and of Benedict's refusal to take responsibility for her and their baby. Yet he appeared to have wiped that from his mind.

How delightful it must be to have no conscience.

She loved him, she no longer denied it, but she still could not forgive him and that memory festered. She longed to shout at him, to scream out her anger and frustration over what he had done to her, and yet she could not process her thoughts swiftly enough to work out what reaction that might provoke. What if it caused him to break off their betrothal? What would she do then, and how…*how*…could she survive if he rejected her again?

One day—when she was brave enough, and strong enough, to broach the subject—she would have to tell him the truth of how she felt. But once that truth was spoken, would there be any future for them? Could they work together to rebuild her trust in him, or would their troubled past destroy any hope of a happy life together?

At the masquerade, she had been certain marriage to Benedict would solve all her problems. And so it would—her practical problems. But what of her feelings, and what of his? Her emotions pushed and pulled at her heart until she could no longer be sure what was for the best and what it was she really wanted.

She could not decide what to say for the best, and so she said nothing.

She waited.

Benedict paced the room before he returned to tower over her. She tensed against the instinct to shrink away from him.

'Why did Malcolm settle such a large sum on you?'

'I do not know. I did not know that the money came from your cousin.'

Uncertainty churned her insides. *Why is he angry?* Shadows from the past rose up to haunt her. *Is it my fault?*

Benedict paced the room again as he continued to fire questions at her.

'So you *did* know there was a settlement.'

'No. Yes.' She remembered the dreadful meeting with Mr Drake. 'But I only found out recently—that day you came to my aid outside the solicitor's office. I assumed the money was settled on me by my husband.'

'Did you never think to ask?'

'I… No. I—'

'Why were the dividends paid to Brierley?'

Her head was spinning. She gripped her hands so tightly together in her lap her knuckles turned white. 'I don't know.'

What had Mr Drake told her? There was a condition attached to the settlement, that Brierley would pass the dividends onto Harriet as long as she did nothing bring the Brierley name into disrepute. Except, of course, her late husband had never seen fit to pay her those dividends.

Nausea churned her stomach and forced its way higher to burn her throat as she felt the full weight of her worthlessness bear down upon her. She tore her hands apart and pressed her fingers to her lips to prevent a sob from escaping. Benedict had not wanted her—still did not want her, not truly—and Brierley, that lecherous, brutish old goat, would not even take her without a handsome bribe.

'You must ask Edward,' she said finally, for want of something better to say. 'I know nothing more than I have already told you.'

She rubbed her hand across her forehead and rose to her feet, her legs shaking. 'I am sorry,' she said. 'I am unwell. I must go and lie down.'

Benedict was by her side in an instant. He scooped up her hands and clasped them to his chest. 'No, do not say sorry. It is I who must apologise,' he said. 'I have done nothing but fire questions at you since my arrival. I will do as you suggest, and talk to Brierley.'

Chapter Twenty-Three

'What did Edward say?' Harriet asked later, as she and Benedict travelled in his carriage to dinner at Stanton House in Cavendish Square.

'He was at the Lords,' Benedict said, 'taking part in a debate that's expected to continue into the small hours. I left him a message that I will call on him tomorrow morning.'

Harriet had spent all afternoon sifting through the past in the light of the information that Sir Malcolm had paid Brierley to marry her. She should be accustomed to humiliation. No wonder Brierley's favourite taunt had been that Harriet belonged to him, body and soul. But, if she considered the transaction from Brierley's position, it made sense. He would be faced with the expense of raising another man's child except, in the end, it had cost him nothing. But it had cost her everything.

She cast a glance at Benedict. He was frowning. Again. It appeared to be his constant expression since Kitty's ball, she realised with a start. He was not happy about their betrothal, that was clear, but what she could not fathom was why he was so incredulous that Sir Malcolm had paid money to provide for her. He knew she had been with child. What had he expected? Did he think when he rejected her that there would be no further consequences, and that his guardian would cast her adrift with no means of support, like so many gentlemen did to their maidservants in the same circumstances?

The incredulity that had smouldered ever since Benedict had told her about the dowry finally sparked into rage, exploding through her. This was Benedict, not Brierley. She must not fear punishment for speaking her mind. If he objected to her words enough to break off their betrothal, then so be it. Better to live a pauper than to constantly fear to voice her opinion.

'*Why* do you persist with this fantasy? Is it really so unbelievable that your guardian paid Brierley to marry me?'

Benedict stiffened before twisting to face her. '*Fantasy?* What is that supposed to mean?'

'I mean that you are making this into a drama when you know *damned* well why he did it. You might not have been told that he had provided financial support for me, but you must be able to work it out.

'Not speaking of a thing does not mean it did not happen, Benedict, or have you managed to completely wipe the past from your memory?'

Benedict hauled in a deep breath, battening down the urge to grab Harriet by the shoulders and shake her meaning from her. A glance out of the window revealed the carriage was even now approaching Cavendish Square. He rapped the ceiling of the carriage with his cane and it drew to a halt. He opened the door and leaned out to speak to the coachman. The carriage lurched on its way, and Benedict sat down.

'I've told Atkins to take a turn around the park,' he

said, 'whilst you explain to me exactly what you are talking about.'

He crossed his arms across his chest and waited. Harriet's ragged breathing was loud in the carriage, but he battled his instinct to take her in his arms and soothe her distress. Or was it anger? Whichever it was, she had spoken from the heart and she must continue to do so if he was ever to learn the truth of the past.

'The money was for the baby.'

The air whooshed from his lungs. *Baby?* He could not speak. His heart jolted and lurched in his chest as her words reverberated right through him. *No. It could not be.* But... He dragged in a tortured breath, his chest swelling and burning with the effort. He looked back over the years... They had been inseparable, confident in the throes of first love and the unassailable belief of youth that nothing could spoil their vision for the future. They had made love. The first time, for each of them...

'What baby?' His voice was strained as it emerged from his thick throat.

'*Our* baby.' She glared at him. 'Do not pretend you did not know. Papa *told* me.'

His thoughts charged onward, skimming over what had taken place that summer and the following autumn: the best, followed by the worst, time of his life. He had blocked what had happened from his mind for the most part; he had not examined those events but buried them securely in a compartment in the depths of his mind. Now he must bring them into the light and look again. What was the truth?

He had returned from Cambridge that Christmas to find her gone. Had he ever questioned Malcolm's glib announcement that she had married Brierley for his title and for the riches he could provide?

'What did your father tell you?'

'He told me what you said to him.' Tears sparkled in her eyes and glistened on her lashes. 'I w-was a bit of f-fun. You were sowing your *wild oats*.' The disgust in her voice affected him even more than even those words did. 'Y-you wanted n-nothing to do with m-me or…or our b-baby.'

Fury blacker than he had ever known thundered through Benedict. He clenched his fist and slammed it into the carriage door, which shivered in its frame. The carriage once more lurched to a halt. *Damn and blast it!* He stuck his head from the door again. 'Keep driving until I *tell* you to stop!'

He turned to Harriet, who sat shaking, her arms wrapped around her torso, head bowed.

'It's not true.'

She lifted her head and glared at him. 'Papa wouldn't lie. Not about something like that.'

He sat down again, prised her arms away from her body and enfolded her in his arms. 'I am not lying to you, Harry. I knew nothing about the baby. What… But where is the baby?'

Tremors racked her body and a sob escaped her.

'Harriet?'

'She—she died. Before she was even born.'

Benedict freed one of his hands to scrub it over his face. He couldn't take it in. He'd only just learned he'd fathered a baby, and now it was as if she had been snatched from his arms. Grief engulfed him for a tiny life he had not even known existed until a few minutes ago.

'Why didn't you tell me?' His words sounded harsher than he intended. He cupped Harriet under the chin and forced her head up to meet his gaze. 'Why?'

'You *knew*!'

'Harriet…no. I didn't know. I swear.'

Before his eyes, she withdrew, retreating behind a mask that foiled the eye of the observer quite as effectively as the mask she had worn for the masquerade.

'Talk to me, Harriet, please. I—'

'We will be late,' she said. 'Richard and Felicity are expecting us.'

Richard! The same jealousy spiked through him and burst from him before he could consider his words. 'Stanton! Heaven forbid we upset *Stanton*. Are the rumours true? Is he your lover?'

She jerked away from his touch. 'We are not lovers.'

'But you were?'

'That is neither here nor there.' Her voice wobbled.

He worked hard to tamp down his anger and moderate his tone. 'We should go home and talk about this.'

'I am not ready to talk about it. Not yet.'

'How much time do you need? You've had eleven years to think about it…to talk about—'

'I've had eleven years of *not* talking about it. To anyone. Do you understand?' A bitter laugh escaped her. 'No, of course you do not. You have had eleven years of living a life of blissful ignorance. Now, please, may we continue to Cavendish Square? I do not want to be late.'

To look at her, nobody would now suspect anything was wrong. She hadn't been that way when he'd first known her—he had often joked she was like an open book—but since they had met again, there had only been an occasional glimpse of the spirited Harriet he used to know. Such as just now, when she had lost her temper. Why did she retreat behind a mask whenever there was a danger of confrontation or whenever her emotions ran high? It was as though she was scared of letting go…of saying what she really thought. She had erected a barrier as effective as a brick wall, and he could not find a way to breach it.

Or could he? He could take her in his arms and kiss her, encourage her to talk about her deepest feelings… but would it be a mistake to push her now, at a time when both of their feelings were raw and time was limited? He was afraid of widening the gap between them rather than breaching it. Maybe it would be better to tackle it tomorrow, when they'd both had time to calm down.

As he instructed the coachman to drive back to Cavendish Square he promised himself that tomorrow morning—early—they would sit down and they would talk this thing through.

And then he would take her in his arms and kiss her and tell her—for the first time in eleven years—how much he loved her.

What was she to do?

Harriet sat in her boudoir, gazing unseeingly from the window, until the rosy light of dawn fingered the rooftops opposite. She was numb, her brain frozen with indecision. She had picked over her memories until the bones of the past were stripped bare. Either Papa had lied or Benedict now lied. She wanted neither of those two to be true. And that was impossible.

How she had survived the evening before without screaming out her pain and frustration she did not know. But she had. And her heart had twisted a little tighter each time she'd observed Matthew and Eleanor or Richard and Felicity together, and recognised the love that bound them, shining out for all to see. She had watched Benedict, too. Read the signs of strain in his features;

traced with her eyes the furrows on his brow; recognised his discontent in the downward turn of his mouth.

He escorted her home from the Stantons' house in near silence, depositing her at her home and then leaving in his carriage. And Harriet had climbed the stairs and dismissed Janet and had sat and thought.

It was not just their argument about the baby and about Stanton that had caused Benedict's low mood. He had been frowning and unhappy before that—she had noticed it more than once since Kitty's ball. And the thought crept unbidden into her mind that she was the cause. She viewed the decisions she had made and the actions she had taken since Benedict's return to London and she reached the conclusion she was no better than Bridget Marstone.

Oh, she could fool herself that she had not deliberately trapped him into a proposal at Kitty's ball. She had convinced herself at the time that the whole farce was his fault because he'd followed her into Edward's library. And yet…she could not deny she'd deliberately set out to seduce Benedict on the night of the masquerade with every intention of prising a proposal from him—because she'd felt aggrieved, because she'd blamed him for everything that had gone wrong in her life and because she'd thought he deserved to suffer as she had.

Her plan had not worked. He had seen right through her and he had *chosen* not to propose to her. He did not want to marry her but now he was trapped and… What if he was telling the truth? What if he had *not* known she was with child? Did she want him to suffer in a marriage he did not want? Could she live with herself, knowing what she did about her motives and knowing that there would be no betrothal had it been Benedict's free decision? And would he ever forgive her when he found out the truth about her and Stanton?

He was due to call on her at ten.

She loved him. She did not want him bound to her from a sense of obligation or duty.

Benedict no longer had a choice, but she did. Suddenly, she knew what she must do.

Chapter Twenty-Four

Don't worry?

Benedict ripped the letter in half and in half again, and dashed the pieces to the floor of Harriet's salon. She'd done it again—led him on and then betrayed him! Broken off their betrothal and gone. He rammed his fingers through his hair and paced up and down, fury boiling in his gut. Then his steps slowed as common sense began to penetrate his anger. Her wording—she had *released* him… Had she gone for his sake? He must believe she had. He must not allow the lies of the past to cloud his judgement.

Where would she go?

To Brierley? Hardly.

The Stantons? Possibly.

That charity house of hers? Where was it again? Cheapside? Again, possible.

What had she said again? He retrieved the ripped letter, strode to a table by the window and laid the pieces out, fitting them back together.

Dear Benedict,

I have been unfair, both in not believing you last night and in accepting your proposal. I therefore release you from our betrothal: I have come to realise that to be forced into an unwanted union can never provide a solid foundation for a happy marriage such as our friends demonstrate.

I have gone to find the truth of what happened eleven years ago.

Do not worry, I beg of you. I am no longer your concern and I shall be perfectly safe. I have written to Edward to inform him that our betrothal is at an end and that I shall accept his offer of a cottage at Brierley Place, so you will no longer need to worry about me. If what the solicitor told you is true as to the source of the monies, I imagine Edward will not be so churlish as to withhold my allowance for very long! And I dare to hope that, after Kitty is settled, he will again countenance my presence in London.

I wish you good fortune in your search for a bride, and I hope that your union will be blessed with children and you will lead a happy and contented life together.

Do not worry about me. I will see you upon my return and tell you what I have discovered.

Your good friend,
Harriet

Three times she had told him not to worry. What did the foolish woman think he would do other than worry? Why the *hell* hadn't he made her talk to him last night? Why had he decided it would be better this morning after they'd both had a chance to calm down and think things through?

Because you were scared of what you must admit, and of what you might hear, if you both spoke from the heart.

Now she had gone and the ache in his heart rippled through his body until he could feel it in his toes and the tips of his fingers and in his jaw, which was clenched tight against his tears.

Where would she go?

Thoughts flitted in and out of his mind, never settling for long enough to allow him to examine them.

Calm down, slow down, think!

He sat on a nearby chair, head bowed, his hand resting on the torn letter as if he could absorb her thoughts through his fingertips.

Think logically.

I have gone to find the truth of what happened...

Who would know? Malcolm, Brierley and her father were all dead. The present Lord Brierley? He shook his head, frustration mounting. Who else was involved? Harriet herself. The solicitors!

He surged to his feet and was halfway across the room before he realised the three men who had planned this would have had no need to confide the whole truth to their solicitors.

Planning—what had they planned? If it was true about the baby, and he could not, having witnessed Harriet's distress, disbelieve it then the men—her father, his guardian and her future husband—had conspired to keep Benedict in the dark about Harriet's pregnancy, and Harriet in the dark about Benedict not knowing. They'd told Harriet that Benedict had rejected her and they married her off to Brierley. The whole thing stank of Malcolm. He had made no secret of his disapproval of Benedict spending time with the village children and of his plan to find a suitably well-bred bride for his heir. But Harriet's father was complicit in the deception.

And *that* must be where Harriet had gone—to see her mother—the only person who might still know the truth of what had actually happened.

He dredged up a memory… Harriet, talking about her mother and her aunt… The sea air… Whitstable. That was it.

Benedict headed for the door.

'What time did her ladyship leave?' he asked Stevens, who was hovering outside the salon door, an anxious expression on his face. 'Did she say where she was going?'

'She took a hackney at seven this morning, sir, carrying a portmanteau. Janet says her bed wasn't slept in and that she packed her bag herself. I heard her direct the hackney to Lad Lane so I can only assume she is going to Brierley Place, but she did not say so.'

Or Whitstable. The Swan with Two Necks was in Lad Lane, and the stagecoach that ran from there to Canterbury would pass through Faversham, a scant five miles or so from Whitstable.

Benedict whipped up his horses and arrived back in Grosvenor Street in record time.

'Order the carriage round,' he said to Reeves as he strode into his house. 'I am going into Kent. Fletcher!' He had kept Malcolm's valet on as well, after his kinsman's death, despite having little use for one. Fletcher appeared at the top of the stairs as Benedict took them two at a time. 'Pack a bag—enough for a couple of nights away, please.'

'Am I to accompany you, sir?'

'No. No need.' He did a quick calculation in his

head. With any luck, and frequent team changes, he should be in Whitstable by six.

'She is not here, as you can see.' Mrs Rowlands showed Benedict into the empty sitting room of the small house she shared with her widowed sister. On the opposite side of the hallway he had glimpsed a dining room through an open door. It, too, had been unoccupied. Involuntarily, he glanced at the ceiling.

'My sister is resting in her bedchamber.'

Benedict gazed at Harriet's mother in frustration. Small likenesses to Harriet, glimpsed in isolation, smote at his heart—her elegant posture, the shape of her brow, the set of her chin. They stood facing one another. Mrs Rowlands had not taken a seat—the implication being that Benedict was not welcome to stay—and neither had she offered him refreshments.

'Have you heard from her?'

'I received a letter about a week ago.'

'Well—have you any idea where she might have gone?' he asked in desperation.

The woman was as uncommunicative as it was possible to be, without out-and-out rudeness.

'I am afraid I cannot help you,' Mrs Rowlands said. 'I suggest you return to London and wait for Harriet to contact you, if she chooses to do so.'

The woman was a poor liar, but he could not fault her for trying to protect her daughter. Harriet was here. He felt it in his gut but, short of forcibly searching the house, there was little he could do. Did Harriet know he was here and was hiding from him? Or had Mrs Rowlands taken it upon herself to shield her daughter from him?

'She told me about the baby.'

Mrs Rowlands flinched. 'We do not speak of that.'

So it *was* true. 'Why was I never told?'

'What could *you* have offered my daughter? You were just a youth, with nothing in the way of prospects until Sir Malcolm died, and *he* held all the power. You ruined our daughter's life and broke our hearts. We lost her when she married that man.'

'Lost her? How?'

Mrs Rowlands walked to the door. 'It can do no good raking over the past. Leave it where it belongs. If Harriet wishes you to know, I am sure she will tell you when she is ready to. I am sorry for your wasted journey.'

'It is of no consequence. If you *do* happen to see Harriet, tell her I was here. Tell her that I am gone to Tenterfield Court, when she is ready to talk to me.'

He had no choice now but to leave. He trod down the short path to his carriage and then looked back at Harriet's mother. 'And tell her that, in my eyes, our betrothal still stands.'

'Betrothal?' Mrs Rowlands' voice rose in sharp enquiry. 'What betrothal?'

He ignored her and opened the carriage door.

'Where to now, sir?' Atkins called from the box as Benedict mounted the carriage steps.

'Tenterfield Court.'

He settled against the squabs as the carriage rocked into motion.

...to be forced into an unwanted union can never provide a solid foundation for a happy marriage...

Those words had haunted him the whole journey from London. An unwanted union. Did she mean unwanted by her? If so, he must accept he was chasing a lost dream. Or did she—as he hoped and prayed she did—mean unwanted by him? He must trust Mrs Rowlands to give Harriet his message and he must trust Harriet to understand why he had given her this opportunity to come to him freely. It was time they were open about the past, and about their present feelings, if they were to have any chance of happiness.

He would give her until the day after tomorrow. If she did not come, he would return to Whitstable and, this time, he would find her. But he hoped against hope that she would come of her own accord.

When Harriet awoke, sunlight was flooding through the open curtains in an unfamiliar bedchamber. She squinted and rubbed at her temples, which throbbed. A loud gurgling accompanied a churn of her stomach and the events of the day before came tumbling out of her memory and into her conscious thoughts. She was at Mama's, in Whitstable. As if in confirmation, the haunting cry of a seagull echoed outside the window.

Her stomach rumbled again, reminding her she had not eaten since yesterday, when she had managed to grab a quick slice of bread and cheese at one of the inns when the stagecoach had pulled in for a change of horses. She frowned. That would explain the headache, but why had she not eaten when she arrived here in the middle of the afternoon? Those memories—her actual arrival—remained hazy. But she recalled with absolute clarity the reason for her impromptu journey to the Kent coast.

Benedict. Their betrothal. The burning question she hoped her mother could answer.

She got up and crossed to the washstand in the corner of the neat, impersonal guest bedchamber. There was clean water standing in the jug and she poured it into the basin. It was cool, but it would help to wake her up. She washed quickly and pulled on the same dress she had travelled in yesterday. Someone, she noted, had brushed the dusty evidence of six hours of travel from the blue fabric. She brushed her hair and roughly plaited it before going downstairs.

The clock on the mantelshelf in the sitting room read quarter to eleven.

'Good morning, Mama.' Harriet crossed the room to the window, where her mother sat—embroidery in hand—and bent to kiss her cheek.

Her mother smiled. 'You are looking better, my dear. That tincture of laudanum worked—you have slept for almost seventeen hours. You had better have something to eat. Go and ask Joan to prepare toast and tea, will you, please?'

'Mama, I need to ask—'

'Yes, yes, my dear, but first you must have something to eat.'

She put her embroidery on the arm of her chair and rose to her feet. She framed Harriet's face with her hands and shook her head, smiling. 'Listen to your mama, stubborn girl.'

Tears welled up to thicken Harriet's throat and she turned away before Mama saw. 'Yes, Mama,' she said.

Oh, how she wished she could return to her childhood, to a time when life was uncomplicated and full of promise. How she wished she could forget everything— Benedict included—and stay here in peace with her mother and her aunt. She silently berated herself for her ingratitude, and vowed to cease this self-pitying nonsense. Look at all the women and girls who had fared so much worse than she had. The workhouses were full of them, single mothers who had no option but to rely upon the parish to survive.

When she returned from speaking to Joan, Harriet said, 'I cannot remember what I said—or did, for that matter—when I arrived yesterday. How is Aunt Jane?'

Mrs Rowlands filled her in on her sister's various ailments until Joan brought in tea for two and buttered toast for Harriet. Once she had left the room, Harriet opened her mouth to question her mother, but she was beaten to it.

'He came looking for you.'

Harriet gaped at her mother. 'Who? Benedict?' She started to her feet. 'Where is he?'

Mrs Rowlands grabbed at Harriet's sleeve. 'Sit down. He is not here. He came yesterday in the early evening.'

'What did he say? How did he seem?' She studied her mother's expression. 'You did tell him I was here?' There was a beat of silence, during which Harriet drew her own conclusion. 'Oh, Mama! How could you? Where did he go?'

'I did not tell him you were here because I had no way of knowing whether or not you would wish to see him,' Mrs Rowlands said, her exasperation clear. 'What was I supposed to think? You arrived here without warning, exhausted, distraught and nigh on incoherent. The words you did say made no sense. The only information I could glean was that, once again, Benedict Poole appeared to be the cause of your distress. Of *course* I told him you weren't here.'

'I'm sorry, Mama.' She recalled the nightmare of a journey on the stagecoach. She hadn't expected to feel so vulnerable, or so unworldly, when she'd made that spur of the moment decision to come to Whitstable. A sleepless night…over seven hours crammed into an airless coach…no food to speak of…no wonder she could barely recall her arrival. 'I can see you were trying to protect me.'

She squirmed under Mrs Rowlands' penetrating gaze.

'You still carry a torch for him, don't you, Harriet?'

'I cannot help it, even though I know...at least, I thought I knew...how badly he treated me before. Now I am confused, and I want—'

'Now you want the truth?'

'Yes. Did Papa lie to me?' She waited for the answer to the question, not knowing what she wanted to hear, not knowing which option would be the most painful to endure.

'Yes, but Sir Malcolm left him no choice.' She took Harriet's hands in hers, holding her gaze. 'We both lived to regret our decision, but by then it was too late to change anything. Once you had married that...that...' A deep sigh, seemingly torn from the depths of her mother's soul, accompanied a shake of her head. 'Sir Malcolm was adamant he would never permit you and Benedict to wed. We were frantic. You were disgraced, and your baby would be...'

Her mother fell silent and Harriet felt her chest swell with pain at the memory of her tiny, tiny daughter, held once in her arms before being taken from her.

'It was unthinkable to your papa...to *us*...that your child, our grandchild, should grow up with the stigma of being born out of wedlock. Sir Malcolm offered a solution. The *only* solution, as far as we could see, but only on condition we backed his story that Benedict had rejected marrying you. He even offered to settle money on you—we had nothing to offer as a dowry—and he threatened...he threatened...' Mama's voice cracked and her eyes filled. Harriet squeezed her hands. 'You must believe me, darling... If we had *known*, no threat to take Papa's living from him would have made us agree. But…but…'

She hauled in a shaky breath.

'I thank God you have another chance. Go to him, Harriet. Go to Benedict and try to put right that dreadful decision Papa and I made all those years ago.'

Harriet gazed from the window of the chaise and four, eager for her first sighting of Tenterfield Court. She hoped and prayed Benedict would still be there, for what if he had tired of waiting and was even now on his way to London? She picked at her soft kid gloves, impatient to be doing and not just sitting and yet dreading the conversation to come. If she—if *they*—were to sort out this mess and ever find happiness, she knew she must find the courage to tell Benedict the whole truth.

Her mother's words rang in her head. *He said to tell you that, in his eyes, your betrothal still stands.*

That message gave Harriet hope—and yet she didn't dare to hope too much—that Benedict might still harbour some tender feelings for her, apart from his obvious lust. But if that was so, why had he not offered for her after the masquerade ball? It made no sense and yet, during that journey, she gradually realised she still did not know the whole story. She now knew why Papa had lied to her, but she still had no idea what Benedict had been told to explain her marriage to Brierley. Was that the key?

The chaise jolted to a halt in front of Tenterfield Court. Harriet gazed up at the imposing red-brick mansion and her heart flipped before climbing into her throat. Her entire future would be decided in the next few minutes. A footman opened the carriage door for her and handed her down.

'Thank you, Cooper,' she said with a smile.

'It is a pleasure to see you again, my lady.'

Crabtree was at the door, waiting. He bowed as she approached.

'Good afternoon, Crabtree. Is Sir Benedict at home?'

Her stomach knotted as she waited for his reply. *Please let him still be here.*

'No, milady.'

Harriet's heart plummeted. She was too late. He had tired of waiting for her and returned to London. The butler's measured tones penetrated her inner panic.

'I beg your pardon, Crabtree. I missed that.'

'I said, before he went out, the master left instructions that if anyone should ask for him, I should say he is at the folly.'

Harriet bit at her lip, excitement stirring deep within her. He was waiting for her. 'I will go to him there,' she called over her shoulder as she dashed out of the front door and down the steps.

The slope up to the folly seemed steeper than ever to Harriet as she dragged air into her lungs and her calves ached with fatigue. *Or you are not used to such strenuous exercise.* She paused, her hand to her heaving chest, the thud of her heart tangible beneath her fingers. The folly towered above her, silent and grim, silhouetted against the grey sky. Doubt assailed her. It looked deserted. Was she a fool to read such hope in his message?

Her breathing eased, but her heart still raced—from nerves now rather than exertion. There was no choice. She had come this far. If they could not reconcile the happenings of the past now, they would never do so. She walked to the door, her steps leaden with trepidation.

The door was unlatched. Harriet pushed it open.

Chapter Twenty-Five

The interior of the folly had changed beyond recognition. Candles flickered, banishing the gloom of the day and illuminating the red Chinese-style carpet that had been spread on the floor, and the cushions of all colours that had been arranged into two facing heaps. In the centre of the rug, between the piles of cushions, was a wicker basket, the neck of a bottle protruding. A flicker of movement caught Harriet's eye. Benedict, eyes glittering in the light from the candles as he sat on the old tub chair pushed back against the wall on the far side of the tower from the door. He watched her. Waiting.

She stretched her trembling lips into a smile. 'I owe you an explanation,' she said.

'You do.' In one lithe movement he was on his feet but he did not approach her. Instead, he gestured to the cushions. 'It is comfortable enough,' he said, 'although the resilience and enthusiasm of youth made it seem more comfortable back then than we might find it today.'

Harriet folded her legs and sank down onto the cushions. Benedict did likewise, the basket between them. So near and yet so far. Would he understand?

'Have you eaten?'

She shook her head. He unpacked the basket and spread bread, cheese and fruit before her and then uncorked the wine and poured each of them a glass. He appeared totally at ease, lounging on the cushions, propped up one elbow, wine glass in hand.

'Why could you not talk to me the other night?'

Brutal honesty was required, however hard it was for her and however shameful. She knew instinctively that he would struggle to ever fully trust her if she could not now summon enough confidence to tell him everything.

'I was afraid.' She bent her legs and hugged her knees close to her chest.

His brows snapped together. 'Of me?'

'You were so angry when I told you about the baby. I panicked and I couldn't work out what to say in case it made you angrier.' She gulped a mouthful of wine.

'What about the truth? All I wanted was the truth. What did it matter even if it did make me angrier?' He straightened, leaning towards her, staring at her, probing. 'What has made you fear a man's anger, Harriet? Brierley?'

Even his name made her want to curl into a tiny ball and disappear from view. She nodded.

'But you must know I would never hurt you,' he whispered achingly.

There was pain in his eyes, and the urge to comfort him overrode her dread of finally talking of her ordeal.

'Oh, I do.' She reached out impulsively and he met her gesture halfway, taking her hand and rubbing his thumb across her knuckles. She stared down at their joined hands. 'Sometimes…' She paused, trying out the words inside her head. 'Sometimes…something happens that brings the past back and it is as though I cannot separate the now and the then.' She looked up, anxious that he would understand. 'When we met again. At Tenterfield. That night you ran up the stairs behind me and I...I...'

Her throat squeezed shut, leaving a torrent of words dammed up inside, as they had been for years. She dragged her hand from his and pressed her palms to her face, pushing her fingers to her closed lids.

'Harry? My love?' There was a rustle and Benedict was beside her, nestling her into the crook of his arm, stroking her hair.

'Tell me, sweetheart.'

'He th-threw me down the stairs.' She clutched at Benedict, her words muffled against his chest. 'I was s-seven m-months' pregnant. I l-lost our b-baby.' Huge sobs racked her as he held her and soothed her, rocking gently. 'I didn't think I c-could b-bear to carry on living—I didn't w-want to survive. I had lost you, but knowing that I carried your baby s-somehow made it b-better. I s-still had a part of you and then...I had n-nothing. Nothing b-but p-pain and misery and fear and disgust.'

She wept on his shoulder, his deep murmurs soothing her until eventually her sobs subsided and she pulled back to look up into his beloved face. His jaw was taut, his features etched with pain. A tear sparkled on his lashes. Wonderingly, she reached up and wiped it away. He feathered a kiss to her forehead.

'Oh, Harry, my darling, I can't bear to think of you going through all that alone.' His words vibrated with anguish. 'Our poor, defenceless baby, robbed of the chance of life. You don't need to mourn her alone anymore, my love. I mourn with you. I am here for you. I will be with you forever.'

Hope blossomed with his words, and yet there was something she must say…something Benedict must know before he committed himself and felt honour-bound to stand by his word.

'Ben…what if…what if I can no longer carry a child?' Her worst fear, out in the open. 'You n-need an heir. And in seven years with…*him*…I never got with child. What if I am b-barren?'

'Then, we will adopt children and we will love them as our own. Oh, *God*, Harriet! All that wasted time!'

A muscle in his jaw bunched and his chest expanded as he dragged in a breath.

'*Why* did I trust Malcolm?' he gritted out. 'Why was I so ready to believe you would betray me by marrying for wealth and a title? I should have known better. I should have known *you* better.'

She placed her palm to the side of his face. 'You were young. We both were. Is that what they told you? That I married Brierley for status and money?' She read the shame that dulled his eyes. 'You were young,' she said again. 'I would rather learn now that you made such a mistake than still believe you heartlessly abandoned me.'

'Which is the thought you have lived with all these years.' He hugged her close, resting his cheek on her hair. 'All those wasted years over one lie… All that wasted energy, resenting one another for something that did not happen.'

He pulled away and tilted her chin, looking deep into her eyes. 'I can understand why Malcolm lied. He made no secret of his ambition for a great match for me, perhaps to atone for his own failure to wed and produce an heir. I doubt he would have spent a single second feeling guilty, but…your father—I cannot understand why he didn't tell you the truth. Why would such a pious, honest man lie about something so fundamental to his only daughter's happiness? Did your mother explain *why* he went along with Malcolm's lie? For I swear to you I never said those ugly things to him.'

She stretched up to press her lips to his. 'I know you did not,' she whispered. 'I knew, in my heart, that you were telling the truth the other night, but I was torn. I hated that my memory of my father would be tainted by these lies…but now…I realise I did not go to my mother for proof you were telling the truth but to understand *why* my father had lied.'

She moved away from him, shrugging his arm from her shoulders, then shifted her position so she fully faced him. He watched her intently, his green eyes sombre, as she took his hands in hers.

'My mother guessed my condition before I even knew it myself. I had missed my courses, and then I began to be sick in the mornings. She confronted me…' Harriet paused, recalling the horror of that conversation, and her shame when her father had discovered the truth. Poor Papa. He had been devastated.

'When Papa went to your cousin to tell him I was with child and to demand you marry me, Sir Malcolm was adamant he would never allow us to wed. As you said, he had much higher ambitions for you and, as your guardian, you would need his permission to marry. My father was equally determined that his first grandchild should not be born out of wedlock—that would have offended every precept in which he believed. So my parents' only option was to find someone who would marry me before the child was born.

'As you might imagine, Sir Malcolm was only too keen to help them out with finding someone, and he suggested Brierley. My father was so grateful for his help and to have his daughter married to an earl, and his grandchild brought up in such splendour... That was far more than he, or my mother, could ever have imagined for me.

'I was utterly horrified when they told me I was to marry Brierley. I refused. I cried. I told them we loved each other and that I knew you would marry me—that we would elope if Malcolm wouldn't give us permission.'

She smiled, shaking her head at the memory. 'I had a very hazy notion of what elopement might entail,' she said. 'All my knowledge had come from reading novels, much to my mother's despair. Anyway, that is when they decided a white lie was in my best interests, according to Mama. If I thought you wanted nothing to do with me or our baby, then I would stop hankering after you. I would find my peace and settle into my new life more easily.'

He squeezed her hands, then lifted them to press his lips to her skin. 'Poor Harry. I wish you had written to tell me what was happening.'

'I wish that, too, but it all happened so very fast after Mama realised I was with child that by the time I caught my breath, the arrangements had been made with Brierley and I had been told—and I believed—you did not want me. If I had written, it would have been to tell you how I hated you.'

A rumble rose from deep within his chest as he pulled her back into his arms. 'I would have come back straight away to shake some sense into you. Tell me about Brierley.'

'I can hardly bear to even think of that man,' Harriet said, shuddering. She must be brave, though. No more secrets. 'He hid his true character well, although the fact that he was a friend of Sir Malcolm's should perhaps have been warning enough. But my parents were not worldly people and I do not think it occurred to them Brierley might be so very cruel. Not even Edward fully realises his father's depravity—from what I have gathered over the years, Edward's mother was a most upright, moral woman and his father worshipped her.'

She swallowed, the memories looming large, threatening to overshadow her new-found joy. 'Perhaps it was I who caused such vile behaviour—I could never match the perfection of his first wife. He constantly compared my appearance and my behaviour to hers, accusing me of not being fit to take her place.'

She hesitated, dredging her past for the truths she must now reveal if she and Benedict were to have a chance of happiness together.

'He would punish me,' she whispered into his chest. It was easier to admit to such sordid details when she could not read the disgust in his eyes. 'It started with the occasional blow if I displeased him, but eventually I could *never* please him, no matter how hard I tried. And he seemed to…seemed to…'

She stopped, unable to control the wobble in her voice, tears flowing again. Benedict rocked her. 'Shh,' he murmured into her hair. 'You don't have to tell me. Leave it in the past where it belongs. You're safe now.'

Harriet rubbed her eyes and forced another swallow past the lump in her throat. 'No,' she said. 'I need to tell you. I need you to know about Stanton.'

He stiffened. She could *feel* the anger radiating from him. Her courage almost failed her, but she had come this far; she did need to tell him all. She could not allow suspicions to fester between them.

'Are the rumours true?'

She forced away her instinct to appease him by saying what he might want to hear, to deflect his anger by lying.

It's Benedict. Even if he is furious, he will never hurt you. Not physically.

'Yes,' she said, her heart quailing as she accepted that, although he might not hurt her physically, he had the power to crucify her emotionally, once he knew the truth of her *affaire* with Stanton.

The silence seemed to stretch forever, his chest rising and falling beneath her cheek.

'Tell me,' he said eventually.

She dragged in a torturous breath. 'Brierley... When he...he couldn't...' She could not say the words. She hoped Benedict would understand. 'He *liked* to hurt me. When he...when he...'

'When you were intimate?'

'Yes.' Harriet felt her cheeks burn. Confessing such things, even to the man she loved—or perhaps *especially* to the man she loved—was as hard as she had imagined. 'He made me...*do* things and, if I did not please him, he would punish me again. He would... restrain me, sometimes for hours. Usually naked. To await his pleasure, he would say. Because it was all I was good for. And he would force me to accept his advances, at all times of the day or night. I know a wife is expected to accommodate her husband's needs, but I grew to hate and fear any sort of intimacy and I hated *him*.'

She sighed. 'I have never admitted this, but I was *glad* when he died, God forgive me. He cut me off from everyone. I was only permitted to go out if he was with me. I was not allowed to visit my parents, and he read their letters to me and would only frank my letters to them after he had read them. I was entirely dependent on him and his servants.'

'And Stanton?'

Ah. Stanton. Will he understand?

She must be brave. Harriet levered herself upright so she could look into Benedict's eyes.

'I have always wanted a family and I was heartbroken when I lost our baby—'

Benedict put his fingers to her lips. 'You did not lose our daughter. Place the blame where it belongs. Brierley killed her. You and she were both innocent victims.'

The burden of guilt in her heart eased a little. How many times had she wondered if—had she said or done something differently—Brierley would not have lost his temper with her and pushed her on the stairs? How many times had she blamed herself, as Brierley had?

'Thank you for understanding.' She sucked in a deep breath, praying for the strength to continue; to admit her calculated decision to use another man to help her forget. 'Although I longed for a baby, I never wanted a child with Brierley and I thank God I did not have one. But then, after he died, I thought I might…' She paused, chewing on her lip. 'I thought of remarrying, but I found I was too afraid to trust *any* man. I could not even contemplate allowing any man such control over me, so I put my desire for a family to the back of my mind and I focused my energies on the charity I founded.

'And then I was invited to a house party. Lord Stanton was there, and I heard some of the other ladies discussing his prowess.'

Benedict glowered at those words and, despite knowing what else she must admit to, Harriet had to bite back a smile at his expression.

'He was well known as a ladies' man before he married Felicity,' she continued, 'but nobody expected him to marry when he did—he was known as the Elusive Earl for his ability to avoid the snares put out for him. And I began to wonder if someone like him—if *he*—might help me to overcome my distaste for...for the marital act.'

Her cheeks burned. 'This sounds so sordid and... and calculating,' she said. 'I'm sorry.'

'For what?'

For what indeed? She forced a laugh. 'If I am honest, I suppose am sorry for myself. I am sorry that I must admit out loud that I would even contemplate asking a man to help me with such a thing, let alone actually do so. So I made a point of getting to know Stanton. We became friends and, when I felt I could trust him, I asked him to help me.'

'You told a man you barely knew about things you have been unable to tell me?'

'It's odd, is it not, that I found it easier to approach Stanton than to tell you? Mayhap it was because my feelings were not involved. And I did not tell him much: I...I told him my husband had found me unsatisfactory, but after a few times I think Stanton guessed there was more to it than that.'

'I don't think I care to hear any more,' Benedict growled, leaping to his feet to take a hasty turn around the room.

Harriet watched him anxiously. Would he be able to accept the past, and what she had done? She was well aware that men set great store on their brides being chaste and pure. Not only was she a widow, but she had just confessed to having a lover—one that she had pursued, and one with whom she still enjoyed a close friendship. She could not guess what was going through his mind now, but she had confessed thus far and she would finish her tale.

'We agreed no one should ever know, and we only met at my house. I will not lie to you, Benedict. Stanton and I did become close, but there was never any question of love on either side. When Stanton became betrothed to Felicity—quite unexpectedly—he ended our arrangement.' She huffed a laugh. 'He was mortified when Felicity and I became friends.'

Benedict stood staring out of the window, silent except for the harsh sound of his breaths. Harriet rose from the cushions to go to him. She did not touch him; she did not quite dare, he was so stiff and unyielding.

'Can you forgive me?'

He spun round to face her. 'Forgive *you*?' He placed his hands on her shoulders. 'Harry, how can you ask such a thing—there is nothing to forgive you for. It is I who should beg *your* forgiveness.'

He kissed her fiercely, his lips and tongue possessing her mouth as he cradled her face.

'I cannot forgive myself for all you have gone through. I am astounded you can even bear the sight of me, let alone... You are an amazing, beautiful, generous woman.'

His words demolished the last remaining barrier around her heart, allowing a flood of hope and joy to cascade through her, filling her with wonder and love.

'Now—' he stepped back and looked at her, a teasing glow in his green eyes as his hands slid from her face, across her shoulders and down her arms to clasp her hands '—what is this nonsense about releasing me from our betrothal?'

'It is not nonsense. It is another thing which I am

not proud of, although I honestly did not plan to en-trap you at Kitty's ball… You were right…I *did* plan… I did intend… Well, it did not work—' she caught at her breath, which was coming out in frantic-sounding gasps '—and you did not fall for my scheming at the m-masquerade…but I am still g-guilty and I cannot bear for you to be t-trapped into a marriage you do not want.'

A light lit his eyes. 'That masquerade,' he said slowly. He tasted her lips again with a low, satisfied hum. 'How could I ever forget?'

'You do not want to marry me,' Harriet said desper-ately. 'You would have asked me then.'

Benedict threw his head back and laughed. 'Sweet-heart, you do not understand me very well if you think I would *ever* allow myself to be trapped into making a proposal against my own wishes.'

'B-but…you *were* forced into proposing after Kitty's ball. You cannot deny it, and *I* cannot l-live with that knowledge.'

'That is true,' he said slowly, frowning. 'And if you truly cannot live with the guilt that you have entrapped me, I must thank you for releasing me from any obliga-tion to marry you. I accept.

'Our betrothal, as of this moment, is over.'

Harriet's heart cleaved in two and tears blurred her vision. He might have forgiven her, but he did not love her.

'Harriet. Look at me, please.' She raised her eyes to his, feeling a tear slide down her cheek.

Benedict lifted her hands to his lips. 'My darling Harriet, will you please do me the honour of becom-ing my wife?'

'But…'

'You goose! Did you really believe I proposed to you

against my will? I was *relieved* to be forced into it—I could then excuse myself from being a fool for trusting you again and pretend I was merely acting the gentleman.' He hesitated then, his face suddenly serious. 'You do *want* to marry me?'

She gasped. 'Of *course* I do. There is nothing I want more. I love you, Benedict Poole, with all my heart.'

'Then, that is that,' he said with a huge smile as he took her into his arms. 'For I love you, too, with all my heart.'

She tilted her face to his and silence reigned for several satisfying minutes.

'Do you think you can learn to accept my friendship with the Stantons?' Harriet asked when they eventually came up for air.

He gave her a little shake. 'Will you please stop fretting? Yes. If Felicity can live with what happened before she and Stanton wed, then I'm damned sure I can. I cannot blame either of you for what happened before we met again…and I thank God that we did meet again,' he added, smiling down at her.

'And I, too. And,' she added, feeling decidedly naughty now her worries had been put to rest, 'it turns out Brierley did me one favour.'

She laughed as Benedict lifted a brow. A weight had been lifted from her and her life now stretched before her, full of hope and pleasure and love.

'I have certain skills.' She lowered her voice to a purr, half closing her eyes as she traced a path down Benedict's chest to his groin and closed her fingers around his manhood. 'Skills to please gentlemen.' With her other hand, she pulled his head lower to flick her tongue in his ear.

A strangled noise sounded deep in Benedict's chest

and he hauled her to him, capturing her lips in another passionate kiss.

'Skills to please *this* gentleman alone,' he growled. 'You are *my* woman from now on. Mine alone. You are the breath in my lungs and the song in my heart.

'I love you, Harriet. I've always loved you. It's only ever been you.'

Epilogue

October 1813

'Four…five…six.'

Benedict slammed to a halt mere inches from the drawing room door, which stayed stubbornly closed, even in the face of his most ferocious glare. He spun on his heel and paced back across the room. Six lousy paces. He swore viciously under his breath. He had become accustomed to the screams. But there had been nothing but silence for ages. That was even worse.

A hand landed on his shoulder.

'You'll wear a hole in the carpet if you don't stop this,' Matthew said. 'Come and sit down. Ellie will come and tell you as soon as there's any news.'

'I *can't* sit and do nothing. I've a mind to go up there and…'

'Whoa! You'll scandalise the whole neighbourhood if you go near Harry while she's…while she's…well… you know. It's not men's business. Why don't we go to the club and have a drink? Take your mind off things.'

Benedict turned and stared at his friend. 'Take my *mind* off… Did *you* go off drinking whilst Ellie was going through this torture?'

'Well. No. Now you come to mention it, I do believe I wore a track in our drawing room carpet, too,' Matthew said, his blue eyes twinkling. 'But it's worth it. You'll see. You'll have a littl'un like our Thomas and life will be ten…no, a *hundred* times better than you ever thought possible.'

'I hope so,' Benedict muttered. Never in his life had he felt so utterly helpless. 'Why's it taking so long?'

Matthew shrugged. 'It always does. It's nature's way.'

'As long as Harry is all right.' Benedict's throat squeezed tight at the thought of all the things that could go wrong. He gripped Matthew's arm with sudden urgency. 'I don't know what I'd do if—'

He broke off at a sound from the hallway. Running feet. Then the door flew open and Eleanor burst into the room, her cheeks flushed, her eyes bright, a huge smile on her face.

'Come on, Papa Poole. It's all over, barring the introductions.'

Benedict was past her in a trice, across the hall and up the stairs two at a time. The bedchamber door was closed and, as he reached it, he hesitated, suddenly uncertain. The unmistakable mewl of a baby sounded from inside the room, shaking him from his momentary attack of nerves. His son. Or daughter. He opened the door. Walked in. There were others in the room but he had eyes only for Harriet.

His Harriet. His beautiful wife—tired and flushed, but beaming.

Her arms were full. He couldn't… *What?* Benedict stared, his brain trying to make sense of the sight of his gorgeous, beloved wife and the babies in her arms. He looked again, resisting the urge to rub at his eyes.

'Twins?' he whispered.

Harriet's smile widened. 'Twins,' she said. 'One of each. A boy and a girl.'

Benedict crossed to the bed as if in a dream. He reached to stroke Harriet's cheek. Harriet, who had made his life complete and who had banished all the hurt and loneliness of his past, and now... He reached out tentatively with one finger and touched the rounded cheek of the baby nearest to him. How soft. How delicate. How *perfect*. He watched as the pink lips pursed and a tiny frown flickered across the babe's forehead and his heart swelled, so full of love it felt as though it might explode. Wispy strawberry blonde curls peeped out from the edge of the white shawl it was wrapped in.

'Your daughter,' Harriet said. 'Is she not perfect?'

Benedict tore his eyes from his daughter to search Harriet's face. Always sensitive to her moods, he caught the faintest whisper of pain in her voice. Pain for what might have been. He bent and pressed his lips to her forehead. 'We will never forget our first girl, my love. Never. But we will give these two the most joyous, secure childhood they could wish for.'

'We will,' Harriet said as Benedict brushed a kiss on first his daughter's head and then his son's, his chest near bursting with pride and with love.

'It is fortunate we selected names for both a boy and a girl, is it not?' Harriet said with a weary smile. 'William and Rebecca—they sound very well together, do they not?'

'They do indeed.'

Benedict reached for William, taking the tiny bundle of his son into his arms and cradling him to his chest as he perched on the side of the bed, unable to tear his gaze from his tiny hand as it waved in the air, fingers splayed. He tickled his palm with the tip of his little finger, amazed at how huge it looked, then gasped with delight as William closed his tiny fingers around his.

His vision blurred and he blinked hard. A gentle hand touched his and he looked up into the glorious violet eyes of his wife, watching him with tenderness and love.

'I love you, Ben,' she whispered, and her eyes were now heavy with sleep. 'So very much.'

He leaned over and kissed her gently. 'I love you, too, my Harriet. Sleep now. You need your rest.'

'Will you stay with me…with us…awhile?'

'For as long as you want, sweetheart. You have made me the happiest man on earth, and there is nowhere else I would rather be.'

* * * * *